The Poseidon Project

Paul Alan Rosen

The Poseidon Project

DEDICATION

For my Father
I wish you were here to see this.
I love you.
I miss you.

Michael Dorn Rosen
February 26th, 1943 - January 12th, 1994

ACKNOWLEDGEMENTS

I would like to thank Ensign Gantz and Leshnover of the Coast Guard for their information and time. I learned a lot. Thank you also, to all the men and women of the Mohawk. It was an honor to tour your ship.

Thank you, Dr. Marten and the rest of the crew at Earthtrust in Hawaii. I never thought someone would let an undergraduate work with dolphins. I had a great experience I will never forget. Ken, turn the air down.

Thank you Dr. Gallup. I loved working with you on my thesis, but I still think I should have received an 'A' in Experimental Psychology.

I would like to thank all of my friends for their interest in my book. I know I didn't let you read most of it until it was finished, but I hope it was worth the wait. Ben, I promise never to write about the leg shaking, you know what I mean. Oh, and by the way, she's looking at me. Ari, congratulations on your marriage. I hope you guys have a long and happy life together and I hope I can visit often. (You know I only wrote this so you'll buy the book.)

And of course, thanks to my family. Thanks, uncle Ken for all your help. Mom and Irv, thank you for telling me that no matter what I did in life, you would support my decision. That made all the difference. With your support I was able to achieve my goals and dreams. I'll try to keep your parenting style in mind when I have my own family. I love all of my brothers and sisters, even if I don't see or talk to you guys a lot, know that I'm thinking of you.

A big thank you to all of you who read the manuscripts along the way and told me what to fix. Finally, thank you to my editor Nicole Stein. You helped me with the most important edit of all, the last one. I hope we will be able to work again on my next project.

RESEARCH NOTE

The self-awareness research described in this book is an actual, empirical process created by the author to test self-recognition in bottlenose dolphins. If any further research is done to test self-recognition in cetaceans using this process or anything related to this process, please credit the author of this book properly.

Thank you and enjoy the book,

Paul Alan Rosen

THE POSEIDON PROJECT
PROLOGUE

Señor Jesus Lopez's silver plated, nine-millimeter Glock® pistol sparkled in the sun as he held it on his guest. They were sitting on the deck of his one hundred-foot yacht. The sun beat down on them with unrelenting force and they were sweating profusely, sweat soaking through their light clothes. Javier, his guest, had already given up hope for survival.

"Is it not beautiful out here," Lopez asked, not expecting a response. "Nothing and no one for miles around. It is just us, the sky and the sea." He waved his gun around like a little toy as he spoke. "We are at the mercy of God and all of His elements. A storm could brew up at any moment and kill the both of us."

Javier wished that would happen but he knew his fate was to be more gruesome. At least if I'm going to die, he thought, I would rather be killed by the hand of God and not by the gun of a madman. But, he knew, that a storm would not come soon enough.

Lopez had invited Javier on a weekend long shark-fishing trip, but now, Javier realized the true intentions of the invitation. Periodically he would beg Señor Lopez to let him go free but it would do no good. Lopez's mind was set.

"Sometimes, I come out here just to think. I don't really like fishing anyway. Do you like to fish," Lopez asked, not paying much attention to Javier. "It's not really fair to the fish, or in our case the sharks. Think about it. They hunt for food and we hunt for sport. Sometimes I wonder, who is the real animal?" His eyes were glazed over in deep thought but Javier would never have known. Lopez's glasses masked his eyes, feelings, and intentions. He slowly came back to reality, pointed the gun in his prisoner's direction intently, and asked him again.

"Javier, my men tell me that they have found all of the papers that they need." Lopez sat up in his chair and continued. "Are they correct in telling me this, or have you made other copies that I do not know about?"

Javier did not answer but sat in a trance like a chicken that knew it was about to be slaughtered. He couldn't hear his captor but he could hear and see his beautiful wife and three-year-old son.

Javier had accepted the job just after his marriage. His architectural business wasn't working out and bills were piling up. It wasn't because he wasn't good; he was one of the best in Colombia, but at the time, no one had enough money to build with his extremely expensive plans.

Señor Lopez had come to him as he was preparing to close shop and offered him the job of a lifetime. Javier knew his name (as did every child in Colombia) from scary bedtime stories but figured this was a terrible coincidence. The more he had worked with Señor Lopez, the nicer he became until the project was finished.

After he drew up the final plans, he was not allowed to see the project come to life. Javier was upset about this and had complained to his boss many times. All that Señor Lopez told him was, "These payments are in place of you being able to see your completed project, and it should be compensation enough." This was very true. The money he made from the project was enough to last his family for two lifetimes.

For a while, Javier and his young family lived happily in new homes, with new cars and possessions, but it kept eating him up inside. He had to see his project. Javier demanded that Señor Lopez let him see the new facility and with some thought, Señor Lopez agreed.

Now, Javier knew his captor's promise would never be kept. This *was* the man from scary childhood stories. He was now living in his own nightmare.

"It would be a shame for that beautiful wife of yours to meet an untimely end as well," Lopez said, still waiting for his answer but Javier was still in his trance. "And that cute little son of yours? I wonder how long he would last?"

Javier looked up finally with tears slowly rolling down his face. "You will not touch my family!" He said strongly, through gritted teeth.

"Well, that all depends on you."

Javier was still staring hatefully at his captor. He wanted to jump up, take his captor's gun, shoot him with as many bullets as the gun had, then throw him overboard and let the gathering sharks devour him, but he knew he would never make it out of his chair alive. Lopez was pointing the gun at him and was paying close attention to him.

"Well, what is it going to be? Your final testimony to me, or should I send your sweet family to come join you?" Javier put his head in his hands and shook it slowly. "So, there are no other copies?"

"No." Javier squeezed out, looking angrily at his captor again.

"Are you sure now? You wouldn't want to die right after telling a lie, would you? What would God think?"

"Fuck you," Javier screamed.

"That is no way to treat your old boss now, is it?" Lopez stood up and backed away from his prisoner. "Would you do me a favor and go up there to

2

check how many sharks our little bucket of bait has drawn," Lopez asked, pointing to the front of the boat with his pistol.

Javier did not move. He sat in his chair, with his head hung low, still cradled in his hands.

"Go now," Lopez screamed, showing anger for the first time in their conversation. "Go!"

Javier got up slowly. As he did, his tears ceased. He knew his time had come and there was nothing to do but pray. Pray for his family's safety and for his soul. He moved slowly towards the front of the yacht, praying softly to God. His lips were moving but Señor Lopez could not hear his prayers. Only God could hear him now.

"If you've lied to me, you'll be seeing your family very soon," Lopez said as Javier reached the front of the boat. "Now, count. Count the sharks that are going to feast on you!"

Javier did not look at the water. His head turned towards the heavens and his God. "One," he began softly.

PROLOGUE 2

Captain James Hunter had loved boats since he was a child. He was the only black kid he knew who went sailing, not to mention going out every weekend with his father.

Growing up in Miami, James's walls were always covered with pictures and drawings of boats. He loved being surrounded by thoughts of the ocean. His friends, on the other hand, had different ideas of what fun meant.

Most of James's childhood friends played basketball, football and other sports. Some of them even dealt drugs to get ahead. There weren't many ways out of the "hood" as most people referred to it, but James had hope. When James and his father were out together in the open sea, the mean streets of Miami that they called home disappeared.

His parents weren't wealthy by any means, but what his father could scrape together, was spent on their small sailboat. James loved sailing so much; sometimes his father would wonder if James liked being with him only because they were on the boat.

One weekend when James was thirteen, his father drove him all the way to Key West to go sailing. His father didn't know the area very well, and that is what caused the accident.

James still remembered that day as if he had seen it in a movie recently. The water was crystal clear. The wind was perfect, cooperating with them every step of the way. There was not a cloud in the sky and it was so blue he could have mistaken it for the water.

His father was in the front of the boat securing the rig on the main sail when James yelled.

"Yo, Dad, coming about!"

His father turned around and saw the boom bar coming at him as James turned the boat to starboard. He ducked, and the bar barely missed knocking his head off.

"James, try to give me a little more notice than that," his father said, smiling back at the young captain.

"Sorry Dad," James replied, just before he was thrown against the steering wheel. Neither of them knew that they had just run aground on a coral reef. The impact knocked the breath out of James's lungs and then threw him back down to the deck.

When he stood up, his father was gone. "Dad," he yelled. "Dad, Where are you?" He ran desperately to the front of the beached boat. As he was running, James noticed blood on the deck. He looked into the water in front of the boat and saw his dad floating, face up in the water.

"Dad," James yelled again helplessly as he started to cry. James knew he wasn't strong enough to lift him from the water onto the boat, and even if he could, how would he get him to shore with this disabled sailing boat?

"Dad," he yelled again, crying harder. Just then he remembered the radio. He had used it many times before to talk with other passing boats in Miami, but he had never had to use it in an emergency.

What was the frequency, he asked himself? How would he remember? His father had told him what it was just in case. James's adrenaline was pumping, flushing his dark face.

As he ran to the back of the boat his brain began to clear a little. He picked up the receiver thinking out loud. "Sixteen, Sixteen!" His heart was racing a million miles a minute.

"Help, help," James screamed into the receiver as soon as he tuned it to channel sixteen. "Help, my dad's hurt, please help!"

"This is the U.S. Coast Guard Cutter Titan, what seems to be the problem?"

"My dad, he's hurt," James cried over the receiver.

"What do you mean, son?"

"Our boat crashed and he fell off. He's in the water and he looks dead, please help me!"

"What's your name, son?"

"James," he said, starting to calm down.

"All right James, we're coming to help your father, but we need your help too. Can you help us James?"

"Yes," James replied, sniveling.

"Okay, James, I need you to tell me if your dad is facing up in the water."

"Yes, he is."

"That's good. That's very good, James. Can you get him onto the boat?"

"No, he's too big," James said, starting to cry again.

"That's all right, James. Don't worry!" The man on the other end said to try and calm the boy. "If he's face up in the water he'll probably be fine. Can you do me one more favor?"

"Yes."

"Do you see any numbers near the radio? Anything telling your position?"

"I see numbers but I don't know what they mean."

"That's okay, James. Can you just read them to me?"

The Coast Guard held James on the line until they could get to the boat. It only took fifteen minutes, but to James it seemed like a year had passed.

6

When the Coast Guard finally arrived, James's father had floated a few yards away from the boat. They immediately retrieved his father from the water and checked his vital signs. He wasn't breathing and didn't have a pulse. If it had been fifteen minutes since his last breath, he was already brain dead and nothing could have been done, but they started CPR anyway.

Shortly after a Coast Guard man boarded the sailboat, he found James shivering near the receiver. James looked up and smiled at the man because he thought his father was going to be saved.

"Yo, you helped my dad, right? He's okay, right?"

"I'm sorry, James."

Had he killed his own father? James took in a breath, held it, and his eyes started to tear. He couldn't hold it in and began to cry uncontrollably. The Coast Guard man tried to pick James up from his fetal position but James resisted. He was angry with himself for running aground on a coral reef and angry with the Coast Guard for getting there too late to save his father!

Through the years James began to realize that what had happened was not his fault. He also realized that blaming the Coast Guard was not right either. He was actually very thankful for the Coast Guard for trying to help his father.

This thankfulness turned into love and James realized that he wanted to become a part of the Coast Guard. He felt that saving people's lives would, in some way, bring his father back.

When James finally graduated from the United States Coast Guard Academy, he could feel his father watching over him. It made him sad to think that his father was gone, but he knew that, in spirit, his father would be with him whenever he was out on the sea.

It must have been his father's presence that gave James the ability to succeed so quickly. At thirty-three, he became the youngest African-American captain in the Coast Guard fleet. If asked, James would say his father was actually by his side, guiding him around at sea.

Everyone James had ever met knew the famous story of how his father's presence had once saved his life. James never missed a chance to tell every new officer on his ship. An officer's first night was always the same, and Ensign Mark Huerta's was no different.

The first moment that Mark saw the 270-foot, medium endurance cutter, he was taken aback. He had graduated near the top of his class from the Academy in New London, Connecticut, and had received his first choice on his "dream sheet."

The cold weather in Connecticut wasn't that much different from winters in New York City, but he wanted warmer weather. Mark got it when he was assigned to the Seventh District, in Key West.

He couldn't believe that he was about to start his first assignment. Mark had been out on boats before but this was different. Now he was going to be able to do what he had always dreamed. He still remembered exactly what the application for the Seventh District had said:

> On an average day the Seventh District:
> Completes 22 search and rescue cases,
> Saves 3 lives,
> Saves or assists $729,000 in property at sea,
> Services 14 aids to navigation facilitating $221 million in cargo movement,
> Seizes 96 million pounds of marijuana and 186 pounds of cocaine,
> Conducts 33 general law enforcement boardings of vessels at sea, with an additional 10 boardings specifically to enforce living marine resource laws,
> Inspects 14 commercial vessels for safety, and
> Responds to 4 oil or chemical spills.

This was his first chance to change the world in his own way, and he couldn't wait to get on board.

Mark stood on the dock, in front of the quarterdeck, in his blue uniform. The telecommunications specialist had taken his information from inside the white shack and had called for the officer of the day. She attended to other work as he smiled at the ship in front of him.

The boat was docked on the starboard side and the gangplank was resting on the aft deck. There was a blue banner on both handrails proudly presenting the ship as the USCGC Tomahawk, number 613. He knew that the Tomahawk was the thirteenth medium endurance cutter in the fleet, but the number didn't bother him at all.

As he was waiting, perusing the ship from the dock, Mark saw someone emerge from the hangar. It was a woman, and from the markings on her hat, Mark could tell she was the officer of the day. He waited until she was close enough, then saluted as she walked down the gangplank to greet him.

Mark was a little overzealous and kept his salute up even after the officer of the day had saluted him back.

"You can take your hand down now," she said with a relaxed attitude, pointing to his head. Mark looked up, took his hand down and the woman continued.

"I'm the XO, Jessica Carp. Can I see your papers?"

"Yes, ma'am, here they are," Mark said, handing his orders over quickly. "Everything seems to be in order here Ensign Huerta. Welcome to the Tomahawk," she said with a smile.

"Thank you, ma'am."

"Follow me, I'll show you around. Oh, but before I forget, here's your cover. Remember, always wear it outside and only inside if you're on duty." She handed Mark his very own blue hat with the USCGC Tomahawk patch sewn on over the bill.

Mark took the hat gladly and placed it on his head. Jessica was already aboard the boat when she looked back to find the new ensign admiring how the hat fit on his head.

"Are you coming?"

"Yes, ma'am," Mark said, snapping back into reality. Her soft manner with him did not calm his fears of being perfect. His nervousness showed through clearly in his stiff movements and quick, short answers.

Mark ran on board with his small duffel bag. He followed Jessica up the short, white ladder to the flight deck, which was only six feet above aft deck. Below his feet, he saw a white bull's eye to aid in the landing of helicopters.

The hangar in front of him was retracted and he followed Jessica inside. There was equipment everywhere in the hangar. It looked like it had no order to where everything went, but Mark knew there was a place for everything.

"This is also the recreation area, or at least one of them." Jessica pointed to the exercise equipment in the center of the hangar where there was a bench press and other equipment that looked like they had been worth the purchase.

Moving toward the back of the hangar and behind some large electrical equipment, they came to a closed porthole that led to the interior of the ship. Jessica turned the handle on the left side of the door and opened it with ease. She moved aside for Mark to step in. After he was inside, Jessica shut the heavy door and locked it.

"We're in the climate control area now. Make sure you keep these doors shut to keep out the hot air."

"Yes, ma'am." He was still visibly nervous.

Jessica did not move forward but instead was gesturing at Mark's head. "Remember what I told you. You're not on duty right now and we're inside."

"Oh, yeah!" Mark quickly removed his blue hat. "I'm sorry."

"It's okay. It takes a while to get used to all the rules. Come on, let me show you where your stateroom is." Jessica continued forward and Mark continued to follow her.

Taking in as much as he could, Mark noticed small details that others on the ship probably took for granted if they had been on board for any amount of time. Over head, which was less than a foot away, he saw metal tubes hanging in a controlled path just below the ceiling. The hallway they were in was narrow and curvy. He could not see the end of the hallway but figured the wires ran the length of it.

They passed other members of the crew along the way but Jessica did not introduce Mark to anyone, she figured that would come later.

Jessica and Mark turned left down another, shorter hallway which looked no different from the one they had just left except for the lack of wires above their heads. They stopped at the first doorway on the right and Jessica motioned him to enter.

Mark entered the small stateroom. It looked exactly like every college dorm he had ever seen. There was a bunk bed to his right and two desks, one on the far wall and one on his left. Everything was made out of metal, but the room was a refreshing change from the ship he had seen so far. There was a nice blue carpet in this room and the reminder of college life added a homey feel for Mark. There was even a small poster of a marijuana leaf above the top bunk. Someone had circled the leaf and struck through it with a black marker. Mark smiled.

"Your roommate isn't here at the moment, but yours is the bottom bunk, in case you were wondering." Jessica pointed to the empty mattress. "And your closet and desk is the one against the forward bulkhead. Put your stuff down and make yourself comfortable. You'll meet the rest of the officers tonight at dinner, everyone's going to be here." She paused for a moment to make sure Mark was all right. "You don't have to stay here, you can tour the ship by yourself. You have been on a cutter before in the Academy, haven't you?"

Her politeness bothered him but kept him on his toes. He was sure that she would start barking orders at him at any minute.

"Yes, ma'am, but it's been a while. I'll find my way around, thanks."

"Okay, then, we'll see you at dinner which is really early, usually around four-thirty or so." Jessica left Mark alone in his new stateroom and he couldn't believe she hadn't yelled at him once.

Mark passed it off as just one person who must be extremely nice on the ship and put his bag down without unpacking a thing. There was something he wanted to see.

Mark ran around the forward deck like a little boy checking out a new jungle gym. His eyes were wide with wonder and his hands caressed the 75-mm gun on the front deck. A large white dome that only came off during exercises and in emergencies covered the trigger and most of the gun, but the shaft was enough for him. He was in love with the ship.

As Mark quickly and carelessly circled the white dome, he ran into someone.

"Shit, son, you need to be more careful," Captain Hunter yelled, as his coffee mug smashed onto the deck spilling coffee and white porcelain fragments on the metal surface.

Mark was mortified when he noticed the captain's stripes. He immediately stood at salute as his face turned white. He couldn't believe that he had just run into one of the most famous captains of the USCG on his first morning of serving with him. He knew his good luck wouldn't last long.

"Welcome to the Tomahawk." Captain Hunter hesitated while looking at the man's nametag. "Ensign Huerta," James said as if he was trying to remember his name for when he needed someone to polish his shoes.

"Hello, sir," Mark said in a shaky voice. "I just want to tell you..."

"Don't you think you should ask permission to speak, Ensign," James asked quietly as he leaned in and squinted his eyes at the new officer.

"Yes, sir."

"Well then, go ahead."

"Well, sir, I just wanted to say that..."

"I didn't mean go ahead and talk, I meant go ahead and ask for permission to talk. You got it straight this time?"

Mark could hardly stand still. The captain looked so angry, Mark thought that he might throw him overboard.

"Yes, sir. Permission to speak freely, Captain?"

"Permission granted, and you can also stand at ease if you wish."

Mark had forgotten that he was still saluting the captain. He quickly looked up and pulled his hand down from his forehead.

"Sir, I'm so sorry about your coffee. It was an accident and I'll clean it up right away."

He bent down to start cleaning up the mess on the deck but James stopped him.

"Don't worry about it. Someone else will clean it." He sounded agitated.

"Yes, sir. Thank you, sir," Mark said, as he saluted Captain Hunter again.

"You don't need to keep saluting me, Ensign."

"Yes, sir," Mark replied, taking his hand down from his forehead.

"And stop calling me sir, we're not in the army."

"Yes, sir." Mark cringed.

"Just call me Captain."

"Yes, Captain."

"You a little nervous, Ensign Huerta?"

"This is my first mission and I'm very honored to be working with you. I've heard great things about you sir and..."

"Ensign Huerta!" James interrupted loud enough to be heard across the boat.

"Yes, sir? I mean Captain."

"I know this is your first mission. I just wanted to know if you're nervous?"

"Yes, sir, very nervous." He had not even realize he had said "sir" again.

James shook his head before he continued. He couldn't believe how nervous this guy was. He could tell Huerta meant well but he was going to have to calm down first in order to be a good officer on his ship.

"You seem nervous. I wasn't sure. I thought maybe you had to go to the bathroom or something," he said jokingly, without a smile. James remained silent for a second, waiting for a reaction that he knew would never come, and then he continued. "This isn't how you act when you have to go to the bathroom, is it?"

"No, sir!"

"Captain."

"Captain," Mark answered, still standing as stiff as a board.

"Good, I'm glad. And, uh, don't worry. The nervousness goes away. It's kind of like having stage fright."

James started circling the new ensign, getting a better look at him. He was still acting like a hard ass but he loved seeing the new crewmembers squirm. It was almost a ritual, something like being shoved in a locker on the first day as a freshman in high school.

"During the first scene you're really nervous, but once you say your first line, you'll be okay."

By this time he had completely circled Mark. "Do you understand?"

"Yes, Captain."

"Very good, you're learning."

James stood there silently, staring at him for a few seconds. "Why did you join the Coast Guard?"

Mark wanted to smile but he was afraid the captain would yell at him. He had wanted to tell Captain James Hunter what his intentions were in the USCG for years. Mark thought that the reason he joined was so valiant that he'd been practicing exactly what he was going to say for months.

"Well, Captain," he started excitedly. "I come from a bad neighborhood in Manhattan, in New York City."

"Yes, I know where Manhattan is."

"Sorry, Captain."

"It's okay, continue."

"Well, in my neighborhood drugs rule, you know? And everyone I know has been affected by it, especially my family. My older brothers were all killed. Shot in the streets because they were involved in drugs. And my oldest brother died in my arms. We were walking down the street one day and out of nowhere, bam, yo!" As he spoke, Mark made a gun with his hand and an action that reminded James of gang signs from his neighborhood that people made when they were signaling that they were going to shoot someone. "He got shot in the chest! He told me while he was dying, never to get into this mess. He knew that I was the last hope to make my mother proud of us. My brother made me promise that I would help fight back for my brothers, only not on the streets. I would go to the source of the problem and do it the right way! I would stop drugs coming into the country before they could ruin other people's lives. And that's why I wanted to work in the Seventh District, because I know you's guys catch a lot of drug dealers down here!"

As he was talking, Mark had gotten all hyped up. When he finished his speech, he realized he was not standing at attention anymore and stiffened up again.

"That's very honorable of you, ensign. And you're right, we do catch some scum from time to time."

He paused for a moment, leaned forward, smiled and said. "Don't worry, you'll get your chance." James leaned back. "Why don't you go explore the rest of the ship. You know the guns aren't the most important part? Keep that in mind. We try and avoid violence at all cost."

"Yes, Captain."

"Well, go on then!"

"Yes, Captain!"

Mark saluted the captain and ran back inside the ship, opening and closing the heavy door as he went. Captain Hunter watched him leave and smiled at how tormenting he had been. He then bent down and started cleaning up the mess.

"Why do you have to be like that to the new crewmembers," James's Executive Officer asked as she came around the corner. Captain Hunter looked up and laughed at Jessica.

"What do you mean," he asked innocently.

"Oh, come on! You did it to me. You do it to everyone!"

"It's all in fun. He'll figure out soon enough that I'm not that harsh."

"Yeah, but in the meantime he'll be scared shitless. Trust me, I know exactly how he feels."

"I wasn't that bad to you when you first got here, was I?"

"What, you don't remember making me cry my first day?"

"I did not," Captain Hunter pleaded as he stood up with the broken pieces of mug in his hands.

"Yes you did, *Captain.*" As she finished, Jessica slapped a piece of paper into his chest. He smiled.

"What's this," James asked, as Jessica walked away.

"It's our new assignment, straight from the Commandant," she continued as she entered the interior of the ship. "It came in a few minutes ago. And you don't have to tell him your famous story either," she yelled as she shut the door.

"Of course I do," he yelled back. "Thanks for reminding me," he said to himself as he began reading the transmission.

> Tomahawk,
> Proceed to Jamaica... Dock... Refuel... Patrol area 30 miles East of Maurant Point, in the Windward Pass... Heightened Colombian presence has been detected in the area... Drug smuggling suspected...
> USCG Commandant,
> Robert Burrall

"Well, well, well," Captain Hunter said to himself. "Won't Mr. Huerta be pleased."

*****

Later that afternoon, the Tomahawk was sailing towards Jamaica. Mark had settled into his new stateroom and was resting in his bunk when Lieutenant Joe Napier ducked his head into the room.

"So, you must be the new guy," Joe asked, thrusting his hand in Mark's direction.

Mark stood quickly and saluted him. "Yes, sir," he shouted happily.

Joe saluted the new shipmate. "What are you doing?"

"I was just resting, sir."

"What's your name," Joe asked, offering his hand again.

"Mark Huerta, sir," he said shaking his hand.

"Uh, you don't have to call me, sir. Just call me Joe. You haven't met Captain Hunter yet, have you?" They were still shaking hands.

"Yeah, he's tough!" Mark was sure of his judgment.

Joe started to laugh. "Oh, man. He always does that to new crewmembers. James's not really like that. He was just gettin' a rise out of you."

"You mean you guys call the captain by his first name?"

"Yeah, man. We're not as formal as most crews. It's pretty laid back on the Tomahawk."

"Oh, okay." Mark was finally getting the point. And thinking about it, Mark realized that Jessica had been pretty laid back as well.

"James didn't tell you his story by any chance did he?"

"What story?" Mark was scared by the look on Joe's face.

"Oh, he didn't. But he will, I guarantee it!"

"What do you mean? What story?" Just then a bell rang over the intercom system. "Dinner is now being served in the Ward Room and on the Mess Deck."

"It's dinner time," Joe said. "Come on, let's go."

A few seconds later, they entered a small, carpeted room that looked like a cross between a company boardroom and a lounge. There were couches on one side of the room and a long table surrounded by chairs on the other.

At the far end of the room was a small opening in the bulkhead that led to the galley. There was food on the counter top of the opening, next to plates and silverware. Joe and Mark headed for the food.

Out of the corner of his eye Mark noticed the captain sitting at the head of the table surrounded by other officers. He thought that the higher-ranking officers would sit right next to the captain but there was a space just to the captain's left. As Mark was moving towards the food the captain caught his attention.

"Ensign Huerta," James called, as the whole dining room went quiet. "So nice to see you again. Did you get settled?" Mark stopped cold in his tracks, cringed and then turned around to face the captain.

"Yes, Captain, thank you," Mark answered as everyone stared at him. He wasn't as stiff as he had been before because of what Joe had said.

"Everyone say hello to Ensign Huerta."

"Hello, Ensign Huerta," everyone said in unison and laughed. There were twelve officers in the room and all of them were fixated on the new crewmember.

"Go get your dinner and come sit down," James said, pointing to the empty seat. Everyone in the room except for Mark knew what was going to happen.

Mark went to the counter to receive his food. The cook looked at him as if he was sorry for Mark. Mark looked back at the cook with a confused expression.

"Don't worry, you'll be okay," Joe said to Mark quietly. "Have a good dinner." He walked off and left Mark alone to face the captain.

As Mark sat down, the captain put his arm around his shoulder and shook him.

"Listen, I'm sorry about today. I was just kidding around. I hope I didn't scare you," James asked, seeming much less overbearing than he was earlier.

"No, it's okay, Captain," Mark replied, still a little uneasy that the captain was acting so nice.

The captain continued talking with the rest of the crew at the table while Mark poked at his green beans and mashed potatoes. He was slowly becoming more comfortable with his surroundings but he didn't feel like it was his home yet. He felt like it was his first day in training again. It was the kind of feeling most people get on the first few days of sleep-away camp. He still wasn't able to do normal things, like showering or eating, without being shy about it.

All of a sudden, Mark's table burst out in laughter. He hadn't been paying attention but laughed anyway. The captain turned to him and smiled. "You'll be happy to know we're headed down south to a high drug trafficking area, The Windward Pass. This could be your chance to catch all those bad drug people." The captain's eyes widened abruptly, he seemed excited. "Say," he said, still looking at Mark. "Have you ever heard the story about how my father saved me once when I was on a drug mission?"

Just then everyone at the table needed to leave for various reasons. The captain looked up and questioned everyone. "Hey, where are you guys going?"

"I've got to prepare the charts for tomorrow," one crewmember said, and walked off with his tray.

Captain Hunter looked around for some other explanations. "What about you," he asked an older officer.

"Excuse me Captain, I have to go to the head," he said, bowing his head in embarrassment.

"And you? I'm sure you have a great excuse," the captain yelled to the cook who was walking away from the service window. "Dinner's over. You don't have anything to cook!"

"No, Captain, I don't," the cook said, already closing the window. "I've got a shuffleboard game with some of the guys." He laughed.

Captain Hunter laughed to himself then looked down at Mark. "Well, I guess it's just you and me."

"I guess so, Captain." His facial expressions were mixed. Mark tried to hide the fact that he was worried about having to listen to the captain's story, but at the same time he tried to look happy. His cover-up didn't work.

"You don't look too enthusiastic about hearing my story."

"No, Captain, I'm very interested, please." Mark almost sounded sincere.

Captain Hunter stared at him for a second to catch his sarcasm, but he could not. "All right then, here's the story. Don't worry, I'll tell you the abridged version."

James got comfortable and then began. "We had a call over the radio of a suspicious ship heading towards Florida from the Gulf. They said it might be a drug shipment so we got a boarding party together, myself included."

The captain took a sip of his tea, and then continued. "So we get on this small ship, maybe only one-hundred feet long or so. We asked the captain of the ship to escort us to his cargo hold. And, by the way, all the people on this ship were scary looking. They had that look in their eyes that told you to be careful. You got the feeling they didn't want us on their boat," he said as a side point.

"Anyway, the captain took us down to the cargo hold and I got this strange feeling. It was very spooky, kind of like something passed through me or over me. Until this day I'm not sure what it was exactly, but I did know one thing. Whatever it was, it had my father's presence in it." James paused for a moment as his eyes focused on a far away image of his father.

"So anyway, it pulled me around to look the other way, and the first thing I saw was a metal bar coming at my head. I ducked just in time, grabbed the pipe and pushed the guy to the ground. My heart was racing like a horse. Not just because I could've been killed, but also because I felt my father there!"

The captain took in a deep breath and let it out as if he was reliving the story but relieved that it was over.

Mark was staring at him. "So," he asked impatiently.

"So, what?"

"What happened with the drugs?" Mark was waiting for the answer with wide-eyed anticipation.

"Is that all you're worried about? The point of the story was about how my father saved my life!"

"Yes, I know Captain, but what happened with the drugs? Did you find any?"

Captain Hunter sighed and shook his head. "No, we didn't find any drugs. It turned out to be a decoy ship. The only thing we found was pure cane sugar."

"What do you mean it was a decoy ship?" His voice and face showed his interest in the complexities of the drug trade.

"Well, sometimes drug lords will send out decoy ships so that the real drug carriers can get through. That's one of their ways of distracting us, and it works."

"Wow," Mark exclaimed. He was staring at the captain as if he had never seen a human before.

"Are you all right," the captain asked, waving his hand in front of Mark's face.

Mark snapped out of his trance. "Yes, sorry, I'm fine."

"Captain Hunter, your presence is requested on the bridge," a voice said over the intercom. James turned back to Mark. "Well, I guess that's me." He picked up his tray and stood to go. "See, that story wasn't so bad. I have no idea why everyone can't stand it." James walked away.

"Bye, Captain."

*****

Captain Hunter could not sleep that night. He woke up in a sweat from bad dreams but could not remember them, though he tried. Finally, at about 0200 hours, he decided not to fight it anymore. James threw on some warm clothes and went out on the deck. It was a very cool night for the Gulf of Mexico. James looked down at his watch and then up in the air. He calculated the speed and distance and figured that they were not too far from Jamaica.

James loved being out on the deck at night. The stars were so magnificent in the middle of the ocean. There were never any lights for miles.

James found his way to the bow. He was looking down at the water being pushed aside by the force of his ship when he saw a faint light coming from the water. It must have only been a hundred yards and closing, he thought. He leaned over to get a closer look. The light was heading straight for his ship, or they were heading straight for the light, James couldn't decide which was happening. The light was getting closer by the second; it was now only fifty yards from the ship.

Suddenly, James felt a familiar presence. Chills washed across his body. The intensity of the feeling revealed that James's father was back to help him.

He still did not know what the light was but James knew that it must mean danger. The captain knew he had to warn the bridge. He turned around and started to run but it was too late.

The boat halted to a dead stop and in that instant the captain's inertia threw him back and off the front of the ship. They won't even know I'm gone until it's too late, he thought as he flew through the air. It only took the captain's body five seconds to hit the water, and in that instant, he was no longer conscious.

The sudden halt of the ship had injured most of the crew and killed about half. Most of the crew had been thrown into steel bulkheads, through glass windows, or even off the ship like the captain they thought was sleeping.

Jessica, the Officer of the Day, and Mark were laying on the floor of the bridge. They had been thrown against the console in the middle of the bridge and had bounced off when the ship stopped. The other two crewmembers on the bridge had been thrown through the windows and had died on impact.

Neither Jessica nor Mark were unconscious but both were in terrible pain. Jessica tried to get up but could not. Both of her legs were broken.

She called out to Mark, the only other crewmember she could see. "Mark," she cried in pain. There was no answer.

"Mark," she said again more forcefully.

"Yeah?" The answer came slowly.

"Are you okay?" All the lights were out and the darkness was ominous. It hung over everything like the grim reaper himself was there to claim all of their souls. Jessica could see Mark but not well enough to determine if he was injured as badly as she was.

"Yes," Mark responded, as he slid closer to her. "Are you," he asked, touching her shoulder.

Jessica screamed in pain as she felt the touch. She realized that she must have broken more than her legs.

"Can you walk," she asked through clenched teeth.

"I think so," Mark answered hesitantly.

"Then go down and see if you can find the captain. I'll radio for help."

"Yes, Ma'am." Mark slowly got to his feet. He tried to pull him himself up with his right arm and cringed. He didn't want Jessica to know he was hurt.

Mark became very dizzy as he stood. He ran one of his hands over his head and felt blood running freely near his right ear. He grabbed onto a console in front of him to keep his balance, then felt his way aft of the bridge and down towards the lower decks.

When he neared the door, Mark saw light coming from beneath the ship. He wondered if he was hallucinating, but he quickly pushed the thought out of his mind and focused on the task at hand.

Jessica was still trying to gather enough strength and courage to move. When she did, her whole body hurt like hell. She felt as if everything in her body was broken except her left arm. Although the lights were out, she knew where she was on the bridge and she knew the radio wasn't far away.

Jessica closed her eyes and pulled her broken, bleeding body across the floor. She slid easily over the rough, cold metallic surface. There was no water around and she figured that it was her blood that was easing the friction between her and the floor.

Slowly and painfully, she made her way to the receiver, which she could hear as it slid back and forth across the wall. It had been thrown from its cradle when the boat halted.

As she reached up for the receiver, she heard a loud clang come from the bottom of the ship and the floor began gyrating beneath her. Her body was banging up and down on the floor and her broken bones were receiving no sympathy from the movements.

She threw her left arm up and grabbed the receiver while she screamed in pain. She was starting to get dizzy and knew that she must send out a distress call soon.

It was getting hard for her to talk and Jessica hoped she had enough energy left to send out a message. As she pressed the side of the receiver to send the message Jessica had another strange feeling. She felt as if the boat was sinking.

"Mayday, mayday," she said weakly into the receiver. "This is XO Jessica Carp of the Coast Guard Cutter Tomahawk. Please respond."

"This is U.S. Coast Guard Cutter Endurance," a voice came crackling over the radio. "What's going on there, Tomahawk?"

Just then, Jessica heard a loud splash and the sound of rushing water. She felt the floor getting cold and wet. Water was coming in from the outside. The ship *was* sinking. She realized that Mark must have been trapped below deck; otherwise he would have come to warn her. Water was coming in faster and faster and she knew she was about to pass out. It's better to die unconscious than drown, she thought.

"We're going under... All dead... Stopped," she said into the receiver not making any sense now. The water was about to engulf her, but she passed out just before the water covered her mouth.

The Tomahawk was never heard from or seen again.

CHAPTER 1

Aaron had loved dolphins since he was a child. His parents used to take him every year to a Florida Keys research facility to watch them. After a few years, everyone who worked at the research facility knew Aaron by name.

As he grew older, the researchers in Florida let him work with them during the summers and Aaron was thrilled. He did most of the everyday chores and he didn't get paid, but being around the dolphins and swimming with them was payment enough.

Aaron continued to work for the researchers every summer until he was eighteen. That summer, both of his parents died in a plane crash over the Rocky Mountains along with two hundred other passengers.

The news of his parents' death had crippled him. He did not go to college that year but instead moved to Israel to get away from any memories he had of his parents. He loved them and missed them terribly, but every time he turned the corner, something else reminded him of their absence.

In Israel, Aaron joined the army with his best friend, Jason, and as luck would have it they were placed in the same division — the Golani. The Golani were a special forces unit that served near the Lebanese border and often across it. They served for three years, side by side and came out mostly mentally and physically unscathed but many of their friends had lost their lives defending their Jewish homeland.

Aaron often thought about dying in combat and at the time it didn't bother him. He was still in anguish over his parents' death but after three years of being surrounded by death, he was tired of it.

After his service with the Golani ended he returned to America to start a normal life again and pursue his dream of working with dolphins but Jason did not join him. He remained in Israel and was recruited by the Israeli Foreign Intelligence — the Mossad.

Their geographical separation didn't hamper their friendship but they didn't speak as much. Jason wasn't one for keeping in touch but once in a while he would set Aaron up on blind dates with his leftovers. They never worked out but at least it gave them something to talk about besides the past.

In three years, Aaron finished his undergraduate studies in psychology at The University at Albany with a perfect grade point average and was accepted to Harvard with a full scholarship, excluding room and board. He had more than enough money from his parents' estate to put him through college and graduate school but he never told schools about it. He felt guilty having to use any portion of what his parents had left him and worked to support himself instead. He didn't go to Harvard just for the prestige factor. There were a few schools that would have been a better choice as far as dolphin research went but Aaron was attracted to Boston's youthful atmosphere. The city was overrun with people his age, and he figured it might be a good place to meet a nice Jewish girl that he would, one day, settle down with.

Upon acceptance to the graduate program, Aaron began reviewing the physiology of bottlenose dolphins with his professor, Dr. John J. Jeffries. It was important, and necessary if he was going to do his research. Aaron took up too much time studying dolphins according to his professor, but Triple J., Dr. Jeffries, couldn't complain. Aaron always finished the work he was asked to do, but when Dr. Jeffries caught Aaron polishing up on the sensory systems of dolphins during experimental psychology, he couldn't help but reprimand him.

"Mr. Silver, what do you think this is, study hall," Dr. Jeffries bellowed in his British baritone accent.

"What," Aaron asked, looking up as the class laughed at him.

"Mr. Silver, do you need extra time to study during the day? If so, I can arrange for you to be transferred to another psychology program. They may not ask as much of you somewhere else."

Aaron mumbled a response under his breath and the small class laughed at him again.

"Excuse me," Dr. Jeffries replied.

"Nothing, never mind," Aaron answered, not embarrassed.

"Indeed, well, that's all the time we have for now."

The whole class was almost out the door when Aaron was caught by Jeffries's words. "Aaron, may I talk to you for a second?" Aaron turned around, to face his professor who didn't look British, if there was a British look.

Dr. Jeffries was wearing a tweed jacket and blue jeans with penny loafers. He was the same height as Aaron but looked much wiser with his pepper colored hair and slightly wrinkled face. He was the kind of man who was easy to talk to about psychology but never once did he ever mention anything about his family history. He looked like the sort of professor who slept with every student he could get his hands on but Aaron never heard any rumors like that. In fact, there were more rumors about his married life floating around but Aaron didn't want to crack the mystery. He stayed more of an enigma that way and that was what he liked about Dr. Jeffries.

"Aaron, I don't mind if you study dolphins. In fact, you *should* be studying them, but you need to learn other things as well. Don't let me catch you doing this again during class time. Understood." He was speaking to Aaron over his spectacles.

"I'm sorry Triple J. I just wanted to finish the chapter I was reading. It won't happen again."

"Good. Now walk me back to my office," Jeffries said with a smile.

They continued talking as they walked down the hall. The professor took a liking to Aaron soon after they met because he reminded Jeffries of how he used to be as a young psychology student. He was driven.

"You look a little fidgety, Aaron. What's going on," Jeffries asked after they retreated from the hallway into his office.

"I just want to get back to studying."

Aaron really did want to get back to his reading, but that's not why he was fidgety. Jason had set him up on another blind date that he knew wouldn't work out.

"So, what are you working on," Dr. Jeffries asked for the second time.

"What," Aaron asked, coming out of a trance.

"You know, sometimes I wonder if you're ever listening to me."

"I'm sorry, my mind is always churning."

"What are you working on?"

"I could tell you but then I'd have to kill you," Aaron said mysteriously. Dr. Jeffries wasn't amused.

"I'm working on Dolphin self-recognition," Aaron continued seriously.

"Why are you wasting your time, you'll never find anything. Dolphins may be smart, they may be able to learn tricks, but you'll never find a dolphin who'll recognize itself in a mirror."

"I'm not going to research it that way."

"So, how are you going to test self-recognition in dolphins?" Dr. Jeffries sat down in his old chair. It made a high-pitched squeak as he made himself comfortable and Aaron continued.

"Well, I've read up on your self-recognition research in primates, as well as the research done on humans, and there's something in common with both of them."

"Which is?"

"Both primates and humans are land animals, and one of the most important sensory mechanisms for us is sight, but that doesn't apply to dolphins. The major sensory mechanism for dolphins is their sense of hearing."

"And how are you tying this into self-recognition?" Jeffries was intrigued.

"Well, you know that dolphins use echo location to find things and other noises to communicate, or so it seems?" It was a rhetorical question, knowing very well that his professor knew the answer.

"Yes," Dr. Jeffries asked, leaning back in his chair and wanting to hear more.

"Yeah, well, we could program pictures of different dolphins on an underwater touch screen. One of the pictures would be of the dolphin in question. The other pictures would be of other dolphins from the same tank. Obviously there would be a training phase for the dolphins to learn to use the touch screen and to let them look at themselves in mirrors."

"Obviously."

"After that, you put pictures of different dolphins on the touch screen with one dolphin in the tank. While it's swimming around you play pre-recorded vocalizations from that dolphin and the other dolphins."

"And?"

"And, if the dolphin continuously chooses the correct pictures of his buddies and especially himself…"

"Then they seem to have the ability of self-recognition," Dr. Jeffries interrupted. "Very creative, but I still don't think you'll get any interesting results."

"But, you see, it's just like listening to a recording of yourself. You know when it sounds like you, and you know when it sounds like somebody else. The dolphins would be doing the same thing except they would be using two senses, sight and hearing, the latter of which has been proven to be their strongest asset!"

"I understand what you're saying, but there's never been any evidence that dolphins can conceive of themselves."

Aaron was trying to drive the final nail in the coffin but with Dr. Jeffries, it was like trying to drive a nail in a lead coffin. He would always play devil's advocate with his students to get them thinking about what they were doing.

"I think it's still worth a shot, because after all…" He began imitating Dr. Jeffries. "The absence of evidence is not the evidence of absence."

"So, you *do* listen in class. I'm amazed."

Dr. Jeffries sat quietly for a moment contemplating the idea. He leaned back in his squeaky old chair and rubbed his clean-shaven face. Aaron sat, wondering why he didn't get a new chair. This chair had holes in it that were covered in silver duct tape. It must have been there since Dr. Jeffries started working at Harvard about twenty years ago. Sometimes it almost seemed as if Dr. Jeffries himself hadn't moved in years.

His office was a pigsty. There were papers piled all over the office, one could hardly move around. It reminded Aaron of how his room used to look when he was younger.

Whenever he asked the good doctor why he never cleaned his office, Dr. Jeffries responded by saying that he was waiting for the university to get him a secretary. Just by glancing at his office anyone could tell he'd been waiting too long.

"I think there might actually be a way for you to do this research this summer."

"Really? How," Aaron asked with enthusiasm. He couldn't believe that Dr. Jeffries wasn't still grilling him on his project.

"You can apply for a grant to work with dolphins. I don't know off hand of any research facility that has the equipment you would need, but I'm sure it's out there."

Aaron thought of the research center he had gone to all those summers as a teenager. They didn't have that kind of equipment but he wouldn't want to go there even if they did. It would bring back too many memories. Memories that he had tried hard to forget.

"You don't have any idea where they might have the equipment that I need to do this?"

Dr. Jeffries sat back and thought about it some more. "Wait, I do know." He paused for a second, then continued. "You could go to Jamaica. I have some old friends there doing some dolphin research. I think I remember them telling me about some new toys that they had received for their lab."

"Sounds nice to me. I've never been down there." Aaron's eyes looked up and he imagined lying on a white sand beach.

"You wouldn't be going down for a vacation so you can push those thoughts of lying on the beach right out of your mind!"

"You know me too well. What about money though?"

"I told you. You'll apply for a grant."

"Yeah, but from whom?" Aaron knew that it was a pain to apply for grants. He had done it before, but to no avail. One of the hardest things to find was a company willing to give a grant for dolphin research.

"I've got a packet around here somewhere with a whole bunch of private companies who fund animal research."

"Yeah, right!" Aaron laughed. "You'll find it in this mess!"

"Maybe I'll just ask my secretary to find it." Dr. Jeffries was being sarcastic and they both chuckled because he had no secretary.

"Oh, shit," Aaron said suddenly as he glanced down at his watch. "I'm late!" He rose hastily from his chair and started out of the office.

"Late for what," Dr. Jeffries asked as Aaron grabbed his coat and backpack.

"A date." He turned back quickly before leaving the office. "Oh, if you ever do find that packet could you drop it off in my box downstairs?"

"No problem," he answered as Aaron ran out of his office.

"Thanks, Triple J," Aaron screamed from down the hall.

Dr. Jeffries sat in his office laughing. Then he shook his head and said to himself, "That boy's going to win the Nobel Prize one day."

*****

Cheers didn't look anything like it did in the television show except for the wooden Indian in the entrance but Aaron liked it anyway. The bar was always crowded with tourists from all over the country who would get the waiters to take pictures of them surrounded by all the sports and *Cheers* memorabilia. Being surrounded by tourists made him feel like a local and he liked it.

A career waitress, no younger than fifty, took Aaron to a small table situated near the front door. Although the cold spring air blew in every time the doors opened, he wanted to sit near the entrance to make sure his blind date noticed him.

"Can I get ya anything to staat with," the waitress asked in her fifty-year-old Bostonian accent.

"Can I have a Cider Jack® please?"

"Sure thing," she said as she whisked off into the sea of people crowding the bar.

Being in *Cheers* made him reminisce. When he was young, he used to go over to a friend's house every night and watch *Cheers* reruns. It was his favorite show, and being in the bar brought back all the good memories of being at home. Most of those memories were not from school however.

His house in Memphis was next door to his high school. Aaron figured that if he lived closer to the school than anyone else, that he could get up the latest and still be on time for classes. This assumption was correct, but he was never on time for school.

The waitress appeared for a brief second to deliver the cider to Aaron before she vanished again into the crowd. He took a sip and his mind began to wander off again amidst the hustle and bustle of the crowded room.

During the afternoons Aaron would sneak home from school to eat lunch. Most of the time Jason would come with him. They would make huge tuna sandwiches and watch *Simon and Simon*, and the *A-Team*. They really didn't care much about their classes and never got caught anyway.

26

One time, Aaron thought, as a smile crossed his face, one of their teachers told them not to come to class if they didn't finish their homework assignment. Aaron and Jason took her seriously and did not come to her class the next day. Instead, they hid in some bookshelves in the next room until they were caught.

From that day forth they swore to themselves that no matter what stunt they were to pull, they would never get caught again but some years later they broke that agreement after being caught by Aaron's mother upon returning from raiding a summer camp. It was a small sleep away camp just outside of Memphis where many of Aaron and Jason's friends spent the summer. They had concocted a scheme to raid their friends' camp from the outside. That way no one would ever suspect them.

Aaron took involuntary sips of his cider as he thought. His brain had completely shut out the outside world and was focused securely on the past. He didn't like to go there often for fear of conjuring up too many images of his lost parents but once in a while there were some good memories to think about.

Jason had spent the night at Aaron's house that muggy summer night. Aaron's mother suspected something was going on right away because Aaron had always slept over at Jason's house.

Jason had planned the whole strategic raid, right down to the army paint they were to use on their faces for camouflage. They stayed up till two in the morning, and then drove forty-five minutes to the camp. After parking the car just outside the campgrounds, they walked the rest of the way to the bunks. As they got closer, Jason said it would be safer for them to crawl to prevent detection. Aaron followed his order.

They went into each bunk and wreaked havoc. In the bathrooms they put clear plastic wrap under the toilet seats and greased the top of the seats with white shoe polish. Shaving cream was used to write obscenities on the mirrors and after they finished doing their worst, Jason and Aaron turned off the power for each cabin. The raid of the camp went off without a hitch but their return to Aaron's house was a different story.

When they returned, there was a note on the front door from Aaron's mother, which read, "Wake me up when you get back!" She was pissed, but she never told anyone what they had done. They had been caught again, but they knew the third time would be the charm.

"Excuse me," a young woman said, trying to get Aaron's attention but he was still wandering through the past.

"I'm fine, I'm just waiting for someone," Aaron replied with his eyes glazed over.

"Like, hello! I'm not your waitress," the voice said softly.

Aaron looked up to see a young woman about his age smiling at him. She stood there with long flowing blonde hair and deep blue eyes. She didn't look Jewish but Jason would never set Aaron up with someone who wasn't. Jason knew how Aaron felt about that.

"I'm sorry," Aaron said sincerely as he turned beet red. He always embarrassed himself when he met girls, why should this time be any different?

"You must be Marissa," he continued, as he stood abruptly. As Aaron got up to shake her hand, he knocked his cider over and it spilled on her jeans.

"Oh, my God, I'm so sorry! I'm such a klutz."

"It's okay," she answered honestly as she grabbed a napkin from the table and cleaned herself off. Aaron was going to help but when he realized the spill was right around her crotch he just stood there helpless.

"I'm gonna go to the bathroom for a second." Marissa laughed as she walked off trying to cover the spill inconspicuously.

Aaron sat back down with his head in his hands not believing what he had just done. The waitress came back and saw the mess.

"Nice move, Slick," she said. "I'm sure that really impressed her."

"I always do that when I meet women!" Aaron looked up, ashamed.

"What, spill cider on them?"

"Very funny," he said as the waitress started to clean off the table. As she was cleaning, the television on the opposite wall went black and came on again. The flash caught Aaron's eye. It was a World News Network special report.

The anchor came on and started speaking but Aaron couldn't hear what he was saying. The volumes on the televisions were never turned up in *Cheers*. There was no point; the atmosphere was always too loud to hear over anyway. All Aaron could make out was the video of the anchorperson talking with another man who was from the CIA with the background of the sea behind them. He could see "CIA" written at the bottom of the screen but the man's name was too small to read.

"Can you believe that," the waitress asked, now watching the television with Aaron.

"What?"

"There's another Bermuda Triangle in the Gulf of Mexico."

Aaron looked at her, confused.

"Ya know," she said as if he knew already. "Ships are just up and disappearing, but this time in the Gulf of Mexico."

Aaron still looked a little confused.

"You haven't heard about it yet?"

"No."

"It's been in the news for a week already, where you been?"

"In school," he answered as she walked off. Aaron had no idea what was going on in the world when he was in school. He was too busy studying. Just then Aaron saw Marissa walking back from the bathroom. He was about to get up to greet her, but before he was able to, she stopped him. "That's okay, please *don't* get up," she said with a smile and a giggle. Aaron was red but amazed that she hadn't walked out on the date yet. Maybe this one will work out, he thought as he watched her. She was quite pretty.

"It's okay. I was half expecting something like that to happen."

"What do you mean?"

"Jason told me how you get when you first meet women."

"He told you I get klutzy when I meet women," Aaron asked in disbelief. "I can't believe he told you that!" He laughed. "What else did he tell you?"

"Oh, you don't have to be embarrassed. It was good that I was expecting it. That way I wasn't wearing anything too nice."

She was pretty but Marissa's voice portrayed her as a bit of a ditz, even if she was book smart. Aaron had met many women like this and they were not his type. He was beginning to think that maybe Jason was wrong yet again.

The waitress appeared again from nowhere. "Alright, what will it be?"

The couple looked at each other and Marissa signaled for Aaron to order first.

"I'll have a garden salad with ranch dressing. Oh, and, can I have another cider please?"

"Sure thing, but try not to spill this one okay? And you, honey?" She turned towards Marissa.

"I'll have the steak, medium rare. That comes with cheese sticks, right?"

Aaron couldn't believe his ears. He'd never been out with a woman who ate like that, especially on the first date.

"If you order them it does," the waitress replied sarcastically, with her hands on her hips.

"Then I guess I will. And, uh, let me have a beer, too."

"Okay kids, be back soon," the waitress said as she took the menus and left again.

Aaron looked at Marissa and knew that this wasn't going to work out. She didn't seem to care about keeping kosher, and although Aaron wasn't very strict himself, he never ate non-kosher meat. He also liked eating healthy ever since leaving the army. The food they had served in one day in his base on the border of Lebanon could have kept five tanks well oiled for a month.

They talked for a while, but Aaron wasn't interested in what she had to say. Marissa kept talking about how interesting being a librarian was, and it was all

29

Aaron could do to stay awake. He began thinking of all the applications he would have to fill out in order to do his research. First though, he had to wait and see if Dr. Jeffries could find the packet of scholarships in his office. Although these thoughts were not very entertaining, they kept Aaron from dozing off in front of his date.

A few hours later, Aaron took Marissa to her apartment. He didn't have a great time but asked for her number anyway. "Goodnight," he said to Marissa as he kissed her on the cheek.

"Call me," she yelled as she got out of the car and ran up the steps to her apartment. Marissa unlocked the front door, turned around and waved to Aaron cheerily. Aaron waved back, drove off and sighed to himself sadly. "What the hell were you thinking, Jason?"

*****

The next morning, Aaron was rudely awakened by a telephone call that echoed loudly through his modest one-bedroom apartment. He had been sleeping with the pillow over his head to block out the already roaring world outside but it hadn't worked well enough. He fumbled around without looking, picked up the receiver and placed it on the pillow covering his head.

"What," Aaron said groggily. The sound was muffled from the pillow.

"Aaron, are you still sleeping," Dr. Jeffries asked.

"Yes, what do you want?" Aaron was still half asleep.

"I found that packet with all the funding information I was telling you about."

"You found it? Where?" He pulled the pillow off of his head and sat up.

"In my office!"

"Oh, please, can't you find anything better to do than tease me about stuff like that? I'm going back to sleep." Aaron fell back on his bed with the receiver still to his head.

"No, I'm serious. Come in and have a look at it."

"I'll come in later, how about two?"

"That's fine for me."

"Okay, I'll see you then."

Dr. Jeffries hung up and Aaron looked at the phone and chuckled at it. "Yeah, right," he said to himself. "You found it in your office." He put the phone back down and relaxed again on his bed. He was asleep within two minutes.

He had finished all his reading the night before and his job at the dive shop didn't start until eleven. He figured he would run by Dr. Jeffries's office during his lunch break and see if he was telling the truth.

At about two, Aaron walked into Jeffries's office and walked out again, thinking he had walked into the wrong room. The room he had been in was spotless, and someone was cleaning it. This was definitely not Triple J's office, Aaron thought to himself.

He looked up, above the door and the number read 286. Aaron was in shock. This *was* Jeffries's room. Maybe they had changed room numbers, he thought?

As Aaron was looking into the office he felt a hand on his shoulder.

"Isn't it a thing of beauty," Dr. Jeffries asked as he sighed in relief.

"I can't believe it," Aaron said, still staring at the office. "Hell really did freeze over!" He still couldn't believe that John's office was being cleaned. He stood there without moving until Dr. Jeffries started talking again.

"They figured it was about time."

Aaron looked up at Jeffries. "But how?"

"Well, it's kind of like two roommates living together, one's a slob and one's not. Neither one wants to clean up the other's mess, but after a while one gives in because he can't stand the appearance of the place. That's what Harvard did, they finally caved. It took them a while, but they caved." He paused for another moment admiring the cleanliness of his office.

"There's a lesson for you, Aaron."

"I don't have a roommate," Aaron said, still gazing at the office from the hall.

"You will one day my friend. Oh, before I forget." Jeffries walked into his office. "Take the packet I found for you, because when she leaves, this place is going back to normal."

Jeffries picked the forty-page packet up from his desk and walked out to hand it to Aaron. Aaron could not force himself to walk into the office. He was afraid the office would turn back to normal if he went inside and he wanted to behold of the wonder as long as he could.

"Here," Jeffries said, turning to one of the middle pages. "I circled one that looked really promising. The deadline is really close so just apply for this one and see what happens. Besides, remember how I told you about my friends down in Jamaica? Well, this grant, if awarded, can only be used down there."

"What's it called? Oh, here it is," Aaron said, turning to the previous page, his gaze finally stolen from the office. "The International Cetacean Behavior Fund. Yeah, it does sound pretty promising. I'll give it a try."

"Cheers," Jeffries said, signaling the abrupt end of their conversation. It seemed to Aaron that he was always pressed for time.

"Alright, I'm going. Hey, before I forget, can you write me a letter of recommendation for this?"

"We shall see," Dr. Jeffries said as he retreated into his clean office.

Aaron walked down the hallway, dreading having to fill out the Cetacean Fund application. Well, I can always do it at work, he thought to himself. He was never too busy at the dive shop.

CHAPTER 2

Tag Millwood was a middle ranking CIA agent with the Miami bureau. He had been assigned to Miami twenty years ago, and for Tag, that was much too long.

Tag was from Minneapolis, and he still missed the somewhat mild summers and snowy winters. He had been captain of his college ski team but since he graduated, he had not been skiing even once. After his graduate degree in criminology was attained, he figured that the CIA would give him a great job as a field agent. Instead they put him at a desk. Tag knew that he had to give the CIA at least five years of his life.

During those five years he had been married and divorced. His wife left him because he was never home. Tag wanted to be with his wife and only son, but the agency always had extra work for him to do. He missed most of his son's childhood and he hated the CIA for it. Tag could have quit, but that wasn't enough for him. He wanted to leave the agency with a bang. He wanted them to know that people could not just mess with his life and not feel the repercussions.

The stress that built up from all his anger through the years was showing. Tag's face was older than his years and he had almost a full head of gray hair at forty-five. His demeanor changed every year as well. Tag got meaner as he got older. No one in the Miami office wanted to deal with him, but they all had to. Everything that happened in the office went through Tag.

This morning was very different than any morning had been in years. Tag still had his two glasses of cognac to start off the day, but instead of his inexpensive V.S. Courvoisier, he was trying out his new bottle of Succession J.L., a very old and very rare Grande Champagne Cognac.

His first special paycheck had just arrived the other day and he wanted to splurge. Tag knew he was an alcoholic but he didn't care. He drank enough to ease the pain, but very rarely got drunk during work hours.

Tag was pretty sure what he was going to encounter at the office that morning. It had been a month since the first Coast Guard ship had sunk in international waters near Jamaica and he was expecting to hear reports from his field agents.

The CIA had jurisdiction over this investigation because the area was considered a national security risk. The Jamaican government complained about the strong CIA presence in the region but once they were asked to help, things calmed down.

"What in the hell do you mean, you don't know anything," Tag screamed across the short, conference room table to his field agents who had just arrived from the Caribbean. "What the hell did you do down there? I hope you smoked enough weed! 'Cause for God's sake you better have a good reason for not knowing anything!"

"Well, sir, there were some important findings," one of the agents responded calmly. Everyone in the Miami office had learned how to deal with Tag's temper. They just remained calm. That was the only thing that they could do. If they tried to get angry at him, that would be their end at the Miami bureau.

"And what were those, 'some important things'?" Tag relaxed back in his chair. He was waiting to hear nothing of importance. He knew that his agents couldn't have found too much. For one, he thought they were all incompetent, and two, he knew there was no wreckage.

"First, sir, and most importantly, there was no wreckage."

"Really, you noticed that," Tag said sarcastically. "Shit, you guys are better than I thought."

"Well," the agent continued, unfazed. "It's kind of like what happened in the Bermuda Triangle." Tag rolled his eyes at this news.

"We took the last few minutes of the recorded message from the Tomahawk and found what we could. It seemed as if the crew was confused about where they where. They didn't know up from down or their left from their right. Then, after that, the boat just disappeared. That's all we have, sir."

Tag sat there for a minute staring at his agents, his agents staring back waiting for a response. Without any warning, Tag broke out in heavy laughter. The other agents in the room looked at Tag and then at themselves and started to laugh with their boss.

In their fits of laughter no one noticed Tag's raging face. As the agents were laughing, Tag slammed his fists down on the table shaking the whole room.

"Are you guys fucking nuts? What the hell kind of shit are you spewing over this table? Does this look like a bathroom to you? Does it?" He was not expecting a response.

The agents were mortified. Their faces went from dark sun drenched skin to ghost white in a matter of seconds. They were staring at Tag, unable to take their eyes off of him. He had been angry before but they had never seen him like this.

"Answer me! Does this look like a God damn bathroom to you?" Tag slowly, dragged each word out as if his audience was hard of hearing.

"No, sir," one of the agents said slowly.

"What kind of shit for brains, dip shit do you think I am? Huh? What kind, I want to know?"

No one answered him.

"Do you know what headquarters would say if I called them and told them, 'Hey guys, we've got another Bermuda Triangle in the Gulf of Mexico?' Do you know what they'd say? I don't know what a good response to that would be. I was hoping you would, because it sounds fuckin' ridiculous to me!"

Tag's face was red from shouting and the veins in his neck were about to explode. He was breathing heavily, but finally quiet. Without a word he pointed to the door while staring at his agents. They had learned long ago, like good little dogs, what that meant. They quickly gathered their things and headed for the door but just before the agents left the room, Tag blared, "And I don't want to see your asses back in Miami until you have some good information!"

Now that Tag had made the office a little less crowded for a while, he figured he would get some work done. He walked out of the conference room into the narrow, bare hallway to his office. They never kept the appearance of the office up to standards. Tag was in charge of that, but he didn't care, and no one else dared challenge his decision.

The CIA building was very inconspicuous and the mailmen thought that it was some kind of mail processing center. It was a good guess on their part because the mail delivered to the building was addressed to different organizations, including the one that had been delivered that morning, which was addressed to the International Cetacean Behavior Fund.

Tag sat down at his desk and looked at the pile of mail he had to go through. Usually his secretary would sort through it first but she was out on vacation. He started separating the mail by organizations and as he was sorting, he came across an envelope addressed to the International Cetacean Behavior Fund. Tag stopped and looked at the envelope for a second. He had not seen one addressed to this fund in a while and didn't know if the CIA was still secretly funding this kind of research.

Dolphin and whale research had been big in the sixties and seventies, but had died down recently. Many of the documents were still classified, and would probably always be. The research they had done would have brought conservationists screaming at the top of their lungs to Capitol Hill. The only reason that Tag had access to the documents was because he read all the proposals for dolphin research that came through the CIA.

Some of the research projects involved training dolphins to carry small explosives and attach them to enemy vessels. Actually, the testing site for their earliest experiments had been the Bermuda Triangle. The Navy and the CIA

35

would send the dolphins out from Norfolk and wait for the results. Sure enough, the next week there would be a report of a vessel that never returned to port and the government started rumors in order to cover up what was actually going on.

The CIA and the Navy had also sponsored many independent researchers without the researcher's knowledge. These projects though, were much more humane. Most of the projects sponsored secretly by the government were ones involving dolphin communication. This was the key that every country, and many researchers, had been looking for. If anyone could figure out how the dolphins were communicating with one another, it would be the biggest breakthrough in marine biology. Tag thought that they had given up on that a while ago. It had seemed so hopeless that anyone would ever get close to understanding the dolphins' vocalizations that most researchers had stopped trying and had gone on with other ideas.

Tag, realizing that this was the first proposal he had seen in a while, opened the large manila envelope and began reading. The title was *Self-awareness in Bottlenose Dolphins*. He recognized the area of research but knew that it had nothing to do with dolphin communication. As Tag read further however, he saw that this experiment had been set up very differently than the past experiments on self-awareness. This experiment actually used sounds of dolphins, rather than just visual representations. The project seemed interesting to him but he had other things to do. He still didn't know whether to send a "thanks but no thanks" letter, or if it was anything worth funding, so for clarification Tag decided to call the dolphin research project director in Washington.

"This is Bob Jacobs, can I help you," the voice asked over the receiver.

"Bob, hello, this is Tag."

"Tag! What's goin' on down there? Hear you lost another boat," Bob said, hoping to be the bearer of bad tidings.

"What," Tag yelled, obviously surprised.

*****

Although Aaron was an advanced open water diver, the dive shop hired him anyway. They had him do many things, including filling air tanks, selling merchandise, and even helping with the scuba classes. The shop had an inside pool in the back that allowed customers to take the class right in the shop and at the moment, Aaron was helping with one of the classes.

The dive master was teaching the class how to find their regulators in case it was dislodged from their mouths and Aaron was watching to make sure the students were doing alright. He had already helped the stunning blonde next to him twice, and he didn't mind that at all.

As the blonde turned in his direction for help again, Aaron heard a whistle from above the pool. Everyone looked up and the wavy figure on the surface seemed to be pointing at Aaron. Damn, he thought, I think she was beginning to like me.

He put his index finger up to the blonde student as if to say he would return in a second. Then Aaron ascended slowly to the surface.

As he reached the surface of the water, Aaron recognized the figure as Doug, the store owner. He was kneeling over the side of the pool with the whistle in one hand and an envelope in the other.

"The mail just came," he said, trying to hint something to Aaron.

"Yeah, so?"

"You got something."

"Great, what's new?" Aaron had given many people the shop's address so they could send him mail there and Doug didn't mind. He hated giving people his home address because his mailbox wasn't secure and he had had packages stolen in the past.

"I think you might be interested in this one." Doug was referring to the envelope in his hands, with a big smile on his face.

It had been a few weeks since he had sent in the application and Aaron had totally forgotten about the Cetacean Fund.

"Who's it from?"

"You remember you were telling me about the dolphin research you wanted to do this summer?" Aaron's eyes widened. "Well, this came today from the Cetacean Fund." He showed Aaron the front of the envelope. Aaron stared at it for a second but it didn't seem to be stuffed the way acceptance letters generally were.

"You open it," Aaron said, still wading in the pool. "My hands are wet."

"You don't look too excited."

"I don't think it's good news," Aaron said solemnly.

"Well, let's see." Doug tore carefully into the envelope. Aaron could see the back of the papers. It was two pages stapled together. He could tell it was typewritten on the fund's stationary; the logo was easily visible from the back of the second page. Although he didn't really want to read it himself, Aaron was trying very hard to see through to the front page.

Doug started reading with no expression on his face or in his voice. "Dear Mr. Silver, We are pleased..."

"Yes," Aaron screamed as he bobbed up and down in the water. "Yes! Yes! Yes," he said again enthusiastically.

"Don't you want to hear the rest of it?"

"Don't need to. I'll read it later." Aaron swam to the edge of the pool and took off his gear.

"What are you doing?"

"Oh," Aaron said, remembering he was at work and had responsibilities. "Do you mind if I take off a little early? I really need to go tell my professor!"

"Sure, go ahead. Phil can handle this class."

"Great, thanks," Aaron said as he continued to take off his scuba gear.

Not paying attention to anything he was doing because of his excited state, Aaron took his buoyancy device off without disconnecting his regulator or his tank and left them in the pool. He ran to the bathroom to get changed and as he ran out of the pool area his apparatus began to sink slowly to the bottom of the pool. Phil and the rest of the students were very confused. Aaron's equipment was back, but he was nowhere to be seen.

It was Tuesday afternoon and Aaron figured he could catch Dr. Jeffries after his undergraduate experimental psychology course. Aaron had heard that it was a course comparable to organic chemistry with Dr. Jeffries teaching it and was glad to have taken it at another school during his undergraduate career.

As he ran up to the door with the paper clenched in his hand, Aaron could see through the window that the class was still in session. He tried to get Jeffries's attention by waving his hands and the letter in front of the window but it was no use. Jeffries was always so into his classes that he hardly ever looked up as he taught. He didn't like being interrupted until he finished a thought.

Aaron paced around in the quiet hallway until, a few minutes later, one student walked out of the classroom. Yes, Aaron thought to himself, it's over, now I can show him.

He was so anxious to tell Dr. Jeffries that he threw open the door and ran into the room. The lecture room sloped down from the back to the front, where the lectern was. Aaron ran down the isle on the left side of the room, keeping his eyes on the ground so he wouldn't trip. When he got to the front of the room he looked up at Dr. Jeffries who stared silently back at him.

He shoved the letter in his professor's face. "I can't believe it," Aaron said loudly. "They gave me everything: travel, housing and expenses!"

Dr. Jeffries was still looking at Aaron silently, not even smiling. Aaron figured he would after the next bit of news.

"There's only one thing though." Aaron was wearing a fake frown. "For some strange reason they told me I have to go to a specific lab and do the research. I wonder where that would be? Maybe... Jamaica? Booya," he belted out, pushing his arms into the air.

Dr. Jeffries still did not seem impressed. Aaron was wondering why he didn't look happy.

"What? You not impressed," he asked Jeffries jokingly.

The professor's hands were crossed over his chest with chalk still in his right hand. He looked slowly from Aaron towards the classroom, motioning for Aaron to look as well. He did, and realized that all the students were staring at him. Class was not over.

"Oh," Aaron said softly as he turned bright red. "Sorry, I'll leave now."

He walked slowly up to the back of the room, keeping his eyes on the floor. Not because he didn't want to trip, but because he didn't want to make eye contact with anyone in the class. He felt like such a dork.

About five minutes later people started exiting the classroom. Aaron was sitting with his back to the wall only ten feet from the door. He heard some of the students laugh as they went by but did not look in their direction.

"Next time you think you can wait till after I finish my class," Dr. Jeffries asked as he exited the classroom.

Aaron looked up. "I'm sorry, I saw someone leave and I thought it was over."

"It's alright. It was pretty funny, though." He had been amused.

Aaron got up from the floor and walked down the hall with the professor. "What you said sounds pretty good," Dr. Jeffries continued. "Jamaica is a pretty nice place. I'm not really sure about Kingston, though. The research facility is still in Kingston, right?"

"It says," Aaron hesitated while trying to read the letter. "Marine Mammal Research Laboratory, Kingston."

"So, you're in the capital, wow, that's going to be great! Just be careful. It can be a little dangerous there." Dr. Jeffries stopped walking and looked at Aaron. "But don't worry, you're going to have one hell of a summer!"

"Wait. What do you mean? 'It could be dangerous'! "

CHAPTER 3

Aaron's neck was killing him. On both flights he had been sitting on the left side of the plane. He loved looking out the window and viewing the world from thirty thousand feet in the air.

"Can you see anything yet," the passenger next to him asked.

"No, but they should sell a special ticket that allows you to switch seats with people from the other side of the plane so you can look out the other window, too. My neck is killing me," he said, rubbing his neck. "You going down for a vacation?"

"Sure am," the man said in a happy southern drawl.

Aaron had figured as much because of the man's straw hat and white shorts. On top of that he had a camera already strapped around his neck and was reading a tour book on Jamaica. "What about you?"

"I'm going to do dolphin research," Aaron replied and turned again to look out the window afraid he would miss something. He loved telling people he was going to do dolphin research. It made him feel interesting and important. He hoped people would think to themselves how boring their job seemed after they realized they had missed the chance in their lives to do something like dolphin research.

"That's interesting!" Aaron smiled at him and turned back to the window. "How long you goin' to be down there?"

"About three months."

"That's great! What are you trying to find out?"

"We're trying to find out if dolphins are self-aware," Aaron said, now paying attention to the fat man who was probably bald underneath the hat but Aaron couldn't tell. He thought about going into detail about what the project involved, but he didn't want to bore the guy to death.

Aaron looked off to his left again, his neck still telling him to stop. He could just make out a large landmass coming into view.

"Have you been to Jamaica before," he asked the southerner.

"Sure have."

"Well, is that what it looks like," Aaron asked, pointing out the window.

The man took off his seat belt and leaned over Aaron for a closer look. The man's belly almost squashed him against the side of the plane.

"Well, I can't..." the man started. "Oh, yeah, that looks like it might be it," he said, sitting back down. Aaron kept looking out the window at the oncoming terrain, thankful for his space again. It was a welcome sight after an hour of nothing but water and clouds.

"Ladies and gentlemen, we're cleared for landing. The local time in Kingston is 8:26 p.m., winds are calm, and the temperature is eighty degrees. We thank you for flying American Airlines. Enjoy your stay in Jamaica, and when you think of traveling again, please call us."

The man next to Aaron smiled and put his headphones on. He started singing a Bob Marley tune with his eyes closed, and judging by the stares coming his way, Aaron knew he wasn't the only one who could hear him.

From the silhouette of the setting sun, Aaron could make out the shape of the island. He could see that there was a large mountain range in the middle and that it sloped off steeply in some places. He tried to get a glimpse of the infamous beaches, but it was too dark to see them.

As the island got closer and the plane got lower, Aaron was hoping that Dr. Camron, the head researcher at the Kingston facility, had gotten the message. He had been delayed in Miami for three hours because of technical problems. Two of the other researchers were supposed to pick him up at the airport at three that afternoon. If they hadn't received the message, and had been waiting all that time, they might have given up already. If no one was there to pick him up, he would have to find his own transportation but Aaron didn't care because the grant would cover it.

Outside, the colors in the sky were so beautiful starting from a red-orange glow, which bled into lighter blue colors that turned into dark purples, ending in black. Looking down, Kingston seemed like a large city with tall buildings and many lights.

As the plane touched down, the man next to Aaron was grabbing onto his armrests for dear life. "I don't like this part," he said to Aaron with his eyes clenched tight.

Aaron chuckled at him quietly. What a character, he thought to himself.

"Please remain seated until the plane has come to a complete stop at the gate." The lead flight attendant said over the intercom. Just as he finished his sentence the plane was slowing down at the gate, and almost everyone on the plane jumped up to start grabbing their belongings. This was so crazy to Aaron. Where were they all going, he asked himself. It's not as if the doors would open immediately and people could just run out. Besides, the aisles were always a traffic jam for the first few minutes anyway. Aaron always waited until most of the people were off already to start gathering his things and deboarding the plane.

As he exited the breezeway he saw a few people still waiting for passengers to deplane. He looked around to see if anyone would come up to

41

him and ask if he was the researcher from Harvard. He realized then, that he hadn't planned his arrival too well. He didn't have anyone's number except for Dr. Camron's.

"Well, they're not here, I guess," he said with quiet frustration, and walked off towards the baggage claim.

When he got to the carousel, he looked around again to see if anyone was looking for him. Aaron didn't notice anyone so he called Dr. Camron.

"Dr. Camron," he asked as someone answered the phone.

"Hold on," a woman's voice said.

"Hello?"

"Dr. Camron?"

"Yes."

"This is Aaron."

"Hi Aaron, are you here?"

"Yes, I just got in. Did you get my message?"

"Yes, and I relayed it to Mike and Maria. They should be there to pick you up."

"Great!" Aaron was very relieved.

"Listen, Aaron," Dr. Camron asked. "When you find Mike and Maria, ask them if they would like to come over for dinner and talk about the research, that is unless you're too tired."

"No, I'm great!" He was surprised that Dr. Camron wanted to start so early. Aaron thought he was more laid back and that they wouldn't get started on his project for a few days. "The sooner we can get started, the better!"

"Great, have Mike call me on his cell phone when you guys are on your way."

"Okay." Aaron looked at the crowd still surrounding the conveyer belt. "By the way, what do they look like?"

"Well, I don't know how to describe Maria except that she's got long, dark hair and she's about five-four. Mike is a little taller and has short hair and a mustache."

While Dr. Camron was talking, Aaron looked around the crowded room trying to find the pair. "Alright, then, I'll have him call you."

"Great, I'll see you soon then. Welcome to Jamaica."

"Thanks."

Aaron hung up the phone. He figured that they could have been waiting outside so he hurried over to the crowd to claim his baggage. The two huge duffel bags only took a few minutes to come out and he flung them over his shoulders. As he started walking, Aaron hoped that they were outside and that he had not missed them somewhere in the terminal.

As he walked outside he saw a man and a woman, both about thirty, standing next to each other with their arms folded. The man had a mustache and the woman looked as Dr. Camron had described her. He saw them look at each other and figured that it must be his greeting party.

"Are you the ones with the limousine for Aaron Silver," he asked with a smile on his face.

"You can call it what you want, but it's far from a limousine," the man said, pointing to his small, white hatchback.

"Well, I'd shake your hand but mine are full," Aaron said, still carrying his duffel bags on his shoulders.

"Here let me help you with one of those," Mike offered as he took one of the bags.

"You only brought two bags," Maria asked in a noticeably Italian accent.

"Well, I'm not moving down here for good."

Mike helped Aaron get his huge duffel bags into the tiny trunk of his white Mazda. The car must have been at least ten years old. It was the kind of car Aaron had expected to see on the island. For some reason he thought that Jamaica was a developing nation and that everything on the island would be outdated. It was an absurd idea, but one he had nonetheless.

Once they had packed the car, Maria got into the back seat. "You can sit in the front if you want," Aaron said to her.

"No, it's okay." Aaron wasn't going to argue so he hopped in front with his backpack on his lap. He liked to carry his delicate items in it so that the baggage handlers couldn't damage them.

"I'm Mike Harding," he said to Aaron, shaking his hand firmly.

"And I'm Maria Salleo," she said, shaking Aaron's hand from the back as Mike sped off.

"How was your trip," Mike asked.

"It was good." Aaron sighed. "I had this weird guy sitting next to me, but I guess that's to be expected sometimes. Oh, by the way," he said, remembering his recent conversation. "Dr. Camron wants to know if you guys want to get together and talk about the research over dinner?"

"I guess so," Mike said. "What about you, Maria?"

"That is fine with me."

Mike picked his cellular phone off of the dashboard and dialed Dr. Camron. As he started talking to him Aaron looked outside and tried to make out the landscape. He couldn't make out much but he did see that he was wrong about the cars in Jamaica. There was a fair share of old ones but he also noticed many new Toyotas®, Mazdas®, Hondas®, and other models he would have seen back home. Cars were speeding past them to pick up passengers at the airport they had just left.

"We're going to Dr. Camron's place for dinner. His wife made lasagna," Mark said as he pressed a button on his phone and put it down again.

"Good, I'm hungry," Aaron said.

The three of them conversed about Aaron's trip to Jamaica and other issues until they arrived at Dr. Camron's apartment complex. The units looked modest but the grounds were beautiful. Throughout the parking lot there were small islands with tropical plants and flowers of all colors. The apartment complex was a long, two-story building that had been painted light brown and had probably not been touched up since it was first constructed.

"Here we are," Mike said as he pulled his car into a spot in front of one of the units. Aaron stretched as he got out of the car. It felt good to stand up and stretch after such a long trip. He followed the two researchers to a door and waited as they knocked.

"Coming," a voice yelled from inside. A few seconds later, the door opened to reveal a balding man in his fifties. He had freckles all over his face, arms and legs. Heavy glasses hung from his nose. His Hawaiian style, floral shirt was half way unbuttoned, and what was left of his red hair was a mess. "Hi guys," he said to the three standing outside his doorway. "Come in. Come in." He waved his hands, beckoning them inside.

After Dr. Camron's wife, Patricia, served the lasagna in heaping portions, a general conversation began. Maria said that she had received her doctorate in biology from the University of Padua only a year ago and was in Jamaica to do her post-doc. Her dissertation had been on the self-awareness in killer whales and she was now working with dolphins.

Mike was from Iowa originally, but had lived all over the United States before finding his niche in Jamaica. He had no formal training when it came to dolphins but he knew a lot about the computers that were used in the lab and in that way was a big help.

Dr. Camron, whom everyone called Bob, was the only one who was paid for doing research. The others had part time jobs or grants. Looking at his apartment though, Aaron could tell that Bob didn't get paid much.

Dr. Camron had been doing dolphin research since his days as a graduate student at UCLA. He also had his doctorate in biology.

Aaron felt weird being the only psychologist in the group, but confident in the team he was working with. There was so much experience sitting at the table that he couldn't go wrong. Looking around, Aaron realized that he was, by far, the youngest of the group. This made him feel awkward, like he didn't belong in the research team. Although it wasn't his top priority, Aaron wanted to know if there was anyone who worked in the lab that was his age.

As the conversation died down Aaron seized a quiet moment. "No offense, but, by any chance, is there anyone who helps out in the lab who is my age?"

Everyone at the table was quiet. It seemed that everyone knew the answer, but was not saying anything. They all kept looking at someone else to give the answer and finally Bob spoke up.

"I think so. How old are you again?"

"Twenty-four."

"How old is Sarah," Bob asked in Mike's direction.

"I'm not sure." His bottom lip was pushed out indicating that he was about to guess. "Probably about twenty-five or so."

"What does she do," Aaron asked calmly. He was excited that there was a girl who worked at the lab who was his age but didn't want to show it.

"She's a dolphin trainer. She helps us with the experiments," Dr. Camron said. "You'll meet her tomorrow, she's a really nice girl. But now..." He looked directly at Aaron. "Let's get down to business. We've all seen your proposal, but I want to make sure that we're on the same wavelength."

"Okay," Aaron said taking in a deep breath and letting it out again. "First, we need to give the dolphins some mirror exposure so they know what they look like. At the same time we can gather pictures of the dolphins that we have in the tank. There are four now, right," he asked in Bob's direction. Bob nodded his head.

"The pictures will be easy to get," Mike said. "I can take some tomorrow."

"Great," Aaron replied. "Next, we need to get similar sounds from all the dolphins in our tanks."

"Signature whistles," Bob said, interrupting Aaron.

"What?" Aaron knew what signature whistles were, but he thought that they had not been proven to exist yet. Signature whistles were certain vocalizations from dolphins that were like names given by dolphins to other dolphins. "I thought they weren't..." Aaron continued, but was interrupted.

"They're real," Bob said. "You'll see. I've been working on their communication patterns for ten years and I'm almost to the point where I can prove it."

"Okay," Aaron agreed. He didn't want to contradict Dr. Camron, especially on his first meeting with him. He wanted this summer to be productive and arguing wouldn't speed anything along. Besides, even if there weren't signature whistles, the sounds would probably be very similar enough to use in the experiment.

"Then all we have to do is train them to answer our questions."

45

"What do you mean," Bob asked.

"Well, I wouldn't expect the dolphins to just go up to the touch screen and activate it when they hear sounds. We've got to train them to do it. I guess Sarah will be able to help out with that one. And, once we get them to touch the screen after they hear a sound, then we train them to touch the correct picture on the touch screen. For example, if we give them a sound of a seal barking, then show them two different pictures: one of a seal and one of a whale, we will only give them a food reward for touching the picture of the seal. And, when they've got that straight we know they understand what we want them to do." Aaron paused for a second. Dr. Camron and the rest of the crew were staring at him inquisitively. "That makes sense, right?"

"Sounds good," Dr. Camron said, his chin still resting on his hands, which were resting on the table.

Aaron went on to explain the rest of the experiment and everyone seemed to embrace his methods. It seemed as if everything was fitting into place like a puzzle that was almost done. Everyone there had something to offer, even Patricia.

When he was almost done explaining what he wanted to get accomplished, Patricia brought out iced tea and pastries. Aaron was pretty full, but just like anything in life, he thought, no matter how much you eat, there's always room for dessert.

"So where are you staying tonight, Aaron," Bob asked.

"I…" He hesitated, looking up from his plate with the half eaten apple turnover in it. He didn't know what to say because he didn't know where he was staying. Aaron figured that someone would just take him to a nearby hotel, and the next day he would look for a place to live.

"He's staying with me tonight," Mark said. "I've got a place for him on my floor. If that's cool with you," he asked Aaron.

"That's great," he replied honestly.

"Tomorrow you can look for a place, and take a few days if you need to get settled in," Dr. Camron added. "Don't worry about starting the project tomorrow, you've got all summer and we need to take those pictures and record some new sounds before you get started."

"And I can even put the mirror up tomorrow on one of the underwater windows," Maria interjected.

"Good idea," Dr. Camron said. "Well, sounds like a plan," he said, rising to his feet. Everyone had finished their dessert and was ready to leave. Aaron could not wait to get into bed, or floor, as the case was that night. He didn't care, as long as he slept.

Bob and Patricia walked the three out to Mike's car. It was a beautiful night. The climate was the same as it had been indoors, and the stars were out. Aaron wouldn't have minded if they told him he had to sleep on the beach that night.

"It was very nice to meet you," Patricia said to Aaron.

"Nice to meet you too, Mrs. Camron."

"Oh, please," she said, "Call me Patricia. Mrs. Camron is Bob's mother."

"Okay, then, Patricia," Aaron laughed. Every married woman he had ever met said that.

As they finished saying goodbye, Mike opened the passenger door to his car and Maria, again, slipped into the back seat.

"Really," Aaron said. "You can sit in the front."

"No, please," Maria said, motioning for him to take shotgun.

"Alright." He gave up for the second time. As they drove out of the apartment complex Aaron waved goodbye to Dr. Camron and his wife. They were standing side by side with their arms around each other. Just before the car left the parking lot, he could see them kissing as they turned to go back inside the apartment.

"They are so cute," Aaron said to the other two researchers.

They've probably been married for such a long time and you can tell they are still very much in love, Aaron thought to himself. He took in a breath and sighed. I hope I'm like that with my wife when we've been married about thirty years.

CHAPTER 4

The sun had only peeked over the horizon an hour before but it seemed like late morning already. There was not a cloud in the sky and the temperature must have been about seventy-nine degrees, Aaron thought. There was just a slight breeze coming from the south, just enough to rustle the trees and bushes in Mike's front yard. Behind the house were the Blue Mountains. They reached up more than seven thousand feet in the air and came back down to meet the ocean a few miles from where he was sitting.

Aaron desperately wanted to go to the beach and relax by the shore. He brought his scuba equipment with him and could not wait to see the abundance of marine life around the island. He was hungry though. He had woken up before anyone else in Mike's house and didn't feel right rummaging through the kitchen to find something to satisfy his hunger. He might have felt comfortable if Mike was the only one living in the house, but he shared it with a few other people.

Aaron had slept on the floor in Mike's room near the corner, where he had put his bags the night before. When he awoke around sunrise, he tiptoed over to his belongings and took a change of clothes to the bathroom down the hall. He put on a pair of khaki shorts, sandals, and a tie-dye, Woodstock tee-shirt. It was the first time Aaron had worn shorts or sandals in a long time. He didn't like wearing them. He was very self-conscious about his weight. Aaron felt like he was too skinny and that people would make fun of his pale, skinny legs.

The truth was, his legs were fine. They were a little white because they had not seen the sun in about a year, but they were fine.

Besides, Aaron thought to himself, you've got to start somewhere. He figured that by the end of the summer he would have a better tan than any of his friends back in Boston. The fair skinned women were always so jealous of his tan, when he had one. Although he was white, Aaron tanned very easily.

He had been outside on the small lawn for about thirty minutes, enjoying the morning, wishing he knew how to get to the beach, when he decided to head back inside. As Aaron walked up to the door it opened and Mike appeared. He was only half awake, his hair still a mess.

"Oh, there you are," he yawned. "I didn't know where you went."

"Just out here enjoying the morning," Aaron answered.

"Did you have anything to eat yet?"

"Not yet. I was waiting for you."

"Well, let me get ready and we'll go get something." Mike retreated into the house again. Aaron followed and shut the door behind him.

"There's a corner store right down the street with some really good coffee," Mike said as he turned the corner to go down the hall and into his room. Aaron didn't know what to do so he followed him, stood outside his bedroom door, and waited.

"You know about Jamaican coffee," Mike asked through the door.

"No, I'm not a real big coffee buff. I like to drink it sometimes, but I'm not addicted." It was quiet for a few seconds and then Mike came out wearing shorts and a tee-shirt.

"It's some of the best coffee in the world, supposedly," he added. "Come on let's go."

Walking down the street, they passed houses that also had small yards and different assortments of flowers and plants growing in them. The neighborhood seemed nice enough, Aaron thought. Not somewhere he would want to live when he got older, but nice enough for what his needs were as a college student. Aaron always saw himself retiring in a neighborhood with big houses. Houses that had lots of space for old people who had no need for it.

As they turned the corner, Aaron saw a small convenience store. They entered the busy store where no one was buying groceries. They were getting coffee and enjoying their warm cups at small tables in the front of the store. Jamaican businessmen in suits, drinking coffee and reading newspapers occupied many of the tables.

"I'll get us some coffee. Why don't you save us a seat," Mike said as he walked to the counter.

Aaron sat down at the only unoccupied table. Turning to look inside the shop, it reminded him of a *Seven-Eleven* back home. It had small sections for everything: wine, beer, produce, car essentials, snacks, etc. He saw Mike in line to buy the coffee and snacks. Turning around, Aaron looked out towards the city from behind the window. He could see water off in the distance, but he still couldn't see the beach.

"Here we go." Mike placed two cups of coffee and hot crescent rolls on the table. "Let's scarf it down," he added, just before stuffing his face with one of the rolls.

Aaron thought that "scarf" was an interesting word. He had not heard it in such a long time. It was one of those words from an earlier generation. Not too much earlier, but enough to be an anachronism.

"So," Aaron said as he put plenty of sugar and cream in his coffee. "How do I go about finding a place?"

"Hmm," Mike grunted, swallowing his coffee. "I saved the Sunday paper for you. It should have plenty of listings of apartments, studios, and things like that. When we go back to my house you can look through it and use my phone to call people."

"How am I going to get around if I find some place where I might want to live?"

Mike chewed a little slower on another roll, then looked at his watch. "Well," he said, still chewing. "I have a job to go to in about an hour. You can take the bus."

"Take the bus? How's the bus system?"

"Eh," Mike answered, implying that it wasn't the best in the world.

"Eh?" He didn't like that answer.

Mike could tell that Aaron was not a bus person by the expression on his face. "What's the matter? Don't like riding the bus?"

"Not really," Aaron said, sipping his coffee.

"Well, maybe you can find a moped for sale or somethin' like that."

"Maybe," Aaron responded, finishing his own crescent roll.

When they were both satisfied with their small breakfast, they headed back to Mike's house.

"I've got to finish getting ready. Here's the paper." Mike threw it to Aaron and walked off to his room.

Aaron sat down in the dining room at a small table. He turned the paper over to reveal the front page. It was called the *Sunday Gleaner*, and it boasted being Jamaica's oldest paper, having been established in 1834. He looked down the page and read the headlines for the main story.

Where have all the good ships gone? It read. The story was accompanied with a picture of the open sea. Aaron read the caption and it mentioned the U.S. Coast Guard and Jamaican fishing boats that had disappeared somewhere off the eastern coast of Jamaica and had never been recovered.

"Remind me not to take a boat out there," he said to himself, flipping to the classified section. Aaron started to look through the section for apartments when Mike walked in.

"I've got to book it out of here. My job's all the way across town and it'll take a while to get there. Here's a key." Mike laid a house key down on the table with a piece of paper on it. "I'm also giving you my cell phone number just in case you're not here when I get back and need a ride to the lab."

"Oh, yeah. What time are we going to the lab? And, where is it?"

"We usually go around four, and it's at the end of the Palisadoes in a place called Port Royal."

"Should I try to find a place in Port Royal then?"

"No, you don't want to live there. Just try to find a place near this end of the city. It's not too bad here."

"Okay. I'll be back here around four, then."

"Great." Mike grabbed his computer equipment that was next to the door before he left. "Later... Good luck."

"Thanks," Aaron answered, as Mike shut the door. He looked back down at the paper and continued his search

"You know what I just remembered," Mike said, sticking his head back in the front door. "There's a bike you can use in the garage. Just be careful with it. It's Dr. Camron's."

"Great!" Aaron was relieved that would not have to find other means of transportation. Mike left again, and Aaron sighed. "At least it'll be easier to get around."

After a while Aaron found a few rooms for rent in people's homes in Norman Gardens and Arbor View, suburbs just outside Kingston. He got directions to one of the places and pretended to know how to use them. His sense of direction was very good but Aaron figured that he could ask directions if he got lost.

The bike was leaning on one of the walls in the garage. It was old and he hoped that it still worked. At least there was a helmet hanging off of one of the handlebars, he thought. Aaron opened the garage door and rolled the bike outside onto the driveway. The brakes seemed to work so Aaron put on his backpack and the helmet, and took off down the street towards the shop he had eaten at earlier.

Aaron saw a man coming out of the convenience store and asked him how to get to Norman Gardens and Arbor View.

"Ya, man, it's very easy," the man said. "All ya have to do is go a few blocks and take a left on Mountain View Avenue. Take that all the way to the end and then take a right. Then you will be on Windward Avenue, Okay, man?"

Aaron nodded his head.

"Good," the man continued. "That's it! It's easy. And both neighborhoods are in the same direction. Past that, I don't know where you're goin' man. But that should get ya close enough."

"Thanks."

"No problem, man," he said as Aaron rode off.

Aaron rode past Norman Gardens first but did not like what he saw. The neighborhood looked like it *had been* the place to live but was now a run down area like most mid-town areas in large cities.

He rode on and about ten minutes later Aaron turned onto Hot Springs Road in Arbor View. The houses had small front yards with green grass, many different palm trees and flowers. As far as he could tell it was a nice neighborhood and if the room was nice he wouldn't mind paying four-fifty a month.

Aaron rode on until he came to three-forty. When he arrived, he looked at the piece of paper, then again at the house. It seemed nice enough. There was a garage on the left side of the one story house. The light green and white color of the house made it look like it was from the '60s.

He put his bike down on the side of the driveway and walked to the front door. There was a window just to the left of it, but he couldn't see or hear anyone inside. The woman told Aaron that she would be there so he knocked.

A few seconds later an Asian woman in her sixties opened the door. Aaron was taken aback. He didn't expect to see an Asian woman from the voice he heard over the phone.

"Yes," she asked hesitantly, with the door only half opened.

"I'm Aaron. I called you about the room a little while ago," he said softly.

"Oh, hello. Wait right there. Let me get the keys."

"No problem," he said as the woman closed the door and went inside. Aaron turned around to view a little more of the neighborhood. The house was facing land and Aaron could see hills close by and mountains in the distance. Everyone called them the Blue Mountains and it seemed almost plausible that they could be blue. The sky above them was intensely blue and it seemed to tint the green, lush color of the mountains.

The woman came out again with a key chain and some keys on it. "By the way, I'm Debbie," she said, less hesitant than before.

"Nice to meet you, Debbie," Aaron replied, offering his hand.

"Well, follow me," she said, not noticing his gesture. And although no one was watching, Aaron felt embarrassed as he pulled back his hand.

He followed her around the garage and there was a gate on the other side of it, leading to the back yard. Debbie unlocked the gate with one of the keys and entered as she held the gate open for Aaron. Inside the gate was a narrow walkway. On the left was a small tool shed and on the right was the side of the garage with an entrance into it at the end of the walkway. Straight ahead was another wooden gate painted white. Debbie fumbled with something on the side of it, then pushed the heavy gate open.

"Here it is, right here." She pointed to the right, just after passing through the gate. On the wall in front of Aaron was a small dresser next to a small card table and a lawn chair, which was all covered by an overhang that extended from the roof. Just to the left of that was the door to the studio apartment. Debbie went up to it and opened the door with another one of the keys.

She showed Aaron in, and he looked around while she started talking about the apartment. As he first walked in, there was a full bathroom immediately to his right, and in front of him was the bedroom. Both rooms had large brown tiles for flooring.

As he walked into the bedroom, Aaron noticed that it was not only a bedroom, but also a kitchenette and dining room, which was on his right and to the right of the bed. At the foot of the bed was a small table and at the head of the bed was a nightstand.

"So, what are you here for," she asked.

"I'm doing dolphin research for the summer."

"And how long do you need a place for, because I only like to rent if it is going to be at least three months." She wasn't impressed with his summer job.

"Well, we're both in luck. I'm going to be here about three months."

"Uh huh, well, you know it's four hundred-fifty a month with a one month deposit." She didn't think he would be able to afford it.

"How far from the Palisadoes are you?"

"Actually, we're right at the foot of it. Close to Hillshire Beach, too. It's the only decent one around Kingston. Why? Is that important?"

"The research facility is in Port Royal," he said, speaking as if he knew exactly where it was. "And, it would be nice to be close to the research facility."

"Oh, well this is a good location then."

"Great! I'll take the room." It was very small but it had everything he needed and it was in a good location.

"Well, you have to fill out an application and we'll get back to you." She still did not trust that he would be able to afford the room.

"Oh," Aaron said. "Well, what if I offered you the full three months rent in advance." He took a checkbook out of his backpack.

"Here are the keys," Debbie said, changing her tone immediately and smiling for the first time.

After giving her the check, she left Aaron alone in his new room. Exploring, Aaron found that Debbie had left a piece of paper on the bed with the stipulations of living in the room. One of the rules was the prohibition of overnight guests. Aaron didn't like that rule, but he figured he wouldn't have the chance to break it.

He sat on the bed to test it out. It seemed firm, Aaron thought and then he got up again to check out the rest of the room. Half of the cabinets were open, and he could see that there were already pots, pans, dishes, and other utensils there for his use. It was a very small room but he was becoming quickly attached to it.

"Here we are," Debbie said, coming back into the room. She held a small bag of groceries in her hand. "I figured whoever lives here could use a little starter so as not to worry about the first few days." She placed the bags on the small counter top with a smile. She was much nicer than she had been before.

"I noticed that you rode here on a bicycle. Is it yours?"

"No, I borrowed it from one of the other researchers."

"Oh, well, our neighbor has a moped for sale if you're interested."

"Really?" Aaron sounded surprised. "Which one of your neighbors is selling the moped?"

"As you walk out, it's the one on the left. Just tell them Debbie sent you."

"Alright," he said as she left him alone again. Aaron looked around, realized that he had left the bike in the front yard and went to retrieve it, making sure his keys were in his pocket as he left.

The bike was still lying on the front lawn. He picked it up and took it to the side gate. The first gate opened easily with the key and he pushed the bike through. When he got to the second gate he realized that there was no keyhole. He tried to push it open but it wouldn't budge. Aaron remembered that Debbie had fiddled with it somehow to make it open but he had not been paying attention.

Just then the gate opened and Debbie was standing on the other side of it. "I just realized that I never showed you how to get in," she said, rolling her eyes.

"Yeah, that might help," Aaron laughed.

"Here." She held her hand out, asking for the keys. "All you have to do is stick your key in this slot right here and it unlocks the door."

The slot she was referring to was one of a series of slots on the frame of the gate. It looked like an intercom at first glance and Aaron thought it was cool.

"Sweet! It's like a James Bond lock."

"Yes, kind of like James Bond." She smiled and handed Aaron back his new set of keys.

"By the way," he started. "Do you mind if I ask where you're from?"

"Oh, I'm a California girl."

"Really, how long have you been here?"

"Oh, about twenty years now."

"That's great! You must really like it."

"Yes, the weather here is beautiful all year long, just like in southern California."

"I can imagine," Aaron agreed. "Well, I'm going to check on that moped. I'll probably be back sometime tonight."

"You can come and go as you please. This is your place now."

"Thank you," he said as Debbie walked off into the back door of her house. Aaron put the bike down and walked next door to see about the moped.

*****

The moped was old but it was a good deal. It had been deep blue in color but time and usage had chipped off most of the paint. There were also scrapes running along the left side of the bike but it seemed to run well despite its looks.

His new neighbors had gladly accepted his check for one hundred dollars for the old moped and Aaron drove it away, hoping it would last for three months.

As he rode back to Mike's house, a laugh slipped through his smile. It was so beautiful in Jamaica and he wouldn't have given this up for anything. All the other students are spending their summers in labs on campus working with rats and I'm here in Jamaica working with dolphins, he thought. Some people just know how to live.

He was also eagerly anticipating the start of his research. Dolphins were his favorite animals and he couldn't wait to make new, aquatic friends. Looking down at his watch revealed that it was almost four and he was arriving at Mike's just in time.

As he turned the final corner to his destination, a car pulled up behind him. Looking back, Aaron realized that it was Mike in his Mazda. He slowed up to let him pass, but then pulled along the driver's side of Mike's car. As he peered into the car, Mike noticed that it was Aaron on the moped. He pulled the car into his driveway and got out as Aaron pulled in behind him.

"Where the hell did you get that thing," Mike asked. "It looks like shit!"

"It works," Aaron replied, defending his piece of shit. "I got it from my next door neighbors."

"You found a place to live too?" Mike sounded surprised.

"Yeah."

"Damn, you're quick. How much are you paying?"

"For which, the moped or the room?"

"Both."

"I'm paying four-fifty a month for the room and I paid one hundred for this." Aaron beamed at his new motorbike.

Mike walked over to look at the moped. "Wow, it really does look shitty. I thought maybe it was where I was standing, but the closer you get, the worse it looks!"

"Like I said. It works. I don't care what it looks like."

"Hmm," Mike grunted, as he turned back towards his house. "Well, we'll leave in a few minutes. I just have to get a few things together.

"Can you do me a favor," Aaron asked, following him inside.

"What do you need?"

"I was wondering if we could take my stuff over to my new place on the way to the lab."

"Sure, where is it?"

"It's just outside the city, in Arbor View." Aaron closed the front door behind him as he entered.

"Not bad," Mike said, messing with some equipment. "By the way, where's the bike?"

"Oh, I left it at my new place."

"Okay, I guess I'll just pick it up when we drop off your stuff."

They went to Mike's room and got Aaron's duffel bags. When they had everything in the car, they left for the lab. Aaron left his moped at Mike's, and figured he would pick it up when they returned.

"Here," Mike said, handing Aaron a sweatshirt.

"What's this for?" Aaron stared at him from the passenger seat. It was ninety-five degrees out and he didn't think it was going to get that much colder in the evening.

"The lab gets pretty cold when Bob's there. He can't stand the heat."

"You mean he gets it cold enough to wear this," Aaron asked in disbelief, holding up the sweatshirt.

"Yep, pretty cold." Mike laughed.

As they drove on, Aaron recognized the streets Mike was taking. They stopped at Aaron's house, dropped off his belongings and picked up the bike.

As they headed on towards the lab, Aaron could see planes landing nearby. "We near the airport?"

"Yeah, this is the Palisadoes. It's a peninsula that goes all the way out to Port Royal, and the airport is in the middle." Mike took his eyes off the road for a second while answering.

A few minutes later they passed the entrance to the airport, which Aaron recognized from the night before. The drive past the airport continued to bring them by scrubs and cactus at about fifty miles an hour. For a few minutes, there was nothing else to see and they didn't even pass any cars for a while.

Aaron's first sight of Port Royal was an old cemetery. After that, a few scattered restaurants could be seen from the street. Most of them were not much more than shacks. He got the feeling that this was an authentic Jamaican town. The pace was slow. The people who were walking on the streets seemed like they didn't have anywhere to go. They were strolling along with the carefree feeling of school children in the summer.

Before he knew it, they had turned onto a small gravel road. All that was visible were trees and brush to the left and right. And just as quickly as they had entered the jungle, they emerged and entered a clearing with a small building in front of them. Past the building, all Aaron could see was water, the bay to the right and the open ocean on the left. There were two cars parked off to the side and Mike parked next to one of them.

"Good. Sarah's here," Mike said. "You'll get to meet her."

"Great," Aaron replied enthusiastically, stepping out onto the gravel parking lot.

As they walked around the building, Aaron noticed a large tank in the ground that could not be seen from the road. This tank was connected to a smaller one off to the right, and both were filled with saltwater. There was also a connection from the large tank directly into the bay, which looked like a lap-sized pool with two gates, one at each end.

Just to the left of the inlet was a small pier, jutting out into the water. And, docked at the end of the pier was a small boat named *porpoise*.

Walking up to the tanks, Aaron could not see anyone or anything in them but as he got closer and looked over the side of the tank, a dolphin jumped up right in front of him and landed in the middle of the tank. Aaron's heart jumped out of his chest but he pressed it back in when he grabbed his chest to make sure it was still ticking.

"God, damn," Aaron said to himself, looking back at Mike, thankful that he was still alive.

Mike was unlocking a door on the side of the building, which was kept closed with a padlock. "Scared ya, huh?" He laughed, and Aaron just shook his head.

"So, where's this Sarah girl," Aaron asked, feeling normal again.

"Right here," A voice shouted from the other side of the large tank. Aaron turned around and saw a head with a mask and snorkel on it bobbing up and down in the water. "Who are you," the woman asked sarcastically.

"This is Aaron. The guy from Harvard, who's going to be doing the self-awareness testing on the dolphins," Mike replied for him from the doorway.

Aaron was squinting with the sun in his face, but he still couldn't make out what the source of the soft but confident voice looked like.

Aaron walked up to the tank for a better view but as he got to the edge of the tank, one of the dolphins jumped up from the center. It didn't scare him this time because the dolphin came out of the water farther away but, when it landed, he was very wet.

The dolphin had slapped his body back into the water right in front of Aaron. The resulting splash left him soaking down to his bones. He stood there, not believing how foolish he looked. He could hear both Sarah and Mike laughing.

Aaron figured that he had been standing still long enough, so he decided to turn around, walk to Mike, and ask him for a towel.

The first step he took was the wrong one. Aaron didn't realize that the surface around the tank got very slippery when wet. His feet flew right out from under him just like in the cartoons and he landed squarely on his back.

He couldn't breathe, and he couldn't move. The wind was knocked out of him by the fall and the thought of a broken tailbone came to him shortly after the pain from the same area. His butt hurt almost as much as his pride.

Why, he thought to himself. Why does this *always* happen to me when I meet women? All Aaron could do was think, he could hardly breathe.

"Are you okay," a figure asked, half laughing, half-serious. It was Sarah kneeling above him. This was the first glimpse Aaron had of her, and she looked like an angel with the sun behind her head. She had short, dark brown hair, which was slicked back because of the water. Her eyes were pure green and the Jamaican sun had darkened her skin, which was naturally olive.

Aaron could only cough at first, but he nodded his head to indicate that he was alright.

"I guess you met Skilos," Sarah said, helping Aaron to a sitting position. He looked a little confused.

"The dolphin," she explained. "He doesn't get along very well with everyone."

"Does he do that to everybody," Aaron asked, with his lungs finally able to function again.

"Only to people he likes." She smiled and helped Aaron to his feet.

"This is so embarrassing," Aaron said as he wrung out his clothes. Looking around, he noticed that Mike was gone.

"Where's Mike?"

"He went downstairs to get a first aid kit. He was afraid you might have hit your head pretty hard."

"Maybe," Aaron responded, rubbing his behind. "But my ass is what really hurts."

"Since the introductions have already begun, I'm 'that Sarah girl'." She held out her hand.

Aaron was about to shake it, but he pulled back at the last second. "I'd better not. I'm dangerous to be around when I first meet women. And besides, how do I know you won't splash me or something?" He was almost serious.

"Who cares! You're already wet. And I think I'll take the chance on you being a little dangerous."

She held out her hand again. Aaron looked at her hand for a second, then shook it. She had a strong grip, which Aaron thought added to her character.

"Sarah Gordon," she announced as they finished shaking hands.

"Aaron Silver."

"Nice to meet you. Would you like to meet the other dolphins now?"

Aaron chuckled and walked towards the building without answering her.

"I guess that's a 'no'."

"Maybe tomorrow when I have a bathing suit on and some foam on my ass," Aaron said to her while rubbing his butt.

"Well, go on down then. Mike's in there, and I'll be down in a little while. I've got to finish feeding the dolphins."

Aaron nodded his head and then hung it low as he walked down the stairs into the bottom of the building. He almost ran into Mike coming back up with the first aid kit.

"Are you alright?" Mike sounded concerned.

"Not really."

"What's wrong," he asked, looking Aaron over to see where he might be hurt.

"I made a fool of myself!"

"That's it? Damn, I thought for sure you'd busted your head on the side of the tank!"

"It probably would have been better that way. Is this the way to the lab?"

"Yeah. Come on down," Mike said, turning around and leading the way.

"You're the next contestant on the *Price Is Right*," Aaron said, imitating the TV game show and making fun of himself. "Tell him what he's won, Bob! It's a large, painful bump on his ass. That's right! But wait, there's more! He's also won a full summer with a beautiful girl who thinks he's a total dork! Wow, what a lucky guy. How do you feel?"

After Aaron had finished making fun of himself, he looked up and realized they were already in the lab.

"How do you like it," Mike asked.

"Wow, this is awesome!" The lab was a rectangular room that folded around the outside of the tank, below ground. There were two large bubble windows facing the tank, and in between the two windows was a smaller, flat window, which was blocked by a computer screen facing out into the water.

As he scanned the rest of the lab, he noticed that it was very clean. This was new to him. Aaron thought it would look very much like Dr. Jeffries's office at school. But then, his professor was the only other person he had met who did animal research.

There were three, moderately new computers, along the back wall, which was on his right, and a controlled mess of wires running between them. In between the computers was a multitude of audio equipment, which Aaron was not familiar with, except for a soundboard that was separating the two computers closest to him. Looking in front of him Aaron saw an island in the middle of the lab, with more computers and equipment. To the left of the island there was another desk up against the far bubble window with a small television, a fan, papers and other small equipment. On each bubble window, Aaron noticed a hydrophone, each with its own small water well, which helped conduct the sound from the tank to the listening devices.

Through the windows, he saw the dolphins swimming back and forth in the water as a camera facing out into the tank watched their every movement. He was fascinated by the hi-tech facility that he would be able to use for the following few months.

The walls that were not covered by shelves or file cabinets, were padded with a black foam material used in recording studios. Aaron figured it was helpful in doing the research that Bob was doing. They didn't want to record any impure sounds, only the best nature could provide, or the best that the dolphins would give them.

Aaron suddenly realized that he was very cold. Looking up, he saw a large air conditioner on the wall, on the far side of the lab. "Damn, it's cold in here!" Aaron hugged himself to keep warm.

"I told you! Here, dry off," Mike said, throwing him a towel. Aaron took off his shirt and started to dry himself. After his head and torso were dry, he put on the extra sweatshirt that Mike had brought with him.

"Remind me why it has to be so cold in here?" Aaron shivered as he put the towel around his legs like a skirt.

"Because Bob can't…"

"Stand the cold," Bob interrupted as he entered the lab. "You must have met Skilos," he said, taking a better look at Aaron.

"Yeah, I think he likes me." Aaron looked at Bob but did not believe his eyes. Bob was wearing shorts; just shorts. His middle aged, hairy belly was hanging slightly over the belt on his only piece of visible clothing.

"You're hot," Aaron asked in disbelief.

"I used to be able to take the heat." Bob excused himself as he squeezed by Aaron to get to his chair, which was situated under the air conditioner. "But, in my older age, my body just can't take it anymore." As he sat down, Bob flipped on the small table fan on his desk because the air conditioner wasn't enough.

"It feels like we're headed for another ice age down here," Aaron exclaimed. Mike and Bob both laughed. They had both joked about the way he liked the lab, and were used to the remarks people made.

Mike took on the job of orienting Aaron to the lab and the equipment while Bob busied himself with reviewing tapes of former experiments. He had his headphones on so Mike and Aaron would not distract him as they fumbled around the room.

On the tour, Mike showed Aaron how to use the underwater touch screen, the video camera, gadgets, more cameras, lenses, and computer programming techniques. After a while his head was awash with the hundreds of little different jobs he had to do just to set up his experiment. Although it was a lot, Aaron kept nodding his head, realizing that he'd learn it all in time. Besides, he thought to himself, someone else will be here to point me in the right direction.

"Hi, guys," Sarah said as she walked into the lab. Aaron turned to greet her, as did the rest of the crew. She was now completely dry and had on a tee-shirt and blue jeans. Her hair was pulled back in a scrunchie revealing the soft, clear skin that added to the beauty of her face.

Aaron turned back towards the computer screen slowly. He didn't care anymore about what Mike was trying to show him, but he didn't want to stare at Sarah.

"Are you cold enough yet, Bob," she asked.

"Not yet! Gimmie another few years," he joked, as he heard her question even with his headphone on. Sarah turned towards Aaron and Mike, walked behind them and looked over their shoulders to find out what they were doing.

"You guys havin' fun," she asked.

"Yeah, I'm just teaching him a little programming," Mike answered, still typing on the keyboard. He was very into what he was doing as opposed to Aaron who could have fallen asleep thirty minutes before.

Aaron turned to Sarah and mouthed the words. "Help me!" She smiled and began to persuade Mike that Aaron had had enough. Aaron didn't have the heart to do it himself; Mike looked like he was having too much fun.

"Mike, how long have you been showing Aaron around the lab?"

"Only about thirty minutes now," he said defensively.

"Really?" Sarah crossed her arms knowing that was not true. "Why don't you take a look at your watch?"

Mike did, and realized it was six-fifteen. They had been in the lab much longer than thirty minutes.

"Oh, man! Maybe it has been a little longer than I thought." He looked at Aaron and apologized. "Sorry, I get carried away with these things." He shrugged his shoulders. "Do you think you've learned enough for today?"

"Yes," Sarah said. "You've probably taught him too much! I'd bet he hardly remembers half the things you showed him."

Mike looked back at Aaron for confirmation on Sarah's comment.

"Yeah, I think my brain is full for today," Aaron added apologetically.

"Okay. I guess we'll go over more as time goes on. Besides, we can't really start until I get all the pictures and program them into the computer, which, actually you and I can do now. Right," he asked jokingly.

"Ha," Aaron said, standing and stretching next to Sarah.

"Listen," Sarah began. "I've got to go. Aaron why don't you give me your number. I'll call you tomorrow and show you around the city. You've never been here before, have you?"

"Nope, but I don't have a phone yet," he said, upset that he hadn't bought one.

He was surprised that Sarah offered to take him touring. He liked her outgoing personality and she didn't seem old fashioned at all.

"Do you have a place to live yet?"

"Yeah, I can give you the address." Aaron jotted the address down as quickly as he could.

"Great, I'll show you around tomorrow, then. I have a lot more time than Mike does."

"That's for sure," Mike said, still fidgeting with the computer.

"Are you leaving now," Bob asked, finally putting his headphones down.

"Yes," Sarah replied, still standing next to Aaron and Mike.

"Are you going to be here tomorrow," Bob continued.

"Yep, probably before you."

"Good. Has Aaron told you about his project?"

"Not in depth, but I'll see him tomorrow and we'll talk about it."

"Okay, because I want you to be up to speed when we start training the dolphins for his research."

"Don't worry Bob, I'll be ready." She made her way to the lab door. "See you guys, and I'll pick you up at nine-thirty tomorrow," Sarah said, specifically to Aaron, as she waved and went up the stairs.

"She's really cute," Aaron said as he sat back down in the chair and looked at Mike.

"Yes, but off limits." He was paying closer attention to the computer again.

"What do you mean?"

"You're going to be working with her all summer and it's not very professional to date a co-worker," he said quietly, to make sure Bob couldn't hear.

"I guess you're right. I hate being politically correct sometimes. She really is nice though. Didn't you ever want to date her?"

"No," Mike answered uneasily.

"Oh, come on, man. She's hot!" Aaron continued quietly as Mike began to pay more attention to the conversation.

Hesitantly, Mark began to confess. "Okay, fine. Yes, I did want to date her at one time."

"I knew it! So, what happened," Aaron asked, intrigued.

Mike didn't want to finish the rest of the story but he knew the questions would keep coming. "If you must know, she turned me down."

"Oh, man. I'm sorry. That must have sucked!" Aaron couldn't help but chuckle.

"I'm fine with it now. It's been a while. Are you ready to go?" Mike turned off the computer and ended the conversation. He wasn't angry just uneasy about telling his secret to someone he had only met the day before.

"Yeah, I guess so. I've got to start unpacking anyway."

They both turned to Bob who was still listening to and documenting other videos. "Bob," Mike shouted.

"Yeah," Bob said, taking off his headphones and stopping the VCR. "Are you guys leaving?"

"We're takin' off," Mike answered.

"Alright then." He paused for a moment and then asked Aaron how he liked the lab.

"It's really cool! No pun intended. It'll take me a while to learn everything. I feel like I missed that year in school when they were teaching dolphin research lab techniques. But, I think it's going to be a lot of fun," he said with a smile.

"I'm glad you feel that way. I do think it's a lot of fun and I think that you will have a great time." He was quiet for a few seconds and just stared straight through Mike and Aaron as if they weren't there.

"Well," Bob said, fazing back into reality. "I guess I'll see you guys tomorrow. I'll lock up when I leave."

"Groovy, see you tomorrow," Mike said, using another anachronism.

Aaron and Mike walked up the stairs and out of the building. It was still bright and sunny and the hot air felt good after being in the lab. They stepped into Mike's car and drove back to his house with the windows down.

Aaron closed his eyes and felt the wind across his face. He wished everyday could be this warm in Boston. If it were, maybe he never would have left for the summer and would enjoy the winters even more. But thinking about it, he would miss the winters too much and the changing of the seasons if it stayed warm. That's one of the most beautiful things about the northeast, he thought. The colors of the leaves during fall.

"We're here," Mike said, as Aaron opened his eyes.

"Wow, that was fast."

"I guess so," Mike said as he got out of the car. "You've got all your stuff, right?"

"I think so." Aaron shut the car door.

"Do you need anything?"

"Don't think so," Aaron answered after thinking about it.

"We'll I'm going inside. I guess I'll see you tomorrow."

"I guess so," Aaron answered as he waved goodbye.

Mike closed the door to his house behind him as Aaron got on his used motorbike. He arrived at his house ten minutes later, after only getting lost once.

As he walked into his room, after passing the first gate and the James Bond lock, he realized the he was starting to get tired. After all, he thought, he had been up since dawn.

After unpacking, he took a shower to rid himself of the sticky saltwater and sweat that had accumulated on his body. The evening air felt good and he allowed himself to air-dry as he prepared a macaroni and cheese dinner that Debbie had left for him.

After eating, Aaron plopped down on his new bed. His mind started to slow from all its activity from his long day.

"She's pretty cute," he said to himself. The sentence was the last thing to enter his mind and slip through his lips before he dozed into a deeper sleep.

CHAPTER 5

It was the summer of 1973 when he became the man he was. That was the summer he was supposed to die but God had saved him.

He had been playing soccer with his friends after church as he did every Sunday. They were playing on the vacant lot around the corner from the San Pedro Cathedral. The dirt lot filled with dust as Jesus and his friends kicked the makeshift soccer ball around and tried to score a goal between two plastic buckets.

Most of his friends were poorer than he was, not even wearing shoes to church or to play. But, they all got along just the same. Jesus could afford shoes because his father, Pablo, worked for a rising star in the Cali drug trade, Jose Santacruz Londono.

Pablo Lopez was a gangster and had always been since Jesus could remember his father. Jesus had gone on "jobs" with his father a few times and although he never saw Pablo kill anyone, his bloodstained clothing and machete were good clues as to what his father did.

Pablo had odd ideas for a gangster. For one, he hated guns. One time, after completing a job he joined his son in the car and explained to Jesus why he hated guns. "They are for sissies, not real men! You understand, Jesus," he had asked with a growl. "Real men have the heart and determination to do a job themselves and not to rely on modern inventions to do the job for them!"

Another of Pablo's quirks was his infatuation with the church. Pablo took his only son and his wife to church every Sunday at the San Pedro Cathedral. He wanted his son to grow up and have a respectable vocation such as manufacturing or business like other successful people in Cali. This was why Jesus was named for his savior and also why Jesus' second home was the San Pedro. Twice, sometimes three times a week Jesus would spend hours studying the bible and talking to Padre Martinez, the spiritual leader of San Pedro Cathedral.

Jesus only met Jose Santacruz Londono once when he was ten. He remembered exactly what he looked like because he was so fat. Jesus actually called him "*El Gordo*" — the Fat One. Pablo didn't want Londono influencing his son so he kept Jesus, what he called, distanced from his dealings with the drug lord. But, Jesus was not blind or stupid. He met many of his father's associates and knew that they must be hired assassins as well.

He knew by the bells of the cathedral that it was time to go home for supper but he kept playing anyway. Jesus was having a marvelous game. He had scored three goals already and he felt like he could play for the Colombian national team if he wanted to.

Finally, when the bells chimed at six-thirty, Jesus waved to his friends and started running to his small house. He was already fifteen minutes late for dinner and he knew he would get a beating but the game had been worth it.

To try and decrease his chances of a severe beating Jesus took a shortcut through an abandoned plot with a wooden house that was being torn down by the over-growth of the brush around it. As he ran around the right side of the house, ducking to avoid large branches, he heard multiple gunshots from the direction of his house.

Jesus froze for a few minutes. He knew what must be happening and did not want to run into certain death.

The gruesome sight hit his eyes as soon as he came into the clearing behind his house, just minutes after hearing the gunshots. The window of his parents' bedroom was stained with blood and he could not see past the dripping liquid that had stained the glass.

He stood there, staring at the window, knowing what it must mean when he heard a car screech its tires from in front of his house. A split second later he saw a car speed by the small gap between his house and the next. His senses were acute and he caught a glimpse of the man in the passenger seat. It was another one of Londono's men. Someone he had met many times before because his father had worked with him.

Assured that they had not detected him he ran in through the back, sliding door. He ran through the short hallway and threw open his parent's door to see what he expected. Both of his parents had been executed. They had been shot in the head and dismembered with their limbs scattered around the room.

After vomiting at the doorway he staggered to the back door, passing his own bedroom door and noticing it had been kicked in. He knew Londono meant to kill him too but he had come home late for dinner, which he could now smell as the chicken had not been taken out of the oven.

Jesus cried and wished that he *could* receive a beating from his father. How warm and welcoming his belt would feel on his bare butt now, he thought.

He knew he had to leave the city. Londono would certainly find him and kill him in no time but he was going to take his vengeance first. Jesus walked slowly back into his parent's room, ignored the blood, the body parts, brain and intestine strewn all over the room and went straight to the closet. He pulled the footstool out and stood up on it to get a box but even then the thirteen-year-old had to stretch. His fingers knocked the box off of the shelf and wads of money fell to the floor where it slowly soaked up his parents' blood.

With his eyes glazed over he stuffed his pockets with the money and then
went out to his father's car and retrieved his machete from the trunk. After
looking around for the first time he ran to the backyard, past the empty house
and back to San Pedro Cathedral to seek some solace in his "surrogate father"
Padre Martinez.

He told the Padre what had happened and that he planned on taking
revenge for his parents' murder and leave Cali for good in a cold and calculating
voice.

"You know, my son," Padre Martinez began, trying to talk some sense into
the boy. "Revenge is not the will of God. This is not what your father would
want you to do. Don't you know why he brought you here all the time? He was
trying very hard to make you take another path in life."

Jesus listened impatiently as the Padre began to quote the Bible. "My son,
if sinners entice you, do not yield; if they say, 'Come with us, let us set an
ambush to shed blood.' My son, do not set out with them; keep your feet from
their path. For their feet run to do evil; they hurry to shed blood. In the eyes of
every winged creature the outspread net means nothing. But they lie in ambush
for their own blood; they lie in wait for their own lives. Such is the fate of all
who pursue unjust gain; it takes the life of its possessor."

After a pause, looking into the boy's eyes, he asked him. "Do you know
where that is from?"

"Yes, Proverbs," Jesus answered simply. "But you left out a very
important part, Father. You left out the part about going to kill innocent people.
The person who killed my parents is not innocent."

"My son, you are missing the point," Padre Martinez begged, but it was too
late. Jesus was already out the door. He ran down narrow streets to keep out of
the light when he could and it was getting dark, the sun setting over the
mountains. He ran to his parents' murderer's house. Jesus knew where it was
because he and his father had stopped there many times to pick him up for a job.

Once there he found a scrappy looking peasant boy and paid him fifty
pesos to knock on the man's door and somehow lure him out of the doorway.
The boy gladly agreed and Jesus hid in the brush beside the man's door.

The peasant boy banged loudly on the wooden door until a man answered
angrily. The little boy yelled something at the man and the man raised his fist at
the boy who ran off down the street.

Jesus, with his parents' killer faced the other way, swung the machete with
all his might at the back of the man's neck. Without stopping Jesus sheared his
head clean off his shoulders and his body dropped to the ground, twitching.

He heard a woman's voice calling from inside the house and quickly
chopped off his moving extremities before running away. When he was two

doors down he heard a blood-curdling scream and turned around to see a woman standing over his victim with her hands over her mouth. A smile spread across his face as he continued to run and he did not stop until he had found a ride to Cartagena.

*****

As he sat alone in his chapel, Señor Lopez slammed his Bible shut. Reading the first chapter of Proverbs always brought back these memories. He sat quietly for a few more minutes before lighting two candles for his parents and exiting into the complex.

He walked silently down the concrete corridor, past metal door after metal door but stopped and turned at the last door on the left before the elevator. The guard nodded and, without a word, opened the door for Señor Lopez who entered.

The only other person in the room was tied to a metal slab table by his wrists and ankles. He looked worriedly at the man approaching him but could only make muffled sounds due to the cloth gag.

Lopez removed it and the older man began talking immediately, frantically trying to say something that might aid in his cause to be set free.

"Whatever you want to know, I'll tell you," he pleaded. "Anything you want to know about my research is yours, just ask! But, please, please don't hurt me! I promise I'll tell you everything!" The man squirmed and cried as he pleaded with Señor Lopez.

"We shall see if you will tell me what I want to know," Lopez said, strolling to a dark corner of the room.

The room's only light was directly above the table where the man was bound. It was a dim light and being right above the man's face, did not allow him to see much past the table.

"The only thing is," Lopez continued from the darkness but now heading back into the man's view with a machete in his hands. "I do not really care about your research. What I want to know is much more important than your worthless meddling in marine biology," he said just before hacking off the man's left arm.

CHAPTER 6

As the world spun around at its rapid pace, the sun slowly crept towards Jamaica and its rays found their way into Aaron's small room. As the sun's rays hit Aaron's eyelids the signal was sent through the optic chiasm, through the brain, and to the V5 area. There it triggered the rest of his brain to stop secreting melatonin. His eyes slowly opened, and he stretched.

He felt very relaxed, having had a good night's sleep. He sat up in bed and rubbed his eyes. The morning air felt soothing as it blew across his face from the open window. Aaron opened his drawers that he had stuffed with all his clothing the night before, found his gray sweat pants and slipped them over his legs. Slowly, he found his other clothes that he thought would be good for running. After he finished dressing himself, Aaron slipped out of his apartment quietly shutting all the gates behind him, not wanting to wake up his landlords.

After escaping, without a sound, from his new residence, Aaron pushed his moped out onto the street and started the engine. He drove to the end of the street with the wind combing through his short, dark hair and at the corner, took a left and drove down towards Hillshire beach.

When he arrived, the beach was almost empty except for a few other runners and some homeless people. As he looked at his watch, Aaron realized that it was only seven-thirty. He had not realized it was that early. I'll have plenty of time to run, shower and eat before Sarah picks me up at nine-thirty, he thought.

Walking toward the beach, Aaron wondered why he was up so early. Maybe it was the thought of starting in a new place. This was a chance for him to finally start exercising again. Maybe this time I will be able to work out every morning, he thought.

During his stint in the Israeli Army, Aaron and Jason had both been in the best shape of their lives. Aaron hadn't done us much physical training since he left but he liked to at least stay fit, although, he had been busy lately. That's what he told himself to make him feel better about not exercising. But now, he promised himself, he was going to keep up a regiment of at least a mile, a morning.

Aaron bent down to take off his sandals when he came near to the white sand. There were palm trees lining the beach, near the small parking lot and road that ran alongside oceanfront. He stood up with his sandals in his hand and then took his first step onto the Jamaican beach. The sand felt like fine sugar between his toes. As he walked closer to the water, he could tell everyone had been correct. The water was pure blue. It seemed as if the ocean was a large pool that went on forever. Looking up to his left, Aaron could still not see the sun rising over the land, but it was apparent that the big red giant would come looming over the horizon very soon.

Not being conscience of his own body and how it would get worn, he started to run without stretching. As he ran, Aaron took in the beauty of the beach, the trees, and the weather. It was like being inside a gigantic room with the thermostat set to a perfect temperature, he thought. There was no need to change anything.

When Aaron felt his body was about half done, he turned around to run in the direction he had come. As he turned, he could not help but squint from the glaring light of the sun. It was just peeking over the horizon and the warmth of it covered his body. He ran closer to the water's edge, splashing his feet down in the shallow water as he strode towards his destination. Aaron thought seven minutes was enough for him. The last time he ran a mile, it only took him seven minutes, and a mile seemed like a good distance to run.

While Aaron was still running, he looked down at his watch and realized he only had twenty seconds left to go. He put his right arm back down to match his stride, and began to run very fast. He went as long as he could at this pace, and then collapsed onto the wet sand, breathing heavily. The small waves ran up his body and wet his back. He did not have the energy to get up but where he was lying though, was perfectly comfortable, he thought. The water was not too cold, and even if it was, the sun would have warmed his body.

After getting home, Aaron took a shower. It felt good for him to have already exercised and it was not even ten. Feeling refreshed, Aaron stepped out of his small shower and dried himself off with a towel that had been hanging on the wall and kept it on as he proceeded to make breakfast for himself. It was starting to get warmer and it felt good to air-dry.

He pulled the egg carton out of the small fridge. Aaron hardly ever ate eggs at home because he was afraid of the cholesterol content, but this was his new life. If Rocky ate them to get strong, so would he, but not raw. He thought that was disgusting and he had heard too many stories about salmonella poisoning.

As the eggs were frying in the pan, Aaron glanced at his watch. It was already nine-fifteen.

"Crap," he said to himself as he looked down at his towel. Aaron quickly shoved his egg breakfast down his throat, threw on some nice touring clothes, and brushed his teeth.

Fifteen minutes later, he was standing outside his house waiting for Sarah. Aaron had checked his breath twenty times in the last ten minutes to see if it smelled of breakfast. It wasn't normal for him to be so preoccupied with being aesthetically perfect. He knew it was only because of Sarah, and he wanted to make up for making a fool of himself.

As his thoughts wandered, time passed. Aaron paced back and forth on the driveway with his head down, looking at the pavement. His backpack was getting heavy, so he stopped pacing and placed it on the driveway. As he did, Sarah sped into it with her small Jeep and screeched to a halt.

Aaron jumped back in fright. He had only seen the Jeep a second before it turned into the driveway. The bushes immediately to the right of the driveway were blocking the view of the street.

After a few seconds, Aaron exhaled and began to breathe again. He was still staring at the Jeep and had not moved an inch. He had often wondered why it was the human response, like deer, to freeze in such situations. Wouldn't it make more sense for people to get out of the way before disaster struck, he thought.

"Are you happy to see me or did you just have a lobotomy," a voice asked from the driver's window.

Aaron was staring in the direction of the voice, but right through the figure in the driver's seat. He suddenly focused on the beautiful, dark haired, dark skinned driver in the Jeep and smiled.

"Sorry," he said, picking up his backpack. "I was just watching my life flash before my eyes."

"Are you trying to comment on my driving," Sarah asked defensively, as Aaron sat down in the front seat.

"I'll let my actions speak for themselves." He closed the door and got settled in the passenger seat. "Where are we going?"

"I'll ask the questions and do the driving. You just answer." She paused for a few seconds, then motioned for Aaron to don his seat belt. Sarah smiled, sped out of the driveway backwards, and Aaron quickly complied.

As they raced across town, Sarah asked her frightened passenger about his research project. Aaron summarized the project and what he hoped to find. It helped that Sarah was familiar with the past research that had been conducted on humans and chimps.

While she listened to Aaron explain his research, ideas were already formulating in her head of how best to go about training the dolphins. She was impressed with his knowledge about dolphins, past studies, and research techniques. For a first year graduate student, he knew a lot about one particular subject.

She smiled at him while he was concentrating and explaining to her about the project. His tongue was protruding from his mouth and she thought it was funny.

Aaron stuck his tongue out when he concentrated hard enough. He knew that he did it but was never aware of it while he was doing it.

Aaron was still staring out of the passenger window when Sarah started laughing. He turned his head to see what was so funny, with his tongue still hanging out of his mouth.

"What's so funny," he asked, finally putting his tongue back where it belonged. Sarah couldn't stop laughing long enough to tell him what was so funny.

"What," Aaron asked again.

"You," Sarah said, able to speak again after she finished chuckling.

"What? What did I do?" Aaron looked confused.

"Your tongue." She mimicked him in deep thought with her tongue hanging out and her eyebrows furrowed to convey the severity of her thought process. "Do you always do that when you think hard?"

"Very funny," Aaron remarked at her imitation. "Yeah, I do that a lot, I guess." He was not upset that she had made fun of him but Aaron was trying to impress this beautiful woman and now he had made a fool out of himself again. At least she's laughing, Aaron thought.

"I think it's cute that you stick your tongue out when you're in deep concentration," Sarah said, smiling at him.

"I guess I'll take that as a compliment." Aaron smiled back at her even as she turned her concentration back to the road.

She thinks I'm cute, he thought. Maybe I didn't make an idiot out of myself after all. Aaron kept smiling, this time looking out of his window.

They were already driving through downtown Kingston and Aaron was watching the pedestrians, cars, buildings, and shops as they passed. It was not what he had expected. Kingston looked like any other big city. The buildings weren't old and falling apart from neglect. To Aaron's surprise, some new, beautiful buildings were being built as they drove by. They had even passed a downtown park with green grass, some palm trees and colorful flowerbeds.

Aaron was amazed that there was this huge metropolis in the middle of nowhere. It was amazing to him that this civilization came from somewhere else long ago and set up camp here. Down the line it was turned into a trading post. Then, more people moved in from new places. Slowly, the colony turned into a town and over time, a city, a large city in the middle of the Caribbean.

"We're almost there," Sarah said, as she turned the car onto another major downtown street.

Aaron could see the Blue Mountains off in the distance. He looked at Sarah again and she looked at him and smiled. Aaron felt very relaxed with Sarah already.

Feeling the same, Sarah put her right hand on his left leg and patted it a few times. Aaron turned to her and smiled.

Thoughts ran through his head about what could happen between the two of them: a relationship, marriage, kids, old age. Then, his rational side kicked in. You've only known her for a day, he thought.

"Here we are." Sarah pulled the car to a stop. They parked on the street next to an old building that looked as if it was sturdy adobe, painted blue with white trim. The only windows he could see were on the second floor.

"What is it," Aaron asked, stepping out of the car.

"You'll see when we get inside." She had a playful smile on her face.

Aaron grabbed his backpack and shut the Jeep door. He looked at the building as they went towards the entrance. What was the history and significance of this building that she wanted him to see, he wondered.

As they stepped through the doorway, all of his expectations as to what were inside were swept away with a feeling of amazement.

"It's a synagogue," she said, confirming his thoughts. "One of the oldest in the New World. The oldest is in Curaçao but this one is really beautiful."

Aaron agreed with her. This was a beautiful synagogue. The Jews who built it must have had money, he thought. The benches were all made out of wood with intricate carvings on all of them. The windows he had seen from the street were amazing stained glass windows that rivaled the works of Chagall.

Looking forward he set his eyes on the front of the synagogue. There was a small stage with a stunning replica of the Ten Commandments crafted from silver, gold, and wood. Behind that was where they kept the Torah Scrolls. Aaron could not see them because the doors were shut, but he imagined that they were magnificent.

The women's section was upstairs like in most of the old, traditional synagogues he had seen but all the activity was on the first floor. There were a few old men with yarmulkes talking to each other in the front, not paying much attention to the visitors since they had entered the doorway.

"Sometimes, I like to come here to feel at home," Sarah said. "I just come in and talk with the men or go upstairs and sit by myself and let the feeling of the synagogue sink into me."

"Does it work? Do you feel more at home here?" He was confused about why she would feel at home in a synagogue of all places.

"Not really, but it does feel nice. It gives me a little taste of back home."

"Wait a minute." Aaron shook his head trying to figure Sarah out. "You're Jewish," he asked with doubt in his voice.

"Yeah, aren't you?" But, she already knew the answer.

"Yeah, but how'd you know?"

"With a name like Silver? I was almost sure. Besides, why do you think I brought you here?"

"I don't know. I didn't really think about it till just now." Aaron paused for a second. He could not believe that this beauty was Jewish, what luck! Then he remembered what Mike had said about dating a co-worker and his expression changed immediately.

"Are you Orthodox?"

"Do I look Orthodox?" Sarah motioned to her body, which was dressed in shorts and a short-sleeved tee-shirt.

"You don't even look Jewish!"

"Why not? What does a Jewish girl look like anyway," she asked, challenging him for an acceptable answer.

"Not like you, I don't know." Aaron struggled. He knew she was trying to corner him.

Without an answer, Sarah led the way out of the synagogue with a smile, back towards downtown. "Are you going to leave your Jeep there," Aaron asked, trying to change the subject.

"Yeah, it'll be fine," Sarah answered as they left the block with the synagogue. "Are you Orthodox?"

"No, not really." He was relived that she had dropped the subject of Jewish Women.

"What does that mean?"

"Well, I don't like to mix meat with milk and I don't eat non-kosher meats. Basically, I like to eat Kosher style."

"What about seafood?"

"Only fish with scales, no crab, lobster, shell fish, or things like that."

"Me, too!" Sarah was happy that someone else saw things her way when it came to Jewish dietary restrictions.

"Where are we going now," Aaron asked, looking around.

It was hot but there were people in their business suits passing them as they walked. They were no doubt going to some big job in some big office in one of the many large buildings in the area, Aaron thought. If it were not for the mountains behind us, he thought, and the sea below, we could be in New York. Another difference Aaron noticed was the number of white people. There weren't many. This didn't make him nervous like it would many people instantly thrust into a world where they become the minority. Being Jewish, he was used to it. Instead of being a minority in a sea of Christian whites, he was now a minority in a sea of Jamaican blacks. It didn't make much of a difference to him.

"I thought I'd take you for a stroll around downtown, and then we could go to the botanical gardens for lunch. It's a really nice place."

"Sounds nice," he agreed, not really knowing what was in store.

"After we finish lunch it should be about time to head out to the lab. Are you ready for your first real day of setting up for the project? I know everyone is really excited about doing self-recognition!"

"I guess so. I'll just need to stop at my room on the way back and pick up some notes."

"That's fine, your apartment's on the way to the lab."

They spent the rest of the morning walking around downtown Kingston. Aaron loved new and old architecture. He had always been fascinated with history and thought that if he had a second education, he might study history.

At about twelve-thirty they went back to Sarah's car and sped off towards the botanical gardens. It only took fifteen minutes to get there but it seemed shorter because of the great conversation. There had hardly been a moment of silence between the two.

Aaron had begun to let down his defenses and started to become more comfortable with himself around Sarah. He wasn't worried anymore about his actions around her.

Aaron could already tell that they would get along like old friends. It was that confidence that comes after spending only a few minutes with someone, alone in a quiet setting. You can immediately tell whether you click with someone, or whether you'll have to struggle for conversation whenever you're together.

The Botanical Gardens were beautiful. It was teeming with tropical flowers from every colors of the spectrum. There were also tall and sprawling trees surrounding the walkways, blocking the view of the mountains and beaches. As they were walking on, what seemed, the main pathway, Aaron thought how secluded this place was. Even on this large trail one could jump into the brush on either side and vanish from sight in seconds.

They walked around the main path for about twenty minutes, talking and admiring the colorful life that surrounded them. Eventually the path led them back to the entrance and to a small café that looked more like a wood cabin, which he had not noticed on the way in.

"You ready to eat?" Sarah asked, as they walked up onto the wooden porch.

"Is this place expensive?"

"Not too bad, but this'll be my treat. Okay?"

"No, I'll pay for mine, I just don't have infinite funds for the summer," Aaron answered, not wanting to seem cheap.

They sat down at a small table on the porch. There were four other small, round, wooden tables surrounding them, only one of which was being used. A couple that looked as if they were on a honeymoon sat, eating on the other side of the porch from them. As soon as they sat down, a waiter wearing all white came and dropped off two menus.

"What would you like to drink," the waiter asked in his definitive Jamaican accent.

"Water, please," Sarah and Aaron both said. They looked at each other and almost laughed.

"On your honeymoon, eh, man?" The waiter winked to Aaron.

"Yes," Sarah said, before Aaron could even shake his head.

"Congratulations, man," the waiter said in Aaron's direction. "Looks like you picked a good one. I'll be right back with your drinks." He smiled and left the two alone as he returned to the kitchen, inside the building.

"What was that all...?"

"Oh, its just funny to see what you can get away with," Sarah interrupted. "We're white, we seem to be a couple. To locals that either means we are married and on vacation, or we're on a honeymoon. I've had that waiter ask me the same question with three different guys. If he even remembers, I wonder what he thinks about me?" She laughed.

"What about me?"

"What do you mean?"

"Well, first of all, we just got married and I didn't even know we were engaged! Secondly, before we got married you didn't even bother telling me you were married to three other men! What am I supposed to think? You probably don't even really love me. It's the money, isn't it? You married me for the money," he answered, resolving his own question.

"No, it wasn't for the money this time. I have enough already from the other divorces. This time it was for love, really," she said sincerely, putting a hand on his.

"Alright, I guess I can trust you. After all, you are my wife," Aaron said, just as the waiter returned with the water.

"Is the happy couple ready to order now?" He smiled at them.

"Can you give us a few more minutes please," Sarah asked.

"Sure, take your time, man." The waiter left them again but this time tended to the other couple on the porch.

They sat quietly for a few minutes looking over the menu which was plagued with chicken salad, seafood of non-kosher sorts, and jerk chicken specials. Finally, Aaron came upon a vegetable salad, which looked as though it would accommodate his hunger until dinner.

"Will you order me the botanical garden salad if the waiter comes back, please," Sarah asked, as she stood up from the table. "I need to make a call."

"Sure." Aaron smiled as she left.

Sarah walked toward the other end of the porch, where it wrapped around the building. There was a pay phone Aaron could barely see, jutting out of the corner of the wooden restaurant where the porch wrapped around. Sarah made her way over to the phone as Aaron watched her. He sat entranced by her. He loved watching beautiful women walk by him, and he had gotten used to just that. Aaron never thought that he would be talking to, let alone having lunch with someone so beautiful. It wasn't just her face and body. Her personality made her ten times more attractive then her physical features ever could.

He was still looking in Sarah's direction as she turned back to face him. She had already dialed a number but was not speaking to anyone yet. Sarah looked back at the table and Aaron smiled softly. She smiled back. Aaron turned back to his menu as the waiter returned to his table.

"Are you ready to order, sir? Or would you like to wait for the lady?"

"That's Okay, I'll order for her. We've been together so long; I know exactly what she wants," he said as if it were true, for the waiter's benefit. "We'll have two botanical garden salads, please."

"That's it?"

"Yes, thanks." The waiter nodded his head and took the two paper menus.

After the waiter disappeared again, Aaron turned to see if Sarah had finished her phone call. She was apparently talking to someone now and she looked upset. Her back was facing him and her posture and movements gave away her feelings of frustration.

Aaron could only make out a few words of her conversation, and most of that was just "yes" or "no" answers.

In the middle of the conversation, she glanced in Aaron's direction. Seeing that he was looking in her direction, Sarah moved around the corner.

Getting the feeling that Sarah did not want to be watched during her phone call, Aaron stared aimlessly at the thick greenery surrounding the porch. He hoped that when she returned the mood would not be awkward because she had seen him looking at her.

A few minutes later, Sarah returned to the table seemingly free of the frustration that she had so clearly displayed on the phone call.

"Is everything Okay?" Aaron was concerned.

"Oh, it's fine." Sarah had no hint of frustration in her voice.

"Who were you talking to?" He didn't want to bring it up but was curious.

"My father," she said, now with a brief sign of anger in her face.

"Do you guys not get along," Aaron asked, figuring he was too far into the line of questioning to stop.

"We do sometimes, but he never changes."

"What do you mean?"

"He used to be in the service, a lieutenant in the Navy. I guess he feels like I'm his little soldier girl and for as long as I can remember he's been ordering me around," she said angrily.

"Sorry." Aaron didn't know what else to say.

"Yeah." Sarah looked into the gardens and visualized her father ordering her around sometime in the distant past.

"It was always, 'Let's go to that ball game soldier,' or, 'If you don't get your butt out of that bed in five seconds, you'll give me twenty when I get up there!'" Sarah had turned her head back to the table and was staring down, blankly.

"I'm really sorry that you and your father don't have a better relationship." Aaron waited for a few seconds, debating whether the next subject would be a sore one. "What about your mother?"

Just as he asked the question, the food arrived. He was so engrossed in her past that he had lost track of his surroundings and did not notice the waiter until the food was placed in front of his face.

Sarah's face changed suddenly as the food was placed on the table. "Oh, this looks good!" She smiled and rubbed her hands together. "What did you order?" She had asked the question before looking over at Aaron's plate but immediately Sarah realized that he had ordered the same dish.

"I guess we have the same taste," he said, lifting his utensils.

"I figured we'd probably order the same thing," Sarah responded modestly, then took her first bite.

"Oh, why is that?"

"Well..." she began, with a mouth full of salad. Sarah raised her fork in her right hand to indicate that Aaron should wait until she was finished chewing.

"Yeah, I hate when people ask me questions when my mouth is full too."

Sarah was chewing and trying to talk at the same time with lettuce hanging out of her mouth. She didn't even try and cover it up with her hand. Aaron thought it was funny and started to laugh at her.

"What," she asked, with lettuce still hanging out of her mouth.

"I'm not making fun of you," Aaron said, still laughing softly. "It's cute, though. Definitely a good look for you."

"Thanks." Sarah finally got the lettuce into her mouth, smiled and laughed at herself, with Aaron.

Sarah was different than other women he had met before. She was not preoccupied with making a good impression. She did what she wanted to do and didn't worry about what other people thought. At least, that's the way it seemed to Aaron.

If they had met under different circumstances, Aaron thought, this would have been the beginning of a great relationship. They were very comfortable with each other. Aaron thought that if nothing happened between them romantically, that they would at least become very good friends and being friends with Sarah was fine with Aaron. He loved the idea of having someone to hang out with. It would be nice to do something other than research during the summer.

"What I was trying to say before," Sarah continued after she finished chewing. "Is that I figured you were going to order the salad because there isn't that much on the menu that you would eat. Most of it has shell fish, crab meat, or all that other stuff you wouldn't eat, and neither would I."

"Yeah, I guess that makes sense," Aaron realized, as he, too, began to eat his lunch. She had answered his question to his satisfaction and he had not answered hers about what Jewish women are supposed to look like. He wouldn't try and corner her again.

"So, where are you from again," she asked in between bites.

"Memphis."

"You don't have much of a southern accent."

"That's what everyone says."

"Why do you think you don't have one?"

"The main reason I think." He paused for a moment to finish chewing, then continued his explanation. "Is because I've also lived in Israel, Albany, and now Boston. So, I think that if I did have one when I was a kid, maybe it got washed away from living in so many other places."

"Do your parents have a southern accent?"

"They did," Aaron answered. Sarah did not catch the reference to the past.

"That's interesting. You grew up with two people, both of whom had a southern accent and you didn't get one."

"Well, like I said, I probably grew out of it."

"Interesting theory." She paused, letting it sink in. "How did you get so lucky as to live in all those places? Did your parents move around a lot?"

"No. When I graduated high school, I went to the Israeli Army and when I finished I went to Albany for school. Then, when I graduated, I went on to the doctoral program in psychology at Harvard."

"The Israeli Army, wow!" Sarah paused for a moment from eating and stared at him with a questioning face. "Why did you go to the Israeli Army?"

"Hmm." Aaron thought, wondering which answer to give. "It was a mixture of things, I guess." He paused a moment more to gather his thoughts. "I wanted to get away from the states and my best friend was going into the Israeli Amy and I figured I'd join him," he said simply.

"Just like that?" She thought there must be more to the explanation.

"Yeah, just like that." He knew she was probing deeper but he was trying to keep off the subject of his parents.

"Where did you serve?" She noticed he was becoming uncomfortable with the line of questioning and changed the subject.

"The Golani."

"Oh, special forces, huh? That's pretty sexy."

Aaron laughed. He had never seen risking his life every day as something sexy.

"You know, you seem a little skinny to have been in the special forces," Sarah added, sipping on her water.

"I hate that!"

"What?"

"Being skinny. You know, I'm a lot stronger than I look. Come to think of it. Most of the guys I worked with weren't too much bigger than I am. But, to be honest, I was a little bigger back then. We used to work out every day and run to keep in shape. You never knew when the next time you were going to have to run for your life was."

"Did you like Israel?"

"Yeah, I loved it there. Have you ever been?"

"Once. It was the only nice trip that I ever went on with my family. My father would usually butcher the nice things, but that trip was different. He was calmed and humbled by the history and tone of the land." She stopped for a moment and reflected on the past. "I think I might want to live there one day, but I feel like I'll never make it."

"Don't say that," Aaron said encouragingly. "If you really want to live there one day, it'll happen. I know I'll eventually go back one day, probably later than sooner, but I'll make it."

"Wait, a minute," She said after a moment of silence. "So, why did you leave Israel after three years if you liked it so much?"

"Oh. I guess I was ready to go back." He had to look up and search for an answer.

"After three years you were just ready?" She looked confused.

"I think it stemmed from something that happened before I left for Israel." Aaron sighed. He realized that he was not going to be able dodge the subject forever.

"What?" Sarah paused. "That is, if you don't mind me asking?"

"Well." Aaron hesitated. He did mind her asking but didn't want to make her too uncomfortable by telling her so. He also did not want to discuss what happened to his parents with her. Aaron could not remember the last time he talked about it and didn't want to start now but he did.

"Both of my parents died in a plane crash when I was eighteen," he said slowly, and then paused. "And... I guess it just took me three years to get the courage to come back." When he finished speaking he was looking at the table. Thinking of his parents still made him sad and tears started to form but he wiped them away quickly.

Sarah was looking at him as tears welled up in her eyes. She felt such sorrow for her new friend but did not know how she could console him. She knew that nothing she could say would make him feel any better so she just kept quiet. As she was looking at Aaron, she could tell he was not crying, but still saddened by the loss of his parents. Sarah saw his hand on the table and instinctually put her hand over his. He looked up and smiled.

"Thanks." Aaron tried not to get choked up. "I know there's nothing to say."

As he completed his sentence, Aaron reached his other hand over and joined it with the other two already on the table. He looked down at their hands, in a pile on the table and continued to talk.

"I used to think that after it happened to me, that I would know what to say to someone else in the same situation." As Aaron continued talking he started rubbing Sarah's hand between his hands. He felt such a connection to her. Her gesture meant a lot to him, and at that moment he realized how to console someone.

"And, even after my parents passed away, I still didn't know what to say." He paused for a second and looked up slowly to face her again. "Until right now." Aaron paused again, staring directly into her loving, warm eyes, which were staring right back at him.

"Nothing. There's nothing you can do except for what you just did by feeling my pain and connecting."

Without thinking about it, Aaron had opened up about his parents for the first time in years. With that thought his defenses went up, even in front of Sarah.

"Let's stop talking about it," he said definitively as he concealed his negative emotions as he usually did.

Even though he was upset at himself, he felt a connection between the two of them that neither had felt before. Before he even thought, Aaron leaned over, gently cradled Sarah's head in his left hand, pulled her close and kissed her cheek softly. He held her cheek to his lips for a few moments, and then sat normally again, still looking into her eyes.

Sarah was still looking at him, but with a little less intensity than before. She put her head down, because she still wasn't sure what to say.

"I'm sorry," Aaron said, still holding her hand and leaning toward her. "I just got caught up in the moment." He was referring to the kiss. "I... I know we're co-workers, I'm..."

"No," Sarah interrupted softly and looked up at him. "That's not it. I could care less about the co-worker thing. It's just really nice."

"What's really nice?"

"Oh, not that your parents died," she responded quickly and apologetically. "It's just, well, this moment. It was really nice." They were both smiling at each other.

"Yeah, it was." Aaron looked back at Sarah. They stared at each other for a few moments letting the world spin around them while they were captured in time.

Sarah looked down at her watch quickly. "Oh, man, we need to go!" They quickly paid the bill, left enough for a tip and walked back to Sarah's Jeep.

*****

On the way to the lab, Aaron explained how he wanted the dolphins to be trained for his experiment. Sarah took mental notes of his explanation and knew exactly what she would do to prepare the dolphins for the testing phase.

There were no cars in the gravel lot when they pulled into the lab. They both walked downstairs and into the lab, which was empty as well.

"What time is it," Aaron asked. He knew what time it was by the clock on the wall, but he couldn't believe that no one was in the lab.

"I know. They never get here early. It's like they're on dolphin standard time."

"That's right." Aaron realized, remembering his studies. "Because they're more active in the afternoon than in the morning."

"That's right kiddo," she said endearingly, patting him on the cheek.

"Kiddo?" Aaron did not approve of her term for him.

"Well, you are younger than me," Sarah said, while looking through some papers in the file cabinets.

"What are you looking for?" Aaron gave up. If it was "Kiddo" she wanted, "Kiddo" it would be. He hoped they would never get into an argument because he didn't think he would ever win.

"Some copies of old tests that were done, similar to what you want to do. Turn on the computer will ya," she asked, still looking through old papers.

Aaron sat down at the middle computer against the back wall of the lab. He found the power button on the corner of the keyboard and turned it on.

"Do you remember what Mike was trying to teach you yesterday?"

"Not too much of it stuck with me to tell you the truth."

Sarah took out a few papers, placed them on the counter top and continued looking for more.

"Just open up the file, 'Old Tests,' in the desktop section," she said, with her head still in the filing cabinet.

Aaron fidgeted around until he found what he was looking for and opened the Old Tests folder. As he scrolled down the list he found a document entitled, "Touch Screen Training."

"Is this it?" He had the mouse pointing to the file.

Sarah was finished looking through the files and had moved behind him after she placed the papers neatly on the desk next to him. She put her hands on his shoulders and looked over his head, to the screen. "Yeah, that's it."

She sat down next to him and started to explain what they would do to train the dolphins for the experiment. As she went through the procedure, Sarah made Aaron struggle with the computer programs so he would learn how to run the subjects by himself.

After they had been hard at work for about an hour, they heard someone entering the lab from above. "Must be Bob," Sarah said, without taking her gaze away from the computer screen.

Aaron did not answer. He was also fascinated by what they were doing.

As Bob came down the stairs, he flipped a light switch on the stairwell next to the lab door. When the lights came on both Aaron and Sarah came out of their work trances. They turned around and saw Bob straggling in.

"Did you just wake up," Aaron asked.

"Yep," Bob answered, taking a deep breath and letting it out in the form of a yawn.

"You weren't kidding, were you," Aaron asked Sarah as he turned back to the screen.

"How long have you kids been here," he asked as he walked to his table in the far corner.

"About an hour or so," Sarah answered.

"You still showing him the ropes?"

"Yeah, but he's almost as bright as the dolphins, so we might be able to get this thing rolling soon." She got a "very funny" facial reply from Aaron, but he did not say anything and continued to work on the computer.

"Well, then," Bob said, putting his small, leather briefcase down. "Shall we get started?"

"Sure," Aaron said enthusiastically. He was excited about starting the first dolphin research project of his academic career.

"Okay, but first things first," Bob said, taking off his shirt. "We've got to turn on that air conditioner! It's hot in here! I don't know how you two can stand it!" After turning on the air conditioner, Bob also flipped on his desk fan.

"Oh, no," Aaron said. "I'm going to freeze my ass off!"

CHAPTER 7

Dr. Melinowski walked cautiously out of the front doors. They
would have never found him in the small dump he had stayed in that night, even
if they were onto him, he thought. He had no reason to suspect that they were,
but he was being careful nonetheless.

He looked both ways down the empty street and started briskly on his way.
It was a cool morning for the summer, especially in Cartagena. It was not
raining, but it had been pouring the night before and the sky was overcast with
clouds that seemed to have floated right into the city from the Gulf of Mexico.
These surroundings must be a gift from God, Melinowski thought to himself.
He knew it was hard to see with all the fog and hoped that it kept up for a while
until he could reach his destination.

He turned the corner quickly and knocked his plastic bag into the side of a
building. The bag fell to the ground and some of the papers spilled onto the
pavement. His heart started racing as he squatted down to gather his life
threatening materials and pushed them quickly and carelessly into the bag. He
didn't care if they were crushed a little, but he did not want to get caught for
this, for sure they would kill him.

Looking around nervously through his sunglasses, which made him look
more conspicuous, he still could not detect anyone who might be following him.
Picking himself off the ground with the papers safely secured in his bag, he took
off down the street at a faster pace. At his new pace, his long overcoat began
rubbing against itself, making a sound as if a flag was fluttering on a pole in a
steady wind.

He pulled his hat down lower to avoid any eye contact with people on the
street. No one could be trusted, he thought, and the last thing he wanted to do
was to be recognized.

He had told them that he was going on vacation to the Bahamas, but he
didn't know if his cover was good enough. They could be watching me at this
very moment, he thought. These thoughts were driving him mad, but he knew,
no matter what, he was doing the right thing.

"Dr. Melinowski," A voiced asked, as a car screeched to a halt on the street
next to him.

"Jesus, fucking, Christ," Melinowski said, through his gritted teeth,
throwing a hand over his chest and dropping the bag. "What the fuck do you
think you're doing? You could have killed me doing that, then you wouldn't
have had a witness." He took a deep breath and let it out. "Jesus." He knew he

was safe for the moment but was still trying to get over his near death experience. He had recognized the man's voice as the CIA agent from the phone.

"I'm Agent Chumny with the CIA. Would you get in the car please, Dr. Melinowski," the man with the dark suit and sunglasses said quickly. "We don't have much time."

The doctor picked his bag up again and complied with the man's request. He sat down in the car and without a word the driver sped off down the street through the morning fog.

"I thought we were supposed to meet at the park," Melinowski said, taking off his hat and glasses to reveal a man in his mid-fifties, almost bald. What hair he did have left was gray and scraggly and it looked as though he hadn't cut or brushed it in years.

"The plans changed." Chumny wasn't even looking at his precious passenger. He was keeping his eye on the road behind them to make sure they were not being followed.

"Is something wrong? Why were the plans changed," Melinowski asked nervously.

"They didn't fall for the bait." Chumny paused for a few moments to look around again, then returned his attention to his passenger. "They know you're here. They must have found out somehow that you were coming to see us. Did you tell anyone, I mean *anyone*, that you were doing this?"

"No," Melinowski answered nervously.

"Who did you tell, doctor?"

Melinowski looked around at the men in the car nervously. He thought, foolishly, that if he kept the truth from the CIA that his employers wouldn't find out either. "Just another researcher," he said innocently.

"Just another researcher?" Chumny was dumbfounded and extremely upset. "How could you have been so stupid?"

"What?" Melinowski had no idea how this could be such a bad thing. "What's the big deal? I mean, who's Doctor Harrington going to tell, anyway?"

"It's not what he's *going* to tell them, it's what they've *already made* him tell them!"

"Oh, no! What are they going to do to him?"

"Nothing now," Chumny answered. "He's probably already dead."

"Oh, my God! Do you know what this means? Do you?" He started talking to himself out loud, because he was sure the others in the car knew well what it meant.

"I can't go back! I can't!" He paused for a moment, then looked at Chumny. "Oh, my God! They're going to kill me! They know! They know everything! Shit! Shit! Shit! I'm dead! What am I going to do?" He paused again. "Wait, it's not what I'm going to do. Didn't you say you could protect me if anything happened?"

"Yes, but don't worry about it," Chumny said calmly.

"Don't worry! Don't worry? That's easy for you to say! I'm the one that's..."

"Calm down Dr. Melinowski. We've prepared for this and we're getting you out of the country right now. We've already got your new identity and papers ready to go on the plane at the airport, but first things first."

Chumny stopped talking, pulled out a tape recorder and pressed record. "This is Agent Chumny of the CIA. It's June twentieth, zero-seven hundred hours and I'm in the presence of one..." He stopped speaking and shoved the recorder into the doctor's face, prompting him to speak.

"Dr. Earl Melinowski." There was no expression in his voice or on his face.

"Doctor, tell me everything you know about the Poseidon Project."

Earl settled into his seat and began. "I got involved in the project about a year and a half ago. At the time, I was doing marine biology research for the University of Hawaii in Manoa. Deep saltwater fish, kelp, the sea floor biology, you know, all the normal stuff. Anyway, one day I get this letter from the Colombian Government offering me a position in the new research facility they were building in the Gulf of Mexico. Do you remember when that was going on, all that international bureaucracy? They had a hell of a time getting the thing approved. Not many people knew about it."

Earl became more comfortable as he spoke. Agent Chumny wasn't looking around as much and Earl felt safer being in his presence even though there was a sense of urgency.

"Anyway, the offer was quite large, monetarily and to tell you the truth, universities don't pay that well. I also had nothing tying me down in Hawaii so I figured, why not? Boy, was that a mistake when I look back on it now, but how could I have known," he asked himself, then turned his attention back to the tape.

"Well, I moved down to Jamaica for a month. They were supposed to have finished building by the end of last summer, but, as *they* said, they ran into some problems. The scientists lived it up on the money that we made them pay us because we were supposed to be working already. They weren't too happy about that, but looking back, I guess they wanted to keep a low profile and figured they'd better shut us up quickly before we went running for help.

"They finally finished early last fall and we were flown out to the facility off the coast of Jamaica. We were all surprised when we arrived. It looked an awful lot like an oilrig. It was very nice, though. Each of us had our own room, looking out onto the ocean. The equipment we were using for our respective projects was spectacular! It was the kind of equipment you always wished you had at a university lab but always knew they couldn't afford.

"Everything was going well for the first few months. We were being treated very well. Good food, everyone got along, you know. We'd wake up whenever we wanted to and go down to the lab which was on the sea floor. It was connected to the top by an elevator and stairs, in case of emergency. You had to decompress on the way back up so you couldn't stay down all day. That was really the only problem with it.

"Anyway, one day we were having a staff meeting, like we usually did, and I asked if I could bring a friend to the facility. Well, the staff would have nothing to do with that! 'No visitors,' they said. It was as if what we were doing was top secret and no one could know! I mean, I knew that the facility was low key, but I had no idea how low key!

"After that incident, my relationship with the staff on the rig went downhill. I didn't talk to them much anymore and they didn't have much to say to me. It stayed that way for a while and then the boss of the project, I guess it was the boss, came to visit. He was there to do a staff change, which I was very happy about.

"Well the night he was there, we were all ordered to go to sleep early and I was not going to feel like a prisoner on that rig, so I sneaked out of my bunk late at night. Sometime around eleven-thirty, I think. I was walking around the outside of the rig, taking in some fresh air and thinking about how I was going to ask to leave and as I was walking around, I passed a porthole and saw the boss guy, I think they were calling him Señor Lopez. He was speaking to this guy, or, it was more like arguing. Neither of them seemed too sober.

"I was interested in what they were discussing, so I went around to the inside and stuck my head against the door. I thought I was going to hear Spanish, because the only people on the rig who spoke English were the other scientists but to my surprise, the conversation was being conducted in English.

"As I listened, I started to learn a little about the Poseidon Project. All I really learned from the eavesdropping session was that we were only at the facility for a cover-up purpose. I decided not to resign at this point. I was intrigued about what was going on, so I played it cool. It was easier at this point because there was a new staff on board and I could get along with them. That is, as long as I didn't step out of the strict boundaries they always laid out for us."

"What about the other scientists," Chumny asked, interrupting.

"What do you mean?"

"Didn't they get upset with the boundaries set for them?"

"Oh, sure they did. Some of them left after a while and were replaced by others. God only knows what happened to them. Can I continue now?" Earl looked upset because he had been interrupted.

"I'm sorry. Please continue."

"Well, every month or so, the U.S. Coast Guard and the Jamaican Government would come to inspect the rig. I guess it was one of the clauses in the agreement of the building contract."

"Why didn't you tell one of them," Chumny asked. He did not receive an answer, just a nasty look from Earl.

"I wanted to tell them something was up, but I couldn't. For one: I didn't know enough at the time that telling anyone would do any good. And, two: I was scared about what would happen if anyone found out. I didn't know what I was up against.

"I would have probably slipped something to someone eventually, but the Jamaicans and the U.S. stopped coming by! I couldn't believe it! How could they just give up on what was going on there? How could they be so careless," he asked angrily.

"Now to the important part. The evidence and information I was looking for suddenly appeared one night when I was up late doing research in the lab. I was the only one down there and I was drifting off while crunching some numbers when I heard noises coming from the escape pod door! It was distant, but loud enough to bring me out of my sleepy trance. I went over to the door, turned the handle, and opened it slowly. There was a small area between the sub and the lab. I shut the door behind me and opened the submarine hatch.

"They had opened it once when we first arrived, and it seemed normal enough. It was very scary though. They told us never to enter the sub unless there was an emergency. I was afraid the door would trigger an alarm, but nothing happened. As I walked into the small sub, the noise was a little closer, but I couldn't imagine where it was coming from. I could see the whole pod in front of me and it wasn't coming from inside the sub.

"I closed the sub hatch to see if I could pinpoint the source of the noise, and then I found it! There was another hatch in the bottom of the submarine and that's where it was coming from! I opened it slowly and it revealed a small chamber. Just about large enough to hold three people. I got in and shut the top. The noise was definitely coming from under me. I opened the bottom of the air lock and there it was! A ladder leading to a tunnel! I could see the bottom easily; it must have been about a hundred or two hundred feet down, though. I wanted to go down and see what was there but was afraid I'd get caught. Besides, the workers, or whoever was down there would have seen me and I would have been a goner for sure. So, I waited until the next day."

Chumny interrupted him abruptly, clicking off the tape recorder. "I'm sorry. The rest of the story's going to have to wait. We're here," he said, getting out of the car.

Dr. Melinowski looked about him. The car had stopped and they were on the tarmac at a small airport, parked next to a Learjet. He stepped out with his bag of evidence as someone opened the door for him.

"Come on Earl, let's go," Chumny said. "We need to get you out of here. Every minute you stay it gets more dangerous."

"Where are you taking me, anyway," he asked anxiously.

"To our regional headquarters in Miami, first. Then it'll be up to the relocation crew."

Chumny walked behind the doctor as he led him towards the plane. He wanted to make sure that if there were any snipers around, that they'd hit him and not Melinowski, but everything was eerily quiet. There had not been many cars on the road, no one had followed them to the airport, and the tarmac was deserted, save his men. Maybe his crew was doing a great job, which they usually did, but for some reason he half expected to have trouble. He was worried, but he figured that once they got off the ground and in route to Miami, everything would be fine.

When Earl was safely in the cabin, Chumny shut the door and went into the cockpit. Earl sat down across from the two other agents who had boarded with them. They looked at Earl as he made himself comfortable, then went back to their own private conversation. Looking around, Melinowski noticed there was a bar farther back and other sparsely placed seats throughout the cabin. The beige, leather interior was beautiful. Now he knew what his tax dollars were really paying for.

Earl felt a small jolt and he looked out of his window. The plane was moving and he felt sad. He would probably never be able to do his aquatic research again. He also loved the climate that his profession had allowed him to live in. For all he knew, he would be living in Tibet, disguised as a Buddhist monk for the rest of his life.

As they taxied up to the runway, Chumny returned to the cabin and sat down next to Earl. "Earl, d'you meet the boys," he asked jovially.

"No."

"Boys, Earl; Earl, Boys." He gestured to the men in front of him and back to Earl.

"Thanks a lot," Earl said sarcastically.

Chumny pointed to the man on the left. "Carlos will be helping with your new identity crisis. And, Steve will be looking at your materials," he finished, pointing at the man on the right.

The men just sat there, only slightly nodding their heads as they were introduced. "Smart guys," Chumny said. "Just not men of many words."

Chumny was noticeably more comfortable now. They were lifting off from the tarmac and his worries of ambush vanished as quickly as the ground below them.

"Why don't you go ahead and give him your bag?" Chumny pointed to Earl's white, plastic bag.

"Is everything set for me in Miami," he asked, clutching it tightly.

"Everything's fine. Don't worry."

"How can you be so sure?"

"I just got off the phone with my boss, Mr. Millwood. You'll meet him when we get to Miami. He knows everything, well, whatever you told me a week ago, and just now. He'll make sure everything in Miami is set. Plus, we can get started here. That is, as long as you let us." Chumny motioned to Earl's bag, which he was still clutching tightly.

Earl slowly and reluctantly gave up his precious bag. Steve took the materials, walked down to the other end of the cabin, sat down at a table, and began to look over the disheveled papers.

Earl stood up so Steve could see him. "Be careful with those," he shouted. Steve looked up slowly, then went back to work.

"I risked my life for that stuff," he said again. When Earl got no response from the agent working on his papers, he sat back down, defeated by silence.

"Don't worry Earl, we'll take good care of you and your papers. Now, let's get back to it." Chumny took the tape recorder from his jacket pocket and made sure it was in the right spot.

"Okay," Earl said, searching his mind for where he had left off. "Ah, yes, the tunnel." Chumny clicked the recorder on and Earl continued his story.

*****

It was cloudy as far as he could see and he was happy about that. He knew they would be flying in the clouds to keep out of sight as much as possible, and that worked to his advantage because they would be flying by instrumentation, not sight.

He was standing in the control room of the small, undetectable vessel when the plane came onto the radar screen.

"Twenty-five miles south, bearing North at three hundred fifty knots," the man at the console said, as if he were a robot.

"Is the radio tuned in?"

"Yes, sir," the controller answered, sounding more human.

"Well, turn it up then!"

The controller complied with a turn of a dial near his left hand. As he did, all that came over the speaker was loud static.

"Ten miles south, bearing North at three hundred thirty-nine knots," the controller updated his boss. The man did not answer. He calmly picked up his glass, finished off his morning buzz and placed it back on the console next to the empty bottle of tequila.

"Two miles..."

"Sixty seconds," his superior interrupted. Without skipping a beat, the controller began counting down from sixty.

The boss, with his binoculars, walked outside onto the deck and listened to the controller count.

"Forty-nine, forty-eight, forty-seven."

He then turned his attention to the sky. The sound of the plane passing could not yet be heard.

"Thirty-five, thirty-four, thirty-three."

The counting continued with clock-like precision. As the man in charge was listening to the sky, the wind blew softly across his face. If it weren't for the clouds, he thought, it would be a beautiful day.

"Twenty-two, twenty-one, twenty."

There it was, the sound of the speeding plane overhead. They must have just passed us, he thought. He walked into the control room and stood behind the controller who had not strayed from his pace.

"Thirteen, twelve, eleven."

The boss looked over his subordinate's shoulder and saw that the remote control button was ready to go. The controller had flipped up the safety and was preparing to turn it on.

"Eight, seven, six."

Tag could wait no longer. The plane had already passed and he knew it was time. He pushed the controller's arm aside. The controller became confused and stopped counting but it did not matter. Tag had pressed the remote.

Immediately, voices started to panic over the speaker, and Tag began to smile.

"Sir, look at this," a rather calm voice said.

"Everything's going haywire!" Someone else panicked.

"What should we do," the first voice asked, less calmly than before.

"Try and get out of this cloud cover for starters," the captain answered.

"But, how do I know if I'm goin' up or down," the co-pilot panicked.

"Pick one, I'll radio for help. This is GOV7, does anyone read? I repeat, this is GOV7, does anyone read," the captain pleaded into the radio but no one answered.

"The radio's not working, what are we going to do," one of the co-pilots asked, franticly.

"Just keep her straight, I'll try to get through to someone!" There was fear in all their voices as they spoke.

Tag walked out onto the deck of the ship again, put his binoculars to his face, and searched the clouds to the North of them. He could still hear the plane, and it sounded closer.

"How the hell am I supposed to know which way I'm going," one of the voices yelled over the radio.

"Just fly the fuckin' plane," another voice yelled back.

"Shit, man, shit... We'll never make it out of this!"

"Shut up and fly, man. Just shut up!"

With his binoculars pressed up against his face, Tag continued to smile. He knew what the pilots didn't know for sure. They weren't going to make it. He heard the plane getting louder, and kept searching with his visual aids. Over the radio, all that could be heard was loud screaming. Screaming as he had heard only one other time, when he had shot a prisoner in cold blood. Tag had pointed the gun right in the man's face and pulled the trigger. He had made the same sound just before the bullet scattered his brains on the wall behind him. The sound of knowing that death was inevitable and only a few seconds away.

Tag's search with the binoculars continued. He could hear the plane screaming towards them at, what sounded like, faster than the speed of sound. Then, it ended.

He didn't need his binoculars anymore. The plane had smashed into the water only a few miles to the North. Tag lowered his visual aid and stared at the epicenter of the crash. The impact had been so powerful that debris was sent flying through the air as if the plane had smashed into concrete. Tag just stood there a while and stared with no expression on his face. He was taking in the beauty of his project and how no one would ever know what had happened. The device they planted in the plane simulated events that had happened over the Bermuda Triangle and had also disabled the radio. After they got rid of the wreckage, no one would ever know it was foul play. This event was just going to add to the mystery of the area, he thought. Tag was going to make sure of it.

"Alright," Tag screamed to the controller. "Go get my mess cleaned up!"

*****

"Can you tell us what happened, Mr. Millwood," the reporter asked from the audience.

The live video conference had been called as soon as the press could get their greedy little hands on tickets to get to the search and rescue base the CIA had set up in an abandoned hanger. "Do you think this could be related to the other disappearances that have occurred in almost the exact same locations," another media man asked.

Looking around, Tag recognized all the big names: WNN, CBS, ABC, NBC, they were all covering the tragedy and he couldn't be happier. This was his game and he loved playing it. He was so cocky. Tag sometimes commented that he could convince himself that he was telling the truth when he had to lie. To his credit, no one had caught him yet.

"Ladies and gentlemen, hold on. Okay?" Tag raised his hands to calm the crowd of reporters. "Everyone will get a chance at a later point."

He loved being in the spotlight, weaving his magic in front of the whole world. Tag got off on it.

As the crowd quieted down, Tag began to speak. "I know you want to find out what happened, and believe me, no one wants to get to the bottom of this more than I do." He paused, looking around at the crowd, then continued. "It's been just over twenty-four hours, and we've only just begun to start the search. The next twenty-four hours will be the most critical. Fortunately, the weather is cooperating with us and there doesn't seem to be any bad weather in the forecast. Unfortunately, we haven't found anything yet. We are hopeful though. We received a transmission from the aircraft just before it went down and we can almost pinpoint its last known location. If there are survivors out there, we will find them," Tag said strongly.

"I'm sorry I can't relay any more information at this point, but as soon as we find anything of importance we'll call a conference. Thank you for your patience."

Tag walked off the podium quickly. He did not want to give the media a chance to reply to his comments. Tag was happy with his performance and couldn't wait to keep on telling them that nothing had been found, repeatedly.

As he walked back to his makeshift office, through a crowd of reporters shoving cameras and microphones in his face, his cell phone rang. Tag pulled it out of his pocket and answered. "Millwood, here."

"You look good on TV," the Colombian voice said happily, on the other end.

"Hold on," Tag said angrily, his face showing it. He put the phone by his side and started walking at a faster pace towards his office. The reporters could not get a question in. Even if he had been walking slower, his aids were pushing the vultures out of the way.

As Tag got to his office, he slammed the door behind him. He was the only one in this space for now, but he knew that wouldn't last long. He went across the office and stood behind the old metal desk they had provided him. Everything was so old. Tag felt as if he was back in the '50s from his surroundings.

"What the hell do you think you're doing calling me on this line," Tag screamed into the receiver of his cell phone. Everyone outside heard him scream, but could not understand what he had said. All of the reporters who had just been turned away stared back at the office. The guards at the door, on the other hand, were not fazed by the voice booming through the large, shaded glass windows.

"I told you never to contact me at work," he said, lowering his voice a few decibels.

"Relax," the man on the other end said calmly. "Nothing is going to happen. You are going to be fine."

"That's easy for you to say! You're sittin' pretty somewhere that no one in the world can get their hands on you and I'm right in the middle of the action here!" Tag was calmer now, but only because he didn't want anyone to hear his conversation.

"This line is secure, Mr. Millwood, I assure you."

Tag took in a deep breath and sat down in the old, plush, brown, fake leather chair. "You have no fear, do you Señor," he asked, exhaling.

As they continued to talk, Millwood got up and peeked through the large, old blinds to see if anyone, besides his men, were near his office. He saw the reporters gathered in a corner on the other side of the huge room. They were conversing with each other, gathering information and coffee at the same time.

He figured it was safe and continued to talk to the man on the other end of the receiver, getting more involved in the conversation now. "Did you take care of your end?"

"Yes, I wrapped things up with Doctor Harrington a while ago. No one will ever be able to discover our little research project, and by the time we finish, it will have paid for itself." The man was calm. There was no fear of being caught in his voice as he spoke freely.

"Good, I'll be able to take that little vacation I've been hoping for."

"Señor Millwood, you will be able to take as many vacations as you wish, I assure you."

"Where are you anyway? And when does my next payment arrive?"

"I cannot tell you that, Mr. Millwood. What if this line is not secure?"

"I thought you said..." He started to get angry again and stood abruptly from his seated position.

"That's enough for now, Mr. Millwood, we will meet again soon," Lopez said, cutting Millwood off.

Tag heard a dial tone, and the next thing the press heard was the phone flying through the glass window of his office. Everyone in the old hanger, even his men, was surprised by this action. They had seen him angry at the phone, but never actually angry enough to throw it out of his office window.

CHAPTER 8

Aaron had been working hard on his research for a month but had only started testing the animals two weeks before and it was still unclear to everyone whether his hypothesis would be upheld. This night, like the others, Aaron was watching the test run its course even though it wasn't necessary. The computers could have done everything automatically. Aaron knew this was true but he liked being in the lab nonetheless because for him, the novelty of watching the dolphins had not yet worn off. Often, even after the testing was done for the evening, Aaron would stick around and play catch with the dolphins through the underwater widow. Sometimes, while he was playing with them, Aaron often wondered who was playing with whom.

Skilos didn't like to play catch or participate in the research as much as the others but Aaron had noticed an improvement in Skilos's behavior recently. He had not been as aloof towards Aaron and had even brought him a fish during one of Sarah's feeding sessions. Aaron felt it was a gesture of reconciliation even if the fish was regurgitated.

He had not yet swum in the tank because Bob wanted the dolphins to become accustomed to Aaron so he could safely swim with them. Dolphins were known for being protective of their area if they didn't recognize the intruder, especially Skilos. But, it was enough for Aaron just to watch Sarah interacting with them.

As he sat in the lab now, his thoughts turned to Sarah. They had had an amazing time together during the last few weeks. She had taken him everywhere of interest from out-of-the-way pubs to the University of the West Indies.

He missed her tremendously. She had only been gone a few days and was supposed to return the next day. She often disappeared for days at a time and Aaron thought it was odd but kept forgetting to ask why she had to leave.

Aaron loved spending time with her but didn't want to tell her how he really felt. He was afraid that she thought of him as a little brother or a good friend.

I've heard those excuses from women before and it would be just my luck to hear it again, he thought.

Aaron felt that she was too perfect for him. She loved working with dolphins, she was smart, not to mention gorgeous, and she was Jewish. It was everything he could ever hope for in a woman but he was afraid that he was not everything she was looking for.

They had less than two months left together in Jamaica, and Aaron wondered if that was enough time for him to muster enough courage to tell Sarah how he felt. Maybe, if he told her just before he left, and she didn't feel the same way, it wouldn't be too awkward. On the other hand, if he waited to tell her and she did feel the same way, it would probably be too late.

His stomach hurt while his brain predicted the many ways in which he was going to lose in this most recent love venture. He sighed to release his tension and the thoughts slowly receded from his head and he began to focus on the task at hand.

The tape had stopped rewinding and he took it out of the VCR to label it.

I wish there were a TV and VCR in my room so I could review them at home, he thought, but it's probably better that way. He knew that it wouldn't be right to start analyzing the data until all of the tests were complete. If he found some results, preliminarily, going in the wrong direction, he might, unknowingly, bias the next batch of trials.

Aaron looked at the clock as he was shutting down the lab for the evening; it was eleven o'clock. He had started his day at the lab almost twelve hours before and wasn't tired, but he was ready to go home.

After the lab door was locked he headed up the stairs, and locked the stairwell door behind him. The gravel parking lot seemed lonely, his small bike being the only occupant.

As he secured his backpack to himself someone pulled into the driveway. All he could see was the headlights heading towards him down the narrow pathway.

It must be someone who got lost, he thought. No one else would be coming to work now.

As the Jeep turned to park next to his bike, Aaron was happily proved wrong. It was Sarah.

"What are you doing here? I thought you weren't supposed to come back until tomorrow," Aaron asked pleasantly, as she stepped out of the Jeep.

"I got back early," she said as she moved closer to him. "Our little Harvard boy working late again?"

"I couldn't do it any other way."

They stood there in silence, staring at each other for a moment. It was a warm night, as it usually was, and they were enjoying each other and the peaceful silence between them.

"Oh," Aaron said, snapping back into reality. "I have your keys. I'm sorry."

He handed Sarah her set of lab keys. He had been so busy with his research and hanging out with Sarah, he had not had a chance to make a copy of the lab keys until earlier that day.

"Thanks," she said, as he dropped them into her hand.

"Hey!" Aaron grabbed Sarah's attention as she went to open the stairway. "Do you want to go out on a date with me tomorrow night," he asked confidently.

He was surprised at himself. What just spouted from my lips, he asked silently in disbelief. How did those words dribble out? I'll be so embarrassed if she turns me down but I can't take it back now, he thought.

Sarah stopped and turned towards him. She looked at him awkwardly and then began to smile. Aaron was still embarrassed and was looking at the gravel for consolation. Sarah walked back towards him quickly and before he knew what was happening, she had grabbed his head and kissed him on the cheek.

"You're so cute," she said, and pinched where she had just kissed. Aaron's heart fluttered, flushing his face, and he looked down again. He wanted, more than anything, to reach out at that moment, pull her close, and deliver the most passionate kiss she had ever received. He wanted to, but something held him back. The affection he had just received from Sarah seemed much more like a friendly kiss than anything else.

"I would love to go on a date with you tomorrow night." Sarah repeated his words in a cute reply. "Unfortunately, I already have other plans." She frowned. "I'm sorry."

"It's okay." Aaron felt stupid for having asked. He was obviously upset at himself and the answer he had received, but Sarah didn't seem to notice. She walked back to the stairwell and responded to his distress with only a good night.

If she liked me, Aaron thought, she would have at least given me a rain check. Stupid, stupid, stupid, he thought as he banged his helmet onto his head and turned to get onto his bike.

"Aaron," Sarah yelled, trying to get his attention. He finally heard her and took off his helmet. She was standing by the stairwell door under the lone light of the facility. To him, it made her look like a strong little angel.

"Yeah?"

Sarah started to smile slowly. "Tonight would be better. Do you want to do something tonight?"

"I'd love to. What did you have in mind," he asked calmly as he stepped off of his bike.

"Well, I don't know if I'd consider it a date, but do you want to take a swim with me in the tank?"

"I can't. Doctor Camron said..."

"Oh, screw that," she said apathetically. "I know what he said, but it's been long enough."

"What about Skilos? Do you think he'll be okay with it?" Aaron was worried about the dolphin's possible reaction.

"Skilos will deal with it. He's just jealous."

"Jealous?" Her reasoning confused Aaron.

"Yeah, he thinks you'll take me away from him. He's a little protective, what can I say." She paused. "Do you have your bathing suit with you?"

"Yep." Aaron figured that he had no reason to be worried if Sarah thought swimming with the dolphins was not dangerous.

"Well, get in it and I'll be back up in a sec." She unlocked the stairwell door and disappeared down the stairs.

"You want me to change up here," he asked, but there was no answer. "I guess that's a 'yes'," Aaron said to himself.

He put his helmet on the handlebars of his bike and put his backpack on the gravel surface. After unzipping his bag, he sifted through to find his bathing suit. When he found it, he walked to the other side of the tank to change. The area was not illuminated well and it looked like a good place to change.

Just before taking off his underwear, he took one quick look and did not see or hear Sarah approaching yet. Turning his butt toward the lab, he quickly took off his underwear and threw them with the rest of his clothes where they would not get wet. Almost finished, he started pulling the bathing suit up his legs when the lights in the tank went on.

"Nice butt," Sarah shouted as Aaron pulled his bathing suit on quickly and turned around. Sarah was leaning on the wall near the stairwell door, looking very seductive. She didn't have her regular bathing suit on. Aaron had never seen this one before. Her bikini was small enough to make anyone drool, man or woman, but large enough to leave the rest of her body up to the imagination.

"Hi." Was all he could muster at this point. Aaron was staring at her body, the bouncing reflections of the water illuminating her. He wasn't embarrassed anymore; all of his self-conscious feelings disappeared when he saw her. Aaron had never seen anything like her in real life. He had almost concluded that perfect women only existed on the screen.

"Why don't you come over to this side and get in with me," Sarah asked playfully, as she moved closer to the tank. "It'll be safer that way."

"Okay."

Aaron walked over to where Sarah was easing her feet into the tank. He moved to her left side and sat down at the edge of the tank with her. He could not stop staring at her body. Aaron had seen her in a bathing suit before, but this was different. It was sexy.

"Just put your legs in slowly. Like this." She slid her legs in as an example.

Aaron obeyed. He watched her slim toned legs slip into the water and repeated the action with his own legs.

Aaron had not been paying attention to the water, but something caught his eye. About three feet away, a dolphin's head was just above the crest of the water, watching the two researchers intently. It reminded him of crocodiles he had seen on TV, watching and waiting to kill their prey. This made him a little nervous and he started to pull his legs out.

"No, no." Sarah grabbed his right hand. "Stay, it'll be alright. They won't freak out as long as I'm with you, I promise." She smiled and he relaxed.

She slowly put his hand in the water, still holding onto it. They looked at each other, smiled, and then she turned her attention back to the tank where the dolphin had moved from its last position. Aaron realized that the dolphin, which had been watching from a distance, was now moving slowly towards them. It was Skilos. Aaron got nervous again and pulled back with his hand, but Sarah wouldn't let him. She held his hand in the water until Skilos had passed slowly by and allowed them to caress his belly as he swam.

"He's not going to hurt you. He was jealous at first, but I think he's used to you by now," she said softly.

"I don't get that. Why would a dolphin be jealous? Surely he realizes that he's not going to *mate* with you. You're not the same species," he said, breaking the mood.

"Stop looking at it from the evolutionary perspective and look at it like a loving, caring, feeling, intelligent being. He likes my companionship and doesn't want that taken away from him and transferred to something else." Sarah paused for a second, then continued. "I'm sure you'd feel the same way, if it happened to you." And with that she restored the romantic atmosphere.

"I can see what you mean," he responded in kind.

"Alright, let's get in." Her eyes lit up with excitement.

Sarah lowered her body slowly into the water, then turned to face Aaron who was still sitting on the side with his legs dangling. "Come on!" She motioned him to slide in.

Aaron reluctantly slid into the tank. When he had first come to Jamaica he was so excited about swimming with the dolphins and now he was scared of them but he had no reason to be.

Skilos had started taking a liking to Aaron earlier than he knew but the dolphin had not yet had a chance to show his true feelings towards him. Skilos would not only not harm Aaron but he was willing to start playing as well.

After he was in the tank and treading water, Sarah pulled some snorkeling equipment off the side of the tank and handed the necessary items to her partner. Aaron put them on and waited for Sarah to do the same. When she was ready, she cleared her snorkel, blowing water three feet into the air, then dove towards the bottom of the tank.

Aaron watched her from above and when she got to the bottom, Skilos swam by and let her caress his side.

After Skilos passed, Sarah pushed herself off the bottom of the tank and joined Aaron at the surface. Clearing the waterline, she blew into her snorkel again with a low purging sound and shooting water.

"You wanna do something cool," she asked, taking the snorkel out of her mouth.

"Okay." Aaron was audibly hesitant.

"Alright, put your right arm all the way out, perpendicular to your body. That's right," Sarah said, as Aaron copied her action. "Now, curl your hand in like you were going to grab a handle on a door. Okay, now just wait there for a second, just like that, don't move."

"What are they going to do?" But almost as he had finished his question, Aaron began to move slowly around the tank without putting forth any effort.

"Wow," he shouted, surprised as he began to move faster. He started laughing into his snorkel, his head splitting the water as Skilos pulled him around the tank.

"That was awesome," he shouted as he returned to his point of embarkation near Sarah. "Can I do it again?" He sounded like a child that had just exited his first ride at an amusement park.

"A little later, Okay?" Sarah laughed softly at his question.

She loved seeing him like this. She could feel his joy and it inspired her to show Aaron more. Sarah didn't feel like a grown-up when she was with Aaron. He had a way about him that was so adventuresome and child-like. Maybe that's what kept him looking so young, she thought. She could easily mistake him for a junior or senior in college.

They swam around the tank, watching the dolphins sleep, play, and swim. Every so often, Sarah would motion to one of the dolphins and it would jump over them, swim by them or do any number of acts that Sarah had taught them to do over time. The minutes flew by as they reveled in the wonder of the beautiful animals.

"This salt water's making me a little thirsty," Sarah said. "You wanna go out and grab something to drink before bed?"

"That'd be great!" Aaron was thinking of what a nightcap could mean. "I'm a little parched myself. But, before we go, would you mind if I did that thing one more time?"

"That pull-along trick that Skilos does? It's no problem, unless he doesn't want to."

"How do you know if he doesn't want to?"

"He just won't do it."

"Oh, well, I guess it's worth a shot then." Aaron stretched out his hand out as he had done before. Skilos followed his movements and picked him up in the water where he was floating.

Aaron held onto Skilos until he had almost passed Sarah, but let go just before he had. In one swift movement, Aaron took of his mask, grabbed Sarah around the waist and pinned her against the tank wall. She laughed excitedly when he grabbed her and then giggled as they came to a rest at the side of the tank.

Her mask was still on her head and he removed it while staring into her eyes. Sarah slowly quieted her playful laughing and saw the intent look on his face. A feeling built up quickly in her chest as the same was happening with her partner.

Aaron inched closer to her. With one hand around her waist, supporting her, and one on the edge of the tank, Aaron closed his eyes and pressed his lips gently against Sarah's. It was electric.

They began kissing passionately and Aaron pulled her closer with his right hand and squeezed her against him. All of the pent up frustration that they had both been hiding inside them was pouring out over their kiss, flowing like a river from one to the other. All their cares about not being able to date each other were gone. Nothing mattered.

Their breathing became heavy as they kissed more. Aaron bit her bottom lip softly as she pulled it out of his mouth and took in a deep breath through her clenched teeth. It had been much too long since she had felt like this. She had not been on a date since she had moved to Jamaica. Nice Jewish boys were hard to find in Kingston, but this was a dream come true for her. Aaron was the cutest man she had ever met and was someone she could see herself with long into the future, if things went well. They had bonded so well the last month. She had been waiting for him to make a move, and he finally did. Thank God he did, she thought to herself, thank God.

Thank God I made a move, Aaron thought to himself, thank God. He had also not felt like this in a while. He had been on dates back in Boston, à là

Jason, but those were never the right types of women for him. Aaron wanted a strong, adventurous woman with a mind of her own. Sarah was that woman. She was everything he had ever dreamed of and those thoughts kept them kissing slowly and passionately for what seemed to be a long time.

After a while, they pulled their heads back from each other, looked in each other's eyes, and breathed. Sarah reminded Aaron of sexy pictures of swimsuit models that he and Jason used to drool over during their youth. Her long, dark hair was slicked back by the water and her lips were full and red, water dripping slowly down her face.

"God, you're beautiful," Aaron said softly, touching her face and staring at her.

Sarah smiled but did not say anything.

"What are we going to tell the others," Aaron asked.

"Nothing. We can't."

"What do you mean we can't?"

"What is it that you want to tell them?"

"That I'm dating the most gorgeous, amazing, spectacular, extraordinary, sensual, woman in the world."

"Who said we were dating," Sarah asked in a serious tone.

"But, I thought..." Aaron paused. "Then what was..." He could not finish his question.

"You have to ask me, Aaron! Girls like to be asked." Sarah smiled.

"Oh, I'm sorry," he said innocently. "I thought that was a little out of date. I thought it just happens."

"It does just happen, but, I guess I'm just a little old fashioned that way. Besides, I don't think women planned it so that asking for the woman would go out of style."

"What do you mean, 'women didn't plan it that way?' You make it sound as if all the women of the world are bound together in a sisterhood against men when it comes to love!"

"We are!" Sarah pushed him away playfully. "You haven't figured that out yet, and you're how old? I'm surprised at you! I thought you were smarter than that!"

"I am, just not about some things." He leaned forward to kiss her again and she put her index and middle finger up in front of his lips.

"Well?"

"Okay." He treaded water for a second, without his hands.

"What are you doing?" She was confused by his actions.

"Here," Aaron said, showing her his silver diving watch and resting his other hand on the side of the tank. "Since you're old fashioned, and guys used to give their girls a ring or a jacket and I have neither, I'll give you my watch," he said seriously.

Sarah laughed softly at him. "I'm not going to take your watch."

"Don't laugh," he said, pulling himself up against her. "Besides, I've got another one."

She stopped laughing and Aaron slipped his watch over her wrist and said, "Sarah." He paused and turned his attention from her wrist to her face. "Will you be my girl?"

"Ugh, you are so romantic!" She rolled her eyes with pleasure and slipped her arms around his head. "I'll wear it forever," Sarah said, just before she kissed him again.

*****

It was just after twelve-thirty when they arrived at the tavern. Sarah had taken him to many in the last few weeks, but this one he had never seen. The bar was along the left wall, stretching halfway to the back of the room. The tavern was packed and it was a struggle to get through the crowd. Aaron couldn't see past the dense traffic of people and had to hold onto Sarah's hand, as she dragged him through the rough of drunken people.

As they passed the bar, Aaron could make out a small, black dance floor surrounded by tall, black pizzeria booths. The whole area was on a higher level than the rest of the bar and they stepped up the two-stair staircase and sat down in one of the booths. They had been lucky to grab a bench, he thought. Glancing around he could see that all the benches were full of people and in some cases they were over capacity, seating eight people facing each other.

Their booth had been carved up in many places. Most of the carvings were normal, love inspired carvings, with a heart or a plus sign in between the names. Some read, "For a good time ring…" Not much different from bars or bathrooms in the good old U.S., Aaron thought.

Sarah had gone to the bar to get his Red Stripe® Beer. He had never been much of a beer person, but figured that if he was in Jamaica, he might as well try some Jamaican beer. Aaron was glad she went to the bar. He would have a hard time fighting the crowd, but she would not. A good-looking girl like that, the bartender would go right to her. He looked towards the bar but did not see her yet. She had disappeared into the crowd.

With Sarah not in sight, his attention turned towards the dance floor. It was not too heavily populated, but the people who were dancing were having a good time.

The people dancing moved with such grace to a song with such pounding rhythm, Aaron thought. Bam! Bam! Bam! His eardrums rocked with every bass sound.

He didn't think he could dance well to that music although no one had ever told him that he wasn't good at it. Aaron had been to a few parties where he had danced to this music but he usually got drunk beforehand so that if he wasn't doing a good job, people could attribute it to the alcohol. The truth was that he was a fine dancer, it was his dancing self-esteem that didn't allow him to agree.

Sarah sat back down next to Aaron and put his Red Stripe® Beer in front of him.

"Thanks. Where's yours," he asked loudly so his voice would cut through the loud music.

"I'm not drinking," she yelled back.

"Why not?" Aaron was talking right in her ear so he wouldn't have to scream.

"I'm driving and we left your bike at the lab so you can have as much as you want."

"Oh ,yeah." Aaron shook his head. "I just wasn't thinking, I guess."

"Do you do that a lot?"

"What? Not think?"

She nodded her head.

After thinking about it for a moment, Aaron replied, "Yeah, too often, I think."

"Or, you don't think."

"Very funny," he mouthed.

Aaron pulled her closer with his left hand and kissed her. She kissed back and the passion flowed. The music and lights slowed down and the world melted away for a few seconds.

"Thank you for the beer," he said, as they separated.

"Don't thank me, you paid for it."

"I know, but thanks for getting it," he yelled, implying that that is what he meant originally.

"Any time," she said happily, as he took a large swig. "Is it good?"

"Not really, but then, I really don't like beer," he said with a sour face.

"Then why did you get it," she laughed.

"I don't know. I know I don't like beer, but every time there's a new one to try, I figure it'll be different. And of course, it never is." He took another large gulp of the Red Stripe®, and Sarah laughed at him.

"You're so funny," Sarah said as she looked out onto the dance floor and started moving her body to the beat where she was sitting. She looked back at Aaron who was trying desperately to finish a drink he did not like.

"Do you want to?" She was still moving her body to the beat and motioning to the dance floor.

He knew that was coming and he tried to finish his beer quickly. As he pushed the small bottle up to try and get the last of the alcohol to kill some brain cells, he held up one finger, motioning for her to wait. Just after swallowing the last drop, she pulled him onto the dance floor.

As he stood up, the beer hit him hard. He lost his balance for a second but regained it just as quickly. The small dance floor was crowded now and there wasn't much room for people to move, much less to look at him dancing. His fragile dancing ego used this to its advantage and Aaron let go of his inhibitions and just moved.

The beat in the music gave him the instruction he needed to be able to move with it. His ears were focused on the music and his eyes were focused on his partner. She was right up against him moving with the music just like the others. He put his arm around her and pulled her even closer. Their heads came together and were barely moving in contrast to the rest of their bodies.

Sarah's hand was around Aaron's shoulder now as they began to move their lower bodies in unison. Aaron kissed her, but they never took their eyes off one another. His hands started to follow his eyes up and down the side of her body, caressing the short skirt and tank top she had put on after changing out of her bathing suit. The heat of the crowded bar and the dancing was catching up to them and sweat started to form on their skin. It would have started to drip down the little bit of cleavage that was showing from Sarah's tank top, but Aaron stopped it.

He had moved closer to her and was kissing her neck as they continued to dance. Sarah's hands were in the air, allowing him to do as he pleased. He moved slowly from one side of her neck to the other then moved down to the top of her chest. Sarah, with her eyes closed, slowly moved her hands down and carefully stopped him from going any further.

She pulled his head up and looked into his eyes. "Are you okay," she asked, concerned.

"Really tired," he replied, barely audible over the noise.

"I can see that. You look like you can barely keep your eyes open. Do you want to go home?" She seemed worried about his well-being.

"I guess that beer hit me pretty hard," he said slowly. "I'm sorry, this doesn't usually happen to me."

"That's okay, let's get you home." She took his hand and led him out of the bar, towards her car. "Would you mind sleeping over at my place?"

Aaron smiled as he got into the passenger seat. He plopped himself down with the little energy he had left and turned his head towards her with his eyes half shut. "Only if you promise to take advantage of me," he said, with a faint laugh.

"I'm worried about you," she said seriously, as she started the car and began driving, keeping a close eye on her passenger.

"Oh, don't worry about me. I'll be better in the morning." As Aaron finished speaking, his eyes shut completely.

A few minutes later, they arrived at Sarah's apartment. It was not far from where they had been but Aaron was already sleeping.

"Come on." She opened the passenger door and pulled Aaron from the seat. "You still alive?"

"Just barely," he mumbled.

"What?" Sarah had not understood him in his drunken stupor.

"Nothing," he mumbled again. Aaron didn't feel like explaining to her how he felt, he was too tired to talk.

They got up the stairs slowly and at her door, she let Aaron stand on his own. He didn't fall, but she wasn't sure that he wouldn't. After she unlocked her door, she pushed it open and helped Aaron through. Sarah flipped on the entrance light and looked at her apartment. Everything was clean and ready for visitors.

She pulled him over to her couch and helped Aaron lay down. Sarah took off his shoes and placed them on the ground next to him. There was a blue throw blanket on the top of her old couch and she covered Aaron with it. Aaron instinctively grabbed the blanket and wrapped himself in it, turning on his side.

"Good night," Aaron said, almost unconsciously.

"Good night," Sarah responded. She was sitting on the couch, against his stomach and running her fingers through his hair. He seemed so peaceful, and cute. She didn't want to make a lot of noise and wake him up, although she knew he was asleep for the night. She kissed his forehead and began to get up from the couch when she clearly heard him speak.

"I love you," he said unconsciously, but out loud.

Sarah sat back down and tears welled in her eyes and began to roll slowly down her face. She was already in turmoil about their relationship and this didn't help. She loved him but was it worth it, she asked herself? There was so much more to her that he didn't know and probably never would. Sometimes she hated her life and wished that she could have another one, but it wasn't going to happen.

Tomorrow I'll tell Aaron that tonight was a mistake, she thought. I'll tell him we just can't date because it's against the lab rules and I'll return his watch. She was going to lie right to his face and deny the strong feelings she had for him. She felt it was the only way.

Just then, the phone rang. Sarah wiped the tears from her eyes and forced her feelings away. She walked over to the other side of the living room and picked up her cordless receiver.

"Yes? Yes," she said again, looking at Aaron. "I'm sorry, I can't," Sarah yelled, after listening to her caller. "No!" She was very upset, and was being very loud. She saw Aaron turn over, walked into her bedroom, and shut the door.

Aaron heard a bit of the conversation, but it didn't wake him up. He knew she was angry but didn't have the ability to open his eyes or respond to her distress. He slept until the morning.

CHAPTER 9

Aaron awoke slowly, his head pounding and his eyes stinging. He could feel the blood rushing through his head with every beat of his heart. He put his hand against his head while he was still lying on the couch, but to no avail. It didn't stop his pain. Sitting up, the pain got worse.

His clothes smelled of cigarette smoke and the stench made his headache worse. Aaron slowly opened his eyes and looked around, slowly remembering what happened the night before.

He never had a hangover before, but this must be a dandy, he thought. He used to think that all of his friends who didn't go to class because of a hangover were wimps, but now he understood their pain. Thinking back to it though, it didn't make any sense.

I only had one beer, he thought. How could I have a hangover with just one beer?

Looking around Sarah's living room, Aaron saw that the shades where shut, blocking out most of the outside light, which saved him from more of a headache. He had been sleeping on Sarah's couch and she had covered him with a blanket. There was a small coffee table in front of him and his shoes were under it. The windows facing the parking lot made up the wall to his right. In front of him was Sarah's small television placed in the middle shelf of a nice metal bookcase. The rest of the bookcase was filled with books, pictures and trinkets she must have collected throughout her travels. There was one lamp in the living room, a floor lamp standing next to the bookcase.

Next to the couch was a small nightstand with a telephone and some magazines on it. The only other rooms he could see from his vantage point were the dining room and kitchen, which weren't separated from the room he was in now. To the left of the couch was a short kitchen table that looked to Aaron like it would seat two, maybe three people. It seemed as if she could have purchased it at Goodwill, if they had those kinds of stores in Jamaica.

The top of the table was white with light green spots all over it, part of the original decoration. It also had one, big burn spot in the middle. The side of the table was wrapped in metal, which was starting to come unglued from one of the sides, and it created a dangerous sharp edge.

The kitchen was more like a space, than a room. All of the cabinets and utilities were lined up against the back wall of the apartment, linoleum stretching only a foot past the cabinets. There was not a lot of cabinet space or counter space either. The stove was in the corner and the small fridge was to the left of that. It wasn't much of a kitchen, but it was a large step above what he had for the summer, Aaron thought. At least Sarah's bedroom was separate from the rest of the apartment.

His head started pounding again and Aaron cringed. After cradling his head gently in his hands for a few minutes, he opened his eyes and looked down at the messy coffee table. There was a piece of paper on it with some writing but he hadn't noticed it before because there was so much other crap on the table.

"Aaron," it read. "I'm sorry for what happened last night. I think the bartender must have slipped something into your drink, thinking that I was going to drink it and he could take advantage of me. I called the doctor while you were asleep and I told him your symptoms. He said not to worry, and that you would be fine. If you wake up with a headache, he said to take some painkillers and drink lots of water. I had to run some errands, sorry to leave you alone. Please make yourself at home. The painkillers are in my bathroom, through my bedroom. Watch some TV and relax. I should be back around two. I need to talk to you. See you then. Hope you feel okay. Sarah."

Wow, Aaron thought, I've been drugged. So that explains my hangover.

He got up slowly for fear of the pounding increasing in intensity. Aaron walked slowly to Sarah's bathroom and found the pill bottle behind the mirror. He looked around curiously for prescription medicine but didn't see any.

What are you doing, he thought to himself as he shut the mirror, opened the pill bottle and took out two of the little white pills. Slowly, he moved back into the other room with the pills in his hand, found a glass, filled it with water and downed the pills.

Aaron sat back down on the couch and started to smile through his pain, remembering what had happened the night before. He was very pleased with the outcome, except for his headache.

He looked over at the clock hanging above the television. It was one in the afternoon already. He had one hour, if she came back in time, to make her some lunch. That would be a nice gesture, Aaron thought. She would love it.

Aaron looked around for his wallet but could not find it even in the couch pillows. He was going to get some food at the local market but without his wallet he would just have to see what was in the apartment already. It was odd, he thought, that his wallet was gone. Even with the drugs he knew that he had had it in his pocket the night before.

After about fifteen minutes, the pounding in his head started to recede and he started to prepare lunch. Looking through her cabinets, Aaron found a large wooden bowl that he thought would suffice for a large salad and when he opened the fridge, he found a multitude of vegetables.

Wow, she must really like salad, Aaron thought. She has it whenever we've gone out and she has it in her apartment.

He took out anything he could find that normally went in a salad and put it on the table and counters, wherever he could find space.

Halfway through his masterpiece of a salad, Aaron was feeling much better and turned on the TV for some background noise. The World News Network was on.

Aaron was getting to know and like Sarah even when she wasn't around. He watched this news station all the time back home.

With the background noise of the television, he continued making lunch. He found some interesting things around the kitchen and threw them in the salad including mint leaves, peanuts and sesame seeds. When he finished, he started on the dressing. Aaron found some balsamic vinegar and olive oil and mixed them together. As he did, the news switched to another story that caught his attention.

"Another strange disappearance has taken place off the eastern coast of Jamaica, and authorities still have no answer to the cause of these mysterious disappearances. WNN news correspondent Dave White joins us now from Jamaica. Dave, what's going on out there?"

This got Aaron's attention, and he sat down, leaving his culinary delight unattended. He had heard about this a few times before but hadn't kept up with the story. Aaron thought that they must have figured out what was going on by now, but apparently no one had.

The picture cut to a man with a suit and a microphone standing on the shore. Boats were visible in the distance behind him and he began to speak while glancing periodically at papers in his hand.

"Well, Tom, this mystery started in the early spring with the disappearance of a U.S. Coast Guard ship named the Tomahawk. That ship and its crew disappeared without a trace a few miles offshore somewhere behind me," he said as he pointed to the open sea.

"Since that time, two other Coast Guard ships have disappeared in similar fashion along with five fishing boats from the island of Jamaica. And now, just a few days ago, a plane, believed to be owned by the U.S. Government, has crashed in these same mysterious waters."

Before Dave could continue reporting, the anchorman interrupted him. "Dave, has there been any word about who was on board this plane?"

"No. There has been no word yet about who was on board. The press have been briefed a couple of times by the CIA agent in charge of the investigation, Tag Millwood, but that kind of information has not been announced."

The picture cut briefly to a man in a press conference Aaron recognized. "Tag Millwood," the bottom of the screen read while he confirmed what Dave White had said.

The TV cut back to the reporter and he continued. "In fact, the only information we still have is this." Dave paused and looked down at his sheets of paper and continued. "A U.S. Government owned Learjet was last heard from, heading north off the eastern coast of Jamaica on Monday morning, then vanished from radar," he said, then looked back at the camera and continued.

"As I said before, there is still no mention of who was on board. They have also not told us from where the plane had taken off and where it was heading."

"Dave, given the previous circumstances with this area, are they giving you any idea on the chances of finding survivors," the anchorman interrupted.

"Well, every hour that goes by without any word from the rescue teams makes the situation look dimmer and dimmer. I've talked with some of the rescue workers and they don't even want to be out in the water given the circumstances. So the word for right now is, it doesn't look good as far as survivors and as far as finding the plane, who knows? One thing's for sure, everyone here, and people around the world are starting to think, 'Bermuda Triangle.' This is Dave White in Morant Point, Jamaica for WNN News."

The picture turned back to Tom, in the studio and he continued commenting on the story but Aaron stopped listening. He had turned himself off to the outside world and thought about how close he was to what was going on. When you see it on the news, it seems so far away, he thought. In reality, he was very close. As Aaron continued to think about the disappearing boats and how close he was to the whole situation, the door to the apartment started to open. It was Sarah.

She was wearing gray sweatpants and a sweatshirt and her hair was pulled back with a scrunchie. She looked tired and needed a bath. Her hair was greasy and it looked as though she had been sweating. Sarah did not see Aaron as she entered. Her concentration was set on keeping the door open while taking the key out of the lock and holding a brown grocery bag with her other hand.

"Hey," Aaron said, from the couch.

"Oh my God!" Sarah looked quickly, looking in Aaron's direction. She let go of the bag and it fell to the floor, spilling some of the contents. Her free hand was now covering her chest.

"You scared the shit out of me," she said, finding her breath again.

Aaron laughed. "I'm sorry." He got up to help her with the bag and as he neared her, he went for her lips instead. Aaron pushed her back up against the closed door and began kissing her, but she pushed him away.

"What," he asked, with his hands still cradling her face.

"You're up already? Are you okay?" She seemed concerned but also surprised that he was already awake.

"Yeah, I'm fine. Nothing a little painkillers and water won't help. Where were you? You look…" He could not find a good adjective to describe her without telling her she looked like shit.

"Like shit?" She had finished his thought for him.

"Well, those weren't the words I would have used, but yeah."

"What time did you finally wake up?" Sarah was avoiding the question of where she had been.

"About an hour ago," he said while picking up cans of vegetables from the floor.

"The reason I look like shit, young man, is because I stayed up all night watching and worrying about your sorry ass. I was scared, but it looks like you pulled through nicely," Sarah said as she sat down on the couch.

Aaron took the grocery bag from her as well and placed it on the counter top in the kitchen area. As he unloaded the rest of the contents onto the countertop, Aaron asked a question without turning to look at her. Sarah, taking her chance, slipped his wallet underneath one of the couch pillows.

"Who were you talking to on the phone when we first got back last night?"

"What?" The question flustered Sarah because she didn't know that he had heard the call.

"Did you call a doctor for me? You did," Aaron said, with a smile on his face. "You were worried about me, how cute."

He moved over to the couch, sat down next to his caregiver and kissed her softly on the lips. Sarah returned the affection but with restraint. She liked him so much and wanted to be with him, but she didn't think it would work. How could it, she thought?

This feeling was hurting her and she didn't know how to make it go away. Would she feel better if she just told him that the night before had been a mistake, she asked herself? Maybe if I act like a bitch towards him, he would hate me and there wouldn't be a problem. But, I like being around Aaron so much; I don't want to give that up, she thought. Maybe there is some way to make him realize that they couldn't be together intimately but only as good friends? This question was digging a hole in her stomach as they were still kissing.

Please, give me a sign. What should I do, she asked God silently. Just then, Aaron stopped kissing her. He noticed a lone tear falling slowly down her left cheek.

"A tear of joy, I hope," he said, wiping it off her face.

She started to open her mouth to speak but he covered it with his finger. "You know what I like about you?" She did not answer, but Aaron didn't give her a chance to before he continued.

"I like the fact that you don't give a shit if you're dirty or not, you'll still let me kiss you." He paused for a moment to look in her eyes. She stared back with no expression. "And it's not just that, you're not superficial. You're you, plain and simple. You don't hide behind a mask waiting for people to take it off. You put yourself on the line wherever you are and no matter who you're with. I love that about you."

Aaron had stopped Sarah's outward emotion, and they were still staring at each other when he stood up. "I have a surprise for you."

Aaron walked over towards the kitchen table and picked up the salad bowl with his creation inside. "I made you lunch," Aaron said, positioning the bowl so she could see its ingredients.

"Are you hungry?" He was hoping she was.

Her body, heart and mind were going crazy. Aaron was so sweet, she thought. She looked at him and saw him as he was. His loving kindness for her was apparent. She could not deny the love she had been waiting for, for so long. Her situation didn't matter to her anymore. She was going to give herself to this man, for better or worse. Whatever happens, she thought, I'm going to be with him, at least for now.

"Yes," Sarah said in a sexy voice, rising from the couch. "I am hungry!" She had a determined look on her face.

She marched over to Aaron and tackled him. The salad spilled all around the table and onto the floor, but they didn't seem to care. They were preoccupied with making love on the floor.

CHAPTER 10

It had been over a week since Sarah decided to not give in to her fears of what would happen if they started dating and so far it had worked out for both of them. They were having the time of their lives.

Sarah and Aaron did almost everything together. Their love was growing stronger by the day, but their days together were growing short. There were only a few weeks left until he had to return to Boston with his data. Aaron wanted desperately to extend his trip, but he needed to return before school started and before his grant money ran out.

They had not spoken about it much; they didn't want to think about it. Aaron and Sarah had agreed to keep in touch, but it would be hard for them, after all this time, to be apart. Sometimes, Aaron would run through ideas on how he could visit Sarah during the school year, or even the next summer.

He thought that he might be able to get another grant if his paper got published. Or, maybe, he though, when he graduated that the lab would give him a job. Aaron was also going to ask the administration if he could take classes at the University of the West Indies and do research at the same time, but he knew this would never work. The credits would never transfer.

One thing was for sure, he loved Sarah. He loved Sarah more than anyone he had ever been with, and he was sure she felt the same way about him.

She had been to the lab earlier that day and he had joined her in the tank. They fed the dolphins and played with them while Mike and Maria were inside the lab working on formatting Aaron's tapes. He wondered if they knew. Sarah and Aaron had decided not to tell anyone, for fear of Aaron being dismissed from the project. They also did not want to ruin Aaron's chances of working at the lab in the future.

After Aaron and Sarah fed the dolphins and entertained themselves in the tank, the dolphins were set free and the tank was drained for cleaning. They did this once a week and Aaron loved it because he got to swim with the dolphins before the draining began.

Over the past few drainings, Skilos had started to play more with Aaron and Aaron began to learn more about Skilos. All of the researchers agreed that Sarah was the only human Skilos liked more. Skilos had also started contributing immensely to the research but Aaron had completed the testing phase the day before. He was now working on condensing the videotapes so it would be easier to watch them and extract the pertinent information.

Aaron was sad to see the dolphins go when they were let out each week, especially Skilos. They had forged a friendship with each other over the past week that was usual between a dolphin and a human working together, but unusual for Skilos.

Everyone told him that Skilos always came back but he never was sure until Skilos actually returned every week. Why would captive dolphins, if given the chance to return to the wild, ever come back?

Bob and Mike said it was because Skilos was lazy. "Why should they hunt for food when they can get it at the lab easily? Plus the fact that, in the tank, they didn't have to watch out for predators."

As they drained the water from the tank, Aaron stood at the outer gate that led into the bay. He opened it and let the dolphins out. Skilos stayed in the tank as long as he could, talking to Aaron and Sarah. Finally, before most of the water had drained, he was forced out for fear that he might get caught in the tank with less than enough water left to get him out safely.

As Skilos went out into the ocean, he swam backwards with most of his body out of the water. It seemed as if he was waving goodbye, and it reminded Aaron of the TV show, *Flipper*. Aaron had always watched that show as a kid. He had been fascinated by the dolphins and thought how lucky the actors were to get to work with those beautiful and intelligent animals. This research had been his first chance to work with them closely and it was everything he hoped it would be.

Aaron was upset that they didn't have any dolphins he could work with back at Harvard, but maybe that could work to his benefit, he thought. If he could convince his professors that dolphin research is what he wanted to do then maybe they would let him return and complete his doctoral thesis in Jamaica. This, he thought, would kill two birds with one stone. He could be with Sarah, and do the research he loved at the same time.

After Skilos had left his eyesight, Aaron went back into the lab to start reviewing his tapes in order to delete any unnecessary footage. Aaron thought the editing was going to take forever, but as he started, he realized that there was a lot of empty footage that could be cut. And, although the dolphins had not paid as much attention to the touch-screen as he would have liked, there was enough activity from them for the testing phase to have been successful.

*****

Skilos swam to his usual feeding ground with the rest of the dolphins, south of Kingston Bay. There the water was deep and they had always found many tuna to hunt and feast on. They enjoyed their time away from the research lab. Hunting for food was much more exciting than being fed. They would have left a long time ago but they enjoyed, too much, the bond they had formed with the people at the lab.

They swam around their usual stomping ground for a few minutes until they realized that there were no tuna to be had that evening. Conferring in squeaks and squeals, they decided to head east to a hunting ground they had visited over a year before. It was farther away but they were hungry. They played games along the way to pass the time and arrived a few hours later, exploding out of the water with joy.

There was enough tuna at this old spot to feed them for weeks. The fish were practically jumping out of the water with them.

After eating his fill, Skilos dove down and realized how shallow this area was. He hadn't noticed before. He was also wondering why there had been so many fish here this time. There had always been tuna here before but never as many as there was this evening, he thought.

Stopping at the bottom, he got his answer. Coral reef spread out over a wide area underneath him. Coral meant small animals, small animals meant bigger animals and bigger animals meant sharks so he'd better watch out, he continued his train of thought.

Gliding over the reef playfully, he knew there must be another reason for the teeming life. There was so much activity going on, especially with the scavengers crawling along the bottom.

As the coral reef ended, he saw it. There was a vast area covered by a net that was holding down bloated human body parts that were being devoured by scavengers and sharks. Skilos watched the sharks carefully but they took no notice of him. They were too busy fighting with themselves and the other scavengers for an easy meal.

As he watched, the sea around him started to vibrate. Every living thing he could see started to swim or scuttle past him. At first he thought it was an underwater earthquake. He had felt small ones many times but this was different.

In the distance he saw a bright white light coming from the sea floor and in the light he saw men with machines helping them swim, move in his direction. He swam towards them but as he got close a metal spear whizzed past his body.

He turned quickly to leave. The danger was too great and he didn't want to end up as scavenger food. Skilos knew what was going on was not right in some way and he knew that these men were responsible for the dead bodies. Must tell the people, he thought.

*****

He awoke to darkness in the lab and sat up quickly to look around. I must have been asleep for a few hours, Aaron thought to himself, wiping dribble off the side of his mouth. He looked at his digital diving watch that he had started wearing after he gave his silver analogue to Sarah and saw that it had been longer than he thought. It was two in the morning.

His face was red where he had been resting it on his arm and his hair on that side of his head was disheveled. Aaron rubbed his face to wake himself up, yawned, and stared at the TV screen in front of him for a few seconds.

Aaron tried to remember where he had been in the editing process when he had fallen asleep, but nothing was coming to him at the moment. He decided to get up and stretch, hoping that would jar his memory a bit.

Looking out of the lab windows, he could see the stars, a rare sight. The tank had not been filled yet and it was like looking out of a basement window.

Placing his hands behind his lower back, he walked back to the editing console and looked at the picture on the screen. It was frozen on an image of Skilos in front of the touch-screen.

He stared at the image for a few seconds more and then turned his head in interest, as if he was looking at something very unusual and was trying to figure out what it was. His eyes squinted at the picture as he took his hands from behind his back and sat down in the metal folding chair.

The frozen posture of Skilos looked oddly familiar to him. It reminded him of something Skilos had done earlier that day, before being let out into the ocean.

Aaron hit the play button on the console and the image instantly came to life, along with the sounds that had been recorded by the hydrophones. He saw Skilos slowly back away from the window with quick, jerky movements that almost looked like a bull bucking a cowboy off its back. These movements were accompanied with repetitious sounds.

Remembering what he had already seen on the tapes, Aaron knew this had happened before and rewound the tapes to look for another instance. He rewound the tape until he saw Skilos come up to the screen again. Aaron stopped the tape and played it but Skilos was not doing anything special. He was just watching silently as the screen in front of him was running the test.

He watched Skilos silently observing the screen when, all of the sudden, the image in the bottom left corner of Aaron's screen changed to the next trial. Immediately Skilos started to make the sounds he had made before, but this time he was not moving. Aaron was excited for a moment, but when he realized Skilos was not going to move backward, he felt let down.

Just as he was about to fast forward to where he was before, he saw the other three dolphins race toward the screen that Skilos was watching. Aaron's heart started to race.

Could this be what I think it is, he asked himself? Skilos had made that familiar sound and the other dolphins came racing towards the screen, he thought excitedly. Had Skilos been excited about what he had seen, and beckoned the other dolphins to join him? Had Skilos been asking me to join him in the tank when the movements were incorporated with the sounds, he asked silently?

Aaron knew that if Skilos had been communicating with him and the other dolphins that potentially, it could be an amazing discovery. This, he thought ecstatically, could be the beginning of the unraveling of dolphin communication.

Of course, what Aaron had seen didn't prove anything. It was just an observation. In order to prove it, he would have to set up a whole test involving the recorded sounds and see how the dolphins reacted to them. Even then, if he did find that Skilos was saying, "come here," it would only be one phrase in a whole language. It would be similar to knowing what the word aloha meant, but not knowing anything else about the Hawaiian language. But, it would be an amazing start, more than anyone else had ever found.

He was excited just sitting there, going over the possibilities of notoriety and all of the grants that would be thrown at him. But would Skilos come back, he thought. They said he would, but he didn't trust their judgment.

Aaron heard a noise from up above the lab and it startled him. He looked quickly towards the door but no one was coming down the stairs. The noise, whatever it was, was still up above. He slowly moved toward the lab door, opened it and looked up the stairway. The light was still on and he could clearly see that there was nothing and no one there.

He was walking up the stairs and stopped when he heard the noise again, this time louder than before. It sounded like someone was rummaging through the metal garbage cans on the backside of the lab. Who would be around at two in the morning going through the trash, he asked himself?

Aaron continued slowly up the stairs, his back sliding along the wall. He erroneously thought that this might lower the chances of being seen if someone were to burst into the stairwell. He knew, from his army training, that it would be better to have stayed in the lab, on his own turf, and have someone enter where he could ambush them but he wasn't thinking.

As he got to the top of the stairway, Aaron turned the knob and pushed the door open slowly with his right eye pressed up against the small crack to see if anyone was in the parking lot.

The light that dribbled in from the outside revealed an empty lot, except for his bike. The flood light from the side of the building lit the parking lot well, and all Aaron saw was gravel. At this sight he gathered more courage and slowly opened the door.

When the door was open just enough for him to slip through, he did. Aaron kept it open just in case he needed to dart back into the stairway.

He slid along the wall as if he were walking on a ledge of a tall building. Half way to the corner he heard the noise again and froze where he was standing. Someone was definitely going through the trash, but why, he asked himself again? His curiosity pushed him onward.

Aaron turned, as close as he could to the wall, and put his stomach up against it. He slid closer to the edge, going slower and slower as he neared it. He slowly slid his face over the side of the building and what he saw astonished him.

Nothing. There was nothing there except for the trashcans. The lids were off but there was no one there and this disturbed him even more because he was expecting to see someone.

Had there been someone there a second ago, he thought? Maybe, whoever it was, had heard him coming and was now coming around the other side of the lab to scare him.

As these thoughts ran through his head, a cat jumped out of the can. He screamed and jumped back, startled by the sudden movement.

"Stupid cat," he screamed in the cat's direction, as it ran out of the parking lot. He grunted, ashamed that a cat had scared him. "You scared the shit out of me," he screamed again in the cat's direction, which had already disappeared in the brush surrounding the parking lot.

As Aaron turned back towards the lab he heard a car coming down the driveway and quickly ducked into the bushes near the trashcans. He had no reason for this behavior, except that his nervous system was still in the fight/flight mode.

When the car came into view and into the gravel lot, Aaron realized that it was just Sarah's Jeep. He was about to emerge from his hiding place when he thought better of it. Wasn't it a little strange, he thought, that she would disappear for days and sometimes return to the lab when she thought everyone was gone for the day? She had also come another time before when he was working late and told him that she had forgotten something at the lab. Had she been lying, he asked himself? Was she spying on her own lab partners, he thought, ballooning his own irrational suspicions.

He watched as she stepped out of her Jeep and around it towards the lab. Aaron saw her look at Aaron's bike and then at the half opened lab door. After pondering, she walked over to the stairwell door and then out of Aaron's sight, around the wall.

"Aaron," Sarah called loudly, knowing he must be around but not knowing exactly where. She entered the stairway and called his name again. Aaron could still hear her from the bushes on the other side of the building but he did not answer.

He heard her call his name again, this time from deeper in the stairwell. He figured she was almost in the lab and decided to follow her. Slowly, he emerged from the bushes and softly treaded to the stairwell door when he heard his name again. He still did not answer. Aaron wanted to see what she was doing without him in the lab.

Faint sounds were coming from the lab. It sounded as if she was looking through some drawers in the filing cabinet.

She must have figured I'm not around and this is her chance to do some digging, Aaron concluded.

Sarah left the doors open and Aaron crept in from the outside and descended the stairs slowly. As he went, he heard more papers being shuffled and then silence.

She must be looking at my work on the editing board, he thought. She must be checking up on my research.

He did not want anyone to find out what he thought he had discovered. He knew that they would want to take part in the communication research but he didn't want anyone to find out yet. Aaron wanted to do the preliminary work himself and surprise everyone with his findings. But, if Sarah found out, he knew she would make him spill the beans to the rest of the team, and maybe to someone else. His suspicions grew every second as he went through the implausible conspiracy theories that Sarah might be a part of.

Aaron moved slowly and quietly towards the lab door. He poked his head through to get a look at exactly what she was doing, and he was right. She was sitting in the folding chair, staring at the frozen screen. He knew it wouldn't take her long to start meddling with the video so he moved in.

Aaron slowly moved into the doorway of the lab, leaning himself against the doorpost, with his arms folded. He watched her for a few seconds; she had not noticed his entry.

Sarah became more curious with what was on the screen and she reached for the play button on the console when Aaron cleared his throat. Sarah, startled, stood up quickly, pulled a concealed pistol from inside her windbreaker and pointed it at Aaron. Aaron, even more startled than Sarah, ducked, ran halfway up the stairs and yelled.

"Shit! It's me, Sarah. It's Aaron!"

"Aaron," she asked angrily.

He slowly came back down the stairs with his hands over his head. As he reached the lab she was still holding the gun, but it was pointed at the ground, not at him. Either way, this still made him uncomfortable.

"You scared the shit out of me," she said, returning the gun to its holster.

"Me? *You* scared the shit out of *me*! What the hell are you doing with a gun anyway?" He pointed incriminatingly at her weapon.

"A girl needs to protect herself doesn't she?"

"From what?" Aaron was still visibly upset.

"Well, for situations like this, I suppose."

"I wasn't going to kill you!"

"What if you were some crazy homeless guy, or murderer, or something?"

"Man!" Aaron was still in shock. "I knew you were a strong person, but I never thought you would pull a gun on me!"

Still flustered, Aaron sat down on the floor near the door. He put his head in his hands and took a deep breath. That was the first time in years that he had had a gun pointed in his direction and he didn't like the feelings it brought back from his army service.

Sarah saw that he was upset, walked over to where he was crouched on the floor, and took his head in her arms.

"I'm sorry I scared you. I didn't mean to," she reassured him.

Aaron lifted his head, looked at her and stood up. He walked over to the center of the lab, leaving Sarah kneeling on the ground. When he got far enough away from her that he felt comfortable again, he turned to face her and started questioning.

"What the hell are you doing here anyway," he asked, trying to implicate her of some wrongdoing. He had been suspicious before, but after the gun incident he knew she was up to no good.

"What? I'm not allowed to be here," she responded innocently.

"You always come when you think no one else is around! Why is that?"

"What?" She didn't know what he was getting at.

"You know what I mean! You always come around pretty late, probably when you think no one else is going to be here so you can... I don't know... Spy on us or something."

"What are you talking about, Aaron?"

"And all those times you just disappeared for days? Where the hell did you go? To your "headquarters?" Aaron was pacing around the room, not listening to her short rebuttals because that's all he would let her get in.

"Aaron, I have another job taking photographs for journalists and other companies!" She was trying to defend herself but to no avail.

"Oh, and my wallet too! I bet it wasn't the bar tender who poisoned that drink!" Aaron was now standing stationary on the opposite side of the lab, staring and pointing at Sarah. "You probably did it so you could take my wallet somewhere and... I don't know... Have it analyzed or something!"

"Aaron listen to yourself! You're being idiotic!"

"Right, it just happened to be in the couch where I looked before you came home and it mysteriously appeared there after you got back?"

"Oh, come on!" Sarah was starting to get defensive and angry. "I'm sure you've overlooked things all the time and then found them in the same place later on."

"And, that one time you came and we swam with the dolphins, you probably didn't think anyone was going to be here." As he was talking, Aaron started to pace again, this time closer to her as if he was an inspector presenting the facts of the crime to the suspect, trying to pull out a confession. "Then that time that I was working really late, and you just showed up for no reason. Now tonight? I heard you going through the files and I saw you looking at my research! "

Sarah was still kneeling on the ground where Aaron had been crouched against the wall. She was getting more upset by the moment and it showed on her face. She got up now and started to defend herself.

"Sometimes I actually have things I need to do. Like tonight for example, I have to fill the tank in time to let the dolphins back in tomorrow, if they choose to return. And, has it ever occurred to you that maybe, just maybe, sometimes I come here looking for you? To be with you because I like you and I like spending time with you? Aaron, I know how hard you work, and I figure that you will be here late. Most of the time I even call your room to see if you're there before I ride all the way out here."

As she continued, Sarah moved closer to Aaron. She was trying to make him understand the absurdity of his questioning but this did not work for Aaron. The closer she got, the more uncomfortable he was around her. He felt like she was trying to play things down and pull the wool over his eyes and he wasn't going to let her.

"Maybe you like spending time with me for other reasons! Maybe you don't love me like you'd like me to believe, but it makes it convenient for you to spy on me and my research. You probably despise me! Every time we kiss? God, I hope your boss is paying you well to love me!" He ended slowly, their faces inches apart.

Without an instant passing Sarah reached out and slapped Aaron hard across the face. He was stunned and didn't move or say another word. He just stared at her in disbelief. Aaron never saw it coming.

"How dare you question my love for you! You son of a bitch," she uttered through clenched teeth. She was fuming!

Sarah spun and walked briskly out of the lab. She slammed the lab door hard as she left, without looking back.

Aaron was staring at the space where she had stood. He sat down still staring, still shocked when the ringing started in his left ear. He felt the side of his face and it stung badly.

"Damn," he said to himself. "What the hell did I do?"

CHAPTER 11

"What do you mean, he's gone," the voice asked calmly over the receiver.

"Just what I said, sir. He's been missing since he went out alone yesterday." Agent Schwabb answered, relieved that his superior didn't sound too upset.

"I see. And, why did you let him go out alone?"

"He is my boss, sir, you know him. Even if I told him not to, he'd do it anyway."

"Alright. Let me think for a second."

Agent Schwabb held on the line while the director of the CIA thought out the situation. He was a cool headed man, unlike Tag, and thank God for that, thought Schwabb. If Tag were dealing with this sort of situation, there would have been hell to pay.

"How many people know that he's missing?"

"No one yet, sir."

"Good. Keep it that way until tonight. Call a meeting of the rest of your staff and tell them. Make sure they know this is strictly confidential. I don't want any media people getting a hold of this information. Do you understand me?"

"Yes, sir."

"Tomorrow, call a press conference and tell all of the reporters that you will be relaying information to them from now on. Tell them that Tag had to go see about another project, of which the details are classified. Then you get every available agent you have and look for him."

"Sir. We're looking already," Schwabb interjected.

"I'm not talking about in the water," he said, knowing what Schwabb meant. "I'm talking about in Jamaica, Miami, the Bahamas and in Colombia."

"Sir?"

"I wouldn't be surprised if you find him alive and well in one of those places."

"I'm sorry, sir. Maybe you weren't following. Tag got on a boat and disappeared somewhere out where the plane was lost." Schwabb was trying to clarify his earlier statement.

"I'm well aware of that." The director paused for a moment before relaying the critical information. "Schwabb, we've been suspicious of Millwood for a while now. He's made it clear, at least to me, that he doesn't like us all

126

that much and I think he might be on the take. He probably, given the circumstances of the last few weeks, is involved in all of these disappearances somehow."

"Are you sure, sir?" Schwabb was confused. He had never heard about this before.

"No, not sure, just suspicious. That means, if one of your agents finds him, give them specific instructions to stay out of sight. I don't want him captured yet; we have nothing on him. Make sure he's followed and whatever information you get, relay it back to me."

"Should I send some agents to his house in Miami, sir?"

"No, I'll take care of that myself. Are we clear on all this?"

"Crystal, sir," Schwabb answered, now clear about what was happening and what he had to do.

"Good."

*****

The plane crash, like all of the mysterious disappearances in the past few months had only been two miles from the underwater research center. The authorities were worried that something would happen to the rig so they had evacuated it.

After everyone had been removed from the rig, Tag had arrived and was now on the rig alone, enjoying his privacy and his drink. He thought about how his old colleagues might soon find the structural drawings of the Poseidon Project he had placed in his apartment in Miami. When they did find them Tag knew it wouldn't be long until they pinpointed the complex's location.

I have to be gone by then, he thought to himself as he stared out the window of the control room, sipping his tequila. By then I should have my payment from Lopez and I will disappear forever. And when they catch Lopez I won't have to worry about him trying to dispose of me. They might not even capture Lopez, Tag thought. Maybe he would die trying to defend his creation. After taking another large shot of tequila Tag agreed with himself that Lopez's death would work out even better for him.

Whatever is going to happen, Tag thought, I'm not worried. Things are going to work out just as I plan, they always do.

He leaned back on the metallic chair and focused again on the crash site. There were boats as far as he could see, searching the sea floor. He laughed softly to himself, knowing full well that they would not find anything.

Tag threw back his tenth shot of tequila which he had started only a half-hour before and placed his glass on the console in front of him. The bottle was only half-empty and he decided to take it with him. He knew Lopez would have none in the complex.

As he descended in the elevator to the underwater lab, Tag couldn't help but think about the whole structure. It was too bad we had to kill the architect, he thought. That guy was a genius. He had figured out how to keep the water pressure at bay, but that wasn't the most amazing thing of all.

Lopez had gotten exactly what he had asked for, a great disguise for an airshaft. The whole research center he was in was just a clever way to hide the air vents that kept the Poseidon Project running.

The air vents ran from a storage room in the complex, through a two-mile long, underground tunnel and then into the research center. From the bottom of the research center, then vents ran up, through the elevator shaft and up to the top of the research rig where it captured the fresh air that it needed. And, in between the more than two miles of vents, were the air locks that kept the Poseidon complex pressurized.

It's amazing, Tag thought, that Lopez spent all this money, not just for the complex, but for the laboratory rig, just to cover an airshaft. But Tag had failed to calculate the amount of profit that had been made because of Lopez's investment. In the few months that it had been in operation, The Poseidon Project had already made Lopez an extra five hundred million dollars.

Tag stepped out of the elevator, and into the empty lab. It was as he remembered it, round and dark but it was a little colder because of its vacancy.

The lights were off and he could only see by the lights on the consoles. They lined the windows that went almost all the way around like a cockpit and it made him feel as if he were in a flying saucer.

The airlock to the escape pod was to his right and he pushed the emergency door open with his free hand. Tag stepped in, closed the door behind him, opened the door to the sub and stepped in. The airlock to the tunnel was below him, and after closing the sub door, he opened it, sat down inside and closed the top. Tag placed his bottle of tequila next to him and tugged on the wheel to unlock the bottom of the airlock. With some force, it budged and then started to turn easily. When it unlocked, he pulled it up to reveal the ladder leading into the tunnel. Tag sat back and sighed. He had forgotten about the ladder and now thought that he would not be able to bring his bottle with him.

Tag looked at his bottle and back down the ladder. After a few moments of hard drunken contemplation, Tag stuck the bottle into his underwear and started down the stairs.

When he reached the bottom, Tag pulled the bottle from his crotch. He figured that the climb had earned him a swig. He took a large gulp, capped the bottle and started to walk.

From where he was, Tag could see the closer end of the tunnel, but the other end was not visible because there were many twists and turns.

The tunnel was three car widths wide and fifteen feet high. It was lined with concrete and well lit. Fluorescent fixtures hanging on the left side of the wall lit the tunnel, and were separated by perfect intervals of wall and encased wires. Some wires, Tag thought, no doubt, led to communication equipment aboard the research rig, aiding the Poseidon Project. The round, metal tubes were so large, it looked like plumbing. Every so often the tube would run into a large metal box, and then continue down the wall as if it had not been interrupted.

There were boxes and crates lined up on the right side of the tunnel wall. They took up a lot of space where Tag was walking but they did not run the length of the tunnel.

Above the boxes were the air ducts, which included the exhaust and the intake. The complex had to get rid of its bad air, but they could not have a continuous stream of bubbles moving to the surface above the Poseidon complex. It would look too suspicious and therefore Lopez had the architect build the exhaust parallel to the incoming air. This compacted design hid their presence yet again.

After passing a tall stack of crates to his right, Tag saw a new, yellow, two-seater electric car. It was plugged into the wall and he figured it must be charged. Seeing the keys in the ignition he unplugged it and started it up.

I'm happy I found this thing, he thought happily. Now I won't have to walk the two miles to the complex. Tag was so proud of himself, he opened the bottle, threw down some tequila and drove.

The car was not meant for driving very fast, and it didn't. This upset the drunk driver and he decided to take his frustrations out on some of the boxes lining the wall. Tag maneuvered the car towards the boxes and smashed them against the wall. Most of the time he didn't have to try. Tag was so drunk that even if he was not trying to hit the boxes, they would have hit him.

It would have only taken him about eight minutes to reach the complex, but in his state, it took Tag about fifteen. By that time, the two-seater had sustained nicks and scratches that would have been deemed excess wear and tear on any leased vehicle.

Tag didn't bother plugging the car into its designated outlet on the wall, instead, he parked it at a forty-five degree angle with the bumper firmly smashed on the side of the tunnel.

Walking was a bit of a chore at this point, but he made it to the large metallic door at the end of the tunnel. The door had a large engraving of a trident standing upright inside an equilateral triangle. On either side of the door were vents that took up almost the whole wall. On the left side the air was entering the tunnel from the complex and the vents on the right side were connected to the ducts, running the length of the tunnel.

Before knocking, Tag paused for a moment and looked at the camera keeping watch of the entrance, just above the door. He smiled drunkenly at the camera and at Lopez who was watching him. Instead of knocking, Tag decided to give everyone in the complex a warm greeting. He pulled his pants down and farted loudly at the camera.

Happy with the fart, Tag zipped his pants, looked into the camera and screamed, "Open sesame!"

Lopez, who was watching Tag from a console in the control room of the complex, told the darker man sitting in front of him to open the door. The man commented on Tag's rude manner in disgust and then did as his boss told him.

The door swung outward slowly and an impatient Tag Millwood stumbled through. He was then standing in a large storeroom and all he could see was a door in front of him bathed in green light, and an elevator to his left. If the room were lit, he would have been able to see the large boxes and scrap metal that almost filled the capacity of the room.

He wasn't sure which way to go and started heading towards the elevator when Lopez's voice chimed in over the intercom system. "The control room," he said in a monotone voice.

Tag stopped in his tracks, spun drunkenly around and headed towards the door with the soft, solitary, green light above it. He placed the tequila bottle on the ground next to him and turned the large wheel in the center of the heavy metal door.

As the door opened, bright, white light flooded into the storage room that Tag was standing in and he shielded his eyes from the blinding light so they could adjust. Tag bent down, picked up his bottle, placed it on the other side of the door and stepped through.

When he had finished locking the wheel of the door, Tag picked up his bottle, turned and marveled at the massive room he was now in. Even when he was drunk it amazed him.

The room was enormous. It could have easily held a major league baseball field, including the stands. The walls made a complete circle, which was about one hundred-fifty yards in diameter. From the floor, the walls went straight up about one hundred and fifty feet and then curved inward to complete the retractable dome ceiling. At its peak, the ceiling was about three hundred feet high, with huge, curved support beams running the length.

The most amazing part of the structure, Tag thought, was that it opened to the bottom of the ocean and the room that he was standing in would fill with millions of gallons of seawater.

The structure alone protected against sonar detection. If equipment scanned the sea floor, that is all it would find, the sea floor. From the top, the roof looked, to the naked eye, like a hill on the sea bottom. The Poseidon Project would only be found by someone who knew it was there.

"Towards the control room, Tag," a voice boomed over invisible speakers. Lopez was obviously annoyed with him. He didn't like Tag's drunken ways, but it didn't matter much. There were plans for Tag later in the project. After Lopez was sure it was still secret, Tag would meet an untimely end. But for now Lopez would keep him alive and well in case he needed more insurance.

Tag staggered as he began walking again. At the opposite side of the large chamber was the control room. The entrance was a large door, exactly like the one he had just entered.

Still staring at the ceiling in amazement, he walked slowly towards the control room until he tripped and almost fell flat on his face. It was good, he thought, that he hadn't.

Someone would have paid, he thought angrily as he began walking again. As he continued he decided to take his eyes off the ceiling and pay attention to where he was going.

Tag had tripped over the largest magnet ever made. It was round, took up almost the entire floor of the chamber and had the same engraving as the metal door in the tunnel but this one was ten times the size. At the moment it was recessed into the floor, but he had seen it in action. It was an amazing sight. The only other objects in the room were large pieces of metal, that used to be ships, and about thirty underwater scooters.

As he staggered towards the control room, Tag thought about how they would sink ships. He thought Lopez had it down to a science. They would track ships and if they came too close Lopez would give the order to flood the large chamber and deploy the magnet. Thirty men on water scooters would accompany it to the surface and collect dead bodies that might have been thrown from the ship.

The ship would then be brought down and the dome would close and fill with air. After that, two sets of workers would come into the chamber. One group would get to work taking the ship apart so it could be sold as scrap metal, disposing the evidence. The other group would take all the dead bodies, strip them and then weight them to the bottom of the ocean where they would stay until the scavengers picked them apart into unrecognizable chunks of meat.

Tag had seen the whole process and was amazed by it but just thinking about the dead bodies being devoured by crabs made his stomach churn. He hesitated for a moment, thinking he might expel his tequila but nothing came out and he moved on slowly.

After, what seemed to Tag, a long walk, he reached the control room door. He was about to put his tequila down and turn the wheel but it started turning on its own. As it was turning, Tag looked over the door and saw the red and green lights above it. They were recessed into the wall and covered with heavy glass, as were all the lights in the room. It's amazing, he thought, that even through all that glass, they could produce so much light. As the large door opened slowly, Tag thought about the whole magnificent structure and how much effort went into building it. As he thought harder, his drunken senses got the better of him. "Ah, I could've designed it by myself," he mumbled loudly. Tag could no longer feel his mouth.

"Designed what," Lopez asked. He was standing in the open doorway. His light clothes had given way to a completely black wardrobe. Tag had seen him in both and he thought that everything looked good on Lopez.

That bastard, Tag thought. Why couldn't anything look good on me? He was staring directly at Lopez contemptibly, without saying a word.

"Would you like to come in," Lopez asked, with his usual charm. "Or would you like to stand there all night?"

Tag's eyes focused slowly as he came out of his drunken stupor. He still did not say a word, but moved slowly and silently into the control room. Lopez could smell the tequila on Tag's breath and he saw the bottle in his hand. Immediately, Lopez called the other man in the control room to help Tag.

As the man put Tag's arm over his shoulder, Tag looked up into Lopez's face. Slowly, Tag raised the arm with the bottle in his hand and pointed his finger at Lopez.

"Take me to your leader," he said seriously, then began laughing hysterically. Lopez didn't think this was funny, but smiled anyway and pointed to the elevator.

The man led Tag to the elevator and pressed the button on the right side of the door. Immediately, the doors slid open and the man helped Tag into the elevator. He was so drunk; Tag could have walked in front of a truck and would not have known.

The door closed and they began to descend into the complex. Only two floors below, the door opened again. The ride had been very smooth, but that didn't prevent Tag from regurgitating everything that was in his stomach two floors up.

Tag and his escort exited the elevator, into a narrow hallway, which ran the length of the chamber on the first floor. On the other end of the hallway was another elevator that Tag wasn't able to focus on because his eyes wouldn't stay open.

Tag's partner was now supporting most of his weight as his feet were almost dragging along behind him. As they continued, the bottle slid out of Tag's hand and crashed to the concrete floor. He didn't notice.

As they continued, they passed identical doors on their left and right. Their only distinguishing marks were numbers, spray painted white, with stencils, above the doors.

They stopped at one of the rooms, and the man pushed the door open. Inside was a plain room. It was gray, like most of the complex. The only pieces of furniture were a twin-sized bed with a plain metal frame and a two-drawer nightstand at its head. The bed had a white pillow and a heavy green cover and it made the room look as though it had been furnished by an army surplus store.

The man pulled Tag into the room and sat him down on the bed. Barf was still fresh on his face and shirt and he didn't bother cleaning it off.

Tag was laid down with his head missing the pillow by no more than an inch. He was asleep.

CHAPTER 12

Aaron was still in a somber mood. He hadn't talked to or seen Sarah after their fight. He tried to call her and go over to her apartment, but she was never around.

He was sitting on the edge of the tank, dangling his feet in the water while feeding the dolphins. They had all returned, like everyone had said they would. Skilos had been the last to return but Mike said it was unusual. Skilos was usually waiting in the bay for them to open the gate.

It was a gorgeous day, about eighty-five degrees. The sun was shining bright and there was a slight breeze coming off the bay. It reminded Aaron of a perfect summer day in New England. There was nothing like it, he thought.

"How's that jaw, buddy," Mike asked, as he came around the corner of the lab. Aaron had told Mike that Sarah had slapped him but he hadn't gotten the details.

"It's fine, thanks," he said, telling the truth with a smile. It's a good thing he didn't ask me about how I am emotionally, Aaron thought to himself. He was still a mess from their fight and wanted very badly to apologize to Sarah.

"What did you say to her anyway?"

"I told you, I don't really want to talk about it," Aaron replied trying to be nice.

"You're goin' out with her, aren't you?"

"What makes you say that," he asked quickly, turning red.

"Oh, come on Aaron, everybody knows it." Mike was watching him feed the dolphins over his shoulder.

Aaron was quiet for a moment and did not look up at Mike; he kept feeding the dolphins.

"So, what happens now?" Aaron expected to hear a response indicating that he could not return to do further research.

"Nothing." Mike almost chuckled as if his question was absurd.

"Nothing?" Aaron didn't believe him.

"Yeah, ever since we saw you two together we thought you would be a great couple."

"Really?" Aaron was surprised.

"Sure! Bob, Maria and I have talked about it. We think you guys are great!" Mike paused for a moment. "Well, that is, except for your fight."

"Yeah, I think we could have done without the fight."

"You stayin' late again," Mike asked as he started walking to his car.

"When don't I?"

"Good point."

Aaron got up from his spot on the side of the tank and caught Mike before he got to his car. "Hey, Mike, do you know where Sarah is?" Aaron thought she was doing another photography job but was still checking up on her.

"She said something about having to go out of town for a few days for another photo job. I guess she didn't tell you because of the fight," he said, then continued towards his car and left the premises.

Aaron looked at the ground in sadness as he walked down into the lab. Their fight, which he knew was his fault, hurt him. He missed her terribly. There was an empty pit in his stomach because she wasn't around and Aaron wanted so much just to talk with her. He was sure that if he could talk to her and apologize that she wouldn't be mad at him anymore.

When he entered the lab, Aaron was immediately colder. He looked up and saw Bob sitting on the far side of the lab working on some papers. He was dressed like Aaron; bathing suit and nothing else, but Bob was sweating. The fan, on as usual, backed up the air conditioner.

"Cold," Bob asked sarcastically, looking up at Aaron who was turning blue.

"How can you ask me that? I still can't understand how you think this temperature is normal." Aaron was hugging himself to stop the shivering.

He walked over to his backpack, reached in and pulled out his towel and a shirt. After making sure he was dry, he donned his shirt, but, as usual, that wasn't enough when Bob was around. For just such emergencies, Aaron kept a sweatshirt at the lab and he put it on.

"What's Doctor Bob's forecast for this evening," Aaron asked, sitting down in the chair and placing his backpack on the ground next to him.

"Currently it's fifty degrees and dry; in here that is. And my sources tell me the temperature will probably get closer to the ambient temperature outside in about thirty minutes. Seventy or seventy-five is my guess. Then at about nine tonight, there'll be another cold front coming through."

"No, you're coming back?" Aaron joked as he put his head on the desk and pretended to cry.

"If you can't stand the cold, stay out of the lab. Besides it's only for a while. Then we're all going out on the boat."

"For what?" As they spoke, Aaron turned on the computer in front of him to start his research for the evening.

"Don't you remember? Today is Patricia's birthday. We're taking her out on the boat for an evening of fun."

"Oh, right!" Aaron tapped his head with his finger, implying that he had forgotten.

"Are you okay," Bob asked sincerely.

"Yeah. Yeah, I'm fine." He sighed.

"Are you still coming out with us?"

"Yes, definitely! I wouldn't miss it!"

"Good, you'll have a good time, I promise." Bob paused for a moment, then continued slowly. "Even if Sarah isn't there."

Aaron looked over at Bob who had now put his head back into his own work. He was going to ask Bob about the whole situation and thought better of it. If Bob did know about him and Sarah and hadn't said anything, it must be okay, he thought.

Aaron sat quietly for a moment while opening programs for his research, then stopped. "How long have you known," he asked, not being able to hold back.

Bob chuckled in his low volume, high pitched chuckle. "For a while. Ah, but you guys are perfect for each other." Bob looked over at Aaron and continued. "Patricia and I have always thought you guys would be good together. And then, just seeing you two interact. It's nice to see. It's too bad you guys had to get in that fight, but it's okay. You'll make up, I'm sure."

"What about all that professionalism stuff. You know, she's a co-worker, it's not good, yadda, yadda?"

"Ah, screw all that stuff! You guys are good enough together to override that petty stipulation."

"Really," Aaron asked happily.

"No." Bob changed his tone abruptly. His smile changed very quickly to a stern frown. "You're fired!"

"What?" Aaron was flustered! His heart started to beat faster, flushing his face.

Bob sat in his chair and didn't move. He kept staring at Aaron with his stern face and did not say a word.

Finally the silence broke with a hearty laugh from Bob. "I'm just kidding! Everybody loves you! Plus, you do great work," Bob said and turned back to his desk. "We were even thinking of offering you a job when you graduate," he said nonchalantly. "And..." Bob added turning back to Aaron. "We'd like you to come back during the summers to help out with research until then."

Aaron was flattered. He had a big smile on his face, but did not say anything. His fight with Sarah entered his mind. What would working with her be like if they didn't get along, he thought? Maybe she would quit if she knew he would return.

"What, you don't want to work for us after all," Bob asked after not receiving an answer.

"It's not that. I'd love to. I just need to think about it. Plus, I'll need to get permission from Professor Jeffries and the chair of the department back home."

"Good point." Bob paused, then went back to his work again. "Well, I'm not worried about it. I'm sure they'll let you come back. Just let us know as soon as you can for next summer."

"Sure thing," Aaron said, unsure of what he really wanted to do because of Sarah. He loved his research and this was an opportunity of a lifetime. Maybe I could get a letter of recommendation from Bob and the rest of the group and go somewhere else to do my research, he thought.

Aaron started working on his research again and tried to block everything else from his mind. Every few minutes he noticed the dolphins exhibiting the behavior he had seen in Skilos. Aaron thought for sure they were communicating specific directions and he noted every time it happened and saved it for a later project.

"I'll see you later," Bob said.

He was standing in front of Aaron's console with his briefcase in his hands. "Listen, why don't you go home and relax a little before tonight. Take a shower, dress up a little nicer than a bathing suit. It'll be a nice get together."

Aaron relaxed in his chair and exhaled. He ran his hands through his short hair and stared at Bob. "Maybe you're right," he agreed.

"Great! We want you to be in a good mood for the party. See you tonight," Bob said as he walked out of the lab and left. After relaxing for a few minutes in his chair, Aaron took Bob's advice and went home.

*****

A long, hot shower relaxed Aaron. He sat in the small stand-up shower and let the hot water pound on his head. Pound on it in order to push out all the bad thoughts about his lack of a future with someone he was beginning to love. Pound out the thoughts of not being able to do research with people who already knew he could do a good job.

After getting dressed, Aaron put on his Australian duster and it was a good thing he did. Bob was right, it was a rather chilly evening. Maybe Bob had actually found a way to make all of Jamaica more comfortable to him, Aaron thought.

On the way to the lab Aaron realized he did not have a present for Patricia and he stopped by a supermarket to pick up some flowers. The only thing they had left that was worth buying was a red rose so Aaron got it. They wrapped it up tight for him because Aaron was afraid it would get blown apart on the ride to the lab.

When he arrived in the parking lot, Aaron saw that everyone had already arrived. The parking lot was full, everyone was there, even Sarah. Apparently she had made it back from whatever work she had been doing elsewhere, Aaron thought.

Maybe she doesn't want me around. Maybe I should leave, he thought. Then his senses took over. He knew that Sarah loved him, or *had* loved him. In either case, he was sure that if he apologized, she would forgive him. There was no reason to run away from her and it would accomplish nothing anyway he decided.

Aaron started walking confidently toward the dock where everyone was already on the boat. It had been decked with different colored lights, which shined softly against the calm waters of the bay.

As he got closer, Bob noticed Aaron approaching. "Come on, Aaron, we've been waiting for you," he yelled.

Aaron waved his left hand high in the air to signal his arrival but no one on the boat could see Aaron very well. It was dark, and he was wearing dark clothing, but they knew it was him. Aaron took the poor visibility to his advantage and quickly unwrapped the rose. He then broke the stem to make it shorter and stuck it in his coat sleeve. The sleeve of the duster was long and loose enough to conceal the flower easily without damaging it.

As he came around the corner of the tank and onto the dock, he was able to see everyone more clearly. They were all dressed for the cool evening, except for Bob of course, who had on a short sleeved Hawaiian shirt with a red and white flowered pattern.

Everyone was in a festive mood as he stepped on board. Sarah was acting normal too but she did not greet Aaron as he arrived. Aaron shook hands with Mike and Bob, and hugged Maria.

"I'm sorry I didn't get you anything for your birthday," Aaron said as he hugged Patricia.

"No need," Patricia said. "But thank you for coming. Now, why don't you get something to drink and we'll shove off," she said with a delightful smile.

"Sounds good to me."

Patricia pointed to a large cooler all the way in the stern of the boat. Its lid was off and Aaron could see it was full of ice and various alcoholic and non-alcoholic beverages. He walked over to the cooler and pulled out a *Coke®*. As he opened the *Coke®*, Aaron looked around the boat. He had never been on it before and it looked a lot different from on board. It was relatively new, but it reminded him of the boat that Jaws had attacked in Stephen Spielberg's movie.

There was a large mast shooting up from the back of the small control room in the middle of the boat. There was another bar perpendicular to the mast about four feet over his head, with a line running from the top of the mast to the end of the perpendicular bar. It looked as though it was made to hoist a net into and out of the water, but there was no sign of a net anywhere. The only thing the line held now were the colorful lights that lit the area around the boat.

Aaron looked around, but did not see Sarah. She must have gone to the bow, he thought. Aaron walked around the port side of the boat as it began to move. He almost lost his balance because of the jolt, but caught himself on the railing.

As he walked around the side, Aaron looked into the small wheelhouse. It was about the size of a large car interior. There were four seats, two in the front and two behind them. The front seats were directly in front of the wheel and other navigational apparatus. Three of the seats were occupied by Bob, who was driving, and a middle-aged couple that was keeping him company.

"You the designated driver this evening," Aaron asked.

Bob raised the can of *Coke®* in his right hand and said, "You betcha!" Bob took a swig of his drink, then continued. "And after I get home, I'll still be the designated driver if you know what I mean?" Bob's friends laughed heartily, but Aaron was disgusted.

"Oh, come on!" Aaron had a nasty look on his face. "You really didn't need to tell me that."

Bob looked at his friends who were still laughing and then back at Aaron. "Aaron, these are our good friends, Mickey and Anne." They waved at Aaron and he returned the gesture.

"Nice to meet you," Aaron said.

Mickey and Anne were obviously American from their accents but Aaron didn't know if they were visiting or if they lived in Jamaica. He didn't have a chance to find out though because they quickly resumed whatever previous conversation they had been having with Bob. Returning to his thoughts, Aaron continued towards the bow.

His duster was still on and it blocked the cool breeze from his body. The wind felt good on his face and whipped through his short hair. As he looked past the boat, Aaron could see they were heading out into the ocean and leaving the lights of Kingston behind.

The bow had a small walking area, which was partially boxed in by wooden benches that looked uncomfortable. The hull was high enough to give good back support but not too high as to obscure the line of vision out towards the water.

Aaron noticed that Sarah was not at the bow and neither was anyone else. He was going to walk around the other side of the boat and return to the stern, but decided not to. Everyone was back there laughing and having a good time, but being in the front of the boat with no one else was relaxing. He sat down where the wooden benches made a corner and looked out to the dark, endless waters. He rested his right hand up on the side of the boat and put his feet up on the bench in front of him. The slow undulation of the boat was peaceful. He felt as if he were sitting in a rocking chair on a slightly breezy day. Aaron closed his eyes and let his mind drift for a few seconds.

Slowly, Aaron opened his eyes, took in a deep breath and sighed. He was more relaxed now and ready to confront Sarah.

Out of the corner of his eye, Aaron saw someone coming into the bow area, around the port side of the wheelhouse. It was Sarah. She was looking back over her shoulder towards the back of the boat and did not notice Aaron sitting in the corner.

"You really think you can avoid me all night on a boat this size," Aaron asked.

Sarah turned around slowly to face Aaron. She looked upset for having run into him with no one else around, but her expression was not one of anger.

"I was hoping to avoid you for a little while, at least," she said as she started to walk around the starboard side of the wheelhouse and past Aaron, but he blocked her.

"Will you please talk to me?" Aaron was pleading with her.

Sarah tried to move around him but Aaron blocked her again. "I have something I want to say to you. And then, if you want to go back there, you can and I won't bother you for the rest of the night," he said calmly.

Sarah stood there staring at him. Her arms were crossed over her chest, but at least she wasn't trying to leave, he thought.

"Please," Aaron asked, his right hand pointing towards the benches.

Sarah didn't say anything, but sat down with her arms still crossed. Aaron sat down in front of her and began to talk, while she glared at him.

"Sarah," Aaron started softly. "I know you're upset at me." He paused for a minute trying to find the right words to say. "I'm so sorry. I had no right to question your love for me. I know you weren't spying on me! I had no idea what I was thinking! I was tired, and it was..." He paused and looked at her face which had not changed expressions.

"No. No excuses, I'm sorry. It hurts me so much to know that I've hurt you. I love you!" Aaron was looking directly into her eyes and not veering away. "I love you so much it hurts, especially when you're not around. And, I miss you. It's only been a few days since we last spoke but I can't stand it! It kills me to know you're angry with me. I sit and I think of how I'm ever going to get through the day without talking to you, much less an entire school year. That thought is almost too much to bear."

Aaron paused his heart-felt speech for a moment and leaned in closer to Sarah, who was not glaring at him anymore. She was looking at him, emotionless. It was impossible for him to read what was going through her mind.

"You know what I miss," he asked but answered himself. "I miss your eyes. I miss your hair. I miss your skin. I miss your face. But most of all, I miss you. I miss spending time with you. Just being around you makes me happy. Please tell me that you still want to be with me, because I don't want to even imagine how I'm going to make it through my life without you. I love you." Aaron began to tear as he finished his speech.

He had never felt like this about anyone and thought he never would again. He slowly raised up his left hand, pulled the red rose from his sleeve and offered it to Sarah.

"Please forgive me," he said, with the rose in between them.

Sarah was starting to tear as well, and then she began to speak. "You know what I hate about you," she asked angrily. "I hate that I love you so much that I can't stay mad at you." She paused again. "I want to. I want to stay mad at you but I can't," she said forcefully as she grabbed the rose from him and sniffed it with her stuffed up nose. "I love you, too," Sarah said, finally softening up to Aaron.

Aaron's face lit up with joy. There was such an overwhelming feeling inside him, which was sweeping his whole body. This must be what it's like to be in love, he thought. This has to be it.

Filled with emotion he threw his arms around her and she did the same. "I love you so much," Aaron said, as they embraced.

Just then, the whole boat burst into cheer and applause. Sarah and Aaron were so entrenched in their conversation they had not noticed that everyone on board had gathered and was listening to them. They were caught off guard and were a little embarrassed. As they separated from their embrace, they wiped their eyes and smiled at everyone.

Everyone on board then started to chant in unison. "Kiss, kiss, kiss..." Sarah and Aaron looked at each other and were not embarrassed anymore. It was just the shock of knowing that everyone had been eavesdropping a moment before.

They leaned closer to each other and kissed softly. Their love for each other was apparent to everyone on board. They all cheered for Sarah and Aaron. Sarah and Aaron turned back towards the crowd after their kiss and their expressions were interpreted quickly. The crowd dispersed and they were alone again.

They continued to embrace each other for a while, sitting quietly, leaning against one another and enjoying being together. They decided to return to the party when they heard everyone singing happy birthday and after receiving cake Sarah and Aaron started being social again. While they were talking with Mike, Patricia and Bob approached and interrupted their conversation.

"You know, you and Sarah remind us of ourselves when we were young," Patricia said. "We're so happy you are together and wish you guys all the best." She raised her glass of wine to them.

"What are you talking about," Aaron laughed. "You make it sound as if we're getting married."

"Hey, you never know," Bob said, as he winked at the young lovers.

The rest of the trip was a pleasant one. Everyone talked, drank, and had a good time.

When the party returned to shore, everyone said goodbye to Patricia and Bob. Bob was going to take Patricia on a birthday trip to Ocho Rios, a popular tourist area on the northeastern side of Jamaica. Patricia loved the crowded beaches there and they had not been in a while.

Sarah and Aaron walked to the parking lot at the lab, hand in hand. They stared at each other lovingly.

"Why don't you come back to my place," Aaron asked, as they reached his bike. "It'll be romantic with the small bed and all." They both laughed softly.

"Okay." Sarah smiled back at him. She knew he had a much smaller place but he was right. It would be a destitute kind of romantic.

Sarah followed Aaron back to his room in her Jeep. They went inside and Aaron immediately grabbed Sarah from behind and started kissing her neck. She breathed heavily and brushed her hands through her hair and then onto Aaron's head. She pulled him around, in front of her so she could kiss him. They kissed hard and fell onto Aaron's twin bed.

*****

Aaron and Sarah were lying next to each other, naked, covered only by his sheets. Her head was lying on Aaron's chest and he was stroking her hair as they smiled through the darkness. They were both awake enjoying the calm that only comes after having sex that is as good physically as it is emotionally.

"You're great," Aaron said. Sarah smiled at this and closed her eyes. She breathed in and let out a sigh.

"I know," she said softly.

Aaron laughed at her response and they continued to talk until the sun rose.

CHAPTER 13

Aaron awoke early that morning but did not disturb Sarah as he got up. She looked so peaceful sleeping next to him. Even in her sleep she seemed happy.

He was feeling energetic and decided to go running on the beach and not skip a morning just because he had been up all night. Before he got to the beach, he stopped at a corner store and bought another red rose for Sarah. He came back to his apartment and placed the rose on the pillow next to Sarah who was still asleep. He felt alive because of his courtship with Sarah. Everything was going well again, and this time he wouldn't mess it up.

When he returned to his room after his run, Sarah was gone along with the rose. But in their place was a note on his pillow. It read, "Aaron, I love you so much. You're so sweet. Waking up next to a rose is almost as good as waking up beside the man who gave it to me. I'll see you later, Sarah."

Aaron smiled as he read the note. She made him happy.

Looking at his watch, Aaron realized it was later than he thought. It was ten in the morning and he had a lot of errands to run before going back to the lab. After a quick shower he headed off to the lab to retrieve the air tank they were letting him borrow. He was running low on air and needed to fill it. Unfortunately the lab didn't have a compressor so Aaron had to take it to a dive shop periodically to get it filled.

No one was around at the lab when he arrived. Aaron turned on the equipment he would need later, grabbed his air tank and left. There was no way he was going to carry the tank while riding his bike, so he strapped it onto his buoyancy control device and put it on. Aaron looked stupid riding around with an air tank on his back, but it was the only way to get it to the dive shop safely.

It was called, *The Local*, and it wasn't much. This dive shop was definitely not where the tourists went. There wasn't much for sale and everything looked like it could have been used in Jacques Cousteau's era. The man behind the desk was a scraggly looking Jamaican man about forty years old. Under the roughage though, he looked like a nice man.

Aaron put the tank up on the old counter and asked if the man could fill it.

"Ya man. No problem," he said, with a wide smile revealing some missing teeth.

"How long is it going to take?"

"'Bout thirty minutes."

Aaron had no idea why it would take thirty minutes to fill his tank. When he walked in, the man was staring at the front door, waiting for something to happen. At least that's what it looked like to Aaron.

"What's your name man," the man yelled from the back room, as Aaron was about to leave.

"Aaron Silver. I'll come back to pick it up later," he said, just before the door closed behind him.

After running some more errands, Aaron returned to the dive shop and the man was in the same place behind the run down counter. Only this time he was sitting down watching a small color television that could not be seen from the entrance. The familiar jabbering of a man filled his ears. It must be the news, Aaron thought.

He walked up to the counter and asked for his tank. The man had not noticed Aaron enter the shop but was not startled by his request. He was engrossed in the story on the news.

As he looked over the counter at the small television, Aaron recognized an anchor from the World News Network. The man was standing beside someone else dressed in a suit and the backdrop was that of the Gulf of Mexico. Aaron immediately knew what subject they were discussing.

"As I said before," the black agent, in the suit continued. "We have not found any survivors or the wreckage. At this point we are certain that there are no survivors. It has been too long for anyone to survive out in the ocean without water. Therefore, we have called off the search." He spoke easily as if he gave these reports every day.

"But Agent Schwabb, if the plane crashed in the area in which you were looking, shouldn't you have found something? Could it be that you were looking in the wrong place the whole time," the anchorman asked and then put the microphone back in front of Agent Schwabb.

"No, according to the last known position of the aircraft we have thoroughly searched every possible location on the sea floor where this wreckage could have been."

"Then why didn't you find it," he asked, trying to upset Schwabb for the camera.

"I am not at liberty to disclose any more information about our theories surrounding this crash, but I will tell you this. Just because we are no longer searching the area, does not mean the investigation is over. We have sufficient data of the area in question and we will take that information back to our labs and analyze it until we have found something," Schwabb answered calmly.

The news anchor turned back to the camera and finished his story. "This time, what is being called, 'The Jamaican Deeps' has fooled the CIA as well as the U.S. and Jamaican Coast Guards. With each disappearance, the area off the eastern coast of Jamaica is shrouded deeper and deeper in mystery. Officials are warning all boats and aircraft to stay out of the area within ten miles of the proposed crash site. Until this mystery is solved, if it ever is, the thought on many people's minds is of the Bermuda Triangle. I'm Dave White with WNN News."

The man behind the counter turned to Aaron with a worried look on his face. "I hope you not goin' divin' out there, man!"

"Not in the near future."

"What's your name," the man asked, as he walked to the back of the store to find the tank.

"Aaron Silver."

*****

Aaron had been at the lab all day, going over his tapes. Most of his time there, for the last few weeks, had consisted of putting the tapes together and constructing his secret research on dolphin communication. He had to keep it secret from everyone, even Sarah. Aaron knew that if anyone got wind of this probable find that every country that bordered the oceans of the world would want his information. Aaron knew himself to be paranoid, but he thought they might even kill for it.

From the soft light coming through the underwater windows, Aaron could tell it was getting dark outside. His back was starting to ache from sitting too much so he stood and stretched. Aaron walked over to the larger window in the center of the lab and watched the dolphins. Skilos noticed that Aaron was paying attention and swam swiftly to him.

The tank had just been cleaned the day before, and it seemed as if Skilos was starved for human attention. Skilos was right up at the window nodding his head at Aaron. Instinctively, Aaron picked up the beach ball and started throwing it at the window.

"I know, I know, you want to play," he said, playing catch with the window but Skilos was not playing catch. He was not trying to catch the ball like the dolphins always did. Skilos was shaking his head; seemingly saying "no" with an urgency Aaron had not seen before.

Was Skilos really saying "no," he asked himself? It was quite possible that the dolphins had observed a negative response by humans and associated that with the shaking of their heads. Maybe Skilos learned to do it as well, Aaron thought.

Aaron faked a throw to Skilos like a baseball player would to a teammate during practice to see if he was ready or wanted the ball to be thrown. Again, Skilos shook his head. This is great, Aaron thought. I've got to get this on tape.

As he moved away from the window to set up the camera, Aaron noticed that Skilos moved away. Damn, he thought, I could have had something there.

Aaron moved back to the window and looked for Skilos. It was still light enough to see clearly across the tank without too much trouble, and Skilos was at the other end. He was near the lock on the other side, which led to the ocean. It looked as if Skilos was telling Aaron to come in that direction. Aaron had seen these movements before and was sure that is what Skilos was trying to communicate to him.

Aaron was very curious as to what Skilos was trying to communicate, but he thought he could get a better idea from the topside. He ran up the steps and out into the warm evening air. The lot was still empty, save his bike. He turned right, towards the tank and walked up to the side. Skilos was swimming with his head out of the water, on the other side of the tank, and Aaron followed him. When he got there, Skilos was squeaking at him and swimming backwards towards the lock. Upon reaching the lock, Skilos stopped, turned around and butted his rostrum softly against the gate.

Aaron knew exactly what he wanted. Skilos wanted out. This had come up in conversation before and Bob had said that if any of the dolphins seemed to want out, to let them out. It would be unethical to not give the dolphins freedom if they wanted it.

Aaron felt sad that this was happening and sad that Skilos really wanted to leave, but it was apparent, and Aaron had been given the authority to let the dolphins out. Bob had said that it had happened before but those dolphins rarely returned.

Skilos stopped swimming and stared at Aaron standing above him on the side of the tank. Aaron stared back.

The other dolphins didn't seem to care what was going on between the two. They seemed quite complacent, almost asleep. Aaron knew that if he opened the gate and the other dolphins wanted to leave that he would have to let them out as well.

Begrudgingly, he pulled the lever for the gate and it opened slowly. Skilos went through and the other dolphins stayed inside the main tank with no change in behavior.

Skilos immediately swam towards the outer gate and looked out of the water to find Aaron. After the inner gate was closed, Aaron reluctantly opened the outer gate. With a heavy heart he saw the shadow of Skilos slip under the opening gate and out into the sea. Aaron thought he had forged a close relationship with Skilos but now Aaron got the feeling that their interaction had meant nothing to Skilos. Maybe he just pretended because he knew he could get more food out of me that way, Aaron thought sadly.

The water in the bay was darker and from where he was standing Aaron could not see where Skilos had gone. Usually Skilos would wave goodbye, but this time there was no sign of him.

Unhappily, Aaron turned back towards the lab. He thought they might never see Skilos again. "That would put a huge damper on my communication research," he said to himself.

As he was walking away from the water, Aaron heard Skilos. He turned excitedly but did not see him. The sounds were coming from near the dock and Aaron ran in that direction. It was almost dark now and it was difficult to locate Skilos. Aaron ran onto the dock and yelled to Skilos. Skilos called back. He was in the water, in front of the research boat.

When Skilos saw Aaron, he started making familiar movements in the water. Aaron was happy they he had not left but this thought left him when he realized what Skilos was doing. Skilos wanted Aaron to follow him in the boat. Aaron knew this without any knowledge of being correct but he wanted to fulfill the dolphin's request. Whatever Skilos wants to show me, he thought, it must be important. Ever since he had caught Aaron's attention Skilos had been acting with a sense of urgency.

Starting to get caught up in the excitement, Aaron thought about what he would need for his journey and ran quickly back to the lab after telling Skilos to wait. He grabbed his scuba equipment as he thought how lucky he was that his tank had just been refilled.

After picking up flares and a flashlight he tried to remember where the keys to the boat were. He stood still, trying to calm his head from the rush and then it came to him.

"The file," he said excitedly as he ran to the file cabinet and looked under "K." He pulled out the keys and slammed the drawer. In a rush more hurried than before he picked up his equipment and ran out towards the boat.

He placed his equipment in the back of the boat, then went to the wheelhouse and started the engine. He ran from the wheelhouse and unhooked the boat from the dock and pushed off as hard as he could. Hurrying back to the controls, Aaron took a peek at the bow and could barely make out Skilos in the dim light from the dock.

Back behind the wheel, Aaron started flipping switches feverishly until he found one that controlled a spotlight at the front of the boat. With a bright flash, he found it. Looking up and over the controls he could easily see Skilos in the large circle of light off the bow. This will be plenty of room to keep track of Skilos' movements, if I don't go too fast, Aaron thought as he pushed the throttle up slowly. The engine gurgled louder and faster. Led by Skilos, the boat moved out to sea.

All of the navigational and communication instruments were on, but Aaron didn't know how to use them very well. If only I had served in the Israeli Navy instead of the infantry, he thought to himself. Inexperienced as he was, Aaron was confident that Skilos would bring him back safely. And, Aaron thought, there wasn't too much to worry about because he could still see lights off to his left. They were traveling eastward, just off the coast.

That's when it hit him. We're traveling east, he thought, right into the restricted area.

*****

Señor Lopez was resting in his quarters when his intercom beeped.
"Si?"
"Señor, we are picking up a small boat just inside sonar range."
"Just keep tracking it and let me know if it gets within ten kilometers. Until then put half of the crew on alert," he said confidently as if he had given the order thousands of times.
"Yes, señor," the voice said as the intercom clicked off.
Lopez continued reading the Bible. As a young child his parents told him that Jesus was his savior and he still believed it to be true. He also knew that the drug cartel was the only way of life for him. A part of him believed that Jesus had chosen this profession for him and had helped to protect him in times of trouble. He was grateful to his God and showed it. Lopez brought religion and religious ideals everywhere he went. He even had a chapel built in the Poseidon complex so that his men could pray. Lopez thought that if his men had a relationship with God, they would work harder and be more loyal and this philosophy had never let him down.
Lopez's quarters were larger than any other quarters in the complex, but it was not more lavish than other rooms. He wanted his men to feel that they were more or less equals. He felt this, also, kept them from getting too jealous and betraying him.
Lopez closed his Bible slowly, kissed it, placed it on his nightstand and got up from his bed.

It was a bare room. His bed was like the others, army style. The nightstand only supported his Bible and a lamp, which was on. The only picture in the room was of Jesus, which was hanging on the inside wall, easily visible from the entrance to the room.

He walked over to his private bathroom, which was connected to his quarters, and looked in the mirror. He had not shaved in a few days and was starting to look scraggly. The stubble looked good against a backdrop of dark skin. He was a handsome man and everyone knew it.

The washbasin was spotless. He cleaned his room and bathroom himself. Lopez liked to keep everything spotless, especially his image.

Lopez opened a small drawer under the sink and extracted a razor blade and shaving cream. He used a classic razor like they used in old barbershops. The plastic things they advertised on television were not right for him. He was an old fashioned man, a classic man.

After placing his shaving utensils on the sink basin, Lopez turned on the hot water. It was a simple sink. He had many nice sinks, in many nice bathrooms at his many homes around the world. Here, he did not need one. Everything around him reminded him of army barracks. It kept him on his toes. Lopez did not want to feel comfortable here. He felt that if he got comfortable he would be lazy and if he were lazy, he would be dead.

The steam started rising from the water, escaping from the faucet. It leapt from the air and clung to the mirror behind the sink, spreading like fire on a wooden wall.

Lopez splashed his face with the scalding water then spread shaving cream over his stubble. Slowly, stroke-by-stroke, he removed his facial hair.

As he washed his face, he heard a voice in his room. Lopez took a small towel to his face and walked into his bedroom.

"Señor Lopez?" It was the voice from the intercom again.

"Si," he answered calmly.

"The craft is still closing, but slower now."

"Have they deployed from the research center yet?"

"Si, señor."

"Very well. I will be right there." Lopez retained his composure. He always tried to remain calm, even if things bothered him, and this slowly approaching craft made him nervous.

*****

It had been a while since the last light disappeared off of the port side and since then Aaron had not even seen a boat. As the trip drew on Aaron got an eerie feeling from the anticipation and had turned on the radio to cut the silence.

Skilos had slowed from his earlier pace and it did not help Aaron's conscience, which had been telling him to turn back for hours. The only thing keeping him from listening to his instinct was the thought that they must be close.

Looking in front of the boat, Aaron didn't see Skilos. His heart jumped as he pulled the throttle back. He heard nothing but the slow gurgle of his engine and moved quickly up to the front of the boat to see if he could find Skilos.

Skilos was still not visible and his heart raced faster. How would he find his way back, he thought quickly, trying to remember something he learned in training that might help him.

Aside from Aaron's light on the front of his boat, there was total darkness. There was no moon and the stars were the only other visible points of light. Millions of stars poked through a black blanket of vast nothingness. It was beautiful, but scary.

Thinking more, Aaron came to the conclusion that Skilos had not left him, but rather was waiting for him under the water. This thought excited him and he ran quickly to his large equipment bag and pulled out a black wet suit and black dive boots. He struggled for a few minutes to get them on, pulling and grunting on the floor of the boat until he pushed his feet through the holes. After pulling the wet suit over his body, Aaron pulled out his fins and snorkel and placed them on top of his bag.

As he was about to place his regulator on his tank, Aaron heard the sound of a dolphin coming up for air. He looked around but didn't see anything until Skilos came back into the searchlight. Aaron breathed again.

Skilos made the motion for Aaron to follow him and he ran back to the controls and moved the boat slowly forward with Skilos. They picked up the pace and were almost to their original cruising speed.

Aaron had been prepared to see whatever Skilos wanted to show him but now he had to wait again. It should have calmed him down and given him more time to prepare but instead it made him even more tense.

*****

Lopez was studying the screen. The boat was moving very slowly and was still headed straight for the complex. This worried him.

"I want that boat destroyed," he said sternly but calmly, to the man sitting in front of him. "Make sure you get it. If the magnet does not stop it, use the magnet mines. If that doesn't work, make sure our crew up above destroys it and anyone on board."

During the conception of the complex, Lopez knew that it would be very rare for boats to head exactly over the complex, even if they were in a high traffic area. As a failsafe, he had magnet mines built. They didn't destroy a ship; they just stopped them like the larger magnet. The mines were anchored deep in the ground and scattered in a one-mile radius around the complex. When released they would float to the surface and stop a boat dead in its tracks. Lopez had used them a few times and they worked to their fullest, lethal potential.

The flash on the sonar screen kept getting closer, and it was still heading for the center. "Flood the chamber," Lopez ordered.

The man sitting beside him did not answer. He flipped a couple of switches and there was a loud hissing sound. On the screen, they both watched the enormous chamber begin to fill with water.

There were already men in the chamber with their scuba gear on, ready for action. They had been standing next to their water scooters. As the chamber began to fill with water, they floated to the top with the rising water level.

Lopez couldn't see them, but he knew that there were also thirty men in the storage room on the other side of the chamber, waiting to take the ill-fated boat apart for transportation. They would also be taking any dead bodies and feeding them to the sharks and scavengers.

*****

Tag had gone back to the research rig to supervise the crew of the secret boat. It had been a few days since his last drunken stupor and he was feeling much better. They had been using this rig from the beginning as a dock for the secret boat. It was used to support the cleanup effort after a ship was taken under.

The boat was stored in a dock near the surface level of the rig. It was a restricted area for the scientists, the only one who had ever seen it was Doctor Melinowski, and he was dead. The boat was stored in an airtight shed where the water level would remain constant, even during a storm. Before the chamber was opened, the water level could be manipulated to match the ambient water level of the ocean.

While Tag was resting in the control room of the rig, one of the workers notified him that there was an approaching ship. Tag was interested as to who would be lurking out in dangerous waters, especially since the area was restricted.

He thought it might be the CIA trying to pull something and went out with the crew on the support ship. If it were the CIA he would know their tactics and would love to help destroy his old colleagues.

The support ship was made out of the same material as the stealth bomber and was pitch black. The lights on the ship were turned off and it was hard to see, even when walking around on the deck. The structure reminded him of a large Coast Guard vessel that had been converted for other purposes.

They had left the rig and were in a holding position about two miles from the Poseidon. Tag was standing on the bridge waiting for the call and from his location he could see a faint light off in the distance. It was moving slowly and he knew that was their target.

*****

They slowed again and Aaron's heart was beating with an intensity he could almost hear over the silence. He knew they must be close and kept checking his fuel situation to make sure he had enough to return.

Already used to the low rumbling of the old engine, Aaron heard another sound penetrating the otherwise serene conditions. He didn't want to slow and leave Skilos too far in front of him, so he tried listening over the sounds of the boat. It sounded like another boat was gurgling along somewhere close by.

Looking around, Aaron did not see other lights. There couldn't be a boat around, he thought. I would at least see its lights. The sound made him nervous, especially since he could not detect the source so he listened harder.

He noticed that the sound had changed. It was getting closer. This worried him greatly. If it wasn't a boat, what was it he asked himself? Would there be another boat out here without its lights on? Am I going to run into it? Will it run into me?

Aaron could not see anything in the view of his spotlight except Skilos, and he was still heading forward. It must be safe, he thought. Skilos wouldn't take me all this way just to lead me into an oncoming ship.

The sound was getting louder and he recognized it. It was not another engine. It was bubbles. Bubbles coming from the water somewhere in front of the boat as if a giant lay under the surface blowing air. Whatever it was, it must be massive, Aaron thought.

The bubbles were very close but he could not see them in the spotlight yet. In fact, when he realized what he was looking at, it was nothing at all, only water. Even Skilos was gone.

Suddenly, there was a blinding light. It was coming from under the boat and it lit up everything. He couldn't see the stars anymore. It was as if he had been instantaneously transported to a circular room of light in the middle of the ocean.

The bubbles now surrounded the boat and it shuddered in the lit water. Aaron knew his life was in danger and that he had to ditch the boat to survive. He wasn't worried about what he would say to Bob or Mike. He wasn't worried about the damage he had done by taking the boat out without permission. Aaron was scared for his life.

He ran out of the control room and around to the back of the boat. He already had his wet suit and booties on, and it was a good thing. He grabbed his flippers, mask and snorkel. There was no time to mess with his regulator, tank and vest.

With his essentials, Aaron jumped up on the back of the boat and jumped off. He almost made it in time.

As he jumped, the boat jerked upward. There was a loud sound as if the boat had run aground. He lost his footing and slipped. With a thud, Aaron's body slammed onto the surface of the water. He had landed on something hard.

Pain shot through the right side of his body. The fins and snorkel flew from his hands. His body let out the sound of the wind being knocked out of him, and he couldn't breathe in for a few seconds.

Looking out, he saw the mask, snorkel and fins floating on the surface of the water. They were only a few feet from him. Without thinking or breathing Aaron slid across the hard, wet metallic surface. With the wet suit on, his body slid easily. As he entered the water, Aaron grabbed his essentials. He put them on as quickly as he could and swam fast to get out of the bubbling water and away from the light. He didn't know what it was, but he knew it was not where he wanted to be.

As he was swimming, Aaron realized he could breathe again, but that it was painful to do so. The adrenaline was wearing off. He hoped he hadn't hurt himself too badly. If there was blood, it wouldn't matter if he was hurt or not. The sharks would eat him alive before he could be picked up by anyone.

The light was about fifty yards away and he kept swimming in the opposite direction. Looking around he realized he could see lights in the distance. They were bobbing up and down and they seemed to go off and on as they went in and out of sight. It must be a boat, Aaron thought, there was no land in sight. It was in the direction he was swimming and he started to kick faster.

As he got closer to the boat, Aaron heard voices. This seemed strange because they weren't coming from the direction of the boat.

Aaron turned back to the light that was coming from the water. It was still there but his boat was not. It had vanished.

He looked around quickly and thought he must be hallucinating. How could his boat have disappeared in a few minutes, he thought? Why was he hearing voices in the middle of the ocean? Maybe there was no boat coming to rescue him. It would not make sense for another boat to be in the same vicinity. What were the chances? As these thoughts raced through his head, he began to panic. His breathing became labored for a few seconds until his army training kicked in.

There must be a rational explanation, he thought and he began to calm himself down again. Turning back around, Aaron still saw a boat heading his way. He rubbed his eyes and it was still there. Then he heard voices again, from the direction of the light. He tried, but could not make out what the voices were saying. It didn't sound as if there was a voice talking to him. It sounded like other people having a conversation.

Maybe he was already dead, he thought? Maybe the voices wanted him to swim to the light and when he did it would all be over. Maybe, if he swam towards the oncoming ship he would wake up in a hospital bed. Or maybe he would wake up, floating face up in the middle of the ocean only to await a slower death. Again, he pushed these thoughts out of his head and began to think rationally.

With his mask on, Aaron looked under the water towards the light. There he found the source of the voices. There were divers, riding around the lit area with underwater scooters. Some of them had surfaced and were talking. He also saw his boat. It was stuck to whatever had stopped it and was being sucked downward. The divers must be assisting in the process, he thought. But they were also looking around. What were they looking for, he asked? Then it hit him.

This was what had happened to all the other boats and that plane. They were searching for bodies. No wonder there had never been survivors. The bodies had been stolen and all the wreckage was taken as well. He could see the bottom of the enormous mechanism that was pulling the boat down and he knew that it must be a magnet. What else could have stopped the metal boats that quickly and with such force?

The light was emanating from the bottom of it, which seemed to go straight into the bottom of the ocean. He had never seen anything like it. The magnet itself was huge. It looked like it was twice as large as the boat it had just sucked under the surface of the ocean. It must have been two hundred feet in diameter, he thought in amazement. He also saw part of an enormous engraved trident on the surface of the magnet and wondered what it meant.

The divers were still searching the area of the light, but were starting to venture farther out. Aaron knew that if they caught him, he would end up with the same fate others had met in the last few months. He knew he was alive, and wanted to keep it that way.

Aaron turned to swim away and his breath left him immediately. He would have screamed but his senses got the better of him. The divers would have heard him if they were above water.

Skilos was right in front of his face as he turned to swim away. He scared the shit out of Aaron, but after the shock wore off, he was the happiest human floating hopelessly at sea.

"Skilos," Aaron said quietly, overjoyed at his companion's return. "Good boy!" Aaron was rubbing Skilos' belly as he turned over to have it rubbed. They were both happy to see each other.

"Let's go, Skilos," Aaron said, motioning away from the light. "Let's go home, okay?" Skilos agreed with Aaron and turned over so he could grab his dorsal fin. Aaron happily attached himself to his savior.

Skilos started swimming in the direction of the oncoming ship. Aaron wasn't sure what the boat was doing in the area and decided to remain quiet. As they got closer he realized the boat was made from solid black material. The only way he could have detected its presence in the darkness were the lights on the deck. If the lights had been turned out, he would have run right into it.

Skilos swam along side the boat, passing it slowly without making a sound. They were thinking on the same wavelength. As they swam, Aaron heard some voices. They were busy with something, but he had no idea what it was. They were all speaking Spanish with heavy Latino accents. Aaron would never be able to understand what they were saying.

He tugged softly on Skilos to make him slow down, as if it would help him understand the foreign language. Aaron listened harder to the conversation above him. Listening, he realized that one of the men speaking did not have an accent. It sounded like an American trying to speak Spanish. He wasn't even trying to disguise his accent.

The man sounded angry and was shouting things in Spanish that Aaron still did not understand. Aaron pulled Skilos around so they were now heading in the same direction as the boat. It was not moving fast and it was easy to keep the same pace. The men continued their heated conversation and Aaron continued to listen, hoping the man would say something in English.

Aaron could hear the men very clearly and he knew they must be standing almost directly above him. He kept Skilos swimming along side the boat so that they would not be detected. Aaron was sure that whatever was going on, this boat also had something to do with it.

The conversation above them was still raging, turning into a heated argument, and the light emanating from the water was drawing nearer again. If he didn't hear anything he could understand soon, he would be forced to turn back. Detection certainly meant death or capture and he could afford neither.

There was a crescendo in the argument above and then things went quiet. There had been no English in the conversation. Aaron was about to turn Skilos around and begin their trek to the shore before something hit the water right next to his head. It was a cigarette butt. It fizzled as soon as it hit the water, then floated backwards as it had no momentum to carry it forward.

Aaron looked up and saw a pair of hands stuck out over the side of the railing directly above his head.

"Fuckin' Spics! I could run a drug cartel better than Lopez, that bastard," the voice said. "You'd better find me some dead bodies," he yelled back towards the crew.

The voice sounded oddly familiar, but Aaron didn't want to stick around any longer and increase his chances of capture. He tugged on Skilos and they slowed, staying right alongside the stealthy black boat. As they lost more speed the boat passed, still heading towards the light emanating from the bottom of the ocean. Aaron did not want to turn Skilos around and continue swimming until he was sure no one on board would notice the movement in the water below.

Watching the boat move slowly away, its name was etched in his memory. The large letters were written in a color that made it barely visible against the black backdrop, but it was still legible: *La Fantasma*. It was written just above a large trident in a triangle, exactly like the one he had seen on the magnet, only smaller. There was no city on the boat, under the name. It just read "Colombia".

*****

After all of the wreckage had been collected, Tag and the support ship went back to the research center. The rest of the crew stayed behind while he traveled through the tunnel, back to the underground compound.

While he was still above water they had not found any bodies and Tag was furious. He was hoping that they would have found a body after he had left the boat. If there was nothing, he thought the CIA might already be on their trail. Maybe they had put a detection device on the boat to track it. Maybe they already knew where the Poseidon complex was. These thoughts and more sped through his head as he sped towards the Poseidon complex.

The man in the control room saw Tag's angry face in the screen, as he came up to the door. He made a comment to himself and let Tag in the compound. Tag rushed into the dark storage room and headed straight for the door to the wet room. The light above the door was already green and he could hear machines and people working on the wreckage.

He opened the door and went through. The wreckage of the boat was lying crooked on the floor. There were already men with blowtorches working on ripping the boat to shreds. He walked briskly over to one of them and asked, in Spanish, if they had found any bodies. The man took off his safety mask and pointed to the other side of the large room where two men were talking with Señor Lopez. Tag took off in their direction.

As he got closer, Tag could tell they were talking about the debris on the floor at their feet. He thought that maybe they had found some sort of tracking device. When he reached the three men, he realized the topic of conversation was an air tank. It looked like any other tank that the divers in the compound used, but Señor Lopez looked worried. His chin was cradled in his palm and he was tapping his face with his fingers. It was the first time Tag had ever seen Señor Lopez worry about anything. But even in this state of worry, Señor Lopez looked calm.

"What is it," Tag asked eagerly. Seeing Lopez calm did not make Tag feel the same way.

Lopez looked up from the air tank at Tag, but did not say anything. He looked back down at the tank and pointed to it, then spoke. "They found this on board."

"So, it's a tank. I'm sure there are a million like it."

"Take a closer look," he said quietly.

Tag looked at the tank and saw a piece of white paper with writing on it taped onto the tank. He moved closer to the tank and leaned down. There were two words that made him shiver: *Aaron Silver*.

Tag stood stone cold. He did not say a word, just kept staring at the tank. Tag knew the name but could not place it. He knew it was not one of his agents, but for some reason he knew that name.

"You know it," Lopez asked coldly.

"Yes." His trance was still undisturbed.

"Who is it?"

At first he wasn't sure. Tag couldn't pick out the name from a former context. Then it came to him

"Dolphin research," he thought out loud, his eyes wide.

Tag remembered exactly who it was. Was the CIA playing games with him, he thought? What the hell would this researcher's boat be doing all the way out here?

"What do you mean, dolphin research?" Lopez moved in front of Tag. Tag's eyes fixed on Lopez's face and he came back to where he was. "Is this man dangerous?"

"Of course he's dangerous," Tag yelled. "We gave him a scholarship to study dolphins in Kingston. He's at the research lab there, doing self-recognition tests if I recall."

"Well he doesn't seem to be there anymore," Lopez screamed, as he got in Tag's face. Lopez was steaming, his face red. He took a few breaths in front of Tag, staring into his eyes. Quietly, he continued. "He seems to be quite close to the heart of my operation."

Lopez waited and calmed himself a little more before speaking again. He backed from his position in Tag's face and continued. "If he's not dead, floating around in the sea somewhere, you must find him. You must go to Kingston and see if he's still alive. If he is, see if he knows anything. It could be, by the grace of God on his behalf, that he knows nothing. If he doesn't, leave him alone. If he knows anything, and I mean anything, you kill him. But only if he knows something, you understand? I don't want any unnecessary trails." Lopez paused for a moment and looked directly at Tag. "Do you understand?"

"Yeah." Tag was still in shock. How did this kid from Harvard end up right above the Poseidon Project he wondered?

"And make sure not to get caught yourself. They're probably looking for you as well."

"Don't worry about that. They're my men. I know everything about them. They'll never see me."

"Go then. And make sure that if he tells anyone, you are the only one left alive to know about it. Go to Kingston and find him!"

CHAPTER 14

Skilos had pulled Aaron to Morant Point by early morning and Aaron was exhausted. He told Skilos to return to the research center and Aaron hitched a ride back to Kingston with a trucker. During the entire ride, Aaron's mind raced with the implications of what had transpired the night before and he could not fall asleep.

He arrived at his house at nine in the morning. Aaron, grateful to the driver, ran inside, grabbed fifty dollars and paid the man for his troubles. The driver was more than overjoyed and thanked Aaron profusely for the money before he drove away.

Still exhausted, Aaron went back to his room and slept. His brain was too tired to focus on his dilemma anymore.

Aaron awoke late in the afternoon with a terrible thirst. He stood up and poured some water into a cup, which was resting on the countertop adjacent to his bed. Finishing it quickly, he sat back down. He wasn't exhausted anymore, but he could have slept longer if his brain had not started working again.

No one has called me, he thought. Which means that no one has noticed that the boat has gone missing. This'll give me a little more time to either come up with a story, or tell the truth.

Aaron needed to clear his head. He took a shower, put on some clean clothes and went to the coffee shop a few minutes away from where he lived.

Although it was late in the afternoon, the sun was still high and bright. Aaron was wearing his sunglasses to combat the strong rays hitting his face. He parked his bike in front of the coffee shop and went inside. There were only a few customers in the small establishment but it made the room seem even smaller.

Aaron ordered a large, black coffee from the man behind the counter. He usually liked lots of sugar and cream, but he needed it to be strong. Grabbing a napkin, Aaron walked outside and sat at a small metal table on the sidewalk. There were two chairs at the table and the whole set was rusted. The white coloring of its former life was barely visible.

After a few seconds, a patron came out of the shop with a cup of coffee and a pastry. He walked around Aaron and sat down at the same rusted table. Aaron wasn't staring at the man but he looked oddly familiar. He looked like every other middle-aged American tourist he had seen throughout the summer. This one was slightly overweight and was wearing the typical Hawaiian shirt and khaki shorts. The oversized legs that stuck out of his shorts were white, matching his face and arms. To block the sun from giving him too much of a tan, the man was wearing sunglasses and a straw hat. There was no doubt that he was wearing sunscreen too. Aaron could smell it over his coffee.

Aaron turned the other way while the man was getting settled in his chair. He didn't want to be disturbed. He came to the coffee shop to think about what was going to transpire over the next few days. He didn't need some stupid tourist asking him questions.

"Nice day, huh," the tourist asked.

Aaron did not respond with words. He just turned his head and nodded in the man's direction, then went back to his thoughts. Looking at his face for a split second more, he noticed the man had a mustache.

"Yeah, I can't wait to get to the other side of the island with my tour and lay out on the beaches of Negril," the man said, cutting the silence again.

Aaron turned back to the man. "If you don't mind, I really just came here to relax and think. I'm sorry." Aaron was annoyed. He was trying to be polite but it did not work. Aaron turned again with his back to the tourist.

"Is there something on your mind?" The man was still being friendly.

Aaron turned back, placed his coffee on the small table and looked directly at the man. "Nothing that I'd really like to discuss with a perfect stranger, thank you very much." He was starting to get agitated.

"Sometimes it's good to tell your problems to perfect strangers. You never know, sometimes they can help," the man said cheerfully.

Aaron thought this man looked and sounded familiar but he could not put his finger on it. It was like seeing someone you knew from sometime in your past but not being able to pinpoint that time or place. He stared at the man in silence for a moment trying to remember.

Maybe the Colombians had found him, Aaron thought for a moment. Then that thought subsided. If they had found him, they would have killed him, he thought, not sat with him and asked questions. But it didn't matter who he was talking to; Aaron was not going to tell anyone what he had seen.

I could lie, though. Maybe this man could help me think of an excuse for why the boat was missing.

"Okay." Aaron sighed. "I'm doing dolphin research here in Kingston and I lost the head researcher's boat."

"You lost a boat? How did you lose a boat?" The man was amused at Aaron's trouble.

Aaron had to think quickly. It was good he had his sunglasses on. He could mask the telltale part of his face, his eyes.

"I was doing some research. You know, diving with some dolphins off the coast and when I came back up the boat was gone," he said simply.

"It was gone? What do you mean it was gone? You think someone stole it while you were down under?" The man sounded confused.

Aaron looked down and started acting like he was embarrassed. "Actually, I think I left the engine running and... Well..."

"Yeah, spit it out."

"Well... I think I forgot to anchor the boat," Aaron finished lying and kept his face down, looking at the table. The man started laughing heartily, but not so loud as to attract any extra attention.

"Forgot to anchor it? That's priceless. I've got to tell that one to the kids."

Aaron had achieved his goal of asking for advice but at the same time kept the truth as to what really happened, a secret.

The man stopped laughing and became serious. "Well, I think you might be in luck. I happen to be in the boat finding business," he said softly.

Something about his tone of voice wasn't right. Something about the man had changed in that instant.

He slowly slid a business card across the table. Aaron looked down and immediately recognized the call letters and insignia. This man was from the CIA. His name was Tag Millwood.

Aaron's defenses kicked in immediately. "Hey, I didn't do anything, okay! You've probably got me mixed up with some other guy. Listen, I don't have to talk to you I know I have rights," Aaron said franticly.

He wasn't sure why this agent had approached him and he was suddenly uncomfortable. "I'm sorry, I've got to..." Aaron stood abruptly but the man put a heavy hand on his shoulder and sat him down again.

"Listen, you're not in trouble."

"Then what do you want to talk to me about?" Aaron looked around nervously, as if they were being watched.

"Look at me. Look here."

Aaron stopped darting his eyes around and looked at the agent next to him.

"I want to talk to you about your boat."

Aaron was looking at the man as he talked and it clicked. "I know you!"

"You do?" Tag tightened his grip on the pistol in his pocket.

If Aaron said anything that he didn't like, he would shoot him and leave. There weren't many people out and it would be easy to do if the victim could not point out the culprit.

"Yeah, you were that guy giving news briefings about the missing boats and planes off the coast," Aaron smiled as if he had met a celebrity.

Tag loosened his grip. "That's right," he said with a smile. "That was me. Actually that is what I want to talk with you about." Tag could tell he had him now. If Aaron knew anything, he would spill the beans, Tag thought. And, if he did, Tag was sure Aaron would not be opposed to taking a ride with him to "headquarters."

Aaron tensed up. Why would someone be asking him questions about the disappearances, he thought nervously? They couldn't have known I was out there, could they?

"We know you were out in the restricted area, son. We need to know if you saw anything. Anything at all that might help us find out what's been going on over there. Time is running out and you can help." Tag paused for a moment and looked Aaron in the sunglasses. "Can you help your country," he asked seriously, trying to get something out of him.

Aaron was silent for a moment. He didn't know what to say. He did know something, but he did not know how the CIA would know, in less than twenty-four hours, that he had been in the restricted area. Aaron was confused.

"I don't know what you're talking about." Aaron sounded sincere. "I mean, I know what's been going on. I see all the reports on TV and I read about it in the papers, but that's about it."

"Don't play dumb with me kid," Tag said, getting upset. "Not very many people can play dumb with intelligence agencies and get away with it."

"Sir, I'm not playing dumb with you. I really don't know what you think I know, that would be helpful." He was lying through his teeth and doing a good job.

"Listen!" Tag looked down into his coffee and then back at Aaron. "We found your wreckage in the restricted area; right near where everything has been disappearing. We also found a dive tank with your name on it," he said conclusively, then remained silent for a minute, staring at Aaron. "I've lost five of my own men in that area and I need to know what's been going on!"

Aaron was suddenly terrified. He knew this man was lying. He recognized him as the man from TV during the news briefings but something was wrong.

Aaron had seen his wreckage being dragged under by the gigantic magnet. There is no way the CIA could have recovered my tank or wreckage, he thought as his heart started pounding and his palms started sweating. Aaron knew this man was working for the CIA but something did not fit and he had to leave before his nervousness gave him away.

Despite his anxiety, Aaron's expression remained calm. If he overreacted it would mean his life.

Aaron looked down at his sweaty palms as he rubbed them together and sighed. "Listen, what I told you before was the truth. I was doing some research with the dolphins out off the coast. I don't know exactly where I was. I left the boat to dive and when I came back, the boat was gone. That's it. I didn't find or see anything out of the ordinary when I was out there. If the boat happened to drift into the restricted area, as you said it did, it was without me on board." Aaron paused and looked calmly and directly at Tag. "I'm sorry I can't help. I really wish I could."

"How do you explain the tank we found with your name on it then? If you were diving you would have had it on, right," Tag asked accusingly.

"The kind of diving I do with the dolphins isn't deep but it does last for a long time so we often take a few tanks with us."

"I see. But how did you get back if you were stranded in the middle of the water with no boat," he asked as his eyes narrowed.

"I was using an underwater scooter. When I came up and there was no boat, I just pointed it towards the land and came back in. We never go out so far that we can't see land; just in case situations like that arise. I was lucky I was in close, I don't know anything about navigation." He was doing an exceptional job of keeping calm for the state he was in but it would not last for long.

Tag sat quietly back in his chair, brooding. He wanted so much to grab the kid by his neck and squeeze out of him what he wanted to know. He wanted to put his gun in Aaron's face and pull the trigger until it was empty, but that would accomplish nothing and probably get him caught. Tag thought the kid was lying but he was following orders. He, too, knew that if there was a long trail of bodies that he would be caught easily.

"If you're lying to me kid. If you're withholding even one piece of evidence that could solve this case, you'll never see the light of day again!" Tag leaned forward and continued. "I guarantee it."

"I'm sorry." Aaron was not fazed by Tag's threat. "I don't know anything that could possibly help."

"No, I'm sorry. I've been under a lot of stress lately with this case. As you can imagine, everyone's on my back about this." He was trying to be sincere. If Tag wanted Aaron to confess he had to make him feel comfortable.

"It's alright. I understand," Aaron lied.

"Listen, if you remember anything, anything at all that could help, please call me. My number is on the card. It's my private line."

"Sure." Aaron placed the card in his pocket.

He still seemed calm. Nothing about his appearance was giving away his mortal fear for the man less than two feet away from him.

"And one more thing before you go. Don't go telling anyone about this. It's sensitive information and we don't want all the Jamaicans thinking they've got CIA agents running around all over the place. It'll make everyone antsy. Alright," Tag asked, with a smile.

"No problem." Aaron then got up and went to his bike on the curb. He threw his coffee out in a trashcan on the street then put his hands directly in his pockets. They were shaking but he calmed them as he pulled them out again to operate his bike.

Just before he drove off, he turned back to Tag. "I'll call you if I remember anything!" Aaron waved as he rode off down the street.

"I'll be watching you, kid," Tag said angrily to himself.

CHAPTER 15

When he arrived at Sarah's apartment, his hands were still shaking. He was scared out of his mind. He had been closer to death in the Israeli Army but he felt almost helpless now without any intelligence or weapons of his own. If he was going to survive, he would need to use the ultimate weapon — his mind.

Aaron thought that disappearing for a few days might help and he wanted Sarah to come with him. She was the only one who could calm him at this point.

He wanted to tell her everything. Aaron knew he could trust her, but she would probably think he was crazy or delusional, he thought.

He ran up the stairs to her apartment after half-heartedly parking his bike next to her Jeep. Before he knocked on the door, Aaron looked around again, suspicious that someone was following him. He didn't see anyone and knocked hesitantly on the door.

Sarah answered a few seconds later. When she opened the door Aaron slipped inside quickly. She could tell something was wrong, but she had no idea how severe the situation was.

"What's wrong," she asked with a look of concern on her face. Sarah walked over to Aaron who was standing nervously by her couch. He was too nervous to sit.

She put her hands on his face and he covered them. "We have to go," he said, short of breath. "I mean, I need to go and I want you to come with me."

"What are you talking about? Are you in some kind of trouble? Aaron your hands are shaking," she said as she pulled his hands down to hold them still.

"I am." He walked to the other side of the room nervously.

"What? What kind of trouble?" She followed him around the room.

"I can't tell you now, but come with me and I'll tell you. Please come with me," he begged, as they now stood by the door.

"You can tell me anything," Sarah said sincerely.

"I know, but not here." He was speaking softly as he moved over to the window and perused the parking lot through the blinds. "We must leave! Is there anyplace you go to get away from things, where no one can find you?"

"Yes, but... Aaron, you're scaring me! What's going on?"

"I'll tell you, but not now. We don't have time. Where is it that you go? Where do you go to get away?" He was pleading with her, holding her arms tight.

"Negril." She was now numbed from the shock of his fright.

"Negril, perfect. Listen, meet me in thirty minutes at the botanical gardens. Remember, where we had lunch on the porch?"

"Yes?"

"Right there, thirty minutes. Make sure you have a full tank of gas. We're going to Negril."

"But…"

"I promise, I'll tell you everything on the way," he finished hurriedly.

Just before he left, Aaron kissed her but she was too shocked to return any affection. Aaron hugged her hard. He didn't know if he would see her again. He didn't know if he'd make it to the botanical gardens at all.

*****

Forty-five minutes later, Sarah was waiting for Aaron on the porch where they had eaten lunch the day after they met. She kept looking at her watch and growing more worried by the second. Aaron had been freaked out and she hoped he was okay.

As she looked down at her watch again, Aaron came around the side of the restaurant. He was wearing sunglasses, a baseball cap, shorts and a tee-shirt. He looked normal but she knew he was distraught about something.

He walked up to her and took her arm firmly. "Let's go," he said quietly. "Where did you park?"

"Outside the park," she answered a split second before he led her to the park entrance. Aaron talked to her as they walked to assess the situation and to keep from looking too suspicious.

"You weren't followed, were you?" He didn't look at her as he spoke.

"Followed? Aaron, what are you talking about? Have you lost your mind?" She was trying to stop but he would not let her.

"I'll take that as a 'no'," he answered angrily. He was upset that she did not seem to understand the severity of the situation although he had not explained anything to her.

Sarah looked at Aaron angrily but walked the rest of the way to her car in silence. They got in her Jeep and headed off to Negril. Every few minutes

Aaron looked back to see if anyone was following them. As far as he could tell, the coast was clear.

After about thirty minutes into the drive, he relaxed and sat back in his seat. Aaron was exhausted from the events of the past two days. He had been wired before only because he knew he was in terrible danger and needed to hide somewhere. Aaron felt safe now with Sarah, even if she was pissed at him for not telling her what was going on. He would tell her soon enough, he thought. If they got to Negril safely, he would tell her.

*****

It was late in the afternoon when they arrived in Negril. Aaron was awake when they pulled into the lot of a small, out-of-the-way motel. There wasn't much that was out-of-the-way for a small town like Negril, but this was it. It wasn't on the beach and it was farther south than most of the major motels. The small motel was a ranch-style building with the rooms lined up in a row on each side of the office.

Aaron got out of the Jeep when it stopped. "I'll pay for it. Wait here," he said to Sarah who did not answer.

He went into the small office and paid for the room with cash. After he was done filling out false information on the paperwork, Aaron returned to Sarah who was waiting impatiently in the Jeep. She was leaning back in her seat when he came to her open window.

"You want to go in?" He dangled the key in front of her.

Again, Sarah did not answer, clearly agitated. She turned around, pulled a small bag from the back seat, and gave it forcefully to Aaron. As she got out of the car, Sarah grabbed her own small bag. Aaron looked around nervously but did not see anyone as they entered room eight of the beige, stucco structure with red tile roofing.

There were two double beds with a dresser and television in their room. In between the beds was a nightstand with a lamp and telephone. Aaron thought it looked like any other motel he had ever been in.

"I'm going to the bathroom," Aaron said, and went to the back of the room, entered and shut the door.

Sarah was exhausted from the drive and she sat down on one of the beds. She was very angry with Aaron and was not going to move until he told her the whole story. She knew from his actions that it was something serious, but how serious could it be, she asked herself? Did they really have to go all the way to Negril?

Sarah sat with her back against the headboard and her hands crossed over her chest until Aaron came out of the bathroom. When he did, Sarah got up and took him by his shoulders and forcefully sat him down on the bed.

"Okay, okay," Aaron pleaded, looking at Sarah. "I'll tell you what happened."

Sarah let go of Aaron and sat down in front of him, waiting.

"To make a long story, short," Aaron began, then thought better of it. "Actually, I need to start from the beginning. But first, you're not going to tell anyone, are you? I need to know I can trust you just to listen to what I have to say and give me good advice. Can you promise me that you won't tell a soul about this? Please?"

"I promise! Now, tell me what happened!"

"Alright. First off, you know the research I've been doing?"

"Yeah, the self-recognition work."

"Yes, well, I've been doing some other research on the side." He noticed her facial expression turn from anger to confusion. "I was watching some of the tapes that we've been taking of the dolphins and I noticed a pattern of behavior that seemed like some sort of communication. I isolated the sounds the dolphins were making and they played right into it. I can tell them, in their own language to move in a particular direction. I broke through the dolphin communication barrier," Aaron said calmly.

Sarah's chin dropped. "That's great, but what the hell are we doing out here?" Aaron had not satisfied her curiosity.

"That's not it. It's just the tip of the iceberg. Two days ago I was at the lab and Skilos wanted to leave. He was beckoning me to go topside and let him out. God, I can't believe it was only two days ago. It seems like it was in another lifetime. Anyway, I went and let him out of the tank. I thought he was gone until I saw him pop up next to the boat. He was still beckoning me. I figured he wanted to show me something out in the bay or in the gulf so I took the boat and followed him."

"You what?"

"I followed him." He knew that taking the boat out without permission was the least of his problems.

"You just took the boat without asking anyone?" It was apparent she disapproved. "What if something had happened?" Looking at his face, she knew that something had.

"Oh, my God! You wrecked the boat? Oh, my God they're going to *kill* you! Where is it now," she asked, not prepared for the answer.

"It sank."

Sarah was silent. She was in shock. She shook her head around quickly to try and dispose of the last statement. She couldn't believe he actually sank the lab's research boat. It was old but expensive. A look of disbelief still covered her face.

"It sank? Are you sure?"

"Yes, I'm pretty sure. I saw it go down."

"Oh, my God," Sarah said louder.

"It gets worse."

"It gets worse? What else did you do? Burn down the lab? Kill the dolphins? How could it possibly get worse?" Sarah was getting hysterical.

"Sarah, I'm in big trouble." Aaron placed a hand on her shoulder and focused her attention back to him.

"I'd say."

"No, the boat situation pales in comparison to what I'm about to tell you," he said, white as the sheets on the bed.

This calm, eerie statement quieted Sarah. She couldn't believe that anything could be worse than what she had just heard. His behavior over the last day seemed almost reasonable for what had happened. She could see why he would be afraid to confront Bob and the rest of the crew about the boat. But, what she was about to hear would not have entered her wildest dreams.

"You know all the boats and planes that have been disappearing off the eastern coast?"

"Yeah." Sarah was totally focused on the Aaron's words.

"I know why."

Sarah didn't say a word. She just kept staring at Aaron with a blank face.

"That's what Skilos wanted me to see. He took me out and wanted to show me what was going on. I guess he had seen it too and thought that we should know about it."

"It? What's, it," she asked, still too shocked for expression.

"It's what sank the boat. I was riding along slowly but I didn't have time to stop when I saw it. There was some light in the water and lots of bubbles coming from beneath me. I knew it couldn't be good so I bailed. When I jumped off, I landed on it and it knocked the wind out of me. I had no idea what it was at the time but when I swam away I looked back. It was a huge magnet! I'm talking, huge, like larger than a football field!" Aaron demonstrated with outstretched arms.

"It was out in the middle of the ocean and it was connected to the bottom of the ocean floor. It looked like it came out of some complex that had been built under the surface of the ocean floor. It was the magnet that sunk the boat and my guess is, everything else that's gone missing!"

Sarah was still speechless. There was nothing to say and it was hard to interrupt Aaron at this point because he was talking too fast.

Getting the story out felt good, and as scared as he was, it was nice to be able to tell someone.

"At first the whole situation didn't register. Nothing made sense, but then Skilos found me. He was taking me back to shore when we passed a boat that looked a lot like a stealth bomber. I slowed down to listen because I thought that I could find out what was going on. There were voices on board and I heard one of them mention a drug cartel and a guy's name." He paused for a moment and looked up, trying to remember. "Lopez! Yeah, that was it!"

"I didn't know what it all meant at the time but I think I do now. Also, when I left the area, I saw the country of origin of the ship. It was from Colombia. I had no idea why some people from Colombia wanted to sink boats and planes mysteriously out in the middle of the ocean, but then it all came together. A drug lord is sinking all the boats!"

"Drug lords," Sarah asked, finding that she could speak again.

"Yeah. I thought about it and if you think of the geography, it's a perfect location for what they are doing."

"What are they doing?"

"They're scaring everyone from going into that area because it's a perfect place for their drug traffic. They can take shipments straight from the Colombian coast to the U.S. It all makes perfect sense. If no one wants to sail in that area, they've got free reign. It's simple, expensive, but simple," Aaron continued at a fast pace. As he spoke, the scenario became even clearer to him.

"I read some articles last year in the *New York Times* about how the drug cartels were using the tuna industry to get their drugs into the U.S. They packaged drugs in most of their tuna cans and were shipping it to U.S. companies. The tuna would go to the companies and the drugs would go to the dealers. I guess they had been doing this for a while until the Coast Guard seized one of their shipments. This 'Bermuda Triangle' idea was their new way of staying ahead of the game," he finished, wide eyed.

"Is this really happening? This seems so surreal," Sarah said. She was too shocked to have any large reaction to what Aaron was telling him.

"That's not all, though," Aaron started again. Sarah couldn't believe there was more.

"I was approached by a CIA agent yesterday in Kingston and he wanted to know if I knew anything about what's going on off the coast!"

Sarah looked confused again. "Who was it?"

"Who was the agent," Aaron repeated.

"Yeah."

"What the hell does that matter? It's not like you would know who he is anyway!"

"Sorry, I was just curious. I mean, what am I supposed to ask? I hardly know what to comment on! I can't believe this is actually happening!"

"Look who's talking!"

"Did you tell him what you saw?" She was more intrigued now than shocked. The weight of the story had already hit her and she wanted more information.

"No, but he seemed a little sketchy."

"Of course he's going to seem sketchy, he's a secret agent," she said, thinking her answer to be obvious.

"Yeah, but he knew information that I don't think he could have known!"

"He works for the CIA, he's going to know more information than you think he does, Aaron!"

"Yeah, I guess that would make sense. But, at the time, I was scared someone would come after me for what I had seen."

"Aaron, I want to comfort you and tell you that no one will look for you and that the whole situation will just go away." Sarah was silent for a second, then continued in a nurturing tone. "But it won't go away. Aaron, you've got to tell the CIA about what's going on! Especially if you think the drug cartel is going to find you! This is your *life* you're dealing with here! All you've got to do is tell them what you saw and they can probably put you in some kind of witness protection program!"

"Right, like the witness protection programs where the bad guys always find you? No thanks!"

"Would you rather take your chances running on your own?"

"But I won't be able to live the life I want to live anymore! It's all over! Two days ago marked the end of my life! I'm living someone else's nightmare now," he said, starting to get scared again.

"Aaron, you wanted my advice and I'm giving it to you! From the outside, telling the CIA looks like the best choice right now! I'm sorry, Aaron," Sarah said softly. "I'm sorry all this had to happen to you." She leaned over and hugged her boyfriend.

He was consumed with a feeling of distress. He held onto Sarah tightly, hoping that it would give him divine inspiration.

Sarah held Aaron for a while until they lay down next to each other on the bed. Aaron's head was on Sarah's chest and she was running her fingers through his hair. They rested in silence for a while until Aaron spoke.

"I wish I could be here forever with you."

Sarah did not respond. She just took in what Aaron had to say for the moment.

"You know how years after something happened, you can go back to that place and time in your mind," Aaron asked. "I want to be able to close my eyes thirty years from now and come back to this motel room. I want to lie next to you and have you run your fingers through my hair. I feel safe right now. Amidst all this madness, I feel safe with you. In thirty years, I want to still feel safe with you."

After another moment of silence, Sarah responded, "You know, if you tell them what they want to know and they put you in a protection program, I would come with you."

Aaron sat up and looked at Sarah with loving eyes. "You would? You would give up your life to be with me? You would give up everything?"

"The way I look at it, I want *you* to be my life. If I didn't join you, I *would* be giving up everything."

"I love you," Aaron said with intent, just before he kissed Sarah passionately. They kissed for a minute then embraced, still resting on the bed.

"Okay," Aaron said with a small amount of confidence. "I'll call them when we get back to Kingston and tell them what I saw."

"You could call them from here."

"No, I'll call them when we get back. I want to spend some time alone with you. Just with you. It'll be like the calm before the storm. I know this'll be a time that I'll remember forever, no mater what happens."

Aaron and Sarah rested on the bed together. They did not speak; they just comforted one another until they fell asleep.

*****

The next evening Sarah and Aaron went to *Rick's Café* for dinner. *Rick's* was located at the southern edge of Negril, not too far from where they were staying. Sarah knew there would be a lot of people there and it would be easy to blend into the crowd of tourists.

They were seated immediately at a table at the far end of the restaurant, which was situated near the edge of cliffs overlooking the Gulf. Aaron had heard that the sunset from *Rick's Café* was the best in the world.

There wasn't a cloud in the sky and the hues were magnificent. To the east it was almost dark, but up above and farther west, the sky was light blue. Then, in the far western part of the sky, there were three distinct shades, each getting brighter, heading towards the sun.

They smiled at each other and held hands across the small, round table. A soft breeze blew across the open-air restaurant and made the palm trees talk to each other. Although the atmosphere in the restaurant was hopping, the only world that existed for Aaron and Sarah was around their small table.

"You know." Aaron paused. "My parents were here," he said, looking out onto the ocean.

Sarah did not respond. She knew it was hard for him to talk about his parents and she was not going to interrupt.

Aaron turned back to Sarah and she saw tears forming in his eyes. "They were at this exact table." He got a lump in his throat as he looked around.

After a few more seconds, Aaron could control himself no longer and began crying freely and he put his head down on the table. As he did, Sarah came around and put her arm around his back. She caressed his back as he continued crying.

"Do you want to leave," she asked into his ear.

Aaron shook his head slowly as he ceased his crying. He picked his head up and wiped his face with the white napkin as he began to speak.

"I didn't even think about it," he started with the lump still in his throat. "Until we sat down, I didn't even remember."

As he continued, Sarah could tell he was going to be okay and she returned to her seat across from him. She listened to him as he continued.

"There is a picture I still have in Boston." Aaron was trying to regain his composure as he spoke. "My parents are sitting here, at this table."

Sarah took some tissues out of her purse and gave them to Aaron. He took them graciously and blew his nose in one and placed it in his pocket.

"The last time I really remember crying about it was about a month after it happened. I was looking at old photographs and I ran across the one of them sitting at this table. When I saw it, I lost it and decided I didn't want to be reminded of them anymore." He paused for a moment, trying to hold back the tears. When he felt comfortable, he continued.

"I put all their pictures in a box and all of their possessions in storage. I never talked about it with anyone and avoided the topic whenever possible." Aaron took a deep breath and let it out slowly. His nose was still running so he used the second tissue and placed it with the other one.

"For years I have avoided any thought of my parents but here I am with you at the same table my parents sat at years ago. I feel like I've come full circle and I can't avoid it anymore. I mean, here I am, about to face one of the toughest moments of my life and I'm just now coming to terms with my biggest loss, my parents." Finishing his thought, he looked up at Sarah whose tears were slowly running down her face.

"Without you I don't think facing my fears would have been possible," he said to Sarah. "Thank you," he said, pausing again.

"Could you marry me," Aaron asked, smiling, trying to change the tone of the conversation. He was not trying to change the topic but he felt that he had finally moved on from his parents' death emotionally. And now that he had moved on, he could move on with facing his next fear and face it with confidence.

Sarah smiled. "I *could* marry anyone I want," she said jokingly, but before Aaron could get too embarrassed, she continued. "I'm just kidding. I *would* marry you." She looked directly at him without averting her eyes for a second.

"I would marry you, too."

They both understood what was coming in the next few days. Neither of them wanted to talk about it, but they knew they might never see each other after tomorrow, if things didn't work out the way they wanted them to.

A few moments later, the waiter came to Aaron and Sarah's table and saw that their eyes were red and how they were holding hands across the table. He thought the tears that he had missed must have been out of happiness as he approached. "Does the newly married couple know what they would like to have this evening," he asked cordially.

They both laughed softly and then Aaron answered. "I think my *wife* and I would like two glasses of your best Muscat wine."

"Sure thing. I'll be back in a moment." The waiter left the two alone again.

The couple was still staring at each other. They had not even looked at the waiter. It was like there was only a voice to answer to, and not a real person.

"That was cute," Sarah said.

"Well, I figured I'd just go with it."

They spent a few hours, eating, talking, laughing and reminiscing about the short summer they had together, and after dessert, they returned to the motel. They spent all night cuddling and caressing one another. They were in a somber mood but at the same time, happy to be together. They both knew that it might be their last night together.

They kissed as they lay on the bed together with all of their clothes on. Aaron was on top of Sarah, pressing himself against her firm body. Sarah ran her hands through his hair and pulled him even closer. Aaron slowly moved from Sarah's lips, to her neck, kissing every centimeter as he moved down to her collarbone.

The shirt she was wearing did not allow Aaron to kiss much farther down her chest, but he pushed the neckline as far down as it would go with his hands as he continued kissing. Knowing that he could go no farther, Aaron lifted Sarah up, pulled her shirt from her body, and unbuckled her bra. Her firm chest was now totally revealed.

Sarah relaxed back on the bed as Aaron continued kissing where he had left off. He moved slowly down her chest now that nothing was covering it. He kissed from the top of her right breast, all the way down to her waistline. She moaned as he continued. He loved kissing her body. Her skin was so smooth. It felt like velvet under his lips.

As he was kissing near her belly button, Sarah leaned up and turned Aaron on his back. She wanted him to feel her love, too. The reciprocation of love lasted late into the night. If this was going to be their last night together, it was going to be a good one.

CHAPTER 16

The ride back to Kingston had been quiet and solemn in
anticipation of what might happen in the days to come. Sarah made Aaron
promise he would tell the authorities what was going on. He knew it was the
right thing to do, but it scared him to think he knew something that could get
him killed. Aaron had been in more immediate danger during his army days but
when he did not know where the bullets might come from, his perceived danger
was greater.

"Call me as soon as you set up a meeting with the CIA," Sarah told Aaron
as they pulled to a stop a few blocks from the botanical gardens. He wanted to
walk the rest of the way to his bike in order to observe the area and make sure it
was not being watched.

"I promise I'll call you as soon as something's set," Aaron said before they
kissed. He looked at her intently, to get one last look just in case it would be his
last. Aaron wanted her face etched in his mind.

After studying her for a moment with his hand on her face, he exited the
Jeep with his backpack, hat and sunglasses on and started walking nonchalantly
towards the gardens. He was still very nervous and walked in a crowd of people
whenever possible. At other times he would purposely take wrong turns and
wait around the corner to see if anyone was following him. It appeared to be
safe.

He walked along the opposite side of the street from the gardens and
surveyed the entrance. Nothing seemed to be out of the ordinary, so he entered
the gardens and went around the side of the restaurant. Watching from the
corner of the building, he could see that no one was in the small gravel parking
lot. Convinced it was safe, Aaron took his helmet out of his bag and donned it.
If there was anyone looking for him, they might not recognize who was getting
on the bike until it was too late, he thought. He moved briskly towards his bike
and started it. Just then some people came out of the back of the restaurant.
Aaron turned his head quickly, scared that it might be too late for him to ride off
into safety.

With his heart pounding, he realized it was just a couple touring the island,
probably on their honeymoon. They're not looking for me, Aaron said, calming
himself. They walked lovingly, arm in arm to their rental car and got in.

Aaron took a deep breath and let it out. He was okay for now.

The bike started easily with one try and Aaron rode towards his home, but
he did not go straight there. He wanted to check the area first to see if his house

was being watched. After turning onto his street, Aaron became aware of everything. There were people walking up and down the street, which was normal. There weren't too many cars parked on the side of the street and there were no vans. He thought this was a good sign. He had always seen vans used as reconnaissance vehicles in the movies.

After another ride around his block, he felt safe and drove into his driveway. The sun was beating down and his head was sweating in the helmet. It felt refreshing to take it off and breathe. He looked around and still didn't see anyone or anything out of the ordinary, but he took his bike to the backyard just in case someone was looking for it.

Aaron entered his room cautiously. None of his possessions had been disturbed. Feeling more comfortable by the moment, he suddenly felt tired. He sat down on his bed and took out the card that Tag had given him. He knew he should call, but when he did, there would be no going back.

His eyes felt heavier and he decided to take a nap. Aaron figured that no one knew he was around and it was safe. He put the card on the nightstand next to his bed and lay down. Aaron was asleep within minutes.

*****

When he woke up Aaron felt cold sweat all over his body. He had sweated through his sheet when it was still hot outside but it was now cool and almost dark. The clock on the nightstand read eight. He rubbed his eyes, sat up and yawned softly. The card was exactly where he had left it, but he didn't pick it up yet.

Still not knowing what was going to happen after the call, he wanted to eat something and take a shower. He made satisfying macaroni and cheese and then got in the shower. The warm water washed off the cool sweat nicely, he thought as he rinsed the soap off of his body.

After drying himself Aaron changed into warmer clothes to suit the cooler night air. He put on a pair of blue jeans and a black, long-sleeved tee shirt. Comfortable and full now, he sat down on his bed and picked up the business card. He took a deep breath, let it out and dialed the number.

When the other line picked up, Aaron thought, his life would never be the same. He would live, if he lived, under an assumed name. He would live in a different place. He would do something different from what he always wanted to do: dolphin research. Aaron was right in thinking all of these things, but his life was about to change in ways that he couldn't even imagine.

"Yeah," the voice said as the phone stopped ringing. Aaron did not answer.

"Hello? Who is this?"

Aaron finally breathed and started talking. "Mr. Millwood?"

"Yeah. Who's this," he asked crassly.

"This is the guy you ran into at the café the other day," Aaron answered cautiously.

"Mr. Silver! Nice to hear from you." Tag was being very cordial now. If Aaron was calling, he must have been holding back and he must know something, he thought. And, if he knew something, Tag must find out what it was.

"Did you happen to remember anything that might be of use to our investigation," Tag asked nicely.

Aaron was frozen again. He knew that giving the information was the right thing to do, but his brain was trying to prevent him from saying anything.

"Mr. Silver? You still there?"

"Yes. I'm just a little nervous," he said honestly.

"I can understand that. Listen, before you start, let me tell you a few things to calm you down. Okay?"

"Alright."

"Okay, first of all you don't have to worry about a thing. If you know something that might be dangerous to you, we can put you in a witness protection program until your safety is guaranteed. And, if the information you have is not dangerous, you have nothing to worry about. All you can do is help. You're not hurting anyone by what you're doing. You would actually be doing a great service to your country and to people everywhere if you could help us solve this mystery. So, whenever you're ready you can tell me what you know and I'll send a car to come pick you up and take you to headquarters. Does that sound reasonable?" Tag finished explaining as he readied his pistol and prepared for Aaron's capture and disposal.

Aaron was more assured now and started telling Tag the surface of the story. "I do know why the boats and planes have been disappearing. I know how and why it's being done. And this information is very dangerous to me and to my girlfriend."

Tag paused a moment before answering. A girlfriend was a new twist. "Have you told anyone else besides your girlfriend?"

"No, just her, and she'll need protection, too," Aaron said decisively.

"Of course, and what's her name?"

"Sarah Gordon."

"Okay, I'm just writing this all down," Tag lied.

"I'd feel much safer if we discussed the rest of this at your office."

"Certainly. Listen, stay right where you are. I'll have a car sent for you in a few minutes and..."

"CIA, freeze," a black man screamed, as he burst through Aaron's door. The man was holding a pistol and pointing it at Aaron. Other men rushed in right behind the leader. Aaron, scared shitless, dropped the phone and put his hands up. He looked around quickly at the commotion before being forced, face first, onto his bed. He tried to struggle but it was no use.

Aaron was terrified and confused at the same time. If he was just talking with the CIA, he thought, why would they burst into his apartment? It didn't make sense.

As Aaron was being held down by one of the other men, the black man picked up the phone and started talking into it. "Who is this? Identify yourself," he demanded as the line went dead. The man dropped the phone on the floor. He no longer had interest in it.

The man who seemed to be the leader bent down and looked at Aaron, whose face was being pressed down on the bed. "You'll talk," was all he said. The man stood up again and said something to the other men.

They tied Aaron's hands behind his back, covered his head with a black cloth and lifted him off the bed. Aaron had no idea where they were taking him. He was too shocked to ask questions but he figured he wasn't going to die, at least not at the moment. They wanted to ask him questions.

They walked him out of the side gates and to the front of the house. He could feel the driveway under his feet and then he was pushed into a car. The rest of the trip was silent. No one spoke but he could feel two large men on either side of him. There was no way to get out. He was going along for the ride whether he liked it or not.

*****

"Fuck," Tag yelled as he threw down the phone. He knew the real CIA had gotten to Aaron before he could. The phone lay in pieces on the brown, shag carpeted floor of the hotel.

It was his fourth hotel in as many nights. He could not risk getting caught but he needed Aaron if he was going to keep the Poseidon Project secure. Tag was sure that they had found the blueprints by now and it was only a matter of time until they found the complex. Tag knew the agents would find him if he stayed in Jamaica too long. He needed to leave quickly or he would be caught.

But before he left, Tag had to take care of one more loose end. If he could secure the loose end, that would buy him more time. More time to pull the wool over Señor Lopez's eyes and slip into anonymity forever.

*****

It took a minute for Aaron's eyes to focus when they took the black cloth off of his head. Aaron squinted a few times and the sudden bright light wasn't piercing anymore. The black man from his room was sitting opposite him at the plain metal table. Other men were sitting around the table at the sides and watching both of them. There was one door to Aaron's right and a two-way mirror on the wall opposite him. He knew they were in a tall building because they had ridden in an elevator to arrive at their destination. He had felt the upward starting motion and the slowing of the cabin as it stopped.

Aaron's hands were still tied behind his back and he tried to shift his body to make the plastic ties more comfortable. He hadn't said anything on the way to this room and wasn't going to say anything until someone else spoke first.

He believed that there was no reason to be scared of these people. It had taken him a while, but he figured that the CIA must have been watching him and he hadn't noticed. Even after all his surveillance, Aaron still had no clue that he had been watched.

They must be working for Tag, he thought. They must have brought me to headquarters to meet him. Aaron thought that they were worried for his safety, bringing him the way they did. He thought their actions were a little overboard, but they were the professionals. They must have known what they were doing.

"Are you comfortable, Mr. Silver," the black man asked.

"Do you think you could take these ties off," Aaron responded calmly.

"Do you think it would be wise for us to remove them?"

"Why not?" Aaron was confused as to why they thought he might be dangerous.

The agent sat quietly for a moment, then motioned to one of his men. The man to Aaron's left got up and took off Aaron's handcuffs.

"We're not going to have any trouble with you, are we?"

"No," Aaron said, as if that were already an established fact. He looked up questioningly at the agent who unleashed him as he rubbed his sore wrists. The man went back to his seat without saying a word.

The black man sitting across the table picked up a small leather briefcase from the floor and placed it on the bare table. Looking around again, Aaron noticed that all of the men were wearing suits. They looked like businessmen, he thought.

"Aaron, my name is Agent Schwabb," the black man said as he opened the briefcase. Its contents were facing Agent Schwabb so that Aaron could not see what was inside.

"You're going to be cooperative and answer all of our questions. Is that clear?"

"I already said I was. Listen, I'm sorry I didn't come forward earlier but I was scared. Surely you can understand that," he said defensively. Aaron could not understand why the agents seemed so upset with him. After all, he thought, I'm cooperating completely.

Schwabb was mildly confused by Aaron's statement, but he didn't let it show. He took out a legal-sized envelope from the leather case and slid it across the table to Aaron.

"Go ahead. Take a look at it."

Aaron reached into the envelope and took out a large photograph. It was a picture of him speaking with Tag at the café.

"I don't get it. So what?" Aaron was totally confused. Why would they be showing me a picture of me talking with Tag, he thought. It doesn't make sense.

"We want to know what you two were talking about," Schwabb asked, getting upset at Aaron's seemingly insubordinate behavior.

Aaron laughed, thinking he had figured out what was going on. "And I thought communication was bad where I worked. Didn't he tell you guys anything?" He looked around the room for confirmation but there were no smiles and no understanding of what he was saying. Aaron looked back to Schwabb.

"He didn't tell you why you were bringing me here?"

"What are you talking about," Schwabb asked. Now he was confused.

"Tag and I already talked about this. He told me you were going to bring me here to discuss what's been going on off the coast and that I would receive protection."

There was no response from the men in the room. All of their expressions were blank.

"I am going to receive protection, right?" Aaron was now unsure of the promises he was made because of the response he was getting.

"This man told you he was an agent with the CIA," Schwabb asked, starting to uncover the basis for confusion.

"Yeah, he gave me his card. Why?" Aaron did not understand what was happening.

Schwabb sat back in his chair and looked around the room at the other men. Without verbal communication they were all thinking the same thing. A few seconds later it hit Aaron.

"He's not an agent, is he," Aaron stated coldly.

"He was. He's now working for someone else. We don't know who, but in any case he can't be trusted."

Aaron was silent. He was letting it all sink in. So much had happened and it seemed that every time, when he thought things were getting better, they were actually getting worse. There seemed no end to this puzzle that was his life. There were pieces at every corner, but they never matched the pieces he already had.

Agent Schwabb continued and Aaron looked up from his thoughts. "What did he talk to you about," he asked nicely, now that he knew Aaron's situation.

"About the disappearances out in the Gulf."

"Yes, we know he has connections to whatever is going on out there, but we don't know who he's working with. He's already killed to keep it secret. Did you tell him that you knew anything?"

"Here, I didn't," Aaron said, pointing to the picture Schwabb had passed across the table.

"That's good."

"But I told him I knew everything right before you broke into my room," Aaron said blankly. Aaron knew he was in trouble, but was calm about it. He was too stunned to have any emotion. "When you saw me on the phone? That's who I was talking to. He knows I know everything." Aaron was speaking in a monotone and was not looking at anyone. He was just staring off into nothingness as if he was thinking aloud to himself.

Schwabb was silent again for a few moments, letting the reality hit Aaron. "Do you know what this means?"

"Yeah, it means I'm in deep shit," Aaron said, trying to sneak some humor into his dismal situation.

"It means your life is in danger." Schwabb leaned towards Aaron again. "Do you truly know anything about what is going on out in the restricted area?" He clasped his hands on the table as he asked.

"Everything," Aaron said in a mechanically cold voice. "I think I know everything."

"Do you know exactly where and why all the boats are disappearing?"

"I know why, but I don't know where exactly."

"What do you mean you don't know where it is? I thought you said you knew everything." Schwabb stood from his chair, staring at Aaron.

Aaron followed him with his eyes. "I said, almost everything," Aaron repeated himself. "Let me tell you why I know all of this stuff and then you'll understand why I don't know where it is. But first, we might need some coffee."

Schwabb waved his hand in the direction of one of the agents and without a word, the agent left the room. Aaron started his story and a few minutes later the agent returned with a tray of four cups of coffee, one for each person in the room.

Aaron explained that Skilos had taken him to the site of all the disappearances. He told the agents that it had been at night and he didn't know how to read the navigational equipment on board. The agents listened to everything that Aaron had to tell and did not interrupt once to ask questions. They were so overwhelmed by the information that they were speechless. It was like three children during story time in kindergarten. The only information he held from them was Sarah's knowledge of the whole story and his involvement in communication research that he had uncovered.

Aaron knew that if the agents knew of his discoveries, they would surely want that information and he did not want them to have it. He also knew that Sarah was in trouble but he wanted to get assurances on protection first.

After Aaron finished, Schwabb started asking questions again.

"So, how did you know that dolphin wanted you to follow it?"

"Any researcher can train a dolphin to do a number of tricks. These dolphins are trained to move in certain ways to tell us what they want," Aaron lied.

"So this has nothing to do with their original form of communication?"

"Are you kidding? Every researcher in the world would love to uncover dolphin communication patterns! They've been doing research on that for years and haven't been able to uncover anything. You think a graduate student could just show up out of nowhere and find something? No, this stuff is all learned behavior," he said, trying to reassure Schwabb.

Schwabb thought about what he said for a moment and then moved to another subject. Aaron was relieved.

"I guess your story makes sense. There've been reports of heightened Colombian activity in the area for quite some time now. It's in a perfect location as well. From where they are, there's a clear shot to the Windward Pass and then on to the U.S. The drug traffic has been going unnoticed since this whole mystery began. They've been scaring everyone off to insure themselves smooth sailing."

"Yeah." This was already old news to Aaron. Now he wanted to secure a future for him and Sarah. They would probably need him to testify, Aaron thought and this was the time to bargain for a new life. "So, I guess you'll need to put me in a witness protection program or something, right," Aaron asked smugly.

"Actually, from what you've told us and from what we know about you. We'll need you and the dolphin to take care of this compound for us," Schwabb said, looking through another folder he had taken from his briefcase.

"What?" Aaron shook his head as if he didn't hear what Schwabb had said. He was dumbfounded. Why would they want *him* to destroy the Colombian compound, he asked himself? They wanted to send him to the last place on earth he wanted to be. "I don't think so," Aaron said authoritatively.

"You're the best man for the job as far as I can tell. You and your dolphin know the exact location." Schwabb paused, then flipped through some pages in his file and continued. "Besides, I see here that you've also had three years experience in the Golani brigade of the IDF." Schwabb looked up at Aaron from his papers. "One of the elite units of one of the best armies in the world if I'm not mistaken. Looks like you've got the right stuff."

"What are you talking about? First of all its pronounced Golani." Aaron corrected him in a perfect Israeli accent. "Second of all I was in the infantry, not the navy. Anyway, you know the general area of where this place is! Get a team of SEALS together and find it yourself!"

"We can't," Schwabb began, trying to convince Aaron steadily that he was their best option. "There's no way to pinpoint this place on sonar and if we spent the money it would take to send a whole team, it would cost us millions of dollars. If we send you, you know where to find it and the mission would be cheaper."

"What you're trying to say is that I'm more easily expendable than your precious SEALS. Sorry, I'm not buying it." Aaron sat back in his seat, arms folded across his chest.

Schwabb was agitated. He had no more patience to try and convince Aaron to do this job for them. He could turn to the navy but Aaron was right, he was more expendable, and to exploit him, Schwabb had one more ace up his sleeve.

"I didn't want to have do this, but you leave me no choice," Schwabb said as he grabbed a sheet of paper from the file in his hand and slid it across the table. Aaron picked it up and looked at it. Immediately he recognized the letterhead.

"Do you recognize the name of that company," Schwabb asked as Aaron studied the paper.

"Yes," Aaron answered, looking back at Schwabb. "It's from The International Cetacean Behavior Fund. It's the company that funds my research." He handed the paper back across the table as he finished. "So what?"

"That company is just a cover for the U.S. Government. The CIA runs that fund and has been interested in dolphin research for years." He leaned forward, towards Aaron. "We've been funding your research," he said softly. "You owe us."

"I don't owe you shit," Aaron declared emphatically.

"The hell you do!" Schwabb banged his fist on the table and stood again. "The hell you do! You'll do this job for us or you'll never work with another dolphin again," he screamed, pointing at Aaron. "We can make sure you never get a grant as long as you live. And, I'm not just talking about the Cetacean Research Fund. I mean you won't get money from anyone, anywhere, for anything. So, you can kiss your life-long dreams goodbye!" Schwabb took a few breaths and calmed down a bit, then continued.

"On the other hand. If you do this for us, the U.S. Government will be very grateful. You'll receive full protection from the CIA and you'll be able to work with dolphins. But it'll have to be at a top-secret government research facility. We can't protect you if you're doing the same kind of work in a public place. The Colombians would find you too easily, even with our protection. And even if you don't do this for us, the Colombians will still look for you. You're probably number one on their hit list right now." Schwabb sat down again. Aaron was listening intently to his proposition.

"So... You have two choices. Run on your own, where I'd give you five days to live even with your army training. Or, complete our simple task, and live the rest of your life safe and secure. Think about it. You've been living in anguish for the past few days. Do you want to feel like this for the rest of your life, which incidentally might not be too long? Or, would you like to get away from all this? We've got some nice dolphin research facilities in Hawaii that would be safe. I'm offering you paradise or death," Schwabb finished, holding out his two hands. "It's your choice."

He knew what Schwabb was saying was true but he did not want to believe it. Unfortunately, he did not have any leverage to argue with. "You can't do that! You can't blackmail me into helping you!"

"I just did," Schwabb said, remaining calm.

"And there's no way you can stop me from receiving money from other organizations!" Aaron was grasping at strings.

"Try me. Not that it really matters. You'd be dead before you left this island."

Aaron sat back in his chair, thinking. It was not enough. He got up and walked around the room, thinking, but there was not enough space. The fact that there were no windows made it even smaller. Aaron felt trapped in the small room. He knew Jason had spent some time aboard Israeli submarines and wondered how he did it. The space he lived in must have been more confining than this room, he thought.

Aaron didn't know much about Jason's service with the Israeli Foreign Intelligence. He knew not to ask. Jason could not tell him, or anyone, the details of his service. It would compromise Israeli national security even to tell someone with Aaron's security clearance.

"Can I think about it," Aaron asked calmly.

"You have twenty-four hours. But until then you will remain under our custody for your own protection."

"Can I go back to my room?"

"Too dangerous," Schwabb said plainly.

"What if your men escorted me?"

Schwabb thought for a few moments. It was probably safe enough, he argued to himself. He didn't think that Tag or anyone he was working with would suspect that Aaron would return to his room.

"Okay, but you can't sleep there. Gather some items that you want and return immediately."

Aaron and four CIA agents left in a large Suburban. Schwabb did not go along for the ride. He had received a call from the director and needed to attend to other business but before he did, Schwabb introduced Aaron to the leader of the excursion.

Agent McBride was a stocky, "donut shop" agent who didn't say much before or during the ride to Aaron's. And, because of the silence, and the visible world around, Aaron could think about his plight more clearly. Aaron knew Schwabb was right. If he was going to run on his own, he might not last long. He needed help, which the CIA was willing to give him, but at a price. They were screwing him out of his life and he wanted it back.

As Aaron thought about different strategies, his contempt for the CIA, Agent Schwabb, and Tag grew. He wished he had never gotten into this situation but he had no choice now. There was no looking back.

Before the Suburban stopped in Aaron's area, it circled the block and drove around the neighborhood, looking for anything suspicious. Aaron hoped they knew what they were doing because it had not helped him earlier.

After a few circles they pulled up to the curb a block away from where Aaron lived. "It'll be safer this way," Agent McBride explained. "We'll go from here on foot, through some backyards and into your room. Schaffer, you stay here with the van. We'll escort Aaron to and from his room." McBride cocked his black pistol and checked his small radio.

"Yes, sir," the driver responded.

"Alright, then, let's go. We shouldn't have a problem. Most people should be sleeping by now. Just keep quiet," he said to Aaron.

It was well after midnight when they stepped out of the van and sneaked into one of the neighbor's backyards. Two of the agents stayed just ahead of Aaron, keeping a lookout to make sure everything was safe and the third stayed behind the group in case of any surprises.

This route to his room made more sense than the one that he had taken earlier, Aaron thought. If indeed someone *were* watching the house, he would not be able to detect an entry if it was made from the back.

At the end of the first backyard they came to a low, metal linked fence. There was no obstruction of their view to the next yard and it seemed clear but the agents in front of Aaron went first to make sure. After determining that it was safe, they signaled for Aaron to follow.

Aaron jumped over easily and the last agent followed closely behind. Aaron felt like he was back in summer camp, on a raid of the girls' cabins. It was fun in a way and the thought took his mind off of his situation briefly.

There were many bushes and small trees in the yard that allowed them to move swiftly without drawing any attention and they reached the other side of the second backyard in less than a minute.

The amount of light to guide their way was sufficient, spilling into the darkness from nearby houses and street lamps. It was a good thing that they did not need flashlights. It would have brought too much attention to their movements and would have been dangerous.

The next obstacle blocked not only their entrance to the next yard but also their sight. Aaron recognized this fence. It led to his backyard, a six-foot tall wooden fence, whose posts were solid and lay edge-to-edge.

McBride motioned to the taller agent to boost him, in order to survey the yard before entering. Once he could see, he peered quietly around Aaron's backyard and then returned to the group below. McBride gave an "okay" sign with his fingers and was boosted up again. This time he pulled the rest of his overweight body over and dropped to the other side with a small, quiet thud.

They all went over in this manner except for the last agent. Being much taller than the others, he jumped up, grabbed the top of the fence and pulled himself over without any help. They continued slowly to Aaron's room, guns drawn, on the right side of the house from where they were.

As they neared the door, McBride motioned to Aaron for the key and Aaron handed it to him. He opened the door quickly but silently and another agent rushed into the cramped area, his gun leading the way. After searching thoroughly, which didn't take long, they allowed Aaron to enter. The tall agent stayed outside and kept watch over the vicinity while Aaron gathered his belongings.

"Five minutes max," McBride whispered to Aaron. "And remember, no lights while we're here." He pointed to the small front window indicating that if anyone were watching, they would surely notice lights going on and off.

Aaron nodded and started gathering only what he could carry. As he looked around in the dark, Aaron heard McBride radio the driver and tell him they would return in five minutes.

The agents had given Aaron a small black bag that could only fit a weekend's worth of clothing but he hardly took any, just something to tide him over for a day. There were other things that he thought were more important. One was a picture of him and Sarah in the lab, sitting at one of the computers with their heads touching. Seeing the picture reminded him of Sarah's danger and he hurried to find the one other thing he wanted.

Going through the dresser drawers, he picked out his small address book. It had much more than addresses. There was a lifetime of memories in it: pens, pictures and small papers with the scribble of old friends.

As he was placing it in the bag, Aaron lost grip of the small green book. It fell from his hands and hit the floor with a slap. Both agents turned and looked at Aaron. They looked angry but did not say anything to him.

Aaron bent down to pick up his address book. After hitting the floor, pieces of paper from inside had scattered. Putting the paper quickly back into his book, one of the pieces caught his eye. Aaron recognized it and turned it over to look at the writing. Even in the darkness he knew what it was. It was Jason's address and phone number in Israel.

Just the sight of Jason's name gave Aaron an idea of how to get out of his mess. His mind worked quickly to devise a plan to escape, temporarily, from the CIA. Aaron knew what he needed to do but in order to set his plan in motion, he needed privacy that the CIA would not allow him.

"One minute," Agent McBride whispered into his walkie-talkie, while looking at Aaron.

"Let's go," Aaron whispered back. They left the room and closed the door softly behind them. The tall agent was still standing guard outside the door and they all walked slowly towards the back fence. McBride was about to step up onto the horizontal support beam to look back over the fence but Aaron protested. He pulled on the man's shirt and beckoned for his ear. "I know a shortcut," he whispered.

McBride looked at him angrily. "We have no time for this," he answered quietly.

"Trust me," Aaron whispered louder.

McBride looked at the other two for a judgment call. Aaron seemed to have their approval.

"Quickly," McBride said impatiently.

"I need your radio," Aaron said, holding out his hand.

"For what?" It was the only one they had and McBride wasn't going to give it up easily.

"We'll be going another way. It's kind of like a long shortcut so I'll have to tell the driver where to meet us." Aaron saw the uncertainty in McBride's eyes and tried to reassure him. "It's discrete, don't worry."

Agent McBride hesitated, then gave Aaron the walkie-talkie.

"Okay, I have to scope it out." Aaron signed with his hands and mouthed the words. The agents looked confused but they let him continue. "There are a few ways we can go, I just want to see which one's the best route for now," Aaron assured his bodyguards.

After receiving their uncertain approval, Aaron boosted himself up the fence on a horizontal support beam to look over. But, instead of stopping to look, Aaron jumped over the fence and before the agents knew what happening, Aaron was in the next yard running.

"We need help Schaffer, now," Aaron spoke loudly into the walkie-talkie as he ran. "And leave the keys in the ignition, we'll need a quick getaway."

He could hear the agents behind him coming over the wall but he had already crossed the first yard. As he jumped the small fence, he saw Schaffer coming towards him. Aaron quickly ducked behind a tree and watched Schaffer run towards the other agents who were still waiting for McBride to climb over the large fence.

Aaron's heart was pounding but he could not feel it because his adrenaline was rushing. He knew that what he was doing could get him killed but it might also save him.

After Schaffer was over the chain-linked fence, Aaron ran towards the van. As he did, Schaffer saw him running in that direction, tried to stop himself, slipped and fell flat on his face.

Aaron ducked into the van with Schaffer and the other agents hot on his tail. He found the keys in the ignition and started the van immediately. He shut the driver's door and sped off just as McBride grabbed the door handle. He tried to hold on, but could not. Aaron was already speeding down the street.

Schaffer pulled out his pistol and fired a shot at the tires to try and stop Aaron. He only got off one shot before McBride knocked the gun from his hands. "Are you a fuckin' idiot? You want to kill him," he yelled.

"I was just aiming for the tires," Schaffer answered innocently.

"I don't care what the hell you were aiming for you imbecile. And don't ever talk back to me again! Shit!" He looked back at the van as it sped around the corner.

"I'm just borrowing it for a little while guys, sorry. I'll meet you back at the office soon. Tell Schwabb I say 'Hi'." Aaron ended with a nervous laugh and then his voice was gone from the walkie-talkie.

Schaffer was holding his receiver out and everyone was looking at it.

"Shit," Schaffer said, as he threw it at the ground.

*****

A few minutes later Aaron pulled into a parking lot about a mile from Sarah's apartment. He knew they would be looking for the van and that it wouldn't be a good idea to be with it when it was found.

He started walking in the direction of Sarah's cautiously, aware of his surroundings as he went. He knew that neither the CIA nor Tag knew where he was and he wanted to keep it that way.

The streets were deserted and it was hard to hide in the shadows of the buildings alone. A few scattered pedestrians helped in his concealment, but not much.

After a few minutes of walking along a main street, Aaron came to a twenty-four hour convenience store and ducked in. The only person there was the attendant who was sitting on a stool behind the counter.

The old black man looked up over his glasses at his new customer and sized him up quickly. He concluded that his customer was no threat and went back to his newspaper.

"Do you have a pay phone," Aaron asked.

The man did not look up from his paper or answer. He simply pointed his finger towards the back of his store and kept reading.

Aaron took the cue and walked towards the other end of the small store. It reminded him of many he had been in before in New York. They sold the basic groceries, beer, cigarettes and magazines.

Making his way down one of two aisles created by a center row of goods, Aaron came to a pay phone. It was on the wall just before the lone bathroom in the back of the store.

Aaron took a quick look back at the clerk. He was still reading, not paying any attention to Aaron.

He opened the black bag, pulled out his address book and dropped the bag on the floor at his feet. From the address book, Aaron pulled out a prepaid calling card and Jason's phone number.

It was mid-morning in Israel and Aaron prayed that Jason was home for some reason. Did the Israeli Foreign Intelligence ever get days off, he asked himself. After punching in the numbers, Aaron murmured to himself, "Please be home, please be home." It took a while for the connection to go through and then he heard the familiar tone of an Israeli telephone ringing.

The phone was answered almost immediately and Aaron was astounded. It's a miracle, he thought, but he wasn't happy for long. The voice on the other end was not Jason's. It was a recorded voice that Aaron had heard many times while in Israel. It was the voice of the Israeli Telephone Company, Bezeq. The recording was telling Aaron, in Hebrew, that the number he had dialed was out of service.

"Shit," Aaron said loudly, in total despair. If the number was out of service, his hopes were crushed. There would be no way to reach Jason to work out a plan.

Just before Aaron hung up the phone, he heard the voice change. "Wait, wait," it said in Hebrew. It was Jason's voice.

"Jason," Aaron asked emphatically.

"Aaron! Yo dude, what's up?" Jason was happy to hear his friend's voice.

"I thought I dialed the wrong number!"

"Oh, yeah, I do that once in a while. What's up man?" Jason sounded happy as always. He had every reason to be. He loved his high-risk job and the Israeli women. Aaron couldn't keep up with the many women his friend had. Jason had been a lady's man ever since cooties were cured. Aaron gave Jason "his" song — *Take It Easy*, by the Eagles. It fit him perfectly, at least the part about the women did.

"I need your help," Aaron pleaded.

"What? That Sarah girl didn't work out? I don't think I know many Jewish babes in Jamaica man, sorry."

"No." Aaron paused and looked back at the attendant. He was still not paying any attention to Aaron. "This is serious!"

"Sure man, what's up," Jason asked lightheartedly.

"No, Jason, this is really serious, I'm in big trouble," Aaron added gravely.

"Okay, okay, what's going on?" Jason was starting to feel the urgency in his friend's voice.

For the third time, Aaron began relaying the events of the prior few days. He told Jason about the disappearances off the Jamaican coast and Jason knew exactly what he was referring to. Aaron also told him who he had run into and what he had told them.

In a matter of minutes Aaron had told Jason everything pertinent to his situation. Jason was quiet for a few moments, as if Aaron's full explanation was still coming through the phone lines.

"Are you serious?" Jason thought that Aaron was pulling his leg. "This is another one of your stupid jokes, right? Like that time you called me up at work and asked me to get the drugs for you in a Latino-American accent! You almost had me on that one!" Jason laughed.

"I'm serious Jason, this is no joke," Aaron said loudly. This time the clerk looked in Aaron's direction. He had disturbed the old man with his last plea for help.

"You have one minute remaining," a woman's recorded voice said over the phone.

"Jason, call me back right now, my life depends on it! I'm in Kingston. I don't know the country code but the number to this phone is (876) 555-5309. Call me back…" Aaron was cut off by the same woman's voice notifying him that his card had been exhausted of its minutes.

Aaron hung up the phone and waited for Jason to return his call. He knew that he might be waiting a few minutes so Aaron decided to purchase a drink to quench his growing thirst.

Aaron left his bag under the phone and went to the refrigerators on the wall. He pulled out a liter of water, went to the register and slightly overpaid.

"Keep the change," Aaron said to the old man who had barely peeked over his paper. Aaron started walking back to the phone when the old man finally responded. "Ya, man. Try and keep it down back there, I'm tryin' to read."

"Sorry," Aaron said sincerely. He didn't want to arouse any suspicion.

On his way back to the phone Aaron opened the small bottle of water and took a swig. He was thirsty and would have finished the bottle quickly but the phone rang.

Aaron screwed the top back on the bottle and picked up the receiver in a hurry.

"Jason?"

"Yeah." The answer came a second later.

"Thank God!"

"Alright. So you've convinced me. Now, what do you think I can do for you," Jason asked earnestly.

"Is there any way you can get me out of this situation and get me asylum in Israel?"

"Wow, you know that's going to be next to impossible?"

"I know, but it's the only thing I can think of."

"Well, the only thing I can do is talk to my superior and see what we can do. I, myself, have no say over this, you have to understand!"

"I know, Jason, but they're trying to screw me here!"

"Yeah, the CIA, what can I say? Man, it's not fair! How the hell did you get yourself into this situation? I mean, I know how you did, but it's really amazing! How come I can't get in situations like that? It's so exciting!"

"Believe me Jason, if I could trade places with you now, I'd do it in a second!"

"You know, there might be something that could help make my boss more interested in your situation."

"Yeah, what would that be?"

"You've been doing dolphin research, right?"

"Obviously," Aaron answered sarcastically.

"Okay, okay. And it sounds as if you've uncovered a little bit of dolphin communication."

"Do you really think that kind of information might be able to help me?" Aaron was hesitant about relaying that information.

"Oh, yeah," Jason answered assuredly. "Everyone in the world would drool over a breakthrough in that area. I'd say if you had some pertinent information on that subject, you'd be a hot commodity!"

Aaron didn't want to tell anyone about his breakthrough yet, but this was his life! If it could save his life it was worth telling, he convinced himself. Besides, he thought, I would rather Israel have it than the CIA.

"Well, I stumbled onto a bit of dolphin communication but it hasn't really been tested enough," Aaron confessed.

"I'd say it has! It got you where you are now didn't it?"

"Guess you're right."

"Alright. Hang tight where you are. Are you safe there?"

"I think so." Aaron looked around again.

"Well, stay there, I'll call you back in an hour to tell you what I've come up with on this end."

"Wait, wait," Aaron blurted out. "I have one more question."

"Yeah?"

"Can I bring someone with me?"

"Are you serious, Aaron? Do you know what kind of hell I'm going through to..."

"Yes, I know," Aaron interrupted. "I know very well the dangers involved on both ends of this thing, but it's important to me! I love her!"

Jason didn't say anything for a moment. It was going to be hard enough to convince my superiors to retrieve Aaron, he thought. How the hell am I going to convince them to let him bring his girlfriend along?

"What's her full name," Jason asked reluctantly.

"Sarah Gordon. Thanks, Jason! I'll never forget this!"

"Don't count your chicken's before they've hatched. I have no idea what's going to come of this yet. I'll call you back at this number in one hour. If you don't hear from me call me back at home."

"No problem. I'll speak to you in an hour," Aaron said and then hung up the phone.

One hour was just enough time for him to check on Sarah and fill her in on what had happened. She would never believe it, he thought.

Aaron picked up his black bag and his water bottle and walked out of the store. He looked back to make sure the store was open twenty-fours hours, and he saw the neon sign above the door.

Turning his attention to his surroundings, Aaron did not detect any eyes on him. He moved stealthily in the direction of Sarah's apartment. Using alleyways and side streets, he arrived across the street from where she lived in less than twenty minutes.

He saw Sarah's Jeep parked in the front lot but Aaron did not see any lights on in her apartment. She must be asleep, he thought.

Aaron waited for a few minutes and watched the street. He watched cars pass by and checked to see if unusual amounts of people were about for that time of night. He didn't see anything unusual but that had not helped him earlier.

Cautiously, he made his way around the complex, moving in a two-block radius. A few minutes later he arrived at the back of the apartment complex. Everything was quiet from the back as well, but he still wanted to be careful.

Looking at his watch, Aaron realized he only had thirty minutes left until Jason was supposed to call. He could not miss that call, he thought. He had to move.

He was hidden from sight in tall bushes at the back of the parking lot. Directly under the other side of the bushes was a drop of about six and a half feet. It was a cement wall that was erected to keep the hill from collapsing onto the apartment lot.

There were cars parked directly under him, which would help disguise his movement. As quickly as he could, Aaron lowered himself from the top of the cement wall with his bag on his back. He let go and hit the ground as softly as possible between two parked cars. Once there, he froze and listened to his surroundings. All he could hear was the sound of electricity from the city lights and the infrequent noise of passing cars.

Using the parked cars as cover, he walked low around the perimeter of the lot, which was surrounded by the cement wall. When he reached the corner of the lot, he stopped to listen but heard nothing unusual. From where he was, the parking lot went straight to the apartment building where Sarah lived. The cement wall to his right, angled downward at a steep slope and was level to the ground where it met the building.

Staying low, Aaron almost crawled to the end of the parking lot. When he got there the only thing left to do was to walk to the open stairway and up to Sarah's apartment door. It was very risky but it was the only way in. He had come this far and he had very little time to be back at the store. I have to go now if I'm going to go, he convinced himself.

Slowly, as not to draw any attention, but fast enough to not look suspicious, Aaron started along the building and then up the stairs. He listened carefully as he went but did not hear a thing. So far, so good he thought.

Upon reaching the top of the stairs, a cold chill ran down Aaron's back. Sarah's door was cracked open. Something was wrong, he thought. Something was very wrong. He knew that no one would leave their door open in the middle of the night in a city like Kingston.

Wanting to rush in to see what had happened was his first instinct, but he knew it was the wrong one. If someone was waiting for him, expecting him to barge in, he would have no chance of escape.

Controlling his emotions, he walked silently along the outside wall of her apartment, slowly moving one foot over the other, careful not to make a sound. When Aaron got close enough to her door, he stopped again and listened. If someone was waiting inside he might be able to hear them, he thought.

There was nothing, no movement and no sounds and Aaron gained his courage to enter the apartment. He placed his hand on the door and pushed it in slowly. From his vantage point he could see the apartment had been torn apart. He felt week in the knees as a million thoughts rushed through his head. Had Tag and his men captured her? Had the CIA already been here looking for something? Was Sarah dead?

The worst thoughts kept coming to him. Aaron knew that if he entered the apartment he might find her dead body, stabbed or shot to death on the bedroom floor. He couldn't stand the thoughts that were still flowing through his mind. They were unbearable.

Aaron blamed himself for her misfortune. If he had mentioned her to the CIA earlier, maybe this wouldn't have happened, he thought.

Suddenly Aaron shook his head. He had no evidence that anything that he was thinking had happened. He had to go in and find out.

He entered cautiously and saw a dark, trashed living room. The lights were out and he didn't want to risk being detected by turning them on. Instead, Aaron quickly rummaged through his backpack and took out a small flashlight he had stolen from the CIA van. Scanning the living room with the flashlight gave him a better view.

It didn't look like anything expensive had been taken. The TV was on the floor and there was a large hole in the wall where it had been plugged in. The couch pillows were thrown all over the room leaving the couch bare, exposing the fabric that was ripped to shreds.

The kitchen was worse. All of the cabinets were open and the contents had been dumped onto the floor or the counter tops. Even the food from the refrigerator had been removed and scattered around.

The scene was spooky and Aaron felt even more unnerved as he started towards the bedroom. The door was open about a foot but he could not see in. He wanted to enter the bedroom but was afraid of what he might find.

Tiptoeing closer, Aaron slowly pushed the door wider. As his eyes focused, Aaron saw a room just as destroyed as the other two. The bed was overturned; drawers were open and empty. The contents of most everything from the bedroom and bathroom were on the floor. Again he noticed that nothing seemed to have been stolen. Someone must have been searching for something specific, Aaron thought.

Although the bedroom was taken apart, Aaron was relieved to find no body. If she wasn't here, he hoped she was alive somewhere. Maybe Sarah had come home and seen this mess and ran? But he thought it was unlikely when he remembered that her Jeep was still in the front parking lot.

Only one more room to check, he thought. Aaron walked slowly towards the bathroom, stepping carefully over the debris. The bathroom was very dark and it was hard to see inside. He entered slowly, closed the door quietly and turned on the lights. As he flipped the switch he held his breath and his heart skipped a few beats in anticipation of what he might find.

There was nothing there besides more mess and Aaron breathed easily again. Aaron turned off the bathroom light and opened the door again, still worried. He had seen nothing that gave him a clue to where Sarah was. Maybe that was a good sign, he thought, maybe she was okay.

Slowly, he made his way back into the living room. Checking his watch, Aaron saw that he had only fifteen minutes until Jason was going to call. Aaron was about to leave when he saw something nailed to the back of the front door. It was a note.

Aaron grabbed at it and quickly tore it from its place. It made a small rip at the top of the page but all of the writing was still intact. It had been written in a hurry.

> Lover Boy, your sweet girlfriend is safe with me. I think you know where to find us. Find a way to get where you were when you lost something big. Come alone! If you're not here by the end of two days, you might lose something else. I think you would agree it would be a shame for a body as pretty as this to be mutilated and eaten by scavengers.
> -Tag

Aaron had no time to think about what the note meant. He ran. He shoved the note into his pocket and ran out of the apartment. He ran through the back parking lot and jumped quickly up the cement wall and into the bushes. Aaron wasn't being as careful as he had been on the way to Sarah's apartment, but he couldn't. If he did not make it to Jason's call, he might not make it out of Jamaica.

Aaron was terrified about what had happened to Sarah, the woman he loved dearly. Scenarios were running through his head as he ran to the store. Would he be able to save her? If he could, how would he do it?

In no time, Aaron was across the street from the store where Jason was going to call. Looking up and down the street, Aaron saw no one. He ran across the street and pulled the door but it was locked. Aaron panicked, how could this be, he thought in a frenzy.

He started pacing nervously outside the store. He needed to be in for the phone call in less than five minutes.

"Where is that fucking attendant," Aaron asked out loud as he paced back and forth. Looking through the glass, Aaron did not see anyone. The man must have left, he thought, but all the lights were on. He looked at the door and saw a handwritten sign that he had not noticed before. "Be back in 5 minutes."

"Shit, man," Aaron said, glancing around impatiently for the attendant. What am I going to do if I miss the call, he asked himself? He could call Jason back but he did not know how many minutes he had left on his last calling card.

There was a car driving down the street in the direction of the shop. Aaron stopped pacing in front of the windows and walked slowly with his head down in the opposite direction of the car. It passed without stopping and Aaron walked back to the store. As he did, Aaron saw the man walking slowly towards the front door.

Aaron rapped quickly on the glass door. The man looked at him and kept walking slowly in his direction. When he reached the door, the old man took off the sign and unlocked the door.

"Where were you," Aaron asked, as if he was the man's boss.

"On a personal break, man! You think I can sit there behind that counter without going to the bathroom for eight hours?"

As the man finished his sentence the phone started ringing. Aaron disregarded the old man and ran to the back of the store.

"Jason?" Aaron picked up the phone, panting.

"Yeah, what's with you?" The answer came a few seconds later.

"I had to go somewhere."

"Well, it's a good thing you got back in time."

"Yeah, it's a good thing I got back at all. Is there any news?" Aaron was still a little out of breath.

"Okay, listen carefully. Can you supply all of your preliminary research on the dolphin communication?"

"Yes, anything they want!"

"Would you be willing to do some more of your research over here for the Israeli Government? You would be highly compensated and would only have to do it for a year. It's just to get other researchers on the right track."

Aaron was bargaining for his life and would take what he could get. He didn't like the idea of giving this line of research to any government, but he felt good that it was Israel.

"Are you guys going to be able to protect me over there from the United States and the drug cartel," Aaron asked, trusting the answer would be positive.

"No one will know where you are. They'll think you're dead."

"Really, how are you going to swing that?"

"Don't worry, we're the Mossad, we can cover it," Jason answered confidently.

"Okay, what about Sarah?" Aaron changed the subject, getting down to business.

"She's fine. There's only one more thing."

"What's that?"

"You need to meet us out in the Gulf of Mexico."

"I don't think that'll be a problem, but how will we meet?"

Jason paused for a moment to reason the plan in his head before he spoke. "They want you to go destroy this place tomorrow night, right?"

"Yes."

"Well, just tell them you're going to do it and screw them like they're trying to screw you. It's not your problem, right?"

"Well," Aaron started. He was going to explain that it was now his problem because Sarah had been captured. He wanted to save her but didn't know if he could. Before he could relay the new information, Jason continued.

"Well, nothing. Just go out like they'll tell you to do and I'm sure they'll give you a global positioning system. Just use it to go to the coordinates I'm going to give you and meet us there. They'll probably want you to go late at night and arrive at the target around one in the morning. Why don't you just meet us where I tell you to at about two?"

"How about three?"

"Why three?"

"I think it might take me a little longer."

"You're not really going to blow up the place are you?" Jason sounded excited.

"I think I might."

"Oh, I'm so proud! I wish I could be there!"

"Yeah, I wish you could, too."

"Be careful, man."

"I will but how will I know it's you?"

"Trust me, you'll know! Who else are you going to meet in the middle of the Gulf of Mexico at three o'clock in the morning in an Israeli attack helicopter?"

"Good point," Aaron said and then thought about what Jason had told him. "How the hell are you going to get an Israeli attack helicopter halfway across the world?"

"I can't tell you that right now but you're just going to have to trust me on this one."

"But a helicopter's range is only…"

"You don't have to tell me what a helicopter's range is," Jason interrupted. "Just trust me."

"Okay," Aaron said hesitantly.

Jason and Aaron continued talking for a few minutes. They finished talking about the plan and Jason gave Aaron the rendezvous coordinates. As soon as he was done, Aaron took his bag, thanked the clerk and left the store.

The old man seemed to have a change of heart about his customer and wanted him to stay. He offered Aaron something to buy on his way out but he declined. It was a good thing for Aaron.

The attendant had pushed a button only minutes before, which called the police. He started getting suspicious of Aaron at the end of the conversation and thought he was up to something illegal.

A few minutes after Aaron left the store, the police arrived. The attendant described Aaron to them and they thanked him. The description matched an all points bulletin for Aaron. Schwabb had put it out when he learned of Aaron's escape. They were on to him, but it didn't matter. Aaron had finished what he needed to do and was headed back to the CIA office.

*****

"What the hell did you think you were doing," Schwabb screamed.

They were back in the interrogation room where they had started the night before. Aaron was sitting in the same chair when Schwabb had been called into the room.

Aaron had been careful not to be seen until he made it back to the building where they had taken him earlier. He had already given one of the other agents the keys to the van and its location. Everything was fine, Aaron was not hurt but Schwabb was furious.

"You could have been killed! What were you doing," Schwabb screamed again.

"Calm down! I'm fine, aren't I?"

"Who cares if you're fine! You can't just go around stealing government property and disappearing like that!" Schwabb went on, staring at Aaron while cursing his actions during the last few hours. He rarely got that angry but the situation could have turned out terribly and Schwabb knew it. If Aaron had turned up dead, he would have lost his grip on the case, not to mention his job.

"I'll do it," Aaron screamed over Schwabb's shouting.

"What did you say," he asked in a low roar. He had not heard Aaron clearly.

"I said, I'll do it!" This time the agents heard him. Schwabb had no reason to be angry anymore but he wanted to be. He huffed and puffed for a few seconds more and then calmed down as he sat across from Aaron and looked at him.

"Good choice. We're glad you saw it our way," he said calmly, still wanting to be upset.

"I just have one request," Aaron said and then continued, not waiting for Schwabb to answer. "I want one million dollars."

Now Schwabb had a reason to be angry again and he wasted no time jumping from his seat. "Who the hell do you think we are," he yelled again as his chair crashed to the ground. "You think you can get away with what you did and get paid a million dollars for it?" Schwabb was screaming, pointing his finger dangerously at Aaron. "I should put you in jail when you get back from this mission! Instead we're giving you a new lease on life! No, way." Schwabb stopped yelling but he continued speaking, still upset. "No, we're giving you all you need. You will be provided for, for the rest of your life. You don't need a million dollars."

"You're fucking me," Aaron said calmly, still seated. "You're giving me an ultimatum. I either do your job for you or I'm on my own and that scenario ends up with me dead in a couple of days, so you say. The other answer is for me to do your dirty work and I'll be protected but I won't be able to do what I've always wanted to do — dolphin research. Either way I'm screwed. I don't trust you."

"What would you do with a million dollars," Schwabb asked loudly.

"Whatever I want to. What do you care? I don't trust the CIA protection, so if I think you're doing a lousy job, I'll do it myself. I think one million is enough to help me disappear for a while." He paused for a moment to let Schwabb take in his request. It seemed he was actually listening but for insurance on a positive response, Aaron threw in a twist.

"How about this? You can give me the money before I do the job and I'll leave it in Kingston where you will have access to it in case I don't come back."

Schwabb thought for a moment about the plea. It wasn't such a bad idea, he thought. If he knew where the money was going to be, he could take it back immediately after Aaron's departure. This way Aaron would be appeased, he thought, and would do the job. And, he continued thinking, even if Aaron returns I won't have to give him the money.

"Okay," Schwabb answered. "It's a deal. I don't trust you and you don't trust me, but this'll work." He extended his hand towards Aaron and they shook on it.

Schwabb was proud of himself. He thought Aaron was actually stupid enough to let him know where the money was. But Schwabb was the real fool. Aaron had a plan up his sleeve that would guarantee the money would stay with him, dead or alive.

"I want it in bank notes, one hundred, ten-thousand dollar bank notes. It should fit easily into a small metal box. And, I need some time alone to hide it. I know you have to guard me and I won't run away again, I promise. But, I need some space."

"Where?"

"In the botanical gardens. I can hide it there and you won't be able to find it before I come back. This way you can protect me but I can do what I need to do."

"Fine," Schwabb said. "We can do that." It occurred to him that it would also be possible to put a tracking device in the box with the money. All Schwabb would have to do is trace it and pick it up after Aaron left.

"You'd better get some sleep now," Schwabb said, moving towards the door. "We have a room down the hall with a bed. You can rest there."

Aaron got up and followed Schwabb out of the room. "When you get up, you'll have a briefing and some training for the mission. We found the structural plans and it shouldn't be impossible."

They came to a door through the busy hallway. Agents were crisscrossing each other, busy with morning work. "Don't worry," Schwabb said. "I know you don't trust us but we want you to succeed at this, we won't let you down."

Aaron agreed to the schedule and would leave late the next night. Alone in the small room with a cot and desk, Aaron put his head on the pillow. He was exhausted and although he was terrified that he might not make it through the next night, Aaron fell asleep quickly.

As he slept, Aaron dreamt of Sarah. He saw her dancing in an open field with her long dark hair flowing as she moved. She was beautiful and so were the surroundings. There was no fear in her and she was at peace with herself and with nature. In the dream, Sarah was wearing a long, flowing white dress that blew in any direction the wind would take it.

The sun was shining brightly on the grassy field where she frolicked. Soon, she was tired and walked to a lone tree on a soft hill in the middle of the vast green field. It was a large, ancient tree and it provided the perfect amount of shade.

She sat down on a white blanket with an open picnic basket on it. The basket had been emptied and the mouthwatering foods: ripe strawberries, juicy watermelon, sweet grapefruits topped with sugar and others were resting on fine china, ready to eat. To drink, Sarah had brought sweet Muscat wine and she had already poured two large glasses and was waiting for Aaron to join her.

Aaron floated towards Sarah wearing a white cotton tee-shirt that exposed his athletic build underneath. When he arrived under the tree they toasted each other without speaking and smiled. After they each drank a glass of wine, Sarah reached for Aaron. Aaron leaned in and they kissed. It was magical. Aaron felt as if they were in heaven together. Everything was perfect, the weather, the food, and the kiss.

After a few moments of soft kissing, Aaron opened his eyes to stare at his beautiful angel of heaven. He wanted to get lost in her emerald eyes and stay there for eternity.

As his eyes focused, he realized that Sarah's eyes were no longer green. They were dark brown. Pulling his head back he saw that it wasn't Sarah's face at all.

Agent Schwabb was sitting in front of him on the blanket, wearing a dark suit. Aaron quickly pushed him down on the ground. Schwabb fell backwards easily but as he hit the ground, he morphed into Tag Millwood. His athletic build grew into a fat form and the dark face became a light Caucasian complexion. After the body finished taking shape, the dark suit turned into Tag's tourist outfit he had been wearing a few days earlier.

Aaron was terrified at what he saw and took off running. He left the tree behind him and ran out towards the open green field. As he ran, the grass turned brown and became brittle under his feet. It was snapping and crackling as he ran but he kept running.

Looking over his shoulder, Aaron saw that Tag was gaining ground. No matter how fast he ran, Tag was gaining on him. He could not move his legs fast enough. Aaron knew he could run faster but his legs wouldn't cooperate with his mind. He was going to be captured.

In the distance Aaron spotted a figure. As he ran closer he saw it was Jason. He wanted to scream to Jason and ask for help but all Aaron could do was wave his hands. Jason waved back and Aaron looked over his shoulder to see Tag at his heels. I'm not going to make it, he thought despairingly.

Looking forward again, Jason was directly in front of Aaron and he skidded to a halt before running into him. Jason had a content look on his face. He was happy. How could Jason be happy about my horrible situation, Aaron thought. He was surely doomed now.

There was a soft tap on Aaron's left shoulder. It must be Tag, Aaron thought. There was no escape. Aaron turned around and faced his captor but it was not Tag.

Sarah was now standing before him in the same white dress she had been wearing only a few moments ago. It is Sarah, Aaron thought, but her hair is different. It was not long and dark anymore. Her hair was short and blonde and he stroked it. Aaron had no idea why she had changed, but it was her. She was smiling brightly at Aaron and held her arms out to be embraced.

Aaron embraced Sarah and almost suffocated her because he was so happy to see her. After a few moments Aaron opened his eyes again and Sarah was still there. She had not changed again, but something else had changed. The grass had gone back to its original brilliant green color.

CHAPTER 17

Before he could enjoy the rest of his dream, Agent Schwabb woke Aaron from his deep slumber. "Come on," he said, nudging him. "It's time to get you trained."

Aaron was groggy from his rest and rubbed his eyes. There were no windows in the room and he could not tell what time it was or how long he had been sleeping. Looking down at his watch, Aaron realized he had slept almost the whole day. It was about five-thirty in the evening and he was hungry.

"Can we eat something first," Aaron yawned.

"Sure," Schwabb said, waiting for him at the doorway.

The hallways were still buzzing with activity. I wonder if it's always like this, Aaron asked himself as people in suits whizzed by him at a dizzying pace through the hall. After passing a few doors and many people in the hallway, Aaron and Schwabb entered a door.

The room looked like a "coffee break" room and Aaron assumed that he was correct.

Schwabb went to one of the counters and opened it. "What do you want," he asked, pointing into the cabinet.

There was a multitude of small cereal boxes, each big enough for one bowl. "Give me *Fruit Loops®* and *Honey Combs®.*"

Schwabb pulled the two small boxes from the shelf and threw them at Aaron. Aaron caught them and put them on the round wooden table in the middle of the room. There was enough room for six people but it looked as if it was just going to be the two of them.

Aaron sat down as Schwabb continued to search for utensils and bowls. When everything was on the table, they began eating. Schwabb also had cereal but neither of them had much of a conversation until they were almost done.

"Eat quickly," Schwabb said. "We don't have much time." He was all business.

Aaron and Schwabb both ate quickly and when they were almost finished, Aaron finally got enough courage to ask the question that had been burning in his mind since he awoke.

"When am I going to get the bank notes?"

Schwabb stopped eating for a moment. He was not ready for that question but had an answer nonetheless. "Right after we eat," Schwabb said and then went quickly back to his meal.

"I'll be able to go to the gardens and put it where I want?"

"Yes, at six." Schwabb finished the last bite of his cereal and looked at his watch. "It's time to go." He got up, put his bowl and spoon in the sink and Aaron followed suit without a word.

"The money should be ready just down here," Schwabb said as they forced their way down the busy hallway again.

It's a beautiful room, Aaron thought as they stepped into a conference room that he had not seen before. The walls were covered with floor to ceiling bookshelves, which were filled with books that gave the room a "law office" feel. Everything was meticulously arranged and cleaned, even the books that seemed to have never been touched had no dust on them.

There was a large oak conference table in the middle of the room surrounded by twelve, plush black leather chairs in perfect intervals. It looked as if the room had not been disturbed since it was built except for a small metal box resting on the table with its lid open.

Inside the airtight container was a neat stack of one hundred, ten thousand dollar bank notes. Aaron had no idea if there were actually one hundred bank notes but it looked complete. Aaron flipped through the stack and each one he saw read "Ten Thousand". He paused for a moment with his hands covering the stack of paper. Aaron had never seen that much money and he was awestruck.

"Do you want to count it," Schwabb asked.

"I'm sure we don't have time for that. And, no. I don't want to count it," Aaron answered, returning to normal.

Aaron was right. There wasn't enough time to count it. He didn't trust Schwabb but his quick glance of the bank notes would have to do.

"Very well." Schwabb opened the conference room door and allowing the noise to spill in. "We've spent the last hour clearing the gardens and making sure they're safe. We'll take you out there and you can roam, dig, hide or do whatever you want to do for thirty minutes. If you're not out in thirty minutes we're coming in to get you. And, this time, I'm leading the field trip," Schwabb said strictly, pointing to himself. "You're not going to jump ship this time I can guarantee you that!"

"I don't plan on it. Like I said, I just had to do some things before I came back." Aaron closed and latched the metal box.

Schwabb was still angry because of Aaron's earlier escape but not showing it. He wanted to seem as nice and as trustworthy as he could.

"Alright then, let's get going. We're on a tight schedule," Schwabb said as they slipped out into the hallway.

The ride to the botanical gardens was uneventful. There were three vans full of agents with Aaron's van in the middle. He was riding in the middle row between two huge men who didn't say a word. Schwabb had made sure Aaron wasn't going to run off this time.

When the three black Chevy Suburbans® arrived at the gardens, Aaron noticed that in addition to the agents he had ridden with, there were already many agents at the gardens. He could see the sweat dripping from their brows, the black suits they were wearing not providing any relief from the hot afternoon sun.

The other two vans emptied and agents poured out like clowns from a circus car. The people in Aaron's car, on the contrary, stayed put.

Schwabb radioed another agent on a walkie-talkie and asked if they had secured the area. The response was adequate and Schwabb nodded to the agents sitting next to Aaron. They opened the car door, exited and motioned for Aaron to do the same.

As Aaron stepped out of the van, Schwabb approached him. "Here we are at the entrance." Schwabb pointed to the entrance of the gardens. "You have exactly thirty minutes from now. If you're a second late, we're coming in for you. Do you understand?"

"Yes," Aaron answered calmly, not phased by his seriousness.

"Then go. And you might need this." Schwabb tossed Aaron a shovel.

Aaron walked quickly into the gardens with the shovel and metal box both gleaming in his hands. As he did, he saw agents lined around the outside perimeter. They were all within eyesight of each other and Aaron knew that Schwabb wasn't taking any chances of him escaping again.

The gardens were completely empty. It was like walking around the Garden of Eden and having been the only one let in.

The air was eerily quiet. Aaron did not even hear any birds, which would be a normal sound. Usually it was easy to hear children's voices and other noises drifting on the wind but now there was nothing.

He walked past the entrance and deeper into the foliage. He wanted to be far away from anyone so they could not detect what he was doing. Aaron passed gardens with a colorful array of flowers and bushes. He looked around but wanted to dig somewhere else.

After five minutes Aaron came to an area, dense with trees. One large Banyan tree good for climbing and he put his things down.

He made sure there was no one around and then bent down and took the clean stack of bank notes out of the box. He placed the money on the ground next to the shovel and then took the empty box in his hand and began climbing the tree. Aaron assumed correctly that Schwabb had "tagged" the box and would come looking for it as soon as he left. Not only will he be pissed when he finds it, Aaron thought of Schwabb, but he'll get pissed just trying to look for it.

Climbing was harder than Aaron had expected with the metal box in his hand but soon he was twenty feet in the air. Looking down, he figured he was high enough and wedged the box in between the trunk and one of the branches. He jiggled the box to make sure it was secure and it did not budge. Appeased, he climbed back down to the ground.

With twenty minutes left he started digging directly underneath the box. I'd better hurry, Aaron thought as he put more elbow grease into his work. Aaron was sweating and breathing heavily but he forced out a laugh as he dug. He pictured Schwabb and his men searching for the box with their homing device and digging right where he was digging. He knew they would be totally puzzled and the vision made him chuckle again.

In ten minutes he had finished digging a hole large enough for the box and then proceeded to fill it back in. With ten minutes left, I'd better hurry, he thought to himself as he moved faster.

Filling proved easier than digging and within minutes, Aaron had completed restoring the dirt. He pounded on the loose earth with the shovel and when it was level, he placed the shovel on the ground and wiped his hands on his jeans.

With clean hands, Aaron picked up the bank notes and judged its thickness. Satisfied with his findings, he stuffed the stack in the front of his underwear and adjusted himself with five minutes left.

With no time left to spare, Aaron walked back through the front entrance. He was sweating profusely and was covered with dirt.

He threw the shovel back to Schwabb. "It's done," Aaron said. "Let's go."

Upon arriving back at the building, Schwabb and Aaron returned to the immaculate seventh floor conference room. The table was covered with a large laminated structural drawing that was being held down at the corners by pistols and ammunition clips. All of the chairs had been removed and there was a black bag of military equipment lying at the foot of a huge man.

This guy looked like he never took shit from anyone, Aaron thought, and he wasn't going to test him. He was dressed in gray sweats with a camouflage army hat and stood six-five with bulging muscles. On his face, the man was sporting a mustache and he had not shaved the rest of his face in days. This guy was the spitting image of GI Joe, Aaron thought.

"Tim Franklin," the large man said business-like, offering his hand. Aaron took it without a word. His grip was crushing but he was expecting it from such a man. "I'm here to give you a crash course on your mission. This will include the understanding of explosives, deep sea diving, and all the other equipment that you will be using this evening. Am I to understand that you have advanced open water certification already?"

"Yes," Aaron responded, looking up at the giant before him.

"I was also told that you served in the Israeli Defense Force."

"Yeah, the Golani unit."

"Good, then you'll probably get through this alive. Let's get started, we've got a lot to cover and we are pressed for time." Aaron did not answer but nodded in agreement and Tim began.

"This is the only kind of sidearm you will be using tonight," he said, pointing to one of the black, twenty-two caliber *Berretas®* on the table. "I know it doesn't look like a lot but that's because it's not."

"It's a little smaller than what I'm used to," Aaron responded, picking up one of the guns and inspecting it as the edge of the laminated paper curled up.

"That's because this isn't a combat mission. You used what, an M-sixteen?"

"Yeah." Aaron aimed the sidearm at the large window and peered through the sights.

"Well, this mission should be covert operations. Hopefully they won't even know you're there," Tim said as Aaron put the gun back on the drawing. "You'll get three of these, each with a fully loaded clip and one silencer. You'll also have extra clips just in case you need them."

"Got it." Aaron was paying close attention now.

"Shall we begin with the plan and I'll describe equipment as we go?"

"Let's get to it." Aaron was now all business as well.

"Let's start with how you're going to get to the sight." Tim pulled a sea chart from his briefcase on the floor. "We know that the complex is connected to the underwater research lab which is located here," he stated confidently while spreading the sheet over the table and pointing to an area off the eastern coast of Jamaica. "But we're going to send you a different way than you went before."

"What do you mean?"

"Well, I know you have no idea where you're going so you'll do it like you did before. We'll get your dolphin to lead you to the Poseidon complex but we're going to send a decoy ship with dead bodies just ahead of you. You will be in a raft that is tied onto the back of the decoy and trail about one hundred yards. You'll control the decoy with this." Tim bent down and produced a remote control from the equipment bag. It didn't seem too hard to control and with Tim's instruction it was not.

"The dead bodies are for the benefit of our target. If they pulled the boat down and there was no one in it, they'd get suspicious very quickly. But, with the bodies, it'll take them a little longer to realize that they've been dead more than a few minutes."

"Now for the diving. From what we can tell, your dive will be anywhere from one-hundred to two-hundred feet. Normal dive limits, as you know, are around one hundred feet but just in case you have to go deeper, we're giving you a tank of tri-mix." Tim paused for a moment to make sure Aaron was absorbing everything and then led him to the other side of the table. As he followed Tim, Aaron could feel the bank notes rubbing uncomfortably against his inner thighs but he walked normally to disguise his pain.

"Do you know how to use one of these?" Tim pointed to a large underwater scooter that Aaron had not noticed before.

"I've seen them but haven't had the chance to use one yet."

"Well, this is your lucky day. This is what you're going to use to get down to the complex," Tim said and then proceeded to show Aaron how it worked.

After the explanation of the underwater scooter Tim stopped before turning to the next subject. "Are you getting everything?" Tim was worried that he was going to fast.

"When your life depends on it, it's amazing how much you can digest in a short period of time."

"I know what you mean, but let's get back to work." Tim moved back around the table. When Aaron joined him, Tim pointed down at the structural drawings and continued.

"This is where you'll enter." He pointed to the open dome. "As they're pulling the boat down, you take your water scooter and sneak in here." Tim pointed to an air vent on the inside of the gigantic bay doors.

"They'll be too busy doing other things to notice you, we hope. When you enter you will be in the ventilation shaft," Tim continued explaining, moving his thick finger along the laminated paper. "This part of the shaft is flooded while there is water in the bay area but it will clear with air when they pump out all the water." Aaron visualized his movements as he explained.

"Now, the air vents are going to be the first thing that fill with air, so as soon as you swim in, go as far down as you can. Once you get to the bottom there will be another grate here." Tim moved his finger down to show Aaron the exact spot. "Take it off and go inside this small room. Wait there until the air starts flowing and force your way into the air duct system. You won't have to equalize. The pressure in the Poseidon complex is the same as the water around it."

As he finished his sentence, the door opened and Schwabb walked in with four bottles of water. He moved over to Tim and Aaron who were staring at him and he placed the bottles on the table in front of them.

"Drink as much as you can before you leave," Schwabb ordered as he turned to leave again. "You'll need it."

"He's an ass," Tim said after the door shut behind Schwabb. "But he's right."

"Yeah, I know," Aaron agreed as he opened one of the liter and a half bottles of *Evian®* and poured a fourth of it down his throat.

Aaron wiped his mouth with his shoulder and Tim continued explaining how to infiltrate the Poseidon complex while referring to the laminated drawing. Most of what Tim was saying was common sense and the other tactical information was easy as well because Aaron had used it before in his army days. Then Tim came to planting the explosive and Aaron made him slow down a bit.

"I have been around explosives before but most of the time on the receiving end so explain this as you would to a group of tourists," Aaron asked of Tim who was using more technical language by the minute.

"No problem. If the bomb explodes here, it'll take pretty much everything with it." He pointed to the lowest level of the complex.

Tim explained what the bomb would do when it exploded. The Poseidon complex and the tunnel connecting it to the surface were both pressurized. The vents leading from the research center, through the tunnel, to the Poseidon complex had a series of air locks in them. They compressed the air that was in the tunnel and complex. If these were destroyed, Tim explained, everything would implode. The ambient pressure would be lost and the sheer weight of the water would crush the dome in an instant. After the dome gave away, everything else inside the complex and the tunnel would be squashed or drowned.

Aaron pictured someone caught in the implosion and cringed inside. It wasn't a pretty thought and Aaron felt bad for anyone who experienced such a terrifying death but he knew it was either him or them.

"This is an exact replica of what you'll be using." Tim showed Aaron a small but heavy black box with a display on it that looked like a digital alarm clock.

"It's really sturdy." He demonstrated by dropping the device to the floor intentionally. "Even the real one won't go off until you set the digital timer."

"And, all you need to do to set it is this." Tim placed the device on the table. "Just like your setting an alarm clock that counts down, like on some digital watches," he continued, pointing at Aaron's dive watch. "Give yourself at least one and a half hours and then press this." Tim pressed the red button. As he did, they both saw the display start to count down.

"After you set the charges, go! There's no way to reset it. That's one of the most important things to remember," Tim said, staring at Aaron. "Are you still getting everything?"

"It's like osmosis," Aaron replied simply, after finishing his second bottle of water. "Let's go on."

"Okay." Tim pointed back to the structural plans. "You're going to want to go out this way," he said, moving his finger along. "You'll still be in the air duct system, as you can see. That is, until here." He stopped and tapped the drawing with his hand. "Once you reach this point there will be large grates you can take off of the wall and escape through this tunnel. You'll be able to see the tunnel through the grates but there's only one problem."

Tim brought out another drawing that showed electronic schematics. "There's a camera right above this door, which, incidentally, is right next to the grate you will be coming out of. But, don't worry, we've got that covered." He picked a hose-like tool out of the equipment bag.

It looked like a large, black power cord. And Aaron thought it was until Tim showed him otherwise. One end, that looked like it should have ended in a power tool, had nothing on it. The other end, however, was connected to a small remote control.

Manipulating one end, Tim made the other end go wherever he wanted. "You will use this. Put this end through the grating and move it up the wall. It has a small camera on the other end so you can see what you're doing. Here's the display." Tim pointed to a small display on the controls. It was barely visible but looking closer revealed a small picture of what the end of the apparatus was seeing.

"Then you use this button to manipulate the scissors," Tim explained and demonstrated.

Aaron saw a small but sturdy pair of wire cutters protrude from the other end of the wire. He wondered how many cool gadgets like this had been invented just for covert operations like his. Scared as he was, he still felt like a kid at a candy store.

"You'll see where you're heading with it. Just cut the wire from the camera, which will be leading into the wall. Once you do that, they won't be able to detect you leaving the compound, but they will be suspicious. But the good thing about cutting the wire is it will give you a few extra seconds before they detect something wrong."

"Now, get through the tunnel a fast as you can." Again, Tim moved his finger along to show Aaron where he would be going. After explaining the tunnel, they got to the end of the mission with the small submarine that was attached to the underwater research rig.

"This is how you will depressurize and rendezvous with us," Tim said of the submarine. "Remember to equalize the pressure of the sub slowly until you reach the surface. If you equalize too fast, you could die and if you don't equalize at all, you might die. I know it sounds gruesome, but if you do it right, you'll be fine."

Aaron knew the dangers of water pressure well and the thought did not bother him. His concern was getting to the sub alive to have the chance to depressurize.

After explaining the finer details of maneuvering the submarine Tim gave Aaron a smaller laminated copy of the Poseidon complex plans and the rendezvous coordinates. This I might need, Aaron thought of the drawings but these coordinates I'm not going to use.

"That's pretty much it. Do you feel prepared for what you're about to do?"

"As prepared as I'll ever be, I guess."

As they were finishing up and packing his gear in a small bag that Aaron would take with him, Schwabb returned.

"You finished, Tim?"

"Yes, sir!"

"Are you tired," Schwabb asked, looking at Aaron.

"A little."

"Well, you're going to have to sleep in the van on the way to the lab. It's time."

Tim gave Aaron the black bag with the equipment and the rest of his water. As he walked out of the conference room with Tim and Schwabb, Aaron asked permission to retreat to his room for a moment. Schwabb excused him.

Aaron went inside the room he had slept in the night before and took the money from his pants, which had been there for hours. It had been uncomfortable and he had even sustained some paper cuts on his inner thigh.

Apart from being crinkled, the bank notes were in good shape. Aaron placed the money in the large zip lock bag with the laminated papers and then put it back in the black bag with the rest of the equipment. It fit easily and he knew that they would never suspect anything else had been added to his bag.

Just before he was about to leave the room, Aaron turned back quickly and grabbed his only picture of Sarah. He kissed it and turned it over. There, on the back, were written the coordinates at which he would meet Jason and the helicopter early the next morning. He hoped he would make it that far.

CHAPTER 18

After retrieving Skilos from the lab, Aaron, Tim and four other agents took a large, black rubber raft out of the bay. Aaron was soothed by Tim's presence. He was attached to him in a strange way, almost like a clergy before a death sentence was to be carried out.

They were not all going to the Poseidon complex; they had to meet up with the decoy boat and Aaron saw it from the minute they left the lab. It was a two hundred-seventy foot boat, painted white with a red and blue stripe at the bow to make it look like a U.S. Coast Guard Cutter. It was anchored three-quarters of a mile off the coast and they were at its port side in minutes.

As they approached the boat, Aaron could make out people moving around on board. The light of the setting sun was outlining the boat in front of a blue sky, which made it easy to pick out people busying themselves on the deck.

As the raft came around the stern of the boat, Tim asked Aaron one more time if he had any questions.

"No," Aaron answered as he smiled faintly. He had all the information he needed and was focused on the mission. Aaron was thankful for the concern but did not voice his thoughts.

On the starboard side of the decoy cutter was a twenty-five foot pontoon boat. Schwabb was there along with many other men dressed in suits. Aaron thought it odd that they would wear suits even on the pontoon boat but it did not break his focus on his mission. His eyes were glazed over as if in deep thought as they docked with the pontoon boat.

After everyone left the small raft, Aaron followed onto the crowded boat. Aside from the unnecessary crowd Aaron spotted the rest of his equipment, which they began loading onto the raft.

"Here's your wet suit and holster," Schwabb said as he threw them to Aaron. He did not respond, his concentration still not broken but instead pulled the wet suit and equipped holster over his body like an android programmed for that sole purpose.

Schwabb came up and smiled at Aaron after he had finished donning his wet suit. "We've given you everything we can, including the training. Good luck. I hope you can pull it off."

"Yeah, my chance of survival isn't really good," Aaron said mechanically, his eyes still fixed on nothing.

"Oh, come on. You need to have a more positive attitude," Schwabb said, patting him on the shoulder.

With lightning speed, Aaron put his left foot behind Schwabb's legs and pushed him down on the ground, pinning him to the boat with his elbow. Then, just as quickly, Aaron pulled one of his *Berretas®* from its holster, cocked it and pointed it at Schwabb's head.

"A more positive attitude," Aaron asked angrily as he squeezed the trigger.

They both heard the click of the empty chamber and after everyone on board came out of their shock of what was going on they pulled Aaron off of Schwabb.

Schwabb got up, dusted himself off and decked Aaron as hard as he could. Aaron coughed to try and catch his breath as he kneeled on the deck.

"You're lucky I don't kill you and pretend you died doing the mission," Schwabb said while straitening his tie. "Get him on his way," he commanded his agents.

The agents picked him up off of the deck and helped him to the raft where his equipment was waiting for him. Tim got on the raft with Aaron and did a final check of the supplies.

"It's time for you to go," Tim said after they found everything. With an enormous hand on Aaron's shoulder Tim continued. "I know what you're going through. I've done missions like this more times than I can imagine and I never felt prepared. Just remember that you're doing this for a good reason. Don't listen to anything that prick Schwabb says." Tim sneered over his shoulder. "Do this for you, but remember. Sometimes people don't make it back from the battlefield, but those are the people who secure the safety of others all over the world. Good luck and Godspeed."

Aaron smiled and shook Tim's hand. "Thanks." Aaron broke his concentration for the first time since he left shore.

Tim left Aaron alone on the raft. It was time to go. He knew that he would never see any of these people again, no matter what happened. He would either die tonight or end up in Israel.

As Aaron watched, the boat with the agents took off for shore. When he could not see their faces anymore he looked to the West where the sun had just set. It was a beautiful sight and Aaron hoped he would see it again. He took a minute to enjoy the dark hues of the sky and the sparkle of the water under the glow of the setting sun. After a few moments, Aaron closed his eyes to capture the tranquil scene in his mind. He took in a deep breath, let it out again and then opened his eyes. He was focused again and ready to tempt fate one last time.

THE POSEIDON PROJECT

*****

Sarah sat in the empty room. There was nothing in it except for her and her new cellmate, and he was asleep.

Sarah thought she had been in the compound for a day but she wasn't sure. There were no windows or clocks and the guard had taken the watch Aaron had given her. She fought him for it, but he had a weapon and she did not. The watch was the only thing she had to remember Aaron by, and that was now gone.

She knew where she was only because Tag told her right after he beat her. She did not think any of her bones were broken but she was in pain regardless. Tag had wanted to know how much she knew about the Poseidon Project. She was convinced that despite what she told him, she would not make it out of this situation alive and therefore she didn't tell Tag anything. She didn't want him to have the satisfaction of knowing he had beaten the information out of her.

As she looked around the room, hopelessness settled over her. She saw nothing in the room to help them escape. To add to the fact that escape was futile, there was a guard with a pistol stationed outside the locked door.

The walls were white and the floor was gray concrete. The only light in the room was emanating from recessed fluorescent bulbs in the ceiling. They were provided with a toilet but there was no door separating the small area from the rest of the room.

Her hands were tied behind her back, as were the other prisoner's. He was in the other corner of the small room, sleeping on his side and she had not spoken to him yet.

Her cellmate was a black man in his thirties. He had an uneven, unshaved beard. His hair was short but dirty, as were his clothes. She could tell they were not his original clothes. Someone had changed him into jeans, which were too big for him. His only other article of clothing was a dirty, white button down shirt. This man looked like he was a New York City bum that had been captured and brought to this room. Sarah expected the room to stink of dirty body odor, but it did not. They must have bathed him periodically, but they didn't bother washing his hair, she thought.

Sarah thought the man looked familiar but she couldn't place him. Maybe I've seen him before but just can't recognize him with the beard and dirty clothes, she thought to herself.

As she was racking her brain, trying to place the man, the door lock was turned and a handsome, dark-skinned man walked in with two armed guards at each side.

The man was carrying a tray with enough food for two people. It was a nice meal, hardly the meal for captives, Sarah thought. There was a large salad, fried fish, and two large glasses of water.

As the man entered, Sarah's cellmate awoke from his nap and sat himself up against the back wall of the room. He stared at Sarah for a moment; confused that he had not heard the guards bringing someone else. His stares did not make her uncomfortable. Sarah saw a warmth in the man's eyes that was unusual for a peering stranger.

The man with the tray looked at both of them and smiled. He placed the tray in the middle of the bare floor and walked over to Sarah. She had her hands tied behind her back and was against the wall, wearing only the white bra and blue jeans they had left on her after the beating. There wasn't much chance of her doing anything to the man and he didn't seem afraid of her.

The handsome man knelt down and introduced himself.

"My name," the man began in a thick Latino accent, "is Señor Lopez. It is my pleasure to make your acquaintance."

The man may have an accent, Sarah thought, but his English was perfect.

"I have to apologize for not being able to meet you earlier, but I hear, and see that Mr. Millwood took good care of you," he said, referring to the bruises starting to form on her ribs and face.

Sarah did not respond to Señor Lopez. She just watched him as he continued.

"You know, you are very beautiful," Lopez said, running his right hand through her dark hair. "It will be a shame when we have to put you two to death. But until then, your dinner is served, please enjoy."

As he backed up to leave the room, Sarah tried to rush him. The guards with the two guns came over and pushed her forcefully back on the floor. She winced in pain as she hit the concrete.

"You will quickly find, Sarah, that there will be no escape from my compound," Lopez said confidently.

"Fuck you," Sarah whispered, barely able to get the words out because the breath had been knocked out of her lungs only moments before.

"That's a nice invitation, but I have work to attend to. Maybe later, my sweet."

As he finished speaking, Lopez motioned to his guards and left the room. The guards left soon after, walking backwards to insure there would be no outbursts from the prisoners. They shut and locked the door behind them.

After they left, Sarah's cellmate moved closer to see if she was all right.

"Are you okay," the man asked gently.

"Yeah, I'll be fine," Sarah responded, still in pain.

"Here, let me help." The man tried to sit Sarah back against the wall. As she sat up she looked at the man again and he was smiling.

"Do I know you from somewhere?"

"I don't think so. My name's James, James Hunter."

"That's it!" Sarah's eyes got wide and she got excited. "I knew I knew you from somewhere! You're the Coast Guard captain whose boat disappeared a few months ago. Everyone thought you were dead."

"I'm alive and well but the rest of my crew is gone and I was responsible for every one of them." James started looking a little somber as he remembered his crew. "I don't really know if I'm lucky or cursed to be alive right now. I think I would have rather gone down with my crew and ship. It's very hard to think about, even though it was a long time ago already." As he finished, he sat down next to Sarah, against the wall.

"I'm sorry," Sarah said sincerely. "I don't know what you're going through but it must be hard."

"How did you know who I was," he asked, turning away from his memories and smiling again.

"You were all over the news. It was a big mystery when your ship was lost. Everyone was looking for the wreck for days."

"And they never found a thing, did they," James asked sadly.

"No. No wreck, no bodies."

"It's a shame." James bowed his head. "My crew was good! They deserve more than what they got."

"I don't understand? How did you get here? Why didn't you…"

"I don't know. Last thing I remember I was standing on the bow of my ship. The next thing I know, I was in different clothes tied up in a dark room. The man who was in here before… Señor Lopez, he's the brains behind this whole operation. And I guess you met Tag, he's a hired thug from the CIA."

"Yeah, I know," Sarah said as if she had known him for years and hated him since the very first day they had met.

"How do you know?"

"He told me everything while he was beating me." She twisted her torso left and right trying to find a more comfortable position.

"What are you here for anyway?"

"They think I know about their whole operation and they don't need me running around telling everyone about it."

"*Do* you know what they're doing here," James asked, hoping that she did.

"Yes."

"How?" James was trying to coax the answer out of her with his probing eyes.

"My boyfriend found out by accident and then told me. He's still out there somewhere but I guess I'm here because they figure that if they have me that he'll come to my rescue and they can kill the both of us."

"Do you think he'll actually try and rescue you?"

"No, he has a lot of army training but I think a search and rescue mission under the sea is a little out of his league." She paused for a moment and a tear rolled down her cheek at the thought of her death and never seeing Aaron again. She could not rub it because her hands were tied behind her back and James wiped her face with his sleeve.

"I love him," she said as a few more tears rolled slowly down her bruised cheeks.

After an awkward moment, James began talking again. "Let's eat before it gets cold. What do you say," he asked, trying to take her mind off of their situation.

Sarah nodded silently and slid her hands under her legs so she could use them to eat. She stopped crying. She was always strong and she wanted to be strong to the very end.

No matter what they're not going to take my soul from me, she thought to strengthen herself. As she ate, she prayed that Aaron would have a good life without her. She would have married him in an instant.

*****

It was almost midnight and Aaron had the remote control for the large boat on autopilot. He knew it wasn't too much longer to where they were heading, and he needed to make sure he was ready to go when they arrived.

Aaron was going over the drawings of the Poseidon complex with the flashlight. He wanted to make sure he had it almost memorized. Aaron didn't want to have to spend time in the air ducts looking at the maps, especially if he was trying to escape before the bomb exploded.

Looking over the structure and the coordinates he would use to meet Jason later, Aaron started thinking about Sarah. He thought about the danger he was putting himself in by attempting this rescue and he knew he might get both of them killed in the process. But, he also knew that he could not live without her. Aaron had finally come to terms with the loss of his parents. If he lost Sarah, too, he did not know how he could live.

Shaking off the thoughts of Sarah's possible demise, Aaron went back to reviewing the plans. After a few minutes of hard concentration, Aaron looked up to catch a quick glimpse of Skilos. He was not at the bow of the raft anymore; Skilos was off the port side and was slowing down.

Aaron's adrenaline started pumping through his veins. He knew he was close so he put the laminated papers, and everything else he would need in the black equipment bag, and grabbed the controls. Aaron slowed the large boat until Skilos was again in front of him.

Aaron returned the boat to autopilot and sifted through the bag to find the other guns encased in their holsters. He loaded the gun that was already around his waist and did the same to the other two. After he finished loading them, Aaron put them all on safety and then put the double holster around his torso like a vest. Even with the wetsuit on he looked like a cowboy with three guns hanging off of his body.

As he zipped the equipment bag shut, he saw the bank notes and the picture of Sarah both secure in the airtight bag. Aaron smiled at the picture and kissed it before closing the bag. The large black bag was made to be strapped to the underwater scooter and Aaron secured it tightly.

Aaron slipped on his flippers, pulled the mask over his head and donned the buoyancy control device, which was already attached to his air tanks. He pulled the velcro straps around his waist and stuck them together, then snapped the jacket shut over his chest. It was heavy, but it wouldn't be in the water.

One thing he would not take with him was the black face paint. It was waterproof and would outlast his trip to the bottom. Aaron spread it over his face and after he was done, he was completely black. There was no way anyone could detect him unless they were face to face. Everything he was traveling with was black: his wet suit, the raft, and all his equipment.

Now ready, Aaron paid close attention to Skilos. It would not be much longer until he had to hit the water. The nervousness was getting to him. It was like standing behind stage, waiting for the play to start. The actors were ready, the audience was ready, but everyone was anxiously awaiting curtain time. Aaron had felt like this before every mission he had been on and he knew that as soon as the action started, there would be no more nervous anticipation. From then on out it would be pure adrenaline.

*****

Señor Lopez was called to the operations center only a few minutes before, but the boat was almost on top of them, and it was moving slowly.

"Why did you not call me earlier," he asked sternly to the man behind the radar screen.

"Señor, we didn't think it was heading in this direction till only a few minutes ago but there is no need to worry. I have started the process," the man answered, defending his actions.

"Never again! Do you understand," he asked angrily. "You are to inform me always when something might happen, always!"

"Si, señor," the man said nervously. Lopez did not get angry often.

"What kind of boat is it?" Lopez was still annoyed but sounded calm again.

"It looks like an American Coast Guard Cutter."

Lopez was going to ask exactly what had been done to prepare for the boat's arrival but he could see very well himself. The man had done a good job. The chamber was already filled with water and the men inside were standing by. *La Fantasma*, the ghost boat had already been deployed with Tag aboard, and the alarm was ringing.

When will these people ever learn, Lopez asked himself? He was angry that the governments would not obey the "no operation zone" near the Poseidon complex. He needed the waters to be clear for the drug shipments to the United States, yet there was another Coast Guard boat coming through.

Lopez had no mercy for these infidels. If they found anyone alive this time, he would kill them himself. And after they had dismembered this ship, he would kill the captain he had been keeping for a rainy day. Lopez was confident that he would not need him for bargaining power. It had been such a long time since he had sunk his first ship, he thought back. No one would ever know the truth about the Poseidon Project and live to tell about it.

*****

There was a dim light ahead of the large boat and Skilos had vanished moments before. Aaron knew exactly what was happening. He untied the raft from the decoy boat and dropped the water scooter over the side. Aaron joined it quickly with his regulator on. He prayed that he would breathe the surface air again soon.

The pure, dry air of the tank filled his lungs and calmed him a little. Aaron turned the throttle and the scooter responded immediately as it pulled him forward and downward, to the light. It was so far away, that Aaron could not see its source clearly but he could see a gigantic shadow in the middle of the light rise from the depths. He knew what it was, but he had not seen it clearly a few days earlier. The sight now was awe-inspiring. The magnet looked like it was ascending to heaven on a beam of light, which radiated for miles.

As he closed the distance between himself and the light, Aaron noticed many small shadows moving around like flies in the distance. They were coming from the Poseidon complex and were rising to the surface to aid in the capture of the large decoy boat. Aaron descended quickly in order to avoid detection.

He aimed the scooter towards the sea floor and it obeyed. Looking at his wrist, Aaron's depth meter read twenty-five feet. He knew he must get lower.

As Aaron descended, Skilos stayed by his side and this made Aaron feel a little safer.

He cruised deeper still, the water turning colder. Aaron noticed that he was breathing much quicker than he was only seconds before. He tried to control his rate of consumption but his efforts only helped a little. Aaron hoped that he could find his way into the complex and into the air ducts before he ran out of air.

Looking back at the dive computer on his wrist, Aaron saw that he was still descending and Skilos was still with him. He was already at seventy-five feet. The water was freezing, even with the wet suit. He needed to find and enter the complex soon or he might contract hypothermia but it was also important to be as close to the sea floor as possible. The higher he was, the easier it would for someone to detect him.

Aaron kept descending and Skilos was staying with him every step of the way. His rate of descent was not increasing, but it was fast enough, he thought. He couldn't see anything around him except for the towering pillar of light. Even Skilos was hard to see and he was only a few feet away. Nothing around him was illuminated and he couldn't see the ground advancing quickly upon him.

There was an enormous clang and Aaron looked up. He knew sound traveled very well under water and that sounds carried for miles, but the emanation of this sound wasn't far at all. The gigantic magnet had attached itself to the large boat and halted it to a dead stop.

Aaron could see the crew of the Poseidon swarming around the wreck with their scooters. They would kill survivors, but he knew they wouldn't find anyone alive.

Aaron looked back at his wrist to check his depth. He did not see it. Instead, his body slammed into his scooter as it hit the ground hard. The breath was knocked out of him, as was his regulator. He scrambled quickly to find it.

He knew it was there somewhere, still attached to his body but his groping hands could not find it and his eyes could not either. It was too dark.

He felt Skilos rubbing up against him, trying to help him, but he could not. How ironic it would be if he died like this, he thought. He had assisted others in the very same situation only a few months before.

His lungs burned for air. Only a few more seconds and he would pass out and certainly die. He reached around his back and found a hose. Aaron didn't know what it was, but he tugged on it anyway. His hand slid quickly over the smooth surface until it stopped at a mouthpiece. Aaron pulled it towards him and shoved it in his mouth. He coughed into it and took in heaving, deep breaths.

He was alive. Thank God I didn't drown alone, in the deep, dark ocean, he thought. If he had died, no one would have found him with all the weight strapped to him. His body would have been weighted down and would have started to rot as the scavengers of the sea picked him to pieces.

He pulled in as much oxygen as his lungs could take until he was satiated. It took less than a minute until he was back to normal and Aaron looked around and noticed Skilos was gone. I hope that he just went for more air, Aaron thought. He wanted to wait for Skilos to return but he could not, his tank was already less than half full.

Looking back at his destination, Aaron saw that the Poseidon complex was still quite some distance ahead and that he didn't have much time to reach it. The large decoy boat was already halfway down to its grizzly destination and if they closed the dome before he arrived he would have no way in. Aaron had to move fast.

Going full throttle, Aaron moved ahead silently through the cold, dark waters. The workers accompanying the ill-fated boat were descending with it and Aaron wanted to beat them down. He wanted there to be no chance of detection. It would make his mission much easier.

Maneuvering his water scooter, Aaron felt like he was in a jet plane flying close to the ground in order to avoid radar detection. He could manipulate the scooter in any direction he wanted and was getting better by the moment.

Aaron was almost directly under the huge magnet and the terrain suddenly started rising. Looking around, Aaron noticed that he could see a lot more now and he realized how much was going on below him.

There were scavengers everywhere and some small sharks slipped in and out of his sight eerily. Looking harder at the sea floor below him Aaron suddenly had a jolt of fear. He saw two human eyes staring at him as a crab crawled away. Now he knew why there was so much activity and as he paid more attention to the sea floor, he saw numerous human body parts that were all held down by a massive net. The sight made him sick and he decided to keep his attention to where he was going and not what was beneath him.

Looking ahead he saw the contours of the ocean floor rising like a dome that covered a sports stadium. It was getting lighter by the second and he knew that if anyone looked in his direction, he would be spotted. His only asset was that he looked a lot like the others with his black scooter and wetsuit.

Just then Skilos swam quickly by him. Aaron was a little scared at first but the dolphin was moving so fast that he knew what it was instantly. Aaron watched Skilos swim up to where the other divers were and distract them. If it wasn't for Skilos, Aaron might not have made it this far.

The light was now intense. Aaron was almost enveloped in its warmth when he looked down to check his air gauge. As his eyes focused, there was a loud clang of metal against metal and Aaron came to a halt again. He had been moving slower and the sudden stop did not hurt him this time.

He had just gone over the crest of the hill and there was a man with a scooter right in front of him. Aaron looked directly into his eyes. The man was angry, but he did not notice anything unusual about Aaron. He made a motion that looked like he was telling Aaron to be more careful and Aaron nodded his head. After staring at Aaron for a few moments, he continued ascending to help the others.

Aaron was still frozen like a deer in headlights. His eyes were wide, his pupils fully dilated and he was breathing quickly again.

I can't believe he didn't realize I wasn't one of them, Aaron thought. Aaron was so relieved that it took him a few seconds to realize where he was and to slow his breathing again. Looking again at his air gauge, Aaron realized he needed to hurry. His tank was already three-fourths empty.

Looking down was an awesome sight. He was hovering hundreds of feet above a huge chamber. The light coming from below him was magnificent. It seemed like he was descending into heaven, or was it hell, Aaron asked himself?

There was no one left in the chamber but it was littered with machinery that looked alien to Aaron. He had no idea what each one did, but he had an idea what they did as a whole.

Above him, the boat and the crew of the Poseidon were closing in fast. Aaron looked around the huge bay doors for the air duct and there was one directly underneath him, about fifty yards away.

Upon reaching the opening to the air vent, Aaron realized there were no screws. He remembered what Tim had told him and he looked for the clamps. Aaron found them just behind the left and right sides of the vent. The grating was held into place by two clips that fit into a wedge in the wall. He stuck his hands in and pulled them close to the grate and it came off easily as he pulled it out of the opening.

Moving quickly, Aaron detached his equipment bag from the scooter. Not needing it anymore, he let the scooter fall into the chamber. It fell faster and faster toward the bottom of the large, flooded room. Aaron hoped they would figure it was one of theirs and would not realize it was extra until it was too late.

Holding onto the grate, Aaron shoved the large black bag into the duct and then slipped inside. The hole was much larger than he was and it was easy for him to slide through. After he was completely in, Aaron turned around with ease and replaced the grate just in time. Looking out into the vast arena of water and light, he saw the workers pouring in, and the boat, not far behind.

There must be at least thirty men on scooters, he thought. They looked like an army of black demons escorting a dead crew and ship to their watery grave.

Skilos was nowhere to be seen and Aaron knew that he might not ever see him again. It was sad, but he had to press on. They would start to fill the chamber with air soon and he needed his head start. Aaron turned around, picked up his bag and swam to the bottom of the air duct.

As he went, the slope got steeper and steeper until he was heading strait down. It would have been very dark except for the vents that branched out every fifty feet; leading back to the main chamber.

Aaron kept swimming downward. He was afraid the air duct would get smaller, but it grew larger. He was heading towards one of the main airflows, which would force air back into the enormous chamber.

Looking straight ahead, Aaron could see another grate he would have to go through. That grate would lead to a small room where the air would be pushed up through a large hole in the floor. I'm in the right place, he thought. I'm not lost yet.

Aaron had almost reached the second grate when he heard a loud humming sound coming from all around him. The water was vibrating. He couldn't see anything moving but he knew that the gigantic dome was closing. He only had a few minutes left to get situated in the small room before the air was turned on.

With everything around him vibrating, Aaron reached down and pulled the grate from its place, entered the small room and replaced the grate. He floated slowly down to the floor, placed his equipment bag at his knees and waited. Aaron prayed it would not be long before the air was forced through the hole in the floor. Looking at he gauge, Aaron guessed that he only had another five minutes of air left.

The hole in the floor where the air would be forced into the small room was closed. It would open soon though, and Aaron must be ready.

The air would come through with such force; Aaron had to make sure he wasn't carried away like a leaf in the wind. He hoped that his tank and equipment bag that he was still holding onto would weigh him down enough and he would be able to slip through the hole in the floor.

It was going to be a rough ride, he thought. As he waited for the air to start flowing, Aaron realized that he and Tim had forgotten something. The air would not fill up in the room he was in, giving him time to slip through the hole in the floor. It was going to continuously escape through the grate in the ceiling. He had to find a way to keep the air from escaping until he could escape from the room with ease.

Thoughts ran through his head about what he had and what he could leave behind that would trap the air in the room. Aaron searched through his bag and as he was looking, an idea flashed in his head.

The laminated papers, he thought. If I can spare one of them, it might fit over the grating and trap the air long enough for me to get out of the room.

Aaron pulled out the papers and looked at them, there were only two large enough to fit over the grating. They were both structural drawings of the Poseidon complex and one of them had the coordinates of the rendezvous point with the CIA. The drawing without the CIA meeting point had the layout of the air duct system. He could sacrifice the other one.

As he swam to the top of the small room, Aaron hoped that everything would go according to plan. If it did not, if he had to leave the air ducts, he might get lost.

He placed the large, laminated page over the grate and it covered the area with room to spare. The page would not stay there on its own, and he would have to hold it there as the air was being forced into the small room.

As Aaron was floating slowly back down to the floor, he felt the world around him stop vibrating. The bay doors must be closed, he thought. The air would start flowing any second.

He heard it coming, but only a split second before the air burst through the floor like a tornado. It tossed him around like a rag doll but Aaron held onto the paper and tried to find his bearings. The strong current finally forced him up against the ceiling. The impact wasn't too forceful and he regained his senses quickly. Looking forward, he saw the air escaping through the grating.

Aaron still had the paper in his hand. He had somehow held onto it regardless of the turbulent waters. If he had let go of it, there would be no way to retrieve it in this chaotic atmosphere.

Moving as fast as he could, Aaron slid the laminated paper over the grate. Immediately, the air started to build up in the small room. His idea was working.

Slowly, the room started to fill with air. Aaron swam down to his bag, which was still on the floor. It was lying too low to the ground to have been affected by the flowing air.

He waited until the air was down to his face and Aaron removed his facemask and regulator. The air had almost come too late. Looking at his air gauge, Aaron noticed that he had been breathing on empty.

The room was almost full with air and Aaron knew he didn't have much time until there was so much pressure that the grate would give away. He quickly removed his buoyancy control device and left everything behind except for his equipment bag and the guns strapped to his body.

He slipped into the large hole in the floor but it wasn't as easy as he had thought. Aaron felt like he was lowering himself into a wind tunnel. The air was blowing past him very fast and he knew he would be dry within minutes.

Aaron held onto the floor of the small room as he lowered himself down. Even with his arms fully extended, there would still be a small drop. He hoped the flowing air would help slow him down.

He landed softly and continued forward in the direction that Tim had told him to go. Only a few steps into his journey, Aaron felt the resistance from the wind stop. It was an eerie feeling. It seemed like it stopped because he was there, not because someone had turned it off.

The grate in the small room gave way to the building pressure. With a loud pop the grate and the paper were propelled up through the duct system and Aaron was thrown backwards.

He held onto the bag like it was a baby as he flew backwards. Although it might cushion his landing, he did not want to land on it. He knew it would not be a good idea to land on the explosives or any other equipment that his life depended on. He would risk getting bruised if it meant his life later.

With a large thud, Aaron landed squarely on his back. His breath was taken out of him immediately and he coughed to try and force some air back into his lungs. This wasn't his day, he thought, but he hoped that he would have the last laugh. He got to his feet and continued where he had left off.

Aaron started walking the length of the air duct until it got so small that he had to crawl. After he started crawling, it was not too much further until he came to a fork in the road.

One of the vents went on, straight ahead. The other dropped to a distance he could not judge. It looked as though he could see the bottom, but the low level of light and the lack of color variations confused his eyes. Aaron knew that he must plant the bomb at the bottom of the structure, but he wanted to find Sarah first if she was still alive.

Aaron took out the drawing and studied it, following his finger with his eyes. He found the place where he was and looked downward. This is where he wanted to be, he thought.

He placed the paper back in his bag and zipped it shut. Lowering his legs first, Aaron secured himself on the ladder, which had been built inside the air system.

After about ten feet of climbing silently downward, there were two vents. One ran out to his left and the other to his right. Aaron could see the light from vents running the distance of each duct. They seemed to be equidistant. He listened for Sarah's voice. If she were talking he would be able to hear it, even if it was faint. It would take too much time to search every vent in the complex and he hoped she would say something while he was listening. It was times like these that he wished he had telepathy. Maybe if he willed her to speak, she would say something, he hoped.

After listening for a few moments but only hearing a couple of Latino accents, Aaron went on to the next set of ducts ten feet below him. After arriving there and listening for five minutes, Aaron heard more talking than before; still in Spanish but none of the voices were Sarah's.

Aaron continued to listen at each ten-foot interval, but he never heard Sarah. It crossed his mind that she might be dead and the thought sent chills down his spine. But I won't accept her death as a possibility unless I see her, he thought, pulling himself together so he could continue.

At the bottom of the vertical duct, Aaron stepped softly onto the metal floor. He listened for a few moments but did not hear anything. His eyes fell to his feet and his shoulder loosened. He had not found her and whether Sarah was alive or not, he was still going to have to set the explosives and leave. There wasn't much time left until he had to meet Jason.

He placed the bag quietly on the floor of the duct and picked up the explosive device. It was amazing how light it was but that it could create such horrific destruction. Aaron placed the device on the wall next to him and turned on the timer.

A digital clock lit up with red numbers. At that moment it read zero, but that would change. Aaron toyed with the controls as Tim had told him and manipulated the time as if it were an alarm clock.

If it was an alarm clock, Aaron thought, it would be one hell of a rude awakening. The magnitude of what he was doing did not faze him. Aaron was calm.

It was now one in the morning, Aaron thought while looking at his watch. Thinking of how long he had left until he met Jason, and how much longer he could spend listening for Sarah, Aaron programmed the clock for two hours, took a deep breath and pressed the "set" button. After pressing the button, he immediately set his stopwatch to count down from two hours.

The two dots between the hour and minute half of the detonation clock started blinking every second. The countdown was underway. There was no turning back now. Tim had told him that once the charge was set, there was no way to turn it off.

Aaron sat and watched the clock to make sure the minutes were changing. As soon as the clock read one hour and fifty-nine minutes, Aaron heard a familiar voice floating through the air and his heart stopped. It was Sarah.

01:58:58

The ship had been in the complex for only thirty minutes and Lopez knew something was wrong. He could feel it. He had been watching the process all the way through as he usually did, but something about this operation wasn't right. Lopez sat in the control room watching the progress of the workers from a chair in the back of the room where he could see everything. The process was moving along fine but something was bugging him and he decided to take a first hand look at what was going on.

"Radio Millwood and tell him to have *La Fantasma* ready for anything," Lopez said, before heading out the large door.

He entered the gigantic chamber and stared out across the wreckage. The smell of dead bodies was stronger than usual. Lopez went to the pile of bodies that had not already been disposed of and they were unusual.

Most of them did not seem to have died only minutes before. Some of them must have been dead for days, he thought while examining the extensive decay and smelling the stronger than normal stench. Usually the crews that died, did so because they slammed into bulkheads or other objects aboard the ship when it stopped suddenly. Most of these bodies seemed to have died from other various injuries, Lopez said to himself. He knew now that something was definitely wrong.

Lopez shouted an order to one of the men supervising the destruction of the ship. He wanted them to look for anything suspicious. They had already failed to notice the bodies, which had apparently been dead for days, so the workers might not notice anything unusual unless he told them to be keen. Being that the men had failed to notice the obvious, Lopez decided to take a walk around and see if he could spot anything else out of the ordinary.

As he was walking around, Lopez surveyed the boat, debris, dead bodies and equipment. After walking around the boat once, Lopez made a discovery. All of the water scooters were on one side of the boat, lined up like they normally were, but there was one on the other side, alone, resting by itself, upside down.

Lopez walked over to the lone water scooter, kneeled, and examined it. The water scooter was not from the Poseidon complex. It looked very similar but it was not one of theirs, Lopez thought angrily, his face turning red.

"Someone is here," Lopez raged. His face turned redder as he screamed, his hands tightly clenched. There was an unwelcome visitor somewhere in his complex. Lopez knew he must find this person and kill him immediately.

Looking around at the workers, he did not notice anyone out of the ordinary, but he knew this intruder could be anywhere in the complex. Lopez was steaming with anger. He had believed that his complex was impenetrable but he was proven wrong and was furious. He realized that the boat they had just sunk was a decoy. It was sent to distract them from realizing someone had entered the complex and the plan had worked but he would not let the intruder live to complete his plan.

Lopez got up and walked briskly towards the workers who were still dismantling the boat. Everyone in the chamber was silent and watching their boss move confidently across the floor. The workers who had been watching him knew he was angry and they didn't want to upset him any more than he was. Noticing their lack of concentration to the task at hand, he gave them some orders in Spanish.

"My people," he preached loudly, raising his hands. "We may have an intruder amongst us. Be careful! This boat we have just sunk for our cause might be booby-trapped, please exit it slowly and with caution. Let our bomb experts examine it and then continue your jobs. For now, take some time off and search the complex for intruders. If you find any, I want them alive if possible. If your life is in danger, you may defend it! Remember that your life is precious! God loves you for the work you are doing and his blessings will be with you always. Now go!"

All of his workers obeyed immediately as if they had just heard a speech told by God through his prophet Señor Lopez. They may not have been the brightest people in the world but they were very loyal. They loved God and they loved their fearless leader. All of the workers believed they were doing the right thing. They believed, like their leader, that God was on their side.

Lopez was almost to the control room when something caught his eye. Off to the right he saw a white, rectangular shaped object. He wasn't sure what it was so he walked over to it and picked it up.

It was the plans for the Poseidon Project. It had been laminated and on the back were coordinates. He wasn't sure exactly what the coordinates were for but he recognized them as not being too far from his complex.

The intruder must have lost this and his comrades might also be at these coordinates, he thought. "They might be there to pick him up, but we will meet him instead," he said with an evil smile. He would send *La Fantasma* and Mr. Millwood to that area to destroy any vessel in sight and to pick up the intruder if they found him. But first, he was going to check on his prisoners. They were too much of a liability now and it was time for them to meet their end.

01:50:17

Sarah's voice sounded as if it wasn't too far away on the same level. Her voice had come from his left, and that is the way he crawled, leaving his equipment and his two extra guns behind. He moved slowly and without a sound with the silenced gun in his left hand. He had passed a few grates and had not seen Sarah. One of the grates Aaron had passed revealed a worker from the Poseidon complex sleeping in his bunk. He was just below the grate on a plain looking bed. Aaron moved especially slowly when he was over the man to make sure he did not wake up.

His heart started racing again. Aaron was expecting to see Sarah and his mind was distracted from his mission. He loved her so much and was so happy at the prospect of her being alive and well that he could not focus even though time was running out.

The fourth grate was coming up slowly. He had not heard Sarah's voice in a few minutes but Aaron knew he was moving in the right direction.

When he reached the fourth grate, Aaron stuck his head over it slowly so as not to draw attention to himself if anyone was below him. What he saw filled his soul with joy. It was Sarah.

She was sitting with her back to the wall only a few feet away. Her head was between her knees and her hands were bound together with twine, resting near her feet.

Aaron's eyes started to fill with tears of joy but he did not say a word. He wanted to push out the grate and scream that he was there to save her and he was only a few feet away. Aaron could hardly hold back from doing just that, but he had to.

As he was thinking of how to get her attention without being too loud, Aaron became aware of someone else's presence in the room with Sarah. He looked slowly beneath where his legs were and saw another man lying on the floor. His hands were also bound.

He must be another prisoner, Aaron thought while studying his ragged appearance. Aaron looked carefully around the rest of the room to make sure it was empty. It was and the only other thing in the room besides Sarah and the other prisoner was a dirty tray, cups and plastic spoons.

They must have been fed recently, Aaron thought. This will work to my advantage. Sarah and the other man will need a lot of energy if I'm going to get them out of here.

Turning his attention back to escape, Aaron pulled one of the guns from its holster and trailed it over the grate slowly. As it hit each rung of the grate it made a soft clicking sound. Aaron made sure to keep it at a steady pace. If someone else heard it, he wanted them to think it was just part of the mechanical workings of the air system. All he wanted Sarah to do was look up, and she did.

Sarah looked up slowly towards the grating where the noise was coming from but did not see anything at first. Aaron had painted his face jet black to prevent anyone from detecting him, but it was working too well.

As her eyes focused she realized there was a person inside the air duct but she couldn't tell who it was. Then, Aaron whispered her name.

Her jaw dropped to the floor. She was in shock and could not say anything; she just shook her head as if to say to herself that it was a figment of her imagination.

Aaron waved with his empty hand and Sarah got to her feet to get a closer look. As she did, Aaron began to quietly remove the grate.

Sarah's movement caught James's attention and he looked in her direction. He had no idea what she was looking at. From his spot on the floor James could not see into the air duct.

It didn't take long for Aaron to take off the grate. He placed it in front of him, in the shaft and held his arms out to Sarah. He was afraid to say anything else for fear of the sounds traveling too far.

Sarah touched Aaron's arms with her bound hands and she started crying. She couldn't believe that he was actually in their room and saving, or attempting to save her. She had no idea how he got the equipment he needed to get into the Poseidon complex, but explanations would come later.

Aaron held up one finger and disappeared back into the darkness for a moment. When he returned, Aaron produced a large diving knife. He dropped it into her hands and Sarah handed it to James.

James, seeing the grate being lifted from the hole had also gotten up to see what was going on, but he didn't dare say anything. Sarah and he both knew that there was a guard outside the door and they did not want to attract any attention.

James started to cut through the twine around Sarah's wrists. When she was free, Sarah did the same for her cellmate. They both massaged their wrists. It was a great feeling to be free.

Aaron was about to speak softly but James cautioned him not to by putting a finger to his mouth and then pointing to the door. Aaron realized that an explanation of any kind would have to wait until they were in the tunnel or even after that. Until then, they were just going to have to trust him.

Sarah handed the knife back to Aaron and he put it back in its sheath on his leg. When he returned to the hole, he reached for Sarah. James cupped his hands and pushed Sarah up to the opening.

Aaron grabbed her arms and helped pull her up. She got in quietly right next to Aaron. There was hardly any room to move with the two of them in one place but it was manageable.

They hugged like they had not seen each other in years, squeezing each other hard. Aaron rubbed the back of her head and pulled her away. He motioned for her to start moving back the way he had come. Aaron pointed to his eyes, then down at the grates towards the bomb and then made a "be silent" motion with his index finger to his mouth. Sarah nodded and began moving slowly and silently back the way Aaron had come.

When she was past his feet, Aaron looked back down to James. He reached his arm down and waited for him to jump. Aaron braced himself as James leapt into the air. Aaron caught one arm but James did not get a good grasp on the opening and he fell to the ground with a loud thud.

Both Aaron and James looked at the door in anticipation of the guard's entrance. Had he heard something, they thought in unison. Would he enter to check it out?

They were both answered when they heard the key clicking in the lock and the door opened quickly. The guard pointed his gun in the room but was not prepared for what he saw. One of the prisoners was missing and one was on the floor with his hands untied.

After taking a second to comprehend what was going on, the guard's eye was caught by movement from the ceiling. There was a man in black hanging from the air vent. He lifted his gun to shoot but it was too late.

Aaron fired two shots, with the silenced gun, into the guard. He grunted, flew back and fell to the hallway floor. He looked dead but it didn't matter, they needed to leave quickly.

James grabbed the man, dragged him into the room and placed him under the vent. He looked at the blood in the hallway but didn't want to waste time trying to clean it up. He locked the door from the outside and shut himself in.

James was about to jump again when Aaron protested. He was pointing adamantly at the guard.

"What," James asked quietly. He was confused about what Aaron wanted. All James wanted to do was escape.

"The watch," Aaron whispered insistently.

"We don't have time for this!" James was disgusted that Aaron would want the watch off of a dead man.

"Just get it, now," Aaron insisted.

James bent down quickly and fumbled with the silver diving watch until he got it off of the guard's wrist. He threw it up to Aaron and Aaron lowered his arm for James to jump again.

James jumped up again and this time he pulled himself successfully into the air vent. Aaron gave James the same instructions as Sarah and he started back as well.

When James was safely behind him, Aaron replaced the grate, turned around and followed the other two. As he passed the explosives, Aaron checked his digital watch and they were still perfectly synchronized.

01:30:48

A few seconds later, they were all safely in the area with the ladder leading up to the top levels of the complex, but Aaron knew they needed to go a different way. He got out the plans again and looked at them with a small flashlight he had retrieved from his bag. The other two waited quietly as Aaron found the escape route. Everyone was tense but excited at the same time.

After Aaron figured out the route, he placed the plans and the flashlight back in his bag and motioned for the others to follow him. Aaron went down the shaft opposite of where he had found Sarah.

It took them a few minutes to get all the way across to the next open space. There was another ladder there but they rested for a few seconds before their climb to the top.

01:26:23

234

Lopez checked the gun in his hand to make sure he had enough rounds left to finish off his prisoners. It was a shame he had to kill them but he knew it was necessary.

Exiting the elevator, Lopez did not see the guard standing firm at his post but instead he saw blood spattered on the wall opposite the prisoners' room. Blood was also streaked across the floor leading into the room. When he came closer, Lopez unlocked the door to the prisoners' room, readied his gun and flung the door open.

There, he found the guard slumped on the ground in the corner in a pool of blood. He had been shot twice, and the prisoners were gone.

The guard was still alive and was reaching for his leader to help him. Lopez screamed with anger and finished the job the escaped prisoners had failed to do. The guard was now dead.

The prisoners have escaped the room but they will not make it out of my complex alive, Lopez promised himself. He had to move quickly. Lopez had no idea where they could be but he was sure that James and Sarah were still somewhere within the Poseidon complex.

He ran to the elevator and took it up to the control room. Once there, he ran straight to the man sitting at the control panel.

"Have you seen anyone that you don't know on these screens," Lopez asked loudly. He was out of breath because he ran but also because he knew he was in trouble.

"No, señor."

"I want you to watch these screens very carefully and if you see the prisoners or anyone you don't recognize, notify me immediately! Do you understand," he ordered, pointing at the monitor.

"Yes, señor," the man answered, scared because his boss was so upset.

Lopez raced across the room, picked up two radios and threw one to the man behind the console. "Radio me if you see anything. I'm going to search the complex, and tell Millwood to check out these coordinates," Lopez said as he threw the laminated paper at the man behind the console. Without any further explanation, he rushed out of the room and into the large area with the half-dismantled boat.

Some of the men were still there, waiting for the bomb experts to finish their job. Lopez yelled at them and told them to join him in the search for the escaped prisoners. The workers hopped up and joined their leader without question.

The posse went through the large door at the other end of the chamber and began searching the building for the prisoners.

01:20:37

Aaron, Sarah and James all heard an angry scream and the piercing sound of a gunshot ring through the air ducts. They turned their heads in the direction of where they had just been. Lopez was onto them and they all knew it. They started up the stairs as quickly and as quietly as they could.

As they climbed, there were crawl spaces behind them but nothing in front of them. They must be on the far edge of the Poseidon complex, Aaron thought. He knew it is where they wanted to be, but not for long. Aaron wanted to get as far away from the Poseidon complex as possible before the bomb disintegrated it. He started climbing faster.

It wasn't long before they reached the top of the stairs. The space was much larger now and Aaron could almost stand. He didn't wait for the other two. He knew they would catch up.

Aaron ran quietly to the end of the air duct. He could see the long tunnel through the vents. They were almost there.

01:07:05

He placed his bag down on the floor and took out the equipment he needed. Aaron started loosening the screws that held the large grate on the wall.

As he was finishing up, Sarah and James both joined him. They sat back and watched.

Aaron readied the cutting device for the camera that he knew was above them, looking out over the tunnel. He turned it on and slipped it through one of the holes in the vent.

A picture came up on the console and Aaron could see the camera above them. He moved the cutting device slowly up the side of the wall until he reached the back of the camera. The wire was in sight. He tried to cut it once but missed. Aaron tried again. This is going to be harder than I thought, Aaron said to himself as he started sweating.

01:04:37

Tag had received the orders from Señor Lopez and was headed in the direction of the coordinates he had been given. *La Fantasma* glided along the ocean like a ghost.

Observing with his binoculars, Tag could not see a thing. It was dark but the coordinates he was given were not far from their current position. He was sure there was nothing there. As he looked in the direction they were headed, Tag thought about what could be happening. Was the CIA already onto them? If they were, did he have time to escape? He was in a position to escape, but could he trick the crew into abandoning the area? They were very loyal to Señor Lopez.

Thinking about their loyalty to Señor Lopez gave Tag an idea. He picked up a headset and pretended to contact the control room in the Poseidon complex.

"What, are you certain?" Tag was talking to himself. "Okay, no problem. Yes, Señor Lopez." Tag put down the headset and started to give his own instructions.

"We have a new set of coordinates," Tag said, giving the crew a set of coordinates that would take them in the opposite direction they were heading. If the CIA was at Lopez's coordinates, Tag wasn't going to greet them.

01:00:12

In the control room, the worker kept a close eye on all the cameras. There were too many to display at one time so the screens in front of him changed every few seconds to give another view. Periodically he would see Lopez and other workers he had corralled, looking for the intruder and escaped prisoners. They had started in the upper levels of the complex but were already searching the third level below the control room.

The cameras switched again and one of the views was of the long tunnel, leading to the research station. It was empty. Everyone who had been there earlier had been called in to search for the intruder and nothing in the tunnel had been disturbed. The crates were neatly beside one wall and the electric car was charging against the other wall.

Again, the cameras switched and the man was looking at the interiors of the Poseidon complex. Lopez was still searching below but had not come across anything.

When the cameras switched back to the tunnel view a few minutes later, there was a problem. The camera was not sending back any picture. The area on the screen that had once produced a picture of the tunnel was now producing only static.

"Señor Lopez," the man shouted into the radio. "Señor!"

"What is it," he asked anxiously.

"There is a problem with the camera in the tunnel! It's not responding!"

"I'm going out there!"

00:56:01

Aaron had cut the wire, but he had lost precious time making attempt after attempt with the cutting device. They had to move quickly. He left the cutting tool where he used it and pulled the grate from the wall. They all exited the Poseidon complex and ran into the tunnel.

There was an electric cart in front of them and they decided to take it. There were only two seats, but there was a flatbed on the back for equipment and James got on it.

As they got on the cart, Aaron placed his equipment bag beside him. He reached in and handed one of the guns to James.

"Don't I get one," Sarah asked.

Aaron did not say a word, but handed Sarah his other gun.

"Do you know how to use these," Aaron asked James. He didn't need to ask Sarah, he knew she knew how to use a gun.

"Sure do," James said excitedly. "It's nice to feel one in my hand after such a long time." He caressed the gun.

"How did you make it here?" Sarah was still could not believe that Aaron had come to save them.

"It's a bit of a long story. I'll tell you later, I promise, but first, let's get the hell out of this place," Aaron said, turning on the car. "The bomb is set to detonate soon and if we're not out of here, we'll go up, too." Aaron pressed on the accelerator and they took off down the tunnel.

"You set a bomb," James asked, surprised.

"Yeah, you didn't see it as we were crawling through the vents," Sarah asked.

"I guess I was too preoccupied with getting the hell out of here I wasn't really paying any attention."

"I love you," Sarah said as she turned her attention back to Aaron and squeezed him. "Thanks for saving us."

Sarah could hardly believe that her life was coming to an end only a few hours before, but now it was just beginning again.

"Who's you're friend," Aaron asked.

"James." She looked back at her cellmate.

James turned around and offered his hand. "James Hunter."

"Aaron," he said, shaking James's hand quickly.

"You with Special Forces or something?"

"No, I'm just Sarah's boyfriend."

James was really surprised at this. He figured that they knew each other but he had no idea that they were in a relationship. "Wow, nice boyfriend."

00:50:53

They were only about a hundred yards away when the large door to the Poseidon complex opened and bullets started whizzing through the air just over their heads. Aaron and Sarah ducked beneath the seats and kept driving straight ahead. Sarah fired shots back towards the complex along with James who was already shooting.

Lopez and his men were running as fast as they could to catch up to the electric cart but it was moving too fast for them. They would soon be out of range, but they needed as much distance between them and Lopez as they could get. Once they reached the ladder, it would be a long climb up to the escape pod and they would be very vulnerable during the ascent.

Lopez grabbed one of the rifles from his men and knelt for stability. He aimed carefully at the electric car and fired.

James screamed and collapsed on the flatbed. His head was right next to Sarah's and he screamed again in agony but they could not stop. If they did stop, it would cost them their lives.

James was still alive, but barely. Bullets kept flying by them. Some were hitting the car but it had not stopped working. They kept driving and very quickly they were out of range. The tunnel had curved to the left and it blocked the sight of their pursuers. They were safe, but that would only last for a few seconds.

Sarah and Aaron sat back on the seats and Sarah attended to James. He was still breathing but did not look like he would last long. The blood coming from his wound was dark and thick. Sarah knew, from her short-lived paramedic training, that he had been hit in the liver and did not have long to live.

James was whispering something but Sarah could not make out what he was trying to say. She tried to comfort him but he was in too much pain.

"We're going to get you out with us," she said. "You're going to be okay."

James shook his head. He, too, knew that he was going to die in the tunnel. After waiting months in captivity, at least I'm going to die a free man, he thought. I will have died fighting for life, not begging for it.

He smiled with the thought that he would soon see his father again and would also reunite with the crew he had let down. He could fix the few things that had gone wrong in his life, he thought through the pain.

00:46:09

The cart came to an abrupt halt at the bottom of a long ladder leading directly up to a hatch. They were in a little alcove that would provide minimal protection from the pursuers. Looking back, Aaron could not yet see the men approaching.

They knew it would be impossible to take James with them. Even if they could make it to the hatch in time, they would not be able to save James. He needed medical attention that would not be available for hours and he only had minutes.

"Leave me here! You'll never make it with me," James said through clenched teeth. "I'm not going to be much good in a few minutes anyway." He uncovered his wound, revealing the oozing crimson blood. "Go! You're not going to make it either if you wait. Go!" A tear rolled down his check as he smiled. James knew it was about that time. He knew his father had not come to save him this time for a reason.

He had a far-away look in his eye and what he saw spread a smile across his face. His father was floating slowly towards him on a small sailboat through calm waters and a perfect blue sky. He looks exactly the same, James thought.

"I'll be there in a sec, Dad," he said to himself.

Aaron and Sarah left him with a gun. If he was still alive when the men came into range, he could slow them down. They started climbing

Halfway up to the hatch, Aaron and Sarah heard gunfire. Looking down they saw James halfheartedly firing in the direction of the men and, in turn, they were firing back at him. They could see the bullets hitting the wall below them. They moved faster.

As they continued up the ladder, the gunshots stopped. James had either been shot or he had died of the previous gunshot wound. Either way, he had passed on, but they didn't look down. The men would start firing on them at any second.

They reached the hatch and Aaron opened it as quickly as he could. Sarah was right behind him, keeping an eye on what was happening below. She could not see the men. They had not reached the alcove where the ladder started but bullets began bombarding the wall below them anyway.

Aaron pushed open the hatch just in time. He climbed into the small chamber and Sarah followed. Aaron shut the hatch as bullets were showering the area. When they shut the hatch, they heard the sound of bullets hitting the other side. They would not come through, though; the metal was too thick.

Although they were temporarily safe, Aaron and Sarah did not stop for a breather. They quickly opened the sub hatch above them and entered.

00:41:13

"Shut the sub hatch and I'll get us going," Aaron told Sarah. They were not out of the woods yet.

Sarah stepped out of the small area between the two hatches and shut the one for the small submarine. As she sealed it, she no longer heard the barrage of bullets. It sounded as if they had stopped shooting. Seeing that the hatch was closed, Aaron immediately started the depressurizing process. They needed as much time as they could get.

"I think they stopped shooting," she said to Aaron who was trying to work out the controls.

"Well, there's no point in trying to shoot through the metal." Aaron was paying more attention to the submarine controls than his girlfriend.

"They'll probably go back to the Poseidon complex and leave from there. I'm sure they must have some sort of submarine like this. We're not going to get away that easily, I can tell you that!"

"How do you know?"

"I've seen too many movies! I know," he responded, starting to feel lighthearted that they were still alive. "Besides, they're not going to give this place up that easily! But what they don't know is that I planted a bomb in their air duct system. It's going to go off in less than an hour!" He checked his watch.

With a jolt, Aaron unhitched the sub from its docked position. He moved the controls around and the sub started to move. It worked just as Tim said it would and he was right, Aaron thought. It *was* easy to maneuver.

"Where are we going," Sarah asked, sitting on the hard gray surface behind Aaron.

"To meet my friend Jason, I hope."

"What?" She was confused because she knew he lived in Israel.

"It's a long story and I really need to concentrate to get us out of here alive. Basically though, I made a deal with the Israeli Government. I'm going to give them the dolphin communication research and in turn, they are going to give both of us asylum. We're going to live our dream of moving to Israel." He neglected the controls for a second while he looked back at her.

He hadn't noticed before because he was so happy to see her, but Sarah looked terrible. She was exhausted and had bruises and small cuts all over face. Looking back at the controls, he assured her that they would escape alive.

"Why don't you try and rest back there while I get us to where we're supposed to be. It might take a little while. Here, you can rest your head on this," Aaron said, handing her the equipment bag after he removed the plastic bag with the coordinates and bank notes.

"Just take the hard stuff out and crumble the bag into a ball. Oh, and I thought you might want this." Aaron handed her his watch he had taken from the dead guard.

"The watch," she said excitedly. "Where did you get it?"

"From your guard. He decided he wanted you to have it back."

"Oh, thank you. I was so upset when they took it from me," she finished with a yawn.

"No problem."

Sarah rested on the floor of the small sub and put her head on the bunched up equipment bag. She put the watch on, stroking it as if she were stroking a beloved pet, and was asleep within minutes.

Aaron placed the coordinates in front of him. He found the navigational equipment to his right and kept an eye on it while speeding off in one direction. One of the numbers was getting closer but another was getting farther from his destination. He turned the sub to port a few degrees and the numbers started closing in on where he needed to be.

Feeling more relaxed, Aaron took his eyes off of the window and console. He stared at Sarah for a few seconds. She was sleeping and looking at her resting near him, he knew they were going to make it. He knew they would live a long life together in Israel and he relaxed with a deep sigh and turned back to the controls.

00:35:07

"Prepare the escape submarine and have *La Fantasma* change course and search for the submarine from the research station," Lopez barked over the radio.

They were still in the tunnel, running as quickly as they could back to the Poseidon complex. Lopez had to find these people and kill them otherwise his whole operation would be worthless and he knew it. If he could get in the submarine and hunt them down he would be fine, Lopez assured himself. They had killed James, the Coast Guard captain and now all they had to do was find Sarah and the intruder who was with her.

The Poseidon Project had cost him millions of dollars, and it had almost paid for itself. Sales had increased to the United Sates since its inception. Buyers had become more confident about shipments. They had noticed that the shipments were not getting seized like they had been in the past. Everything was much more reliable. Reliability meant safety. Safety meant good business for everyone and more good business put more money in Lopez's pocket. I will not let this die Lopez steamed. It will not die.

When Lopez returned from the tunnel, the submarine was ready for boarding. It was sitting on the ground next to the wrecked ship, standing upright on what looked like large helicopter landing gear.

Lopez entered the sub from the hatch on the top. When all of the workers were safely out of the chamber, it started to fill with water.

Lopez had not been in the sub since the Poseidon Project was first completed and it was smaller than he remembered. There was only a crew of four and him. Lopez sat in a chair in the middle of the control deck, which was the only room on the small craft. It was dark except for the lights from the control panel, but as the water level overcame the sub, lights poured in from outside. As soon as the chamber had filled with water and started to open, they were on their way.

00:23:16

The message had come only a few seconds before and it helped Tag's plans. The coordinates were in the direction he was traveling to escape Lopez and the CIA, if they were actually in the area.

The sonar aboard *La Fantasma* picked up the small sub and they were now on its tail. Tag didn't mind traveling in this direction since he was going in the opposite direction of the earlier coordinates. He would have no problem blowing the sub out of the water. Lopez had given a description of the man helping the prisoners escape and Tag knew the description matched Aaron.

The kid must have talked to the CIA, he thought. He knew they must have gotten the information out of him and that is why he was here. Tag would kill Aaron and Sarah before they could escape. Just thinking about them made him angry. After they were finished, he would escape and leave Lopez to deal with the authorities. The Poseidon Project was no longer his problem.

"How close are they now," Tag asked.

"Four kilometers and closing," one of the men on the bridge of *La Fantasma* said.

"Good, keep up this pace and have someone get the guns up here."

00:05:57

Aaron was close to the coordinates, which he had taken from Jason. They were almost there and there had been no sign of anyone following him. They were nearly home free, he thought thankfully.

Aaron smiled at himself and his accomplishments. He was so happy everything worked out. What was even better than that was the fact that Sarah was still alive and that he had found her. Now they could live their lives together in Israel like they had dreamed. As soon as they were safe in the helicopter, Aaron would ask Sarah to marry him. He did not have a ring on him but he would find one later. He would buy one with some of the money he had taken from the CIA. He couldn't wait.

He looked back at Sarah. She was still asleep on the bag. He loved her and thanked God for letting them both live through this experience. It was a miracle, he thought. It would be one that he would never forget but one that he would never want to relive. He hoped that this time he was done with all kinds of military activities. Maybe since I have connections in Israel, Aaron thought, I'll be able to get a desk job when I have to go to the reserves.

Looking back at the controls, Aaron saw that the pressure in the cabin was about equal to normal pressure. It was almost time for the helicopter to be in place as well and it was time to ascend to the surface and look around.

As Aaron ascended to the surface, *La Fantasma* was closing in and so was her sister sub. Aboard *La Fantasma*, Tag had detected the submarine on sonar and had spotted the helicopter.

Aaron woke Sarah from her nap and told her it was time to leave the sub. He prayed to God that Jason and his helicopter were on time.

Sarah started to put the equipment back into the bag but Aaron told her not to. The only thing that he deemed important was the zip lock bag with the bank notes and her picture.

The sub hit the surface with a jolt and Aaron left the controls. He could tell it was either very windy or the helicopter was just above their heads. Some force was pushing around the surface of the water around the sub.

00:02:54

Aaron unlocked the top hatch and flung it open, the air swirling viciously over his head. Just above the sub was a black helicopter with a blue Star of David on the tail that he could see periodically as it flashed in and out of sight with the tail-light.

As he was looking up, a face popped over the side of the helicopter. It was Jason.

A smile spread wide over Aaron's black face as his heart filled with joy at seeing his old friend. Jason waved back but he did not look happy to see his best friend. Worried that something had gone wrong, Aaron quickly slipped back into his mission mode and was focused again on what they needed because their lives depended on his actions.

Jason waved for them to hurry and get on board. Aaron knew that someone must have followed the sub and it was dangerous to stay another second.

He nodded back to Jason and bent down inside the sub. "Sarah, we've got to hurry. Give me the bag," he yelled over the sound of the rotors, opening and closing his hand.

Sarah handed him the bag and Aaron exited the sub exposing himself to the wind of the blades. He balanced himself on the sub and threw the bag up a short distance towards Jason's waiting arms.

Jason caught it, gave it to someone else immediately and motioned for Aaron to hurry. Aaron reached up as far as he could but his arms would not reach his friend's. Jason looked away and then back to his friend quickly. A short rope ladder appeared quickly over the side of the helicopter and Aaron grabbed onto it.

Aaron climbed up the ladder and tried to grab Jason's hands again but he almost lost his footing on one of the rungs. As he steadied himself, Aaron saw a spark on the landing gear of the helicopter. They were being shot at.

00:01:02

Aaron looked for the source of the shots but could not see anything. If they did not hurry it would be all over even after they had come this far.

Aaron thought it was stupid to try and grab his friend's hand when the floor of the helicopter was right in front of him. He grabbed on to it and pulled himself up. As he did, he heard bullets flying past his head over the noise of the helicopter. They were getting too close.

When Aaron finally made it safely onto the helicopter, he heard a machine gun going off only a few feet from his head. They were firing back at whatever was attacking them.

00:00:05

After Aaron was on board, Jason turned his attention to Sarah. She was kneeling low on the submarine's roof, trying to avoid the oncoming bullets. She was about to stand up when there was a huge rumble and everything started shaking.

There was a loud popping noise off in the distance and the sound of rushing water. Almost immediately after the sound, came a huge explosion in the distance. The waterscape lit up like a clap of lightning had been frozen in time.

The bomb had detonated and it had taken the underwater research facility with it. The magnitude of the explosion was magnificent but its shock wave was disturbing.

Everything was moved by the blast. The helicopter was pushed a few feet away from the sub but the people firing at the helicopter had also been knocked off balance.

Sarah had been knocked almost off the submarine, but she scrambled back to her feet after the blast. She knew if she could grab onto the rope ladder, that it would be an opportune time without bullets heading her way.

As Sarah got back up, the helicopter returned to its former position over the sub. Sarah jumped up and grabbed the ladder. As she did, the sub that was under her only a split second before was shoved aside like a toy boat. She looked down and saw that another submarine had crashed into it. She had to hang on. If she let go, it would be the end.

One of the men in the helicopter was still firing at the boat that they could now see. The fiery light of the explosion lit it up, but the helicopter was also illuminated. This made them an easy target as well.

Jason was leaning over the edge of the helicopter trying to grab Sarah's hand. He would not fall; he was harnessed to the interior of the helicopter but he was in danger of being shot. The boat had opened fire again on the aircraft.

Jason reached as far as he could and grabbed onto one of Sarah's hands. He almost had her into the belly of the helicopter when she loosened her grip on his arm. Sarah almost slipped out of his hand, but with all his strength, Jason held on. He needed help.

Aaron realized this and leaned over the edge without being tied to anything. It didn't matter to him if he fell. If Sarah was lost, he might as well be lost with her.

Together they pulled her up to the helicopter and they banked right and fled as quickly as they could.

In a few seconds they were out of range. They were safe. Sarah was lying on the floor of the helicopter and both Aaron and Jason were resting against the walls. They were both exhausted and they figured Sarah was as well.

"We did it again man," Jason screamed with his hand up in the air.

"Yee-haw," Aaron and Jason screamed together while slapping hands as they had done so many times before in the army after living through dangerous missions. The rest of the Israeli crew stared at Aaron and Jason having no idea of their history together and thinking them to be crazy.

Still trying to catch his breath Aaron moved slowly to where Sarah was resting. He wasn't going to wait another second to ask her. He picked her up into his arms and squeezed her tightly. They had made it.

"Sarah," he asked loudly over the roar of the rotors. "Will you marry me?"

He let her go to receive his assured answer but she looked stunned and was not saying a word. Was she that tired, he thought? What was wrong with her he wondered? Aaron took a closer look at his girlfriend and realized her body was limp.

Looking down, Aaron noticed blood, lots of it. She wasn't unconscious but she had no energy left. She was dying in his arms and he didn't even know it.

Aaron lost his ability to breathe or speak. He searched for the entrance wound but could not find it, there was too much blood. He looked at Sarah's face. Her eyes were still open and she was looking at him.

"Yes, I will," she said softly and paused for a moment as if she was in a carefree world. "You know, we almost did it."

Aaron shook his head and held her next to him. "No," he cried into her ear. "No! You're going to be fine," he demanded. "You're going to be fine! We're going to live together and get married! I want you to get married to me! You can't die now," he cried.

Aaron was crying and tears flowed from his eyes, down his cheeks and were landing on Sarah's face.

Sarah reached up and touched his face with her hand. She wiped one of the tears away. "Don't cry Aaron, it's for the best. Everything happens for a reason." As she got out the last word, her hand slipped from his face and her eyes closed.

"No!" Aaron screamed. He held her close to his body but she was limp. "No!"

By this time, Jason and the others had noticed that Sarah was in trouble. They pulled Aaron off of her and he fought them. He didn't want to let her go. If he could hold her, he thought, if he could just hold her she would be okay. Everything would be okay, he thought.

After they got him off of Sarah, some of the soldiers started working on her. In a matter of seconds her vital signs had been checked and she had been administered with an IV.

Jason tried to comfort his friend, but it would not work. Aaron was not listening to anything. He heard nothing. All he felt was despair. Aaron was in hell. If Sarah died, he thought, his life would never be the same. He had just come to terms with his parents' death. How would he handle this, he thought.

Aaron cried uncontrollably but did not take his eyes off of Sarah. He wanted to be with her for the rest of his life, but her situation was critical. Jason put it to him the best way anyone could. Her situation did not look good.

CHAPTER 19
ONE YEAR LATER

It was hot, just like every other day. Living in Eilat, Israel was like living in an oven, especially during the summer months. Eilat was a small town on the southern tip of Israel. It was only a five-hour bus ride from Tel Aviv or Jerusalem, but it was a world apart from the stresses of living in one of the world's most controversial countries.

Here, time had no meaning. It was a small resort town squeezed between the borders of Jordan and Egypt. Tourists from all over the world came here. Most of them came for the same reason, some of the best diving in the world.

The natural coral reefs are what drew divers. Most of the visitors could not understand each other, but when they got underwater, they were all speaking the same language.

In the evenings, tourists ate at fine restaurants located in the hotels near the waterfront. After a nice meal, they would crowd the boardwalk and listen to the relaxing sound of the Red Sea slowly lapping up to the shore. Smells of falafel and other native treats filled the air. It was a quiet place, an out of the way place. It was a good place for Aaron to escape the CIA and the drug cartel and enjoy life.

He had taken the money from the CIA and built his own slice of paradise in his new home — *Dolphin Heaven. Dolphin Heaven* was a mixture of many things: research facility, amusement park, education center, and just plain paradise.

Aaron's creation was built right on the ocean, just outside of the main part of Eilat, on the road to the Egyptian border. It had three fenced in areas inside the water. One for research, shows and snorkeling, one for scuba divers, and one for people who just wanted to swim without any large animals.

The park was open to the public for a fee during regular hours. Families would come and watch the dolphins perform, snorkel with the animals or scuba dive with them. Fathers would relax at the bar and watch their wives and children spend their hard-earned money by interacting with another species, but it was worth it. The kids loved their parents for bringing them to swim with the dolphins.

After hours Aaron continued doing research that was not directed by the government. For his own curiosity, he continued the communication research he had started. It was slow going but he was learning a lot. The Israeli

249

Government had even gone back a few months before and acquired Skilos from the research facility in Jamaica.

His past co-researchers thought he was dead, that was the official report. He had drowned at sea and the body was never recovered. Neither was the million dollars that Aaron had taken from the CIA. They had their suspicions, but there was no way they could trace the money.

Schwabb had found the empty case, and was furious. He knew Aaron had taken it with him and there would never be any way to retrieve it.

Schwabb had seen the explosion from the opposite direction as Aaron had. When Aaron never met them, he figured that he must have died in the explosion or even before that.

After the explosion, Schwabb spotted *La Fantasma* in the glow of the fire. One of their boats tracked it down and captured it with Tag Millwood still on board. The United States Government was going to try and pin him with treason. If they were successful it would be the biggest case since Aldrich Ames, another CIA agent, who was convicted of treason in April 1994.

They had also come upon a disabled submarine. In it, they found Señor Lopez. He was taken into custody and all his possessions and assets had been seized. He would no longer supply the U.S. with drugs but someone else would no doubt pick up where he had left off.

Aaron often thought about the past. He thought about how things could have turned out differently. He played the "If" game too much and had to stop himself from that torture. No matter how nice his life was now, it was still not his. He had been living under an assumed name since his arrival in Israel — Ami Stein. It wasn't a bad name, but it wasn't his.

Sitting at the outside bar with other men and women, Aaron was paying attention to his glass of *Coke®*. The bartender was busy with other customers and did not want to ask his boss what was wrong. He had asked too many times already when Aaron was being nostalgic, but he never got an answer.

Aaron was wearing a tee-shirt with *Dolphin Heaven's* logo. It matched the surroundings. He had built it to remind him of the Caribbean. Everything looked like it was right out of *Gilligan's Island*. Almost everything was made out of bamboo and thatched roof. It made the surroundings soothing and tranquil. If the structure weren't there, all anyone would see would be bare, desolate hills on the other side of the road.

He didn't have to come every day but he wanted to spend time with Skilos. It was another way for Aaron to live in the past. Skilos had gotten better around people. The exposure he had with children at *Dolphin Heaven* calmed him down a bit. Aaron also liked to hang out and make sure everything was running smoothly. If he didn't visit during the day, Aaron would have nothing else to do. Eilat was a small town and for people living there, it wasn't too exciting but Aaron kept to himself; his mind wasn't ready to start its new life.

Turning around, Aaron surveyed his beach. It was nicer than other beaches in the area; his had sand. The others were rocky.

There were plenty of people watching, snorkeling, or just lying on the beach. It was busy for the summer months. Many people didn't vacation here during the summer because it was too hot. Winter was much more popular.

He leaned back on the bar and relaxed. The fan behind the bar and the shade from the overhang didn't provide enough protection from the heat. He could see the air boiling off of the sand.

"You want another one, Ami," the bartender asked.

Aaron didn't respond at first. He was still getting used to the name change.

"Ami," the bartender asked again.

Aaron turned around with an empty glass in his hand. He didn't even notice that he had finished it.

"Yes," Aaron said in Hebrew, looking down at the glass and then handing it to the bartender.

After the bartender took the glass to fill it up, Aaron looked to his right where a group of tourists were preparing to dive with the dolphins. The bartender looked at Aaron with worry and filled the glass.

"Aaron," someone said from behind him.

Aaron spun around quickly. He hadn't heard anyone call him that in a year.

To his surprise, but relief, it was Jason. "Damn, man! Don't call me that! You almost gave me a freaking heart attack!"

Jason laughed and sat down next to him at the bar. "What's going on, man? It's been a while!"

"You want something to drink," Aaron asked.

"Oh, yeah!" Jason exclaimed. He was sweating badly. Just walking around in the heat was strenuous.

"Rafi," Aaron said, getting the bartender's attention. "*Miller Beer®!*"

Without delay, the beer was opened and ready to drink. The bottle steamed with cold as Rafi pulled it out of the cooler. Jason took large gulps and finished half the beer in a few seconds.

"Damn, Jason! Do you always drink like that?"

"Yes," he said emphatically. "And you know exactly what I like!"

"Yeah, well, I still can't stand the stuff. What are you doing down here?"

"Work," Jason said before finishing the rest of the beer.

"What kind of stuff they have you doing down here?"

"You know I can't tell you that."

"Well, can you at least tell me how many people you've assassinated in the last twenty-four hours?"

"Can't tell you that either, but if you don't watch it, you might be next," Jason said seriously.

"That's not very funny! I've had enough of people trying to kill me, thank you very much!"

"I'm just kidding!" Jason slapped Aaron on the back. Aaron gave him a stare and then looked back down at his *Coke®*.

"Really though, how's it going," Jason asked sincerely.

"Ah, whatever. Such is life, right?"

"You're still dwelling on the past? You've got a beautiful life here! You've got everything you've ever wanted! What's wrong?"

"I don't have everything!" Aaron pointed angrily at Jason.

"Hey, we did the best we could," Jason said, lifting his hands in the air in self-defense.

Aaron didn't respond. He looked back down at his glass and started to tear. Jason didn't want to interrupt, but he needed to.

"How is she?"

Aaron looked up at Jason briefly, a tear sliding down his face. Aaron hadn't cried about it in a while, but it had been a while since he spoke about it.

"She's still dead," Aaron said softly with more tears running down his face. He wiped them away quickly with his arms.

"I mean, have you visited the grave lately?"

"Yeah, I go every day." Aaron looked up briefly to try and gain control of his emotions. The world had been stripped away from him again a year ago when Sarah had died. He had just gotten over his parents accident when the person he wanted to start a family with was abruptly murdered and practically died in his arms. He knew he would never be able to love again. Not because he didn't want to. Aaron wanted to share his love so badly but his fear of abandonment was so strong that he could not let anyone get too close to him.

"I don't know what it is Jason, but I can't get Sarah out of my mind! I loved her so much! I still love her, which I know is crazy because she's dead!" Aaron paused for a moment trying not to cry again. "I just don't know what to do." He was barely holding back the tears.

Aaron wasn't crying anymore but it wouldn't take much to get him going again. This was always a sore subject for him and Jason knew it.

"Have you dated anyone yet?"

"No, you know I haven't."

"Why not?"

"I can't, okay! I just can't!" Aaron paused for a moment and then explained. "I guess I'm just not ready. I don't think I'll ever be ready." He was looking down again.

"What if I introduced you to some women? I know some really nice, really good-looking Israelis! Come on, what do you say," Jason asked jokingly. He had a big smile on his face and was acting silly. He was trying to make his friend happy and it was working slowly.

Aaron smiled and laughed softly. "You know you could never find me a girl that I was remotely interested in. Remember that librarian back in Boston? Where the hell did you dig her up? She was boring as hell!"

Jason laughed as Aaron reminded him of his bad picks. "And that other girl from NY? Man, she was totally rancid!"

The two laughed heartily, remembering times of their innocent childhood. Everything was much simpler then.

"Remember how we would play army all the time," Jason asked.

"Yeah?"

"Well, I guess I trained you pretty well."

"Yeah, I guess so." Aaron sighed.

There was a pause for a moment while both friends remembered their childhood separately. It seemed liked a different lifetime and for Aaron, it was.

"Aaron, I know you're not ready for this yet..."

"No," Aaron interrupted. "You're right! I'm not..."

"Just listen for a second, man! Okay?"

Aaron was quiet.

"There's someone I want you to meet."

Aaron started to interrupt again but Jason would not let him.

"There's someone I want you to meet! You don't have to date her, just say hello. That's all I ask. I guarantee you'll like her. You don't have to date her, but at least you'll have a friend and she lives right here in Eilat! Come on," Jason begged. He wanted his friend to at least have some fun.

"She lives here in Eilat," Aaron asked cautiously. Jason nodded. "And, I don't have to date her?" Aaron made it clear as Jason nodded again with a smile. "We can just be friends?"

"Now you're getting the picture? I knew you were a smart kid! So, what do you say?" Jason waited, wide-eyed, hoping for a "yes."

Aaron thought about it while looking back at his glass. It would be nice to have a friend in Eilat, he thought. It'll be a woman, but I don't have to date her which means I don't have to let her get too close. Maybe it would be fun, it would definitely be good for me, he thought. Maybe it'll help me take my mind off of the past.

"OK," Aaron said cautiously. "But, I'm not dating her!"

Jason smiled. "Great! It'll be good for you."

"Do you have her phone number?"

"I've got better than that."

"What do you mean, you've got better than her phone number? You have her address or something?" Aaron was being sarcastic.

"No, I brought her with me."

"She's here?" Aaron's face flushed and he was immediately nervously.

"Yeah, she's on the dock looking at the dolphins." He knew that if he brought her to *Dolphin Heaven* that there would be no way his friend could back out.

Aaron turned around nonchalantly and looked in the direction of the dock. There were many people watching the dolphins, there was a show in progress.

"Which one is she," he asked, trying to pick her out himself.

Jason turned around and looked at the dock. "Well, I guess she's in there somewhere." He was trying to find her with his eyes. "I can't see her right now, but I know she's in that crowd. Do you want to go meet her?" He turned back to Aaron who was still staring at the crowd of people.

"I guess." Aaron was still hesitant but growing more curious about the mystery woman.

They got up from the bar and slowly walked over towards the pier that went all the way around the performance and research area.

"One thing I know for sure," Aaron added as they walked.

"Yeah, what's that?"

"I'm sure if *you're* introducing us that I'll hate her."

"Oh, give her a chance, you haven't even met her yet."

"Does she speak English," Aaron asked as they approached the viewing area.

"Yep. Not that it would be a problem anyway. You speak fluent Hebrew!"

"Yeah, I know. I'm just giving you a hard time."

As they were about to step onto the pier, the show ended and fifty people of all sizes started moving towards them and they couldn't make any progress. Kids and adults alike were pushing to be the first ones to get a drink, lay on the beach or purchase a dolphin souvenir.

Aaron tried to look for women as they passed in the crowd but Jason didn't point out any of them, and then the crowd dissipated. Some enthralled children were still on the pier, staring at the dolphins and beckoning them. At the far end, only about thirty feet away was a woman standing by herself.

She was looking into the tank and Aaron had a profile view of her as they approached. Seeing them out of the corner of her eye, she turned to face Aaron and Jason. She was wearing sunglasses and her lips were squeezed together. She didn't move towards them, she just let them come to her.

The woman was beautiful. Her blonde hair was straight and just above her shoulders. Her skin was dark and Aaron thought the light hair and dark skin made for an interesting mixture.

Her white flowing dress was moving in the hot breeze, only exposing her face and arms. She looked muscular.

Aaron stopped about five feet from her and realized she was crying. Tears were running down her face. She looked familiar, but Aaron couldn't place her with the sunglasses covering much of her features. Looking down, Aaron saw a silver diving watch on her left wrist.

He moved closer to the woman and slowly removed her sunglasses revealing deep green eyes. Aaron stared at the woman's face in amazement. It was Sarah.

Aaron fell to his knees right in front of her and started to cry. He didn't know if he was happy, scared, sad, or dreaming. What was happening, he thought? Was this really Sarah, the woman he wanted to spend the rest of his life with?

He touched the flowing white dress and looked up. Sarah was still standing there with tears flowing from her eyes. Aaron stood up and touched her face. She still had not said a word and he wasn't sure that she wasn't a dream.

Aaron ran his hands over her face while they both cried. He felt her familiar skin, her features and gazed into her eyes without saying a word. Aaron slid his hands over her shoulders and around the back of her neck and down her arms.

"Are you real," he whispered. "Say something?"

"I love you," she whispered back. Her hands stopped his from making sure she was real. Sarah pulled them down and they kissed.

Aaron immediately put his hands back up and pressed her against him. He wanted to feel the body he had longed for during a year of mourning. This was what he missed! Nothing else mattered. He had a new, easy life but it had been nothing without Sarah.

"I dreamt about you," he whispered into her ear again. "Just before I came to get you from the Poseidon." He paused for a few moments as they held each other. "I didn't even remember it till just now." Aaron paused again. "I dreamt this very thing."

Sarah and Aaron hugged tightly like they would never let go again. Aaron didn't care if he was in heaven, a dream, or reality. He didn't care, as long as he could stay with Sarah forever.

"I told you, you'd like her," Jason said in the background, bringing Aaron back to reality. Without warning he swung around and punched Jason in the face. Jason fell to the deck, covering his nose.

"You knew about this for a whole year and you didn't tell me?" Aaron had his fist cocked and ready to go again. "What the Fuck is going on," he demanded as some of the patrons turned to see what was going on.

Sarah reached for Aaron's shoulder and he turned around. He put his fist down.

"I'm sorry, Aaron," she sniffled.

"You were in on this, too?" Aaron was hurt. "How could you hide from me for a year? I died with you! My life ended on that helicopter! How could you do this to me?" Aaron thought for a moment. "Why did you do this to me?"

"There's a lot you don't know, Aaron," Sarah said as she touched his face again. "We had to make you, and everyone else, believe that I was dead."

"They had to make everyone think I was dead, too," Aaron argued, pointing at Jason who had recovered from Aaron's punch. "I wouldn't have told anyone about you! Why did you have to hide from me?"

"She was working for the CIA," Jason said from behind him, still rubbing his nose. "We had to make sure that if anyone found you, that you would really believe that Sarah was dead."

Aaron looked back at Sarah in disbelief. "Is that true? You were working for the CIA," he asked, shaking his head in confusion.

"Yes, I was their watchman for the research facility in Kingston. I'm sorry I didn't tell you! I was going to but wasn't the right time!"

Aaron was hurt that she had kept the truth from him. All the time he was in Jamaica she had been assigned to watch him. He thought back to times he had spent with her and some of the things she did made sense to him now.

"Those times I caught you in the lab late at night, you *were* spying on me, weren't you? And when I got drugged at the bar? You did that, too, didn't you? So you could take my wallet," he said accusingly, hurt by her betrayal.

"Yes, Aaron, but I had to. It was my job to keep up with what you were doing, but I *did* fall in love with you. I spent time with you because I loved you, not because I had to follow you around. All I had to do was keep tabs on your research. I love you." She finished, caressing his face trying to convince him of the truth. She did love him but she also had had a job to do.

All of those out-of-town jobs weren't really jobs; they were the same work she was doing at the lab, he thought. It was hard for him to believe, but he knew it was true. She had been spying on him, but she did love him. He believed that Sarah loved him as much as he loved her.

"Remember when you asked if she could come to Israel," Jason interrupted. "I knew *you* were no problem, it was her I was worried about. After we checked her out, we realized who she was. We knew you didn't know that she was working for the CIA but we couldn't tell you. When she was approved for extraction we knew it would be harder to cover her tracks. We had to make sure you thought she was dead. If she hadn't been shot we would have done something else to make you think that she didn't make it."

Aaron still looked confused and hurt.

"Don't you see, Aaron," Sarah asked, looking at him with a sad face, wanting him to understand the pain he had to endure over the last year. "If they had found you, the CIA would be upset but not too upset. But how pissed do you think they would be if they knew I faked my own death and left the country?"

"So, you weren't really shot?"

Sarah took his hand and pressed it against her body where the wound was. Aaron could feel the scar tissue of the bullet wound.

"It was just a coincidence that Sarah was shot," Jason added. "When we knew she was going to be okay, well, we kept that from you. And, well, you know the rest."

Aaron was still in a state of shock but he was coming to terms with his new situation. He had been living like a zombie for a year. He had pined over Sarah's death and felt like he would never meet anyone like her and he was right.

Aaron didn't like the lies that were revealed to him, but he accepted them. Sarah was alive and with him and that was all that mattered to him. He looked at the woman right in front of his face. Aaron studied her features carefully. He wanted to make up for lost time.

BIBLIOGRAPHY

Anderson, James R.; Gallup, Gordon G. Jr. (1999). Self Recognition in Nonhuman primates: Past and Future Challenges. Haung, Mark (Ed); Whalen, Richard E. (Ed); et-al (1999), Animal Models of Human Emotion and Cognition (pp. 175-194). Washington, DC: American Psychological Association.

Fedarko, Kevin. (1995, July 17). OUTWITTING CALI'S PROFESSOR MORIARTY The mastermind of the world's No. 1 drug cartel, who has awed police for years, finally lands in jail. Time Magazine, 146 (No. 3)

Herman, Louis M., Hovancik, John R., Gory, John D., & Bradshaw, Gary L. (1989). Generalization of Visual Matching by a Bottlenosed Dolphin (Tursiops Turncatus): Evidence for Invariance of Cognitive Performance With Visual and Auditory Materials. *Journal of Experimental Psychology*, 15(2), 124-136.

Rosen, P. A. (1999). Expectancy Violations in Bottlenose Dolphins. Unpublished undergraduate thesis, University at Albany, Albany, New York, USA.

Electronic Media

The United States Coast Guard, Seventh District Home Page. (1998). URL: http://www.uscg.mil/d7/

Printed in the United States
3809

9 781591 130888